Copyright © 2025 by Jevasia Stephenson

Printed in Canada

Library of Congress Control Number: 2025926282

ISBN: 979-8-89587-020-4

Lisa K. Stephenson

Book Two

The

Shadows of the

Grey

Lisa K. Stephenson

ASIAS BRANDS

New York

I.

A NORMAL LIFE

It was early morning, and the soft golden light filtering through the tall windows of the Prime Minister's office cast a warm glow on the papers strewn across Benson Jr.'s desk. At just eighteen, he was already an intern at one of the most prestigious offices in the country, tasked with filing paperwork and managing menial tasks that now felt immense with the weight of responsibility. He paced across the polished wooden floors, his hands gripping a folder tightly, as the rising murmur from outside grew louder.

Benson's appearance had changed little over the years, but the subtle shifts lent him an air of maturity. His voice, once tentative and soft, had deepened into a richer, more self-assured tone that hinted at inner growth. Tall and slender, he preferred a polished business casual look, consisting of knitted cardigans over crisp shirts, each outfit thoughtfully composed and perfectly suited to his professional demeanor.

His ginger hair, once untamed, was now shaped into a neat, two-inch afro that framed his face with purpose and precision. He kept his upper lip clean-shaven, while his beard was carefully trimmed along the jawline, highlighting a face that had grown into its features—handsome, composed, and unmistakably adult. Gone was the anxious boy of earlier years; in his place stood a young man who bore his responsibilities, especially those of a husband, with quiet grace. Yet beneath the refinement remained a calm magnetism—an understated charm that made others pause and listen when he spoke.

Through the thick glass windows, the muffled sounds of the townspeople's bellows could be heard, their voices rising in unison, demanding justice. The recent tax hikes had caused unrest, and the streets were filled with frustrated citizens clamoring for answers. Benson Jr. peered outside momentarily; his youthful face etched with concern as he observed the growing crowd gathering around Parliament Square—a daily occurrence. Signs were raised, chants grew louder, and the tension was visible.

The past couple of years have seen significant developments—new infrastructure, added military personnel, modern amenities, and changes in government policies—but these advancements came at a cost. It was as though the government and the monarchy were preparing for something unbeknownst to its people. The economy was strained once again, and the people, particularly the working class, felt the burden of these changes pressing heavily on their lives. They wanted answers, and the mounting pressure on the Prime Minister to address the issues was becoming impossible to ignore.

Benson Jr. wiped his brow as he shuffled the papers on his desk, trying to focus. A soft voice interrupted his thoughts.

"Benson, have you seen the reports on the public reaction to the new tax hikes?" Priya, the media advisor, asked as she approached him. Her presence was calming, even amidst the turmoil. She was composed, as always, with her sleek dark hair pulled back in a professional bun and her sharp eyes scanning the room.

Benson glanced up, swallowing hard, "I've seen them," he replied, his voice a bit shaky. "It's bad, Priya. The people are furious. Do you think my father is going to address this today?"

Priya sighed, "You mean Prime Minister. I need not tell you no more that you must have respect for His Majesty's Government within these walls," she scolded him. Soon after, her eyes drifted towards the window where the shouts grew louder. "But I suppose today should be the day; it looks as though he no longer has a choice in the matter. The people are demanding answers. However, it's not just about calming them down; surely, it's about showing them a plan, giving them hope, and right now, they feel they're paying for things that benefit the wealthy, not them."

Benson nodded, understanding her words but still feeling overwhelmed by the situation. "And what if our Prime Minister cannot calm them down? What if there is no plan?" Priya shot him a callous look, leaning against the edge of the desk and crossing her arms.

"Rest assured, our Prime Minister knows how to handle these situations. He has been through worse. We will make sure he delivers the right message when the time comes." Benson appreciated her confidence but still felt uneasy.

Prince Amer, now standing at a commanding six feet one, had grown into a figure of striking presence. Where he was once polished and reserved, his appearance had evolved into something bolder—more magnetic, almost rebellious. With his brownish-reddish hair swept back in deliberate waves, it still managed to curl at the ends or fall slightly into his face, lending him a roguish charm. Though styled with care, the look suggested a refusal to conform completely—a sharp contrast to the clean-cut boy he had once been.

His fashion sense had transformed into something entirely his own: sharp, tailored ensembles that straddled the line between elegance and edge. Leather jackets, fitted shirts, dark trousers, and polished boots became his signature—a curated defiance wrapped in refinement. But his transformation wasn't just sartorial. It echoed in his demeanor.

Amer had grown unapologetically direct. His words, often unfiltered, cut with precision and rarely spared discomfort. The diplomacy that once shaped his speech had given way to a brutal candor, laced with clarity rather than cruelty. Though his honesty could unsettle, it stemmed from integrity rather than malice—a refusal to mask truth behind etiquette.

Even his voice had changed.

The warmth and innocence of his youth had given way to a deeper, more assertive tone—measured, and heavy with intent. Every sentence carried a gravity that made others pause, unsure whether to expect insight or confrontation. He no longer filled silences with pleasantries. He used them.

This intensity wasn't an affectation. Amer had learned to wield bluntness like a blade—not to wound, but to slice through unnecessary formality. In meetings, he spoke with conviction, prioritizing clarity over charm. Gone was the eager-to-please boy; in his place stood a young man focused on carving his own path.

Watson had watched the shift take root gradually and welcomed it. In his eyes, this change was not only inevitable—it was essential. Soon, Amer would no longer be just a prince. He would be King.

Now promoted to a Major General, Watson carried himself with a quiet dignity and authority that came with years of service to the monarchy. His uniform, a reflection of his esteemed position, was a sight to behold. The dark, deep navy of his coat contrasted sharply with the gleaming silver and gold accents that adorned it. Intricate embroidery of the royal crest sprawled across his chest, surrounded by rows of medals earned through loyalty, bravery, and service. The epaulets on his shoulders were braided in silver, a symbol of his high rank, and a ceremonial sword, polished to a mirror shine, hung at his side.

As Watson approached Prince Amer to escort him down the learning hall for his high school graduation ceremony, his boots made a soft yet commanding sound against the marble floor. Despite the weight of his decorated uniform, Watson moved with an ease that came from years of discipline and service. His sharp, focused eyes scanned the hallways, ever the protector, while his demeanor remained calm and respectful as he approached Amer.

"Your Highness," Watson greeted, his voice formal yet familiar, bowing slightly before standing at attention in front of the prince.

"Watson," Amer sighed.

As the two walked side by side down the long learning hall, the polished metals on Watson's uniform caught the light, reflecting a lifetime of dedication to the crown.

"You don't look too excited for the day," Watson said, hoping to spark a light conversation. "It's not every day a prince graduates from high school."

"What of it?" Amer snapped.

"Your Highness—"

But Amer cut him off. "Stop. You know, I find it rather insulting how you can just show up here, even though I'm no longer your responsibility." He gestured behind them, eyes shifting to Mavis, who followed at a steady pace.

"It's Mavis. She's my new senior Royal Guard."

Watson turned to her and offered a polite wave.

"Understood, Your Highness. I appointed her. It seems that you haven't calmed your anger toward me."

"Calmed? Anger? Are you implying I have a reason to be upset?"

"Implying?" Watson chuckled nervously. "No—just speculation."

"Well, speculate no more. You're dismissed." With his hands in his pockets, Amer turned sharply and continued walking. Mavis followed, careful not to brush past Watson, who remained still.

"Your Highness, may we speak about that night?" Watson's voice echoed through the hallway. Amer stopped abruptly. His brows drew together as he turned.

"I've never been opposed to it," he snapped.

"Of course." Watson bowed. "Ask, and I'll answer truthfully."

Amer stepped closer with urgency. Though slightly shorter, he studied Watson's expression, searching for any telltale signs of deceit—lines that might betray this as a waste of time. But Watson's face was calm, open.

"What happened to the girl we visited that night?"

Watson's eyes widened. "Why does she matter to you after all this time?"

"That's not your concern. Answer, or I walk away."

Clearing his throat, Watson glanced around the hall. Though Mavis appeared aloof, he knew she was listening.

"The girl you ask about, Your Highness, is a half-breed. From what I've heard, she no longer lives on land."

Amer's eyes narrowed. "A half-breed?"

"Yes, Your Highness."

"Hmm. I mean, does it matter? Aren't we all one people now?"

"Not exactly."

"How so?"

Watson shifted uncomfortably. "There are rules for members of the monarchy regarding half-breeds—"

"I do not understand. For years we have been taught of the allegiance between the Modiri and humans. What is the issue? I like a half-breed. I want to be with her. It's been a while since we last met, but maybe she's been waiting, hoping to see me again." He smiled faintly. "I do not understand why you would betray me like that."

"I never betrayed you."

"You broke your loyalty and never acknowledged it. It is as if it never happened. I can't even remember the events of that night—and no one, not even you, will tell me what happened. I don't know if she hated me or if she cared and was taken away. I remember nothing."

"Please lower your voice, Your Highness—"

"I will not!" Amer shouted. "You owe me an explanation. One moment we were en route to Fiona, and the next, I wake up with no memory. On top of that, you're suddenly part of some classified mission and promoted to Major. You are not being honest—"

Mavis stepped forward, her voice calm and composed. "May I suggest a brief intermission, Your Highness? We'll be late for the ceremony."

Her gaze moved gracefully between them. Amer's eyes burned with fury. He clenched his fists at his sides, then turned to Watson, his voice low but razor-sharp.

"I never want to see you again," he said. The words cut through the air like a blade, his tone cold and final. His chest heaved, nostrils flaring, jaw tight, the muscles in his neck rigid as he fought to contain the storm brewing inside him.

Watson, ever the stoic soldier, stood firm. The prince's words struck deeper than he expected. He blinked rapidly, fighting the sting in his eyes. He had faced battlefields and peril without flinching, but nothing prepared him for this: the pain of losing the trust of the boy he had protected for so many years.

He tried to speak, but no words came; he swallowed hard, his eyes stinging as he cast his gaze downward. His strong, weathered hands twitched at his sides, aching to reach out and fix the unfixable, but he knew better. Amer's fury was unrelenting, and Watson, despite his strength, felt powerless. In that moment, with Amer's back to him and the sound of his steps beginning to recede, he blinked again, "Yes, Your Highness," Watson finally managed to say, his voice barely above a whisper.

In the year 2452, the educational system for members of the monarchy had evolved into an advanced, highly specialized program that blended cutting-edge technology with the demands of royal responsibility. Prince Amer, at the age of seventeen, had just completed his rigorous high school education, a milestone that signified not only academic excellence but also his readiness to assume greater responsibilities within the monarchy.

The system was fully electronic and immersive, driven by advanced artificial intelligence that tailored each student's experience to their unique strengths, challenges, and future roles. Traditional classrooms and textbooks had become relics of the past. In their place were holographic simulations, AI tutors, and interactive virtual environments that allowed students to engage with material in real time from anywhere in the world.

Prince Amer's curriculum was meticulously designed to challenge him on every level. It encompassed governance, diplomacy, military strategy, history, and economics, alongside advanced sciences, literature, and ethics. Beyond academics, the program emphasized leadership, emotional intelligence, and decision-making under pressure—skills essential for a future monarch.

Through complex simulations, Amer faced scenarios that mirrored real-world crises: political upheaval, natural disasters, and delicate diplomatic negotiations. The AI system tracked his progress continuously, adjusting lessons to ensure not just retention, but mastery and application in high-stakes environments.

His peers, scattered across the globe, were connected through a global network where collaboration and competition thrived in equal measure. Exams had evolved into practical challenges, often involving large-scale projects or unforgiving simulations where every decision could impact a virtual nation or kingdom.

Amer spent countless hours in his private study, navigating intricate political scenarios or combing through virtual archives to analyze historical events—each session stirring memories of Fiona and the parade. The pace was merciless, but he thrived under its demands, excelling across every discipline.

In his final year, his capstone project required him to govern a virtual kingdom for an entire simulated year, making decisions on everything from economic reform to military engagement. His performance was assessed by a council of intelligence advisors, joined by instructors from his earlier years.

Now, as a graduate, Prince Amer stood as a product of this visionary system: intelligent, capable, and fully prepared to confront the complexities of monarchy in a modern age.

*

Benson Jr. arrived home in the late night, his footsteps soft yet intentional as he approached the grand, period house in Hampstead Village. The night was still, the only sound being the distant rustle of leaves in the trees and the faint hum of city life. The house was dimly lit, the glow from a single lamp in the living room casting long shadows across the elegant interior. Melissa, several months pregnant and due any day now, had been anxiously awaiting his return.

As the door creaked open, Melissa's face lit up with joy. She had been resting on the plush sofa, her hand gently cradling her round belly. "Benson!" she exclaimed, her voice filled with excitement and relief. "The baby's kicking again! You have to feel it," she said, beckoning him over with a wide, hopeful smile. Benson hesitated at the doorway, his knitted cardigan clinging to his slender figure, emphasizing the tension in his posture. He looked at Melissa, her grey eyes sparkling with anticipation, but he couldn't bring himself to move.

"Sorry, I'm just pretty tired," he muttered. His refusal hung in the air, and Melissa's smile faltered, her hand slowly falling back to her side as she tried to mask her disappointment.

"That's no problem, honey, I understand. I'll go ahead and reheat your dinner," she smiled nervously. Benson walked past her, heading toward the large window overlooking the quiet street, his back stiff and his mind heavy with thoughts. He couldn't shake the turmoil that had been brewing in him for months. On the one hand, he wanted to be the good man he had been raised to be, the dutiful son who followed the traditions laid out before him. But on the other hand, doubt gnawed at him. Was Melissa truly the person he was meant to spend the rest of his life with? Their marriage had been arranged, their bond forged by expectations of his family rather than love, and what of her family? He'd never met them.

He clenched his fists, frustration welling up inside him. He wanted to connect with her, to feel the same joy she felt about their child, but something held him back. In many ways, they were still strangers, trying to build a life neither had fully chosen. Melissa watched him silently, her heart sinking as she read the conflict on his face.

"Did something happen at the office today?" she asked gently, joining him at the window while his supper warmed in the oven.

He slowly perched on the window seat, his eyes on her. He craved the touch of someone—anyone—but it wasn't her.

"Things are a little confusing…" he admitted.

"How so, if you don't mind me asking?" she asked softly, rubbing her belly. The baby kicked—a quiet reminder of the new life they were about to welcome.

Benson exhaled slowly. "Um…" He couldn't hold it in any longer. "This—um—this doesn't feel strange to you?"

"Strange?" Melissa raised an eyebrow.

"Yes. I mean, I know we're going to be parents soon, but it feels like we were just thrown into this life. Like everything's been fast-forwarded. Don't you feel that?"

"No. I've always wanted this. The peace, the stability, consistency... and a husband I love."

"Love?" he echoed with a nervous chuckle. "We barely know each other. One day I'm arriving at your flat, surrounded by maids, and the next thing I know, we're off to the countryside for a wedding on my birthday." His gaze dropped to the floor, his voice tinged with shame. "This is a beautiful home, no doubt, but we did not earn it. It doesn't feel real. It's like we're living in a simulation. You don't feel that way?"

Melissa scoffed and replied bashfully, "No. But let me check on your supper. I'll be right back."

As she shuffled into the kitchen to check the temperature of the meal the chambermaids had prepared earlier, a wave of emotion hit her. Her eyes began to water, but before the tears could fall, she composed herself, rubbed her belly bump, and returned to the main area with a soft smile.

"It's not quite ready yet."

"Listen, I didn't mean to upset you. I just—I have questions. Between missing out on uni, the chance to get drunk, live on campus, and meet women... I feel like I was dropped into this picture-perfect life of 'happy wife, working husband.' I don't know what I'm doing. I'll admit that."

He sighed. "And it's not just that. I'm not even earning a paycheck. I'm up at dawn, back by nightfall, and have nothing to show for it. A man's supposed to protect and provide for his family—but what am I providing as an intern? What protection am I offering when I'm barely home? I haven't even met your parents—"

"Please stop!" she cried.

Like a dam breaking, the tears burst forth. As hard as she tried to stifle her sobs, nothing could contain the flood of emotion. Melissa collapsed to her knees, sobbing in agony.

Benson Jr. stood frozen in the dimly lit room, stunned by her sudden breakdown. He hadn't meant to hurt her, but his words had cut deeper than he realized. Her cries, soft at first, quickly became gut-wrenching. Guilt wrapped around his chest like a vice. He couldn't just stand there.

Without hesitation, he moved to her side and wrapped his arms around her, pulling her close. Her tears soaked through his cardigan, but he didn't care. He held her tightly as she cried, her body trembling. Flashbacks of her family surged through her mind. Kaliope's healing had long since faded—she hadn't been in the water for some time. The emotional blockade had lifted, and she was free to feel, though she didn't yet realize it.

Images of Mary, Kovos, Emaline, and Fiona flashed in her mind, each one piercing her heart. The loss, the distance, the uncertainty—it all overwhelmed her. Her sobs turned desperate, her breath shallow and ragged as she clutched Benson's shirt, holding onto him like her only anchor in the storm.

"I'm scared, Benson," she whispered through her tears.

"I guess that's one thing we have in common," he said softly, managing a small laugh. "Sorry... but really, that makes two of us. I've never seen you this vulnerable before."

Her sobs began to quiet, though her body still shook. "I'm trying to be strong. I want to bury the past and build a normal life. That's all I want," she said. "But with everything you've said, and your mother coming by earlier... telling me the baby belongs to the monarchy—"

Benson sat upright, eyes wide. "My mother? What?"

Melissa sniffled. "Yes. She said... if our baby is a hybrid, the monarchy will destroy it. And if it's finned, they'll take it away—"

Benson jumped to his feet, furious. "My mother said that to you?"

"Yes—"

Before they could say more, a shrill blare pierced the room. The smoke alarm wailed, jolting them both. Melissa winced, heart pounding, as smoke drifted from the kitchen.

Benson bolted toward the oven. "Oh no!"

He flung the door open. A cloud of thick smoke billowed out. Without hesitation, he grabbed the charred remains of dinner and tossed the pan into the sink. He turned the faucet on full blast, steam hissing as water hit the scorched metal. The alarm continued its obnoxious cry.

Snatching a kitchen towel, he waved frantically at the smoke detector. After several frantic moments, the alarm finally fell silent, replaced by the soft crackle of water cooling the burned pan.

He turned around, breathless, and flashed a sheepish grin at Melissa, who had followed him in, eyes wide.

"Guess I'm a protector after all," he joked, holding the ruined pan like a trophy. "Saved you from the fire alarm, at least."

Despite everything, Melissa burst into laughter—the kind that catches you off guard and fills a room. It was genuine. Benson laughed too, the tension easing as they stood there, breathless and smiling.

For the first time since their marriage, they shared a moment of lightness.

"All right," Melissa said, wiping the last tear from her cheek. "Let's skip the meal. How about popcorn instead?"

Benson nodded and reached for the kernels. Together, they prepared it, the rhythmic pop of kernels soothing the air. Leaning against the counter, they shared a few more jokes and stories, letting the evening melt into something gentler.

With the popcorn ready, they curled up on the couch. The fire crackled in the distance, buttery scent filling the room. For now, the fears were set aside. Benson wrapped his arm around Melissa, and for the first time, they felt like a family.

II.

EQUAL SPECIES

The Equal Species, a group born out of growing unease, a gnawing sense that something was deeply wrong in the United Kingdom—specifically, within the walls of Buckingham Palace and the shadows of the monarchy. The group started with just Alice and Linus. Andrew, disinterested and resentful, wanted nothing to do with their mission, fearing it would only bring further pain to their mother, who remained in disbelief, disconnected from the outside world, still grieving the man she once knew. But beyond the walls of their home, word began to spread, fueled by whispers and strange occurrences shown on the television that could no longer be ignored.

The catalyst for its formation had been the King's mysterious absence. He has not been publicly seen in years, and still, no official report has been released, therefore sparking a wave of speculation. Alice, a natural thrill-seeker with an insatiable curiosity, has never been one to ignore a mystery. Alice's father and his actions added to her suspicions—he remained evasive, estranged, and secretive. Creeping home in the dead of night and leaving no sooner after, but Bonnie could feel him, his presence lingering around their home. Alice couldn't shake the feeling that whatever was happening inside the palace was far more dangerous than anyone was letting on.

The bunker had been another alarming revelation, suggesting that preparations for something far more sinister were underway. And then there was Melissa's kidnapping and the assault on Linus—Alice and her friends, Piper, Willow, and Preston had pieced together that these incidents were not isolated and there was a clear, dangerous thread running through all of them, one that connects the royal family, the Modiri, and the events that had been unfolding beneath the public's notice.

At the heart of their group is the belief that the Modiri are victims of inequality and subjects to experiments; they are not treated as equals, and there is a plan to eradicate their kind in totality. The group's name symbolizes their desire for equality and truth, for the acknowledgment that the Modiri are not a threat and their treaty with the humans is in clear violation. They are chasing justice for a world that had long been shrouded in secrecy.

Immediately after completing a day's work at the office, Linus headed to Alice's home, where he raced down the narrow staircase into the basement, his breath quickened with excitement. Andrew had barely gotten a word in when he let him in upstairs, but that did not matter now, for he had big news to share. As his feet hit the carpeted stairs, his eyes immediately caught sight of Alice and Willow, who were huddled within their makeshift command center. Piper and Preston to the rear brewing a small pot of coffee.

The twenty-four-year-old fraternal twins and children of media advisor Priya Clarke are strikingly different, but their bond was once unshakable. Piper stands at five feet, six inches with a lithe, athletic frame. Her hair, a fiery auburn, flows in loose waves down her shoulders, always a little wild, refusing to be tamed by hairbands and pins. Her emerald-green eyes are sharp, constantly scanning the room as if she's searching for something hidden in plain sight.

Piper has a habit of tapping her fingers rhythmically on any surface when she's thinking or nervous, a subtle beat that mirrors the energy always pulsing through her. Dressed casually in denim and plain white tees, she often accessorizes with light silver earrings and bracelets, reflecting her easy-going nature. Her laugh is contagious, loud and unapologetic, and she walks with a kind of bounce, as if ready to sprint off on an adventure at any moment.

Preston, in contrast, stands taller at six feet, one inch, his posture relaxed with an air of quiet confidence. His hair, darker than Piper's with chestnut tones, is neatly trimmed and always styled, reflecting his more composed and methodical personality. His hazel eyes, which flicker between green and brown depending on the light, are thoughtful and steady, often narrowing when he's deep in concentration. Preston has a habit of adjusting his glasses when he's speaking, pushing them up with his index finger as he explains something in his calm, measured voice.

His wardrobe is more refined—button-down shirts and tailored jeans or slacks—hinting at his love for structure and order. While quieter than his sister, Preston's wit is sharp, and he often surprises people with his dry sense of humor. He walks at a slower, more premeditated pace as though carefully considering each step. They often exchange glances during conversations, reading each other's thoughts effortlessly. Piper speaks with her hands, her words fast and impassioned, while Preston often listens, arms crossed over his chest, only chiming in when he has something insightful to add.

"You two are famous now!" Linus exclaimed, rushing to the middle of the room. The basement revealed itself—their command center looked more like the office of an FBI agent trying to crack an unsolved case than a billiard room. The walls were covered with photos, notes, and strings connecting one image to another, each detail meticulously pinned and outlined in bold red marker. There was a large corkboard dominating one wall, cluttered with pictures of Beatrice, Melissa, and an old image of Kovos from his childhood that Linus discovered while rummaging through Beatrice's things. Images of the royal family—the King and Queen—taken from internet searches and archival paparazzi shots.

In the center of it all was the phrase, scrawled in black ink, *The Equal Species*. They left no stone unturned. There were clippings of obscure news reports about hybrids ruling the United Kingdom, and speculation that the Queen herself could be a Modiri half-breed, attempting to wipe out the female hybrids to conceal her identity. It was all so bizarre.

"Look at this! You two were photographed with the other protestors! Reporters are finally starting to take notice." His excitement was palpable. His voice breathless as he pointed at the newspaper article, reading it aloud, "For months, citizens have been demanding answers from our government for the increase in taxes across the country. There is no real reason, as inflation continues to skyrocket, and many Britons are struggling to find work. Protestors and groups like, *The Equal Species* are seen front and center, demanding answers and what appears to be equal rights for all as many continue to speculate that their sterling is being hoarded and used to fund the advancement of the education system within the royal family, whilst children who are taught by the public education system are failing and underperforming in their studies."

Alice looked up, her eyes sparkling with satisfaction. "Well, it's not for the reason we wanted, but good press is better than none at all…finally." Her branded T-shirt, black with the bold white logo of *Equal Species* across the chest, stood out among the crowd in the photograph. The baseball cap sat snugly on her head, casting a shadow over her determined features. Willow, standing beside her in the photo, was just as resolute, her dark hair tucked beneath her cap and her expression one of unshakable purpose.

"The more attention we get, the more people will start to ask questions," Willow said. "And the Prime Minister's office is the perfect place to make some noise."

Alice smirked, crossing her arms over her chest, "Right, it's a small step, but certainly a start. Soon they won't be able to ignore us anymore."

"Any update from your mum?" Willow asked Preston and Piper.

"She's avoiding the press, and we don't have any real answers as to why. But I did tell a friend about our group, and he's opted on stopping by tonight. I told him half past eight…" Piper replied.

"A friend?" questioned Linus.

"Yes, believe me, I think he's the best chance we have at a breakthrough."

Willow sighed, tossing her hands into the air, almost defeated, "What have we got to lose at this point? —"

"Everything from being betrayed by the wrong person," Linus chimed in.

"But how will we know who we can trust if we don't try to hear and let people in?"

"No, not like this. We can't trust everyone."

"Hmm" Willow agreed.

"Listen, he's coming in with good intentions. I met him at work a few months ago. We can't protest, Preston and I, otherwise our mother will find out and then we'll lose access to literally everything,"

"She's right. Let's hear out this guy," Preston said in support of Piper. Linus turned to face Alice, who simply shrugged. She wasn't feeling optimistic, but with the time nearing, they had to reach an agreement.

"Babe, if we're ever going to find your mother and niece, we have to consider every lead we're presented."

Linus nodded. "I suppose." The night went on, and the stillness of the room was only punctuated by the incessant ticking of the wall clock, each second stretching out and growing louder in the quiet basement. Alice sat cross-legged on the couch; her face bathed in the dim glow of her phone screen as she scrolled through job boards. Her focus was sharp, fingers tapping nimbly as she mass-applied through a job site, but every so often, she'd sigh, her frustration mounting with each rejection. "A master's degree in data science and still having to rummage through the bottom of the occupation barrel," she grumbled under her breath. Preston, ever the laid-back one, was sprawled out in an armchair, headphones in, watching anime with one eye while wolfing down a bag of original Ruffles. The crinkle of the bag and the soft crunch of the chips were the only sounds breaking through the ticking clock. His expression shifted with the action on the screen, alternating between grins and occasional raised eyebrows, entirely engrossed in his show.

Piper, on the other hand, was restless. She paced the length of the basement, her anxiety manifesting in her jittery movements. She kept checking her phone and glancing at her watch, her foot tapping impatiently every time she paused. The energy around her was obvious, as if she were waiting for something to happen. Her fingers fidgeted with the hem of her shirt, eyes darting between the clock and the door.

At 8:31 p.m., the soft chime of her phone broke the silence. Piper stopped mid-step, her breath catching in her throat as she read the message. The words *"Outside"* flashed across the screen in a low, curt alert. She glanced at the others, her heartbeat quickening, the reality of the moment settling in. Without a word, she shoved her phone into her pocket.

"He's here," she told them. Piper moved quickly but quietly up the stairs until she reached the foyer. The dim light from the entryway barely illuminated her path as she tiptoed to the window, pulling back the curtain just enough to peek outside. There, approaching the house, was Max, a young boy of about fourteen. He was a wiry figure, dressed in a hoodie that was slightly too big for him, the hood pulled up as if to hide his mischievous grin. His glasses sat crooked on his nose, and his hair, a mess of brown curls, looked like it hadn't been combed in days. He exuded a nerdy yet confident energy, the kind of kid who could hack a computer just as easily as he could pick a lock.

Piper's sharp eyes immediately noticed something from Max's back pocket—a lanyard. Her heart skipped a beat when she recognized the insignia: it belonged to a Modiri Guard. That was no small thing to have. She knew she had to get him inside, but discreetly, as Andrew and Bonnie were away in their rooms and should not be disturbed.

She turned and darted back downstairs to the basement, where the rest of the group sat. Max followed soon after, his footsteps light and quick, like he was always on the move. When he entered the basement, he gave them all a knowing smirk, as if he had a secret the world hadn't yet caught on to. The sound of everyone speaking at once bounced off the walls like gibberish.

"This is a kid!" Alice cried.

"Is this the lead? A child?" Linus criticized.

"Did his parents bring him here? How did he get here and why? It's a school night," Willow bellowed.

"Piper?" Preston commanded.

"Look, why don't you all simply relax and give him a chance?" Piper pleaded. Max remained unfazed by the commotion as he strolled around the room, hands stuffed in his hoodie pockets, taking in the scene. His gaze flicked from the walls filled with photos and notes to the scattered papers and laptops. He whistled low, clearly impressed with the setup. But Piper's eyes were glued to the lanyard that swung gently from his back pocket. It dangled a silent message, its presence unnerving.

As Max wandered the room, his casual demeanor could not hide the weight of what he had brought with him.

"Max!" Piper called to him; her eyes low as if to signal they were ready to have their meeting.

"Piper," he replied, taking a seat on the sofa. They were divided, Max and his lanyard on one side and the *Equal Species* on the other. "Pretty nice setup you all have going here. I'm Max, by the way," he said cheerfully.

"Pleasure to meet you, Max. Now, do you have anything you can tell us about the monarchy and the Modiri?" Alice questioned.

"Slow down, I don't even know your names."

"Alice, Preston, Linus, and Willow," Piper said, her voice tinged with annoyance. "Tell them what you told me at the school."

"School?" Willow asked.

"Yes, he's a student at the school I volunteer for."

"Freshman at Condell High School," he nodded confidently.

"Max, we don't have time for all this small talk. What do you have for us?"

"Listen, I want to share this information with you just as badly as you want it. But coming here and seeing this house, I can't just give it away for free," he stated.

"Great, the kid's trying to shake us down," laughed Linus. "Not only that, but he also knows about the group and our hideaway."

"You've watched way too many American movies, lad. I'm simply asking for something in return for my information, is all."

"Return? Who do you think we are? The Avengers? We don't have powers or government funding backing us. We're a group of working-class young adults trying to figure out what's going on in our country."

Alice, clearing her throat. "...and pending working class." Linus corrected.

Piper interrupted, "I believe there's been some misunderstanding. From what I overheard you telling your mother in the administration's office, your brother is still missing—a Modiri Guard, and she's become far too devastated because of it. Now, we just need to learn a bit more."

"But what do I get?" he dragged.

"We don't have any sterling," Alice shouted.

"The watch, on your wrist. Surely, it's worth something."

"My father gave this to me; there's no way you're getting it." Linus tugged Alice away into a corner, hoping to reason with her.

"Please, darling, let's give the kid what he wants. I promise you, we'll get it back!" he whispered. Alice lifted her head, tears welling in her eyes,

"You better be glad I love you." As the pair made their way back to the center of the room, Alice shakingly removed her watch. The gift was small, delicate, and utterly exquisite, with a band crafted from fine silver links that gleamed in any light. Its face was encircled by tiny diamonds, each one catching the light like stars in a clear night sky, giving the timepiece an ethereal sparkle. The hands of the watch were a soft rose gold, contrasting beautifully against the pale mother-of-pearl dial. It was timeless, yet modern, an heirloom in the making.

Inside, engraved with meticulous precision on the inner side of the clasp, were five simple yet profound words: *"For You, Alice, Love Dad."* The inscription, hidden from the outside world but close to the wearer's skin, carried a sentiment of love and protection. It was more than an accessory; it was a deep personal treasure, a symbol of affection and legacy that spoke volumes without a single word. As she handed it off, Alice turned away.

Linus, now aggravated, "Talk!" he demanded.

"Okay, okay," Max sat upright, preparing himself to express all he'd come to know. "A while back, when the soldiers put out a bill for new guards, they explained that the pay would be well over thirteen hundred pounds for training, fifteen hundred pounds for each Modiri caught breaking the laws, and two thousand pounds for every official termination if they had to accompany a Royal Guard. Our father died when we were much younger, and we needed the sterling, so my mother pushed my brother to sign up. She wasn't too confident he would be selected, but it seems they had a mission planned already and wanted some throwaway soldiers," Max sighed. "He was selected. Three days later, Archie was told he would be placed on a top-secret mission to Modiri Mountain. Once he received his orders, we never saw him again…"

"Modiri Mountain?" Alice questioned.

"Yes," Max confirmed. Everyone listened intently. "I don't know anything else about it. But then the other day this showed up," he removed the lanyard from his back pocket. In the badge holder was a plain white card with a black strip along the rear. Alice's watch fumbled from his pocket, but with haste, he returned it. Ashamed to face her, and through gritted teeth, she cursed him.

"What is that card for?" Preston asked.

"I don't know. I was hoping we could try and find out," Max's eyes widened innocently.

"You mean you're here to seek our help to find your brother?" Linus argued.

Max reclined on the sofa, "In all fairness, I'm the one with the key card. My mother wasn't going to do anything with it. She thinks Archie's dead, and since we're too poor, the soldiers didn't bother to come and tell us or give him a proper funeral. But I don't believe so, I think this is his way of telling us that he's alive and he needs to be saved."

"Saved? If he's a guard or—or soldier, what would he need saving from or what for?" Willow wondered.

"Maybe something happened up there," Linus replied. "This all just sounds so sketchy, to be honest. Where would we even use the keycard?"

"Bunker," Alice said, facing the corkboard.

A skeptical Linus looked to Piper, "He told you all of this beforehand?"

"No, only the part about his brother being a guard and having been missing. Sounds like your niece and mother."

"We should probably go to the bunker then. It's a good thing we wrote down as much as we could back then, and we have the Nuvi," he shrugged. "Hopefully, we can try to get a ride there."

"I'll take us," Preston said. "When do we leave?"

Linus turned to face Alice, "Babe?"

Alice paused before answering, "Tomorrow night."

King Bao, God of the Makaras—the legendary dragons of the sea—exuded an aura of dominance as he pulsed vertically through the Snow Kingdom's waters. Draped in a regal military Conical Hat, its brim low enough to obscure his eyes from all but his bride, he carried himself with the mystery and authority befitting his title. The hat was an ancient symbol of his reign, decorated with intricate patterns of swirling dragons, each etched in gold. His eyes, although never seen, were believed to hold the depths of the dragon's wisdom. The long, dark hairs beneath his lips swayed in rhythm with his speech.

His attire is an Ao Tac split evenly at both sides, revealing his majestic fin. The fabric, woven from rare underwater silks, shimmered with the colors of a smokey mahogany and seafoam green whilst the sleeves of his gown remained tightly sealed, concealing his acetics. The folds of his Ao Tac swirled around him like the currents of the sea, silent but purposeful.

Embedded within the scales of his fin were rare, hazy topaz gems, each one glowing as if alive, symbolizing the bond between the Makaras and their leader. His fin, absent a tail fluke, curled at the tip and was a blend of seafoam green and shadowy grey that shifted like the sea at twilight.

When King Bao spoke, his voice reverberated like the deep, steady beat of a drum. A sound that commanded attention, every word steeped in the power of the sea dragons. Earlier in the day, King Bao had arrived in the Snow Kingdom. His Makara, measuring an immense eight hundred twenty-eight meters, had a massive head crowned with jagged, coral-like horns, and eyes glowing a molten gold, watching everything with a sharp, knowing intelligence. Its body was sinuous, snaking through the water with a graceful lethality. Long fins trailed from its sides, fluttering in the currents like the wings of a bird, while its tail was lined with barbs that could tear through anything in its path.

The dragon's breath clouded the water with heat, creating a swirling mist that added to its mystical, fearsome appearance. Though silent now, its mere presence filled the realm with a sense of awe and trepidation. As Bao pulsed toward the royal sector where King Khione and Rudita patiently awaited him, he couldn't help but glance at Naida, who had now made her way into the waters after being summoned by Seraldine. But as he ventured further inside, the Kingdom's commotion slowly began to fade. King Khione remained seated atop his throne, Rudita beside him.

"King Khione," King Bao bowed. "My brother." The very currents seemed to pause in deference to their presence, two titans of the deep whose legacies had shaped the underwater realms. King Khione, ruler of the Snow Kingdom, radiated an icy stillness. There was a chill that hung around him, an almost palpable frost in the water, as though his very being demanded the cold to settle in the room. Between them, the matter of Naida loomed. The discussion was about her journey East to harness her magic, a mission fraught with peril and potential. Khione's voice cutting through the waters like ice shards,

"My brother, King Bao. It has been far too long," he smiled. "Our kingdom welcomes you."

"King Bao, it is always an honor," Rudita slithered.

Listening from the shadows, Fanira, now in eel form, coiled and drifted, her dark, sinuous body blending into the dim corners of the chamber. Her glowing eyes, sharp and ever watchful, flicked between the two kings as they spoke. The eel's body twisted with nervous energy, her mind absorbing every word.

III.

THE SERUM

Morning in the Snow Kingdom was a serene spectacle. Pale light filtered through the icy waters, casting a gentle glow over the frolicking Lorelies. Their laughter echoed softly as they darted among towering frozen corals—some accompanied the Snows, while others paired off to play with the sea creatures that drifted nearby. The water was crisp, the current cool, but the joy in their movements warmed the kingdom with life.

Amid the lively scene, King Khione and King Bao glided through the kingdom. Bao admired the updated architecture—sleek structures carved from glacial stone and adorned with intricate etchings of ancient snow magic. Though the Snow Kingdom was the smallest, it was rich in detail and fierce in spirit. As the kings passed, the Snows bowed respectfully, their forms graceful against the glittering seascape.

Khione moved with undeniable strength. His broad, sweeping tail carved the water with powerful strokes, his arms trailing behind him, acetics clasped in a posture both humble and regal. Every motion seemed to bend the ocean to his will, sending smooth ripples outward as though the sea itself yielded to his presence.

By contrast, King Bao held the upright posture of the Eastern Modiri, his bearing reminiscent of a poised seahorse. His prehensile tail fluttered with small, precise motions, propelling him forward with quiet efficiency. His movement was a subtle dance—restrained but elegant. Where Khione exuded raw power, Bao radiated controlled magic, his stillness conveying an authority rooted not in strength, but in wisdom and tradition.

"Tell me about the girl," Bao remarked.

Khione drew a long sigh. "The hybrid. She is unique."

"What of them venturing into our waters? Need we worry?"

"I cannot say," Khione admitted. "She is here to honor the hybrid father's wish. Our Sea God demands it."

"Poseidon? Demands the hybrid live among us?" Bao exclaimed, his voice tinged with worry.

"Ahvi," Khione nodded.

"It is choorlish and irresponsible. We should not have one among us, let alone train her. We must think of mutiny."

"I concur, my brother. But we must fulfill the wish of the hybrid. It is tradition. My Lady of the Snows prays for our new Iris—your bride," Khione reasoned. "Without honoring The Ahalty, we risk damnation. Eternal punishment. And our kingdom will never recover."

"These orders come from whom?"

"The Mortis God."

"I need to know more," Bao advised. "Why did the hybrid go to our Ancient Gardens?"

"My lady's anger bested her."

"The life she took—was it the hybrid's father?" Bao asked, concerned.

"Ahvi."

Bao no longer empathized with the Snow King; he felt cross, his expression now betraying his frustration. "She has disrupted centuries of tradition, and you have not banished her to stone?"

"I know, my brother."

"The Iris will never open to her. And a Kingdom Lady, you will never supply me—I gather as much."

"You are mistaken. When we fulfill our promise to The Ahalty, the Iris will open, and you will receive your Lady of the Makaras. We never anticipated this outcome when the treaty was signed—"

Bao scoffed and turned his head with hostility. "The treaty," he grunted. "Choorlish."

"I understand your anger, and your patience is waning. But we must honor the dying wish so we can move forward in our lives," Khione said. "The girl is rare—a hybrid with magic. We have never encountered such a being. Your training is the last of it. Once it is complete, my lady and I will return to the Iris in haste. You have my word."

"…And then what of her? Your kingdom will have two majestic Lorelies, which is unorthodox. It cannot be allowed."

Khione shook his head. "We will leave it to the Sea God to decide. It is not our place to conclude such matters."

As their conversation came to an end and Bao prepared his Makara for departure, he left Khione with his final words:

"Send her to the gate. I will not make exceptions in her training—if her life is lost, so be it."

"Ahvi, my brother."

King Khione offered a slight bow, acknowledging his fellow ruler. A heavy silence settled between them, their final exchange sealed with a nod of mutual understanding. Without another word, Khione turned and finned steadily toward the heart of the Snow Kingdom. A decision had been made, and now the wheels of fate were turning.

Upon reaching the grand hall of the icy palace, he raised a hand toward one of the snow warriors stationed at the entrance. His voice, deep and forceful, echoed through the crystalline corridors.

"Alert Kaliope. She is to bring Naida to the Snow Gate. King Bao and his Makara await her."

The warrior bowed swiftly and disappeared down the glittering passage, the whoosh of his fin fading into the distance. He soon located the helley, where Kaliope sat poised atop a glacier, gazing over the snowy expanse below. Leaning close, he whispered Khione's message.

Kaliope's eyes drifted to where Naida played with her sisters, laughter echoing faintly in the frigid air.

Not long after, Kaliope arrived at the Snow Gate with Naida at her side. The Healing Lorelie moved with quiet purpose, her presence as calm as the waters surrounding them. She pulled Naida into a gentle embrace, holding her close.

"Is everything all right?" Naida asked, sensing something beneath Kaliope's stillness. "Why do you look so sad?"

Naida, still soft-spoken but grounded in quiet strength, had changed little outwardly—but her spirit had grown. At sixteen, she had fully embraced her Modiri heritage, becoming the embodiment of her lineage's grace. Her once-curious, uncertain gaze had transformed into a striking, berry-blue shimmer, filled with anticipation and a flickering excitement. Though traces of youth still danced in her expression, her eyes now carried the quiet wisdom of a girl growing steadily into her power.

Her light ash-brown textured hair flowed in soft curls down her back, carrying a natural shine that shimmered with every movement. The salt and sea had graced her tresses with a luminous luster, as if the ocean itself had laid hands upon her. Her skin, once touched by the faint roughness of youth, had transformed into something velvety and radiant—imbued with the vitality of the sea. It was as though the water had sculpted her anew, softening every edge until she became fierce, wondrous—truly the sea's own daughter.

Her brasloor seashells, once simple, now gleamed in metallic silver, their surfaces inset with diamonds and lined with delicate sapphires that traced the edges of the cups and straps. Her fin had become sleeker, more powerful, with regenerative strength that marked her growth. At her core, she was muscular and well-formed, the build of someone shaped by the tide and made for endurance.

"I am not sad, my dear. I am excited for you. I know this next part of your journey is going to seem hard at first, but you're so determined, I know you're going to do well."

"Am I leaving to learn my magic?"

Kaliope nodded, "Yes."

They exchanged no additional words—there was no need. The look in their eyes said enough: a mixture of pride, fear, and a deep unspoken love. As Naida turned away from the Snow Kingdom, her heart raced, her breath shallow in the cold air. She finned beyond the protection of the ice walls, and there he was, King Bao. The sight of him struck her like a blow. He towered above her small body, eclipsing the icy waters beneath him—his frame dwarfing her. The conical hat he wore obscured his eyes, only adding to the terror that gripped her heart.

Naida froze, her body tense as she took in the sheer size of him. King Bao remained silent for a long moment, his aura suffocating in its intensity. Then, finally, he spoke,

"I am King Bao," his tone ancient, as though the ocean itself spoke through him. "And you, Naida, will come to the East."

Naida's throat tightened, her fear almost paralyzing her, but she forced herself to nod. She knew there was no turning back now. King Bao instructed,

"My Makara will remain with you here. You are never to leave this very place until I send for you."

Confused, Naida knit her brows.

"I thought I was going with you," she said calmly.

"You are an Ushu. A part of you will join me in the East. Once she is there, I will send for you. You will have before the moon rises to bring her to me. Otherwise, you will die here. My Makara cannot go without food for too long." Just then, the Makara growled at Naida, showing its fangs, and before she could bring herself to inquire further with King Bao, he was gone. The young hybrid had become deathly afraid.

As the first light of dawn broke through the heavy clouds, Benson Jr. arrived at the Prime Minister's office, partially drenched by the pouring rain that had persisted throughout the night. He navigated through the throng of protestors, their fervent voices echoing in the air as they rallied against the government's decisions. Some wielded umbrellas, their bright colors contrasting with the dreary weather, while others stood defiantly, faces upturned to the sky, unbothered by the downpour. Among them was Willow, wearing her bold Equal Species shirt, her determination shining through despite the wet conditions. He briefly noticed her animated conversation with Alice, who, over the phone, confirmed their meeting location at the house to go to the bunker that evening.

"We keep what we earn!" they shouted.

Climbing the single white step and pushing open the heavy steel door with the number ten on it, Benson stepped into the shelter of the building, shaking his umbrella vigorously to rid it of excess water before tossing it into a bucket filled with a similar, dripping umbrella. The lobby was eerily quiet compared to the commotion taking place outside. The office was under heavy surveillance, but it felt empty, devoid of the usual buzz of activity. As he prepared the workspace for the day, Benson couldn't shake the feeling of unease that hung in the air. From the back office, he overheard his father's voice rising, sharp and filled with tension, as a conversation escalated into anger. Concern flickered in Benson's chest; he wanted to share his good news and hoped it might lighten the mood. Gently tapping on the door, he called out, "Dad, can I come in?"

Benson Sr. ended his call almost immediately. A few pounds heavier and a desk ornate with half-empty bottles of water and empty whiskey glasses, he began to scramble. Putting away the papers that piled up on his desk, tossing away the water bottles, and collecting the glasses to place under his desk.

"Of course, son, come on in," he shouted. Benson Jr. entered, and he was ecstatic, for he had not had a moment alone with his father for months.

"How are you?" he asked, looking around frantically. He could tell something was amiss.

"Oh, Benny, you know, same old same. How's it going? Is Priya treating you well?" Benson Sr. asked, his speech slurred.

"Things are all right," Benson Jr. quickly replied before stepping further inside, where he took a seat in one of the upholstered armchairs. "I wanted to talk to you about Melissa."

Benson Sr.'s eyes widened, "What of her? If you're not happy," he fanned, "It's no worry. This is no permanent arrangement."

With an eyebrow raised, Benson Jr. replied, "No, I'm all right. I think we've made some progress, to be fair. However, she told me yesterday that mother had been to visit her. Do you know why?"

His hand sliding down his cheek as he struggled to keep his eyes open, Benson Sr. knit his brows, "Your mother? Nava? Went to visit Melissa?"

"Yes."

"Well, I suppose it's normal behavior, is it not? She is, after all, to believe she is carrying our grandchild. Seems a bit off-script, but I can only assume your mother meant well."

"Believe?" Benson Jr. scoffed. "No, she is. She even felt the baby kicking yesterday. Which is something I wanted to share with both you and mum, but I don't know, everything just seems strange."

Benson Sr. sat upright in his chair; a look of sheer disbelief etched across his face as the words from his son began to sink in. His disheveled appearance—a wrinkled suit and tousled hair—spoke volumes about the night before, a night spent imbibing far too much. He felt the effects of the alcohol still clinging to him, and the realization of his current state filled him with a mix of dread and urgency. With the surge of determination, he thrust himself from his seat, stumbling slightly as he made his way to the mini refrigerator tucked away in the corner of his office. Grabbing a bottle of water and a packet of electrolytes, he twisted the cap off with shaky hands, desperate to rehydrate and clear his head. He poured the contents into the water, watching as the powder fizzled and dissolved, hoping it would restore some clarity to his muddled thoughts. Benson Jr. simply looked on as he gulped down the mixture.

The Prime Minister quickly grabbed his phone and dialed Priya, his voice strained and anxious.

"Priya, I need you to fetch me an IV drip pill before my 9 a.m. meeting," he urged, trying to keep his tone steady.

"Is everything all right? Did I say something wrong?" Benson Jr. asked, always looking to impress his father; he dreaded the thought of ever letting him down.

"No, you've done well, son," Benson Sr. smiled before admitting nervously. "I will need to get the serum for your kicking child." He hurriedly scrolled his phone, fingers typing a quick message to Dr. Astor. His eyes lingered on the screen for a moment, waiting for a response before pocketing the phone.

"A serum?" he asked, bewildered. "What on earth for?"

"The baby Benny. It's not what they want; we will need to rid her of it," he said casually. "It's no worry, you can simply try again. Only this time be vigilant. Ensure that she's given her medication two times a day as I instructed, yeh."

"Father," he stuttered. "I don't quite understand. I mean, rid her of it. As in a termination? The baby?"

Benson Sr. lowered his eyes as he sauntered back to his desk chair, where he drew a long sigh. "We are only here to appease those who matter. Unfortunately, this was the arrangement. I do not have much to do with it."

"If I am hearing you correctly, you want me to harm the baby?"

"Terminate, I believe is the correct word you used, and yes. The baby, if finned, would not be kicking. We need to get this over with so we can find you a proper bride," he grumbled. The words inaudible as he slowly drifts off into a slumber. Benson Jr. stood in the dimly lit office, the sound of his father's deep, uneven snoring echoing from the room behind him. It was a sound that transported him back to childhood—those nights when his father would stumble home late, drunk and incoherent. Benson would lie awake, listening to the familiar rhythm of his father's intoxicated slumber, a reminder of their fractured bond. They were rarely together, and when they were, his father was either consumed by work or lost in the haze of his vices.

Conversations were few and far between, and any praise or recognition was often swallowed by the alcohol that controlled his father's life. Despite bearing his father's name, Benson Jr. always felt the chasm between them. He had grown up in the shadow of a man he both revered and resented. The lack of connection, the absence of a real relationship, gnawed at him. His entire life had been shaped by an unspoken vow: to be the son his father wanted but never acknowledged—a poster child for obedience, restraint, and achievement. Benson followed the rules, played his part, and never dared to cause trouble.

But now, as he stood at the threshold of his father's office, the reality of what lay ahead hit him. He had to terminate his own child. The decision sat heavily on his chest, but it was overshadowed by the desperate need for his father's approval. After all these years, his father was finally paying attention to him, acknowledging his existence in ways Benson had long craved. He couldn't risk losing that now, not after coming this far.

Quietly, he pulled the door shut, careful not to disturb the man inside. As the latch clicked into place, a wave of sadness washed over him, threatening to break through the carefully constructed walls he had built around his emotions. For a moment, the pain lingered—a reminder of all he had sacrificed for a man who would never truly be there for him. But just as quickly, Benson shrugged it off. He couldn't afford to feel; not now. He was determined not to ruin everything he had worked for.

What seemed like seconds later, Priya came charging into the office with a swift, determined energy. She barely paused to shake the rain from her umbrella, which sprayed droplets across the floor. The protestors' chants outside were still audible through the thick glass, their cries for justice growing louder by the minute. Priya hissed under her breath, irritated by the constant racket. If it were up to her, she'd wish them all away, but part of her felt a twisted sense of satisfaction. At least the Prime Minister was around to address their concerns, and that meant she could prep him for the speech he'd be giving on the tax hikes.

In her hand, she clutched the IV drip pill, the latest in advanced technology for treating hangovers in the year 2452. The pill was a small, transparent capsule filled with blue gel that shimmered faintly. Inside, it contained a concentrated dose of Ember, electrolytes, vitamins, and synthetic enzymes that mimicked the effects of a traditional IV drip. Once swallowed, it rehydrates the body within minutes, accelerating recovery from alcohol-induced sluggishness and nausea. It was quick, efficient, and—most importantly—discreet. Perfect for the Prime Minister who needed to be on top of his game, despite the previous night's excesses.

As the clock struck 8:57 a.m., Priya glanced at her watch just in time to see a sleek, dark vehicle pull up outside. It wasn't the typical royal car; this one was an Excalibur X-952, a rare, high-security model designed for stealth and safety. Its matte black exterior seemed to absorb the dim morning light, giving it an almost ominous presence. Inside the office, Benson Jr. and the other interns and office officials were already hard at work. The hum of emails being typed and phone calls to donors filled the air, an almost frantic energy taking hold. Benson, still rattled by his earlier encounter with his father, was trying to lose himself in the tasks at hand.

The back door to the Excalibur opened, and out stepped Dr. Astor, his fragile figure immediately drawing attention. He was a man known for his presence, a doctor whose loyalty to the monarchy was unquestionable. Though his arrival was expected, as he approached the office, the tension inside seemed to spike.

"Is he in?" he asks sluggishly.

Priya's eyes widened in disbelief; Dr. Astor looked nothing like the man he once was. His appearance had deteriorated significantly, and as he stepped out of the vehicle, it was clear that whatever had afflicted him was severe. His once sharp presence was now overshadowed by a sickly, frail frame. His eyes, sunken deep into his skull, were framed by heavy bags that cast dark shadows across his gaunt face. The sharpness in his gaze had dulled, and his pupils, once vibrant, now appeared clouded with exhaustion and something more sinister. His hairline receded far back., leaving sparse patches of thinning hair that clung weakly to his scalp. Gone was the distinguished beard he had always worn, his face now bare, pale, and almost ghostly.

Once inside the office with Prime Minister Benson Sr., who, after consuming the IV drip pill, was feeling rejuvenated. He caught up on reports and found himself reciting the speech Priya had written for him to address the people later in the day during a press conference she put together. But as if he'd seen a ghost, Benson stopped,

"Dear God, what has happened to you?" he questioned. Dr. Astor stepped inside, careful to close the office door behind him. His nail beds were blackened and cracked, a disturbing sight of his declining health, and his fingers trembled ever so slightly as he clutched tightly to a worn leather briefcase.

"It is for our king," he murmured. Outside, Priya pressed her left ear to the door, curious about their discussion. Swatting away the onlookers.

"Our king? You're dying, are you not?"

Astor scoffed, "You're all so dramatic. I had to harness the Ember and to find the treatment I needed to infect myself with the N.H.S."

"But the king is already infected, surely you could have simply used it on him."

"Rubbish. The king is not a lab rat."

"Lab rat?" Benson Sr. firmly asked. "Isn't the Ember supposed to be the cure; is that not what all of this has been about? The reason my son is involved in this mess."

"Lower your tone. The Ember from Modiri Mountain that the Modiri use to drop is nothing like the one received from the creature. That was potent, different, and we could not use it for the king without being sure of its properties," Astor explained. "The finned Modiri your son will breed will go into the new grid, once it is asleep and it drips an Ember, we can be sure it will work as the others have in the past."

"So, all this time there's still been no cure?"

"What did you believe, Prime Minister?" Astor asked sarcastically. "Have you seen our king walking about, or planting azaleas in his backyard?"

Angrily, Benson Sr. replied, "Don't be curt with me. You're the one who said you had to infect yourself to treat the NHS. So, is it all lies?"

Astor let a cynical laugh vibrate through his lips, "You know nothing about science." Beneath his shaky exterior, there was an eerie presence: "I will receive the Nobel Prize for my contributions to medicine."

"Is that what this has been about? Your selfish ambitions. My son is wedded to a hybrid! We have contaminated our bloodline for this cause, and all this time you've been lying?" Priya's eyes darted to an oblivious Benson Jr.; she could feel her stomach drop. Astor had had enough of their banter; he lowered his briefcase atop the Minister's desk to remove the serum—a small jar with a black lid holding within it an orange liquid. Despite his movements, his skin seemed to cling to his bones, stretched thin, with blue veins beneath visible like tributaries running across his sunken cheeks. His clothes hung off him, ill-fitting and oversized, as though they had been chosen hastily or were remnants from a time when he had more weight on his frame. The blazer, several sizes too big, sagged on his shoulders, and the pants bunched awkwardly at his ankles.

"This is for the girl," he instructed, placing the jar atop the desk. "She will have some labor contractions almost immediately after ingestion. The chambermaids will know where to bring her."

"I want my son out of this arrangement," Benson Sr. demanded. "He will divorce, and the girl will be sent back to where she came from. We are done after this."

Astor chuckled, "You will need Her Majesty's permission—"

"I don't suppose that will be hard, considering you've been lying to us all."

With her ear pressed to the thick wooden door, Priya strained to catch the final fragments of the heated exchange between the Prime Minister and Dr. Astor. She could sense the tension fading and the conversation drawing to a close.

"All? Do you believe you're some valuable piece to this puzzle? Be obedient, address the people, and give us what we've asked for, Prime Minister," he sneered.

Instinctively, she bolted from her eavesdropping position and rushed to the lobby, her heels clicking frantically against the floor. Once there, she hastily began to shuffle papers and busy herself, feigning nonchalance. Moments later, the latch clicked, and the door to the Prime Minister's office swung open. Benson Sr. and Dr. Astor emerged, their voices soft and overly polite, exchanging pleasantries to mask the earlier intensity of their dispute. As the front door shut behind Dr. Astor, Benson Sr. exhaled deeply, his eyes narrowing. He turned sharply and beckoned for Priya; his voice low but forceful.

"Priya!" he barked, causing her to jump slightly. She rushed to his side, heart pounding. "Where did the details of your press speech come from?" Nervously smoothing her skirt, Priya cleared her throat and replied,

"It came from the royal communications office at Buckingham Palace, sir. It was rather surface-level. It hit on the main talking points, I simply embellished them into a proper speech—technological advancements, infrastructure," her voice wavering slightly, but she maintained her professional tone. She viewed him differently, dangerous.

Benson Sr.'s expression darkened. His hand, holding the speech, crumpled it. He felt deceived, "Used," he muttered under his breath, disgusted with the empty reassurances he's been fed. He crushed the paper even further in his fist, veins protruding from his temples. "Reschedule the speech," he snapped abruptly, tossing the ruined speech notes into the waste bin. "I'm going to the palace." Priya nodded, her nerves on edge, quickly making note of his command. She knew this wasn't just a routine visit—something larger was at play.

As the afternoon dragged on, Benson Jr. reentered the office after pushing his way through the swelling crowd; he felt as if he were navigating through a hive of agitated ants, their voices rising and falling like an angry tide. Signs waved violently in the air, each one a plea for justice, demanding answers, and it was as though their cries continued to fall on deaf ears. Once inside, he shook his umbrella dry, his gaze quickly darted around the space as he was the first to return from lunch. Stepping to the rear of the building into his father's office, he noticed it was still empty, and as he turned to exit, a sudden glint caught his eye.

On the desk sat a small vial, the serum glimmering in the afternoon light. Benson Jr. paused,

"Hmm, this must be the serum," he muttered to himself, furrowing his brow. He glanced around to ensure the coast was clear, the quiet office feeling too still for comfort. Why would his father leave it out in plain sight like this? he pondered, a mix of curiosity and concern swirling in his mind. He felt an urge to act, to step up once again and make his father proud. He reached for the vial, feeling the cool glass against his fingertips as he placed it deep into his pants pocket.

IV.

PRESIDENT

KIRLIN

Before the shadows of illness began to cloud King Eldric's regal presence, he was a dynamic force on the world stage, meeting with influential leaders from across the globe. His stature was impressive, standing tall with an aura of authority that immediately warranted respect. He possessed a sharp intellect and a charisma that drew people in, allowing him to navigate complex political landscapes with ease. The king had a penchant for tailored suits that accentuated his strong build, often choosing deep jewel tones that mirrored the richness of his lineage.

In his encounters with the Australian governor and the president of Zimbabwe, Eldric exuded a diplomatic finesse that captivated audiences and fostered connections. His keen insight into international affairs and the intricate web of trade relations made him a valuable ally and partner to those he engaged with. The conversations often veered toward the extraordinary potential of the Modiri Embers—a resource to be useful in the pharmaceutical industry, particularly coveted by American corporations.

However, this secret remained buried deep within the halls of power, hidden even from the Queen herself.

As Eldric shared knowledge and insights with these leaders, the underlying tension of what the Modiri Embers represented lingered unspoken in the air. This potent resource held the promise of vast wealth and advancements in medicine, yet the moral implications of exploiting such a rare gift weighed heavily on his conscience at times. Despite the honor of his position, the king often found himself in quiet contemplation, grappling with the ethical dilemmas that accompanied the political machinations of his time. Little did he know, this burden would eventually intertwine with his health, altering the course of the kingdom's future in ways he could have never anticipated.

As the rain lashed against the grand stone façade of Buckingham Palace, President Kirlin approached the entrance with a confident stride, flanked by his ever-watchful Secret Service agents. Standing at an imposing six feet, two inches, he received attention effortlessly. His broad shoulders and athletic build were accentuated by a tailored powder blue suit that contrasted sharply with the weather outside. A strong jawline and high cheekbones framed his sharp features, while his closely cropped dark hair was beginning to show streaks of silver, lending him an air of seasoned authority. His deep-set, piercing blue eyes scanned the surroundings, revealing both intensity and charm.

Once inside the palace, the thunder rumbled ominously, echoing the weight of the discussions to come. As President Kirlin entered the grand hall, he was taken aback to find Queen Emmary gracefully descending the staircase toward the drawing room. She looked radiant, her newly slim figure accentuated by a sophisticated cashmere blouse tucked into a form-fitting pencil skirt that fell just below her knees. The outfit was complemented by sleek high heels, giving her a seductive walk. Her hair meticulously arranged in a neat bun, emphasizing her refined features and the calm confidence that surrounded her.

Once inside the drawing room, the President offered a surprise smile as their eyes met, appreciating the unexpected yet warm presence of the Queen amidst the formalities of the state. The atmosphere felt charged, both with the tension of the impending meeting and the genuine respect that lingered between the leaders. The rain continued to patter against the windows, a fitting backdrop for the conversation that was to unfold within the palace walls.

"Good morning, Queen Emmary," President Kirlin smiled.

"Good morning, Mr. President," she replied. Both leaders took their respective seats in the recently sanitized room. "Tell me, what brings you here on such urgent notice?"

Crossing his legs, Kirlin chuckled, the look in his eyes doleful. "Thank you for asking, ma'am; however, I was looking forward to an arrangement with the King. Was he unavailable due to the short notice?"

"No, he is very much available, but I have been sent in his place—"

Intrigued, President Kirlin uncrossed his legs. "What could be the reason?"

"A much more personal matter," Queen Emmary smiled painfully. "But we should not dwell on the things we cannot change. I believe you are running for a second term in the next American election. I've had a chance to review your new policies, and I think it's quite admirable of you to now lean into affordable medicinal properties."

Kirlin, displeased with her response, kept his composure. "We needed to pivot given the recent changes in our arrangements—the King and I. I find it ironic that you would bring up my policies without having King Eldric present for this meeting. A very important meeting, I might add."

"Do you believe I am unfit for such councils?"

"No, no ma'am, I've said no such thing. I am simply inquiring about the whereabouts of your King. I want to win this next election, and for the past two—going on three—years, King Eldric has… well, evaporated into thin air, it would seem."

Clicking her teeth, Queen Emmary nodded in agreement. "I understand your disposition, but we are entitled to some form of privacy, even from leaders such as yourself. We did not decline your invite. I am here. To that, I believe there should be a substantial level of appreciation."

"…And of course there is, ma'am," President Kirlin quickly replied. "I never meant to insult you. I just—well, I don't want to say something you're not privy to and then this whole meeting would have been a waste of both our time, ma'am."

"The Ember," she stated confidently. "As I've mentioned before, I read your policies and the shift in your stance as it pertains to affordable medicines within your nation."

President Kirlin relaxed a bit.

"Yes. I need an update on the shipments. We have not received anything in almost two and a half years. We've managed to make do with the excess we had, raised prices in the meantime to help reduce the demand, but now that I'm running for office again, I'd like to be able to promise our citizens the cost will be lower for their advanced meds—and follow through with it."

"Why? It will be your last term anyway," she remarked, nonchalantly.

"Maybe for me and my family as well. Those Ember-infused medications have changed my life and those around me. It isn't a matter of affordability for us, but more so availability. It doesn't help that your King has gone off somewhere without any update. We've paid good money up front for those medications."

Queen Emmary listened intently, for she was not aware of this arrangement with the Americans.

"Is there a problem? Do you no longer have access to the Embers? Where do we need to go to get more?" The sound of his voice ascended—like that of an addict.

"Please. We have plenty. You will receive your due shipment within a few weeks, tops. You have my word." Despite her inner turmoil, she wore her lies like a second skin.

Clapping his knees, President Kirlin rose to his feet, looking to shake hands with the Queen—but she was in no mood. Rising, she extended her arm toward the exit. He awkwardly took his leave, bowing with uncertainty. Once President Kirlin was no longer in view, her smile quickly faded. The meeting had filled the Queen with indignation. Queen Emmary had perfected the art of deception. Her poised demeanor, always composed, was a mask she wore with practiced ease. Even as her heart thumped in her chest, her face betrayed nothing, though inside, she was panicking. Terrified of how far the Americans might go to secure their Ember-infused medicines. Their healthcare system was a complex network of public and private providers, insurers, and facilities, making the Embers significantly profitable. Higher rates for muscle relaxers, cancer treatments, opioids, and more. Their involvement was no doubt dangerous and worrisome to Her Majesty, the Queen. A resource so valuable that a war could erupt over it. And yet, she was completely in the dark about the specifics of the arrangements her husband had made. Bellowing out for the King's Guard, Emmary asked,

"Guard! Where is Watson?" In a quick, mechanical-like movement, the guard turned to face her,

"Preparing a meeting with the Royal Guards on the ground floor, Your Majesty."

"Bring me there," she instructed. King Eldric had damned them all with his secrets. As the three-inch heel from her shoes clank heavily against the marble floors, two King's Guards to her front and two at her back, the Queen stepped in her signature pose, the handclasp, her head straight and posture upright. Inside, her thoughts felt as if they would overpower her. Thinking of his illness and how it had come at the worst possible time, no sooner after the Embers from Modiri Mountain had stopped falling. It was as if some nefarious plot had been orchestrated to dismantle their rulership, piece by piece. There was no doubt that an impending storm was bearing down on her family, and with her husband showing little to no signs of improvement, the burden of leadership now rested squarely on her shoulders.

But she would not let the rule crumble. Her son, Amer, was destined for the throne, and she would ensure that no foreign power—American or otherwise—would interfere with that. No one could ever suspect the truth. Not the Americans, not her courtiers, and certainly not her enemies. Moments later, Queen Emmary descended into the dimly lit guard's chambers beneath Buckingham Palace, her footsteps echoing off the narrow hallways lined with exposed metal pipes and rivets. The air was cool, slightly damp, and smelled faintly of iron and Earth. The small hallway she walked down led to three imposing doors, each marked with a brass plaque. One held the armory, another the archives, and the third, the one she was heading toward, was the meeting room—the nerve center for the King's most trusted military and security leaders.

A King's Guard opened the door, and the room revealed itself. It was stark and functional, a sharp contrast to the grandeur above. The long rectangular table at the center dominated the space, its surface made of reinforced metal, capable of withstanding any emergency. Twelve high-backed, black leather chairs surrounded the table, their design sleek but rugged, symbolizing both power and utility. Each chair bore the crest of the Royal Guard etched into its headrest, marking the seat's importance. The seats were meant for the most trusted—those who handled the Kingdom's darkest secret, but she knew only one of them could have the answers she needed.

Around the room, multiple advanced screens blinked and shifted, displaying live feeds from high-tech security cameras. The largest screen, mounted on the far wall, showed a split image: Buckingham Palace's perimeter and the sprawling grounds of Balmoral Castle, where the Royal family's castle stood. On one screen, Amer could be seen running around the palace grounds, his long legs carrying him swiftly as he maintained his daily routine. His figure cut a determined silhouette as he dashed along the gravel path, his awareness sharp as ever.

But something caught Emmary's attention—the black car pulled up slowly beside him, her guest had arrived. Before she could smirk, Watson entered from the adjoining room, his brow furrowed, his usual composure tinged with tension. They had more pressing matters to discuss, and Queen Emmary's gaze shifted from the screen to him. The weapons lining the walls, the strategic maps and diagrams spread across the tables and the tactical equipment in the corners of the room, all reminders of his competence and profound leadership qualities. At the table's center, a holographic map of the United Kingdom flickered, highlighting key points of interest—border security, troop placements, and the current status of the Modiri Mountain grid room—still blinking red, *access denied.* As Watson approached, Emmary's fingers lightly tapped the table's edge, her thoughts moving faster than the screens around them.

Watson bowed, "Your Majesty—"

"Tell me, Watson, how long have you been of service to our family?"

"As early as nineteen, ma'am. For many years, my loyalty has been to you and our King."

"Surely," she squinted. "I need you to be straightforward with me, as now is not the moment to upset me with your lies." Confused, Watson's eyes widened in dismay,

"I would never lie to you, my Queen."

"Good," she expressed with a sigh of relief. "What do you know about my husband's affairs with the Americans regarding the Embers?" Perturbed, Watson scratched his brow, "Americans?" he questioned.

"Yes."

"There were no affairs outside of the ordinary— security and defenses, the economy—"

"Medicine, technological enhancements?"

"No, no, Your Majesty, I know nothing of those sorts. Is something the matter?" Queen Emmary neared him, whispering almost to avoid the ears of her King's Guards.

"The Americans were paying for our Embers," she revealed. "For their medicine and other substances, from what I've gathered. But what if they used it for more? Weapons," she stated, her eyes wandering around the room. "We would no longer be the superior nation."

"Is there evidence of its use in their armory?"

"I am unsure," she said, putting distance between them once again. "But we've benefited from its use through our military system. Saved trillions in tax revenue, and through it, we've built a staggering army. But we weren't alone, apparently."

"Do you believe they can be a threat to our country?"

"Yes. If we do not supply them with more. But allies or not, why would we strengthen their nation to weaken our own? Weaponry, medicine, treasury…"

"Hmm,"

"They found a way to spread it for their citizens," she clicked her teeth. "Loathsome capitalists."

"I do not follow."

"Their healthcare system is not universal—unlike ours, they do not reap any financial benefits when a life is lost, the sicker one becomes, the more expensive their treatment. To earn more revenue from their citizens, they've marketed the Ember-infused medications as advanced; they make them sick and addicted, then upcharge them for the cure, taking in more sterling than ever—far more than what they've compensated us for it, I'm sure."

"How would we know?"

"The Chancellor. I will visit her."

"Shall I accompany you?"

"Surely," she confirmed.

"Until then, what do we do about the Americans?"

"We supply a placebo. Where is Dr. Astor?"

"You assigned him the Benson boy and the hybrid girl," Watson reminded her, kindly.

"I need an update. We shall find him first."

"Copy, Your Majesty."

As Queen Emmary and Watson made their way through the winding halls of Buckingham Palace, their departure was shrouded in silent urgency. The rain outside pounded against the palace windows, but neither spoke of the dreary weather; both were consumed with the looming visit to Dr. Astor's office in Kensington. The sleek, black car was waiting for them at the private entrance, hovering patiently to whisk them away into the heart of the city. Watson, ever the vigilant guard, opened the door for Emmary, glancing at the skies as the thunder rolled threateningly in the distance.

Meanwhile, in the lush hills of Balmoral Castle, Lady Mary of Sambridge and her chambermaid Clara arrived in the same dark car that followed Amer during his run. The car's tires crushed the gravel as it pulled up to the grand entrance of the home. Amer, completing his final lap around the estate, ignored their arrival. His mind focused on the grueling morning routine he set for himself. His feet hit the ground in rhythmic precision, his breath controlled as he made his way to the enormous swimming area, his private escape.

The natatorium was nothing short of magnificent. Enclosed within towering stone walls, the ceiling arched high above with intricately carved beams and chandeliers that cast a warm light across the glistening surface of the water. Tall windows lined the southern wall, revealing misty views of the estate's vast grounds, though, at times, the rain streaked across the glass in heavy sheets. The pool itself stretched on like an endless river, its Olympic-sized dimensions daunting to anyone but Amer, who thrived on the challenge. The dark blue tiles shimmered beneath the water, creating the illusion of depthless currents swirling beneath him. Marble statues of ancient warriors lined the edges, guardians of his sacred morning ritual.

Mavis, his loyal guard, stood near the entrance, arms folded, her expression tight with concern. She admired the prince's discipline, but worried over his motives. Timing himself for how long he could hold his breath underwater and the toll it was taking on his body. Still, she remained silent, knowing how futile it would be to interrupt his routine. Amer stretched at the water's edge, preparing for his forty-five laps in the cold, crystalline waters, the light ripples barely disturbing the surface as his form sliced through them with ease.

In the grand foyer, just outside the pool room, Clara and Lady Mary were exchanging pleasantries with the castle's housemaid, who appeared to be taking breakfast up to the King's quarters. The warmth of their light, but quick conversation was appreciated by the young Sattler. Clara, polite and dutiful, spoke softly while Mary carried herself with the grace of nobility, their words filling the air as they awaited Amer's attention.

A while later, he emerged momentarily from the pool, water dripping from his broad, athletic frame. He paused briefly, his sharp eyes catching sight of the woman and young girl, whom he deemed her daughter. His wet hair clung to his forehead, and his toned arms hung at his sides, droplets of water still cascading down his skin. His jaw clenched slightly, irritation flickering in his gaze, as if their presence disrupted the calm of his self-imposed isolation. He offered no greeting, only a cold nod before turning away, disappearing deeper into the castle, leaving Clara and Lady Mary with their uneasy smiles frozen in place.

Lady Mary of Sambridge, once the spirited young girl from Sattle, now carried herself with the poise of someone far beyond her eleven years. She was the spitting image of her late mother, Emaline, her fiery red, wavy tresses now reaching just above her lower back, neatly slicked into a perfectly smooth ponytail. Her striking hair was an unmistakable reminder of her lineage, a living echo of the woman whose grace and beauty still lingered in the memories of all who knew her.

Despite her youth, Lady Mary displayed an air of maturity that was hard to ignore. At a slender four feet, eight inches, her stature was delicate, but her posture was that of someone far taller—elegant and composed. Draped in a baby pink tweed Chanel coat that matched her mini skirt, she looked every bit the image of a young aristocrat. Her white stockings were pristine, without a wrinkle or a tear, and her spotless white ballet flats added a touch of understated elegance to her ensemble. Not a single scuff marred their surface, a nod to the careful attention paid to her appearance.

Her face, smooth and blemish-free, was highlighted by her perfect smile. Though still developing into the young woman she would one day become, there was something about her demeanor that spoke of quiet self-control—as though she were always aware of how she appeared to the world. Her brown eyes held a sense of assuredness. Lady Mary was well looked after, and though she was still a child, there was no doubt that she was already becoming a true Princess Consort. She tugged on Clara's gown,

"I do not think he likes me," she whispered.

"Oh, dear no," Clara chuckled nervously. "Her Majesty invited us for dinner tonight to get acquainted with His Highness. Allow me a moment to bring his attention to you." Clara stepped anxiously to the pool room where Amer sat atop the tile, waving his foot around in the water while scrolling his phone. Mavis stood watch, relaxing a bit, her eyes on Clara, who motioned for permission to approach him. With an affirming nod, Mavis obliged.

"Your Highness," she curtsied.

Amer crunched his protein bar obnoxiously. "Yes, how can I help you?"

"Sure, my name is Clara. I am the chambermaid to our Lady Mary of Sambridge. I believe you may have missed her earlier. She is a Princess Consort, and I wanted to—"

"Ha! Princess Consort! To whom?" he cried. Amer, ever so amused by the thought, fell backwards, holding his stomach, immersed in a fit of laughter. His phone rolled from his hand, and his foot flicked upward, wetting Clara slightly. She and Mavis exchanged a concerned look.

"In all seriousness, Your Highness, please be polite. We've traveled all this way—"

"You are hilarious, chambermaid," he said to her as his laughter ceased. "She is but a child."

"I beg your finest pardon," Clara straightened up. She had developed a loving relationship with Mary and felt defensive of her.

"That girl is a child." Amer rose in haste, hurrying from the pool room, making his way down the corridor. Clara and Mavis stood behind him, her armor clanking about loudly. He gulped the last piece of his protein bar before making it to the foyer. With the crumpled wrapper in his hand, he laid eyes on Mary, and he approached her, pointing directly into her face, "This is a child!"

Mary withdrew, curling her body as Clara ran to block her. Amer, Clara, and Mary all stood in the grand entrance of the Castle as if engaged in a standoff.

"What in the world is wrong with this family? Why would anyone expect me to marry a child?" Mary looked around nervously, stepping away from Clara's protection, she introduced herself with confidence.

"Your Highness," she curtsied, her voice soft, angelic. "My name is Lady Mary of Sambridge." Amer's eyes widened in disbelief and anger.

"You are a child," he said, turning to face her. "You do not belong here. Where are your friends? Your—your little Barbie doll playing friends?"

Clara had heard enough. "Please stop berating her. She's done nothing to deserve your ill manners."

Amer took a deep breath, hoping to compose himself, "How can I say this so that everyone is in understanding. I will not wed a child. I am no pervert." The room gasped, Mavis and Clara holding their breath, the butler who entered with a pot of tea for Matilda exited the foyer quickly.

"Watch your language!" Clara bellowed, but just then Mavis intervened.

"I believe it best we end here. Take the girl to her quarters." The chambermaid obeyed.

"Come, Mary. We will await the Queen upstairs."

V.

BALMORAL HILLS

Watson, Queen Emmary, and the two King's Guards arrived at Dr. Astor's office in Kensington, stepping from the sleek black car into the warm, rain-soaked air. The rain drummed steadily on the cobblestone streets as they made their way inside. The small office seemed out of place in the elegant neighborhood, resembling more of an overstuffed library than a doctor's facility. Piles of books lined the walls, towering in precarious stacks on every available surface. Loose papers, scientific reports, and old maps littered the desks, creating a chaotic atmosphere that reeked of neglect.

The dim lighting cast shadows across the room, highlighting the dust motes floating through the air. Shelves overflowing with glass vials and equipment gave the space a claustrophobic feel, each vial filled with an amber liquid—extracted from Aiolos's Ember. The sight made Queen Emmary pause, her chest tightening with unease. These weren't just scientific curiosities; they were the result of dangerous, secret experimentation, and seeing them in such abundance sparked immediate concern.

Dr. Astor stood behind a cluttered desk, frail and gaunt, his clothes hanging loose on his frame. His sunken eyes darted nervously toward the Queen as she entered.

His hands, shaking from either illness or exhaustion, fumbled clumsily with papers as he tried to clean up. His body seemed ready to collapse under the effort, his legs trembling as though they could barely hold him upright.

"Your Majesty," he stammered, his voice hoarse and strained as he hurriedly pushed aside a stack of documents that clattered to the floor. "I wasn't expecting—please, forgive the mess."

Watson exchanged a glance with the Queen, whose expression grew even more troubled as she eyed the half-empty syringes, the liquid inside ominously swirling. Queen Emmary stepped forward, her gaze hardening as she spoke.

"Dr. Astor," she said, her voice cold but controlled.

"Yes, Your Majesty. May I offer you a seat?" he asked, rummaging about, hoping to clear the chairs.

"No, no," she replied quickly, drawing a long sigh. "You're looking more and more dead every day."

"Thank you for the compliment, ma'am," he chuckled nervously. A bewildered look sprang across Watson's face.

"Surely," she muttered. "What do you know about the Americans and our Ember?"

Dr. Astor stood perturbed, searching his mind for an appropriate response.

"Do not fib."

"I dare not, my Queen. The Americans and King Eldric have traded resources for many years."

"The Ember?"

"Sold, Your Majesty."

Queen Emmary's eyes lowered in anger. "Sold to whom and for what purpose?"

"Many country leaders—Australians, Americans… I am not certain of the others, but I am sure there are plenty, Your Majesty. It was simply my responsibility to harness the properties for proper shipping."

"Under our King's law?" she questioned sadly.

"Yes."

"What could be the reason?" Queen Emmary now needed to take a seat. She moved slowly to the chair, lowering herself in disbelief.

"As history would have it, ma'am, it was the Australians who first shared their lands with the Modiri. It wasn't until years later that the creatures began to disperse—some of whom made their way to Scotland—"

Her eyes snapped to him. "Scotland?"

"Why yes."

"Modiri in Scotland?"

"Why… yes, but not quite."

"Are they still there?"

"In hiding…I believe so."

"They've lived among us this entire time?" she yelled. "Preposterous."

It became clear to Dr. Astor that Queen Emmary had not learned her history. He stepped lightly to his bookshelf, which contained decades of research from his father, grandfather, and those before them.

"It is well studied and documented, my Queen, that not all of the Modiri sent to our lands remained in Australia following the signing of the treaty. Their husbands were soldiers of the time, needing to deploy to parts all over the world."

"What of the Ember?"

"It began a long time ago. Like the Americans and the Asians, our King was terminating the finned Modiri. But it was during the reign of King Phillis that they discovered the Ember falling from a freshly birthed finned Modiri. It was taken to the lab for further testing and, lo and behold, it was my ancestor who discovered the healing properties of the Ember. We have since harnessed it for ourselves."

"Well, if all the countries have their Modiri, why are we selling to the Americans?"

"They purified their bloodlines centuries ago. And to keep the peace, our leaders have been selling the Ember to avoid a war—one in which they might invade our waters for the Modiri. They are well aware we still have them."

"Are the hybrids and finned Modiri all gone from their lands?"

Dr. Astor shrugged. "According to their reports, it would appear so, Your Majesty. There have not been any sightings for many decades. Those who were once marked were terminated, tortured, and regarded as threats to their nation."

"We risk war if we stop supplying them?"

"Oh, but of course, ma'am."

She rose, finding her confidence once more. "So be it. We will provide a placebo."

Dr. Astor shook his head in horror.

"Your Majesty, no—I beg of you. They will know the difference. Might I make another suggestion?" He stumbled to the vials. "These are the new power," he pointed. "The Ember which fell from the creature at the mountain. It will make us unstoppable. I have been testing it on myself, you see."

He lifted his shirt sleeve, exposing a trail of injection bruises along his forearm.

"I may look feeble, but I no longer tire. I am working from sunup to sundown. I no longer hunger—it's as though I am a machine. A human machine."

Watson grimaced.

"What are you proposing?"

"The regular Embers from the finned Modiri—we get them from the girl. We use those to keep the other countries at bay, whilst we reserve the strongest for ourselves," he recommended. "The more time I spend perfecting this one, the more we will be able to create an army that never needs sleep or food—only brute strength—and can outlast everyone and everything. If we go to war with the Americans, we will prevail. We will be the strongest and healthiest nation in the world."

Queen Emmary crossed her arms, her expression one of cold scrutiny. Dr. Astor had just finished his proposal, but she remained unconvinced. His frail form, with sunken cheeks and brittle limbs, stood in stark contrast to the robust army she envisioned. She needed warriors, not men who looked like they could shatter under pressure. Her eyes narrowed as she met his gaze, her voice sharp and dismissive.

"No," she said. "A placebo. Those are my orders."

But Astor's refusal to accept her rejection came swiftly. His gaunt legs moved with surprising speed, his body a blur as he rushed toward Watson. His legs moved so quickly they seemed ready to snap, yet there was an unnatural strength behind his frail appearance. Watson, agile and prepared, evaded the attack with ease, swinging around and delivering a punch to Astor's face.

The impact was solid, but Astor did not budge. Watson's fist sank into his face, but rather than crumbling, the hole left by the blow closed up almost instantly, the skin filling in as though it had never been struck. Watson gasped, pulling back his hand, which now throbbed in pain. His knuckles stung as if he'd struck something harder than bone—it was as though Astor's frail appearance concealed a body made of metal.

Queen Emmary, initially enraged by the audacity of the attack, found herself momentarily stunned. Her eyes widened in disbelief as she watched the hole in Astor's face disappear. The Major General recoiled, shaking his hand as if trying to rid himself of the pain, but the doctor stood tall, unmoved—his brittle appearance suddenly menacing.

Her intrigue began to take hold. Clearing her throat, she said, "Perhaps we can try it your way."

"Yes, of course," an elated Dr. Astor bowed.

As Queen Emmary and Watson moved toward the door, the air in Dr. Astor's cluttered office remained thick with tension. The soft thud of the rain outside continued, muffled against the walls, adding to the eerie quiet within. Watson straightened his coat, the residual pain from his encounter with the doctor still visible in the way he flexed his fingers. The King's Guards, silent and poised, stepped swiftly behind them, their polished boots clicking against the floor in unison.

Just as they all reached the threshold, Queen Emmary paused, snapping the fingers on her right hand as if recalling something. A flicker of curiosity—almost too quick to catch—crossed her face. She turned, her cold, calculating eyes narrowing in on Dr. Astor, who stood amongst his piles of books and vials.

"Doctor."

Astor's lips twisted into a faint, unsettling smile, eager to return to his studies. "Yes, Your Majesty?"

"What of the hybrid girl?"

"Oh—"

"Is there a problem?" she questioned, the sound of her voice like a sharp blade.

The guards stiffened, sensing the shift in atmosphere, while Watson—expression neutral but wary—turned his head slightly to hear the response.

"She is with a hybrid or human child, Your Majesty," he said, his disappointment palpable.

"Hmph. Well, when is it due?"

"If all goes well, by late tonight."

Emmary's eyes widened in shock. "How so?"

"The Prime Minister is in possession of my vial."

"The same vial from earlier? I do not follow. What will it do to her?"

"Simply induce the labor, ma'am. She's a hybrid, so the effects are not the same as they would be for us humans. This Ember's properties are far different from what we're used to. The right dosage will surely cause her no harm."

"I thought you said the serum was going to guarantee us a finned Modiri. What of our King and his cure?"

Queen Emmary snarled, her nostrils flaring. "We've waited two years for this child, and it's not even the right one. What deceptive ploys are you playing at?"

The guards took their positions to protect Her Majesty as Astor took a few steps back, fearful they might attack him.

"Your Majesty, please—this is not a simple process. It has proven to be far more intricate than I could have anticipated. We will have the finned Modiri, you have my word," he stammered. "Besides, she's still very young—a good age to procreate as much as needed."

"The Americans need the Ember medicine, as you've so convinced me—and so does our King. The regular Ember, not this mutant medicine you're injecting into yourself. You went on some rogue mission that was never approved by The Crown, and now the orders you were given have yet to be carried out," Queen Emmary held her powerful gaze, her eyes burning mad. "Tell me, Astor, why should I spare your life? A thump to your noggin did not suffice, but I know a sharp blade to your throat will prove victorious."

Dr. Astor, throwing himself to his knees, pleaded for mercy. "Your Majesty, I beg—please grant me your patience. I will show you that all has not been in vain, and we will make the world bend to our will. The girl should be in the bunker lab by nightfall, if all goes according to plan. You are welcome to join us there. I want to show you the progress we have made. You will have dominion over all."

"My dominion or that of our King? Either way, get me what you promised. I need to have a word with my husband, and I will not continue to speak to a vegetable."

With that, she exited swiftly, her dark silhouette vanishing into the dimly lit corridor beyond. Watson followed closely behind, casting one last glance at Astor before the guards fell into formation. Their movements were swift and precise. Inside the hovered vehicle, neither the Queen nor Watson made eye contact; their gazes remained fixed forward.

"How far are you willing to go to prove your loyalty to The Crown?" she questioned.

"Wherever needed, Your Majesty."

"Good. Remember those words," she confirmed before bellowing to the self-driving navigation system, "We will go to the port for Scotland."

Their journey lasted a mere three hours, but for Queen Emmary, it felt far longer as her mind churned over the conversation with Dr. Astor. The roaring sound from the jet engine did little to soothe her growing unease. Astor's cryptic words and his unnatural resilience haunted her thoughts. She clenched her hands in her lap, her knuckles whitening, though outwardly, her face remained a mask of calm. A queen must never betray her emotions, even in the face of treachery. She had long mastered the art of hiding fear behind a veil of regality.

As Balmoral Castle came into view—the sprawling stone fortress standing tall against the backdrop of the misty Highlands—a small crowd of tourists could be seen lingering at the gates. The sound of camera shutters clicking filled the air, though their conversations were muffled and indistinct from inside the car. Emmary's sharp ears picked up a few scattered words, likely about Emaline's scandalous video—the one that had circulated the globe. The world would not soon forget, and how could they? Tourism had dwindled since the video was released, a reminder of the world's thirst for royal disgrace.

Still, no official statement had been made. Queen Emmary knew that silence could be powerful, but now that silence felt heavy—suffocating even. Astor's words lingered like a dark cloud, and the Queen found herself questioning everyone around her. The doctor was all too cunning, too dangerous, and could no longer be trusted. But she needed him.

The hovering car slowed, approaching the castle's grand driveway, the towering gates swinging open with a groan. The Queen's eyes scanned the familiar grounds—the manicured lawns and ancient trees—but her mind was elsewhere. She needed guidance. But who could she turn to in a world where trust had become a currency so rare?

As the car came to a stop, Emmary and Watson emerged, but before they could step past the threshold, the heavy thud of boots echoed through the hall. Prince Amer came stomping toward the foyer, his face flushed with frustration. The young prince's usually composed demeanor was gone, replaced by the fire of youthful rebellion. His sharp eyes, however, never landed on Watson—as though the man was invisible, a mere shadow in the grand hall.

Amer's gaze was fixed on his mother, his voice trembling with anger. "Who is this Mary, Mother?" he demanded. "Why is she here, in our home, uninvited?

That lady with her, spewing nonsense about being a bride? A bride to whom?"

Just then, Watson shot him a look. He winced at the thought of Kovos as the hybrid flashed across his mind. Though his words were fierce, there was something vulnerable beneath them—a flicker of the young boy who once idolized his mother and father.

"I am no child to be dictated to. I will choose my own bride, just as past kings have before me—as Father did!"

In front of Emmary, Amer seemed to shrink, his anger masking a deeper hurt. He didn't want to be forced into a future he had no say in. But his mother could not bring herself to quarrel with her son—not after the taxing journey and the mounting uncertainties gnawing at her. She simply waved a hand, dismissing him with a fan-like gesture, her eyes cold but tired.

"My dearest boy, please," she said coolly, her voice devoid of emotion, as if she were brushing away a minor inconvenience.

Amer's shoulders tightened, his fists clenched, but he said nothing more. He recoiled, his imposing presence crumbling back into that of a frustrated young man seeking approval. As Clara, the chambermaid, descended the stairs with graceful steps, Amer cast one more glance at his mother, his expression a mixture of defiance and desperation.

But the Queen had already turned away.

Her attention was no longer on him.

"Where is the girl?" she questioned.

"In her quarters, ma'am," Clara curtsied.

Amer's protests hung in the air, unanswered, as he stormed off deeper into the castle, leaving a trail of unspoken words and wounded pride behind. Queen Emmary instructed Watson to remain stationed—she needed a word with their king. Within a split second, she brushed past Clara, who stood bewildered but remained silent, her hands clasped before her in dutiful patience. Emmary's focus was elsewhere, her heart thumping rapidly as she aimed her steps toward her bedroom with urgency. The grandeur of the hall—the golden frames and tapestries of royalty—blurred as she made her way.

Inside the bedroom, the scene was tranquil yet haunting. King Eldric sat on the balcony, his frail body slumped in the wheelchair that had become his constant companion. Matilda, his devoted nurse, sat beside him, her voice soft as she read from the afternoon post.

The newspaper rustled in her hands as she recited the latest headlines, her words drifting on the gentle breeze. Though his face remained expressionless, King Eldric's mind still grasped fragments of the world around him— an article here, a name there. The N.H.S. had not completely overtaken him, but with each passing day, it crept further, stealing away the man who once ruled with strength.

The open balcony doors invited the scents of late spring into the room. The afternoon air was blissful and carried the faint warmth of summer's approach. Beyond the balcony, the landscape unfolded like a painting—a patchwork of rolling hills blanketed in the softest green, the royal gardens below bursting with life. The roses, meticulously tended, bloomed in perfect reds and whites.

The tall oak trees swayed gently, their leaves rustling in harmony with the chirping of birds that flitted among the branches. Overhead, the sky was a serene expanse of pale blue, with only a few scattered clouds drifting lazily.

As Queen Emmary entered, her presence immediately silenced Matilda, who stood at attention.

"Your Majesty," Matilda curtsied quickly, her gaze flickering between the Queen and the King. Without needing to ask, she understood, and with a hurried bow, she exited the room, leaving them alone.

Once the door clicked shut, Queen Emmary spared not a single second. She approached the balcony and sank to her knees before her husband, her composure crumbling. Her delicate, manicured hands clutched the armrests of his wheelchair, her face contorting with anguish as tears streamed down her cheeks. The Queen—always so strong and imperious—had finally broken in the presence of the one person who could no longer respond.

Outside, the world continued in its peaceful rhythm—the birds chirped in sweet melodies, the wind softly played with the curtains, and the sunlight bathed them in her golden hue. Through trembling lips, Queen Emmary's words flowed like a soliloquy, raw and unfiltered.

"My king," she began, her voice barely above a whisper, "for years I underestimated your strength and took for granted your leadership."

She paused, her hands placed gently atop his, as though she could draw some of his former might back into the present.

"These decisions are tiresome, never-ending, like a parasite that eats away at your soul," she continued, her breath catching with each word.

Her gaze, tear-streaked and filled with torment, fixed on the distant horizon beyond the balcony, as if searching for answers in the landscape of Balmoral's hills.

"So many decisions made without my knowing or understanding. You have kept me in the dark, but I see now, perhaps, it could have been for my own protection… and that of our son and future King."

She glanced back at him.

"The tourists here in Aberdeenshire… and our Ember to so-called allies, our military, our infrastructure, the medicine…"

She shook her head as though the weight of it all threatened to crush her.

"So much to digest that it stalls my appetite entirely."

Emmary's eyes—once filled with hope and ferocity—were now clouded with sadness and doubt.

"Eldric, the natural-born leader you are," she murmured, her voice wavering, "so confident, so fearless—and dare I say it, foolish."

A quiet whimper escaped her as she averted her gaze, unable to fully confront her king in such a weakened state.

"Was it I you did not trust with your secrets, or that of my potential criticism, so much so that you let your arrogance take hold of you?"

She wiped at her eyes, her hands trembling as her mind raced through the recent revelations.

"I cannot grasp the concept of selling or trading our Ember with the Americans, who have somehow purified their bloodlines once more—as if before the start of the war," she said, her voice rising with incredulity.

"If the artificial intelligence humanoids turned against us once, do you not suppose it could happen again? Yet we arm them with the very tools they would need to overcome us in battle—both man and machine?"

The bitterness in her tone was unmistakable as she added,

"The Asians—I-I dare not even speak of it."

Her chest heaved with frustration and desperation as she repositioned herself beside him, her hands tightening around his unresponsive arm.

"Our alliance should always be to our people first, Eldric. What were you thinking?" Her voice was pained but filled with a lingering love and reverence.

"I voice my concerns with love, as I would not ridicule you, my King. But I need to know what we should be doing now, in this moment. How do I protect us from the things you've set in motion?"

The gravity of the unknown began to bear down on her, pressing into this moment of vulnerability.

"I cannot save our country from potential threats if, with each passing day, those threats reveal themselves to me in mere bits and pieces."

Tears flowed freely now as she shook his limp form gently, her voice growing more desperate.

"You need to snap out of this. I need you back," she cried, repeating the words as though they might stir him. "I need you back."

Despite her pleading tone, King Eldric remained still, his eyes blank, as the birds outside continued their song—indifferent to the turmoil in the hearts of the royal family.

Feeling almost delusional for hoping he might respond, Queen Emmary rose, her tears drying as she composed herself. Her gaze lingered on King Eldric's lifeless eyes, yearning for some flicker of recognition, but none came. The longing in her heart, like a painful ache, burned brightly in her chest. In an instant, her expression shifted. Something within her decided. A new resolve took hold.

Outside, Amer, growing ever defiant, had once again managed to slip away unnoticed. His steps led him down the sloping lawn of Balmoral, past the ancient trees, and toward the TomTom River, where the waters glistened in the fading afternoon light. His mind wandered, thoughts swirling around Fiona and the secrets that beckoned beneath the surface. Standing at the riverbank, he stared out into the depths, the cool breeze brushing his skin. He knew he had little time before Mavis or the guards realized his absence and came searching for him.

Without a moment's hesitation, and with the recklessness of a young prince determined to defy his fate, Amer plunged into the river. The cold water engulfed him as he swam down, deeper and deeper, with no direction, but he prayed his heart would be a compass. His strokes were strong, the pit of his stomach churning with fear, but he would find her, even if it meant risking his life.

Inside the castle, Queen Emmary strode with purpose, her earlier emotions now tightly locked away behind her royal mask of composure. She descended the stairs into the grand foyer, her heels clicking against the polished floor with a rhythm synchronized with her thoughts.

"Clara," she called. The maid appeared at once, curtsying nervously before the Queen.

"Fetch me Mary," Emmary ordered, her tone leaving no room for misunderstanding.

"F-for dinner?" the maid asked, bewildered.

"No. Just bring her here," Emmary's voice was sharp—scary, even.

There was no time to waste.

She had a plan.

VI.

NUVI

Hours later, beneath the dark, icy waters a few miles from the Snow Kingdom's gate, Naida lay motionless on the seabed. The sea's chill was numbing. Her acetics drifted slowly around her, tangling with the few fish that survived in the kingdom's deepest reaches.

Fear gnawed at her—an aching dread that her time was near. The Makara—a beast whose name had never been spoken to her—haunted her thoughts, its eyes seeming to fix on her through the dark, waiting for the perfect moment to strike.

To keep herself grounded, Naida let her acetics brush the backs of the circling fish, some of them already drifting into a deep slumber. But even the comfort of their scales couldn't quiet the rising terror. Her mind wandered, wrestling with the possibility that this might be her end.

Then, a shadow moved—lithe and quick—dodging through the water. Her eyes darted toward it. Instinctively, she reached out, her acetic energy flaring in an attempt to put it to sleep. But the eel, swift and cunning, slipped through her grasp, as though it too sensed her vulnerability.

"What are you doing?" Fanira snarled, her tone stiff and surly.

Naida twitched in horror, but her fright soon turned to relief.

"Oh, Fanira, you're here!" she smiled.

Fanira circled her; the Makara, drifting in and out of its slumber, perked its ears to listen keenly to their private confab.

"Why are you not training?"

"Training?" Naida yelped, slithering upright, her fin flapping gracefully next to her, tapping the seabed lightly. "The King… King Bao, he simply left me here and told me to meet him in the East, but not me, me, the other me. Whatever that means."

Fanira wandered for a moment, finning back and forth, around in circles, as if an abrupt stop would cause her to fall lifelessly to the sea's bottom.

"Is that all he told you?"

Naida shook her head. "Yes. Oh—and he called me an Ushu." Her voice was weary, but cheerful.

"An Ushu?" Fanira questioned, her yellow eyes glowing as if she'd heard something of great significance.

"Yes," Naida confirmed. "What does that mean?"

Fanira slithered in slow, deliberate circles around Naida, her slender, sinuous body moving through the cold waters like a predator stalking its prey. Her eyes observed the small, timid hybrid girl, trembling beneath her gaze. This girl—this fragile creature—was supposed to be an ancient Ushu? Fanira could hardly believe it.

The Ushu were legendary—majestic beings of the Modiri, revered for their extraordinary ability to Sila'rum. Normally, when an Ushu slept, their bodies could split—their soul and physical form dividing into two entities, yet still acting in unison. It was a curse long thought lost with the fall of the Wor Modiri magic, a power feared and respected for the level of control it required. The soul would travel great distances, while the body remained grounded in slumber. And this power, as ancient as the Ushu themselves, lay dormant in the girl before her.

"You dare take such news faintly?" the witch hissed, circling tighter, her voice dripping with disdain and curiosity. "Small, timid, and yet, you are an Ushu." She paused, her eyes locking onto Naida's, searching for the power hidden within. "Do you even know what you are? What you could be?"

Naida's heart raced, her breathing shallow.

"N-no," she stuttered.

The Makara stirred, sensing the rising tension as Fanira circled Naida, who was growing concerned as the witch came closer—her presence suffocating.

"Your body will stay, but your soul must go," she hissed.

In an instant, Fanira's demeanor shifted from calculated menace to unrestrained predator. Without warning, she lunged at Naida, her sleek body coiling and striking with terrifying speed.

Naida barely had time to flinch before the eel was upon her, her sharp eyes glinting with intent to harm. But before she could close the distance, a powerful force surged through the water. The ocean floor trembled as the massive form of the Makara shot forward, his long, serpentine body cutting through the deep with an agility that belied his size. Ripples cascaded in all directions, sending sea creatures scattering and sand billowing up from the seabed.

With a swift and mighty swing of his head, the Makara knocked Naida to safety, shielding her behind his towering form. His massive presence loomed over both of them—the ancient sea dragon now a living wall between Naida and Fanira. His eyes, glowing with an eerie intensity, locked onto Fanira with a warning that needed no words.

Naida gasped, her heart pounding in her chest. She had trusted Fanira, seen her as a friend, but now... now she was something else—an enemy? Her betrayal was as sharp as the fangs she had nearly bared, and Naida's voice cracked with disbelief.

"Why?" she cried. "Why do you want to hurt me?" Her eyes had darkened, her true intentions overtaking whatever bond they had once shared. But she could act no further—the deep, thunderous voice of the Makara filled the water. It was brisk, accompanied by a low rumble that seemed to shake the very ocean around them.

"You will not harm the hybrid."

Naida looked up in disbelief. "You talk?"

His words cut through the tension like a blade, and even Fanira, fierce as she was, hesitated. The Makara's presence was too commanding, too overwhelming. He glared at her, daring her to defy him.

"I will yield... for now. King Bao will hear from me and the Shadows," she warned.

Before Naida could breathe a sigh of relief, Fanira's form began to blur into the shadows of the sea, her body slowly vanishing from sight. The Makara lowered his head, bringing his ancient, glowing eyes level to hers. She tilted her head back to meet his gaze, fear rippling through her.

"Why did you help me?" she asked, her voice a hoarse whisper.

The Makara's eyes flickered like smoldering embers beneath the waves.

"You now belong to the East," he rumbled. "King Bao is the only one who shall see to your demise."

Naida's heart stilled. "But why?" she stammered, panic rising in her chest. "The moon is soon to approach and I am no more the wiser. Should I use my acetics and put myself to sleep? Can't you tell me anything? I don't want to die here."

She trailed off as her eyes caught the shift in the waters around them. The afternoon light had begun to fade, giving way to the muted blues and purples of dusk. The sea, which had once sparkled with bright clarity by day, now grew darker, deeper. Flecks of silver danced across the surface, catching the last remnants of sunlight as evening lowered.

The water itself seemed to hum, alive with anticipation, the approaching moon casting a vague glow. The silence of the sea was heavy, almost tangible, as if the ocean were holding its breath. Shadows stretched long and eerie, twisting through the coral beds and over the rocks. A slow, chilling current moved through the deep, brushing past Naida's skin like a warning.

No longer protected by the Makara, the hybrid let her body drift downward, sinking lifelessly back to the seabed. Her eyes lowered in quiet surrender, as if she were yielding to the inevitable. She resumed her lonely ritual, using her acetics to gently lull the small fish around her into a deep sleep—the only thing she could control in the vast, unforgiving sea. Darkness enveloped her, the moon creeping slowly into the sky, its pale light casting a cold shimmer down below. The Makara, hovering above, licked its lips, its eyes trained on her like a predator awaiting the final moment.

As Naida closed her eyes, she embraced the thought of dying, hoping for a painless end. But instead of fear, there was a strange calm. Her mind slipped away, and she fell into a deep slumber. In her dreams, she found herself back at the old boardwalk in her hometown of Sattle, the sea air warm and familiar. At the far end of the boardwalk stood her mother, Emaline, her hand extended, a soft grin decorating her face. The sight of her filled Naida with a sadness she hadn't felt in years, her lips downturned, quivering as if to weep.

But as she reached out, something shifted in the dream. The breeze off the water seemed to change—no longer warm but cool and firm, as if it carried with it a presence. Slowly, another face entered her mind, brushing aside the comfort of her mother. Kalkisis. His face appeared clearly, and with it, like the wind itself.

"Go to King Bao," he whispered, his voice guiding her like an invisible tether.

Naida's eyes shot open. The Makara's jaw, wide and ready to swallow her whole, loomed just above her. But something had changed. Her eyes, once a stormy grey, now shifted to a berry blue, their depths swirling with new power. Her body remained still, lifeless to an observer, but inside, she had done it. In a flash, she vanished, her physical form slipping from the ocean's grip. She had teleported her body and soul across the seas to the East Oriental Kingdom, leaving the Makara to snap its jaws on nothing but empty water. The sea dragon let out a deep, frustrated rumble—its prey gone in an instant.

And there, far from the seabed where she had surrendered, Naida now glided in the heart of King Bao's kingdom, where he awaited her. But his expression was stern, his displeasure unmistakable. His conical hat hid his eyes, but Naida could feel the weight of his disappointment as he regarded her. Her attempt to teleport had succeeded, but it was not correct.

"You dare disobey me? The Great King Bao?" he scolded. "I did not send for you. Bring me the Ushu!"

Without another word, he removed his left acetic, and with one wave, the waters around her stirred violently, pulling her from the Makara's kingdom and casting her back to the seabed from whence she came.

The Makara was waiting, its long, sinuous body coiled in the depths, its eyes burning with fury. Naida had escaped him once, and that had only intensified his hunger. Now, with her return, he saw his chance for revenge.

In an instant, she appeared back in the Arctic waters, her heart pounding as the sea dragon's immense form cut through the water with terrifying speed. His powerful body churned the ocean's bottom, sending sand and debris flying in his wake. She could feel his anger—palpable and sharp—as he closed in on her.

Desperation overtook the young girl as she finned frantically through the murky depths, looking over her shoulder to see the Makara's glowing eyes fixed on her.

"Please!" she cried, her voice trembling as the water rushed past her. "Spare me! I am only a child!"

But the Makara's rumbling voice, now a sinister growl, echoed through the ocean.

"You are supper, girl. There will be no mercy."

It taunted her as he gained speed, his massive jaws snapping just behind her tail fluke. Naida weaved through the coral beds and crevices, her small body darting between obstacles in a desperate attempt to evade him. Each time she looked back, the Makara drew closer, his eyes filled with hunger. Ever one to play with his food, he found Naida's resistance gratifying.

Fear clouded her mind, and her fin burned with the effort of escape. Finally, just as she began to tire, she spotted a small hole in the seabed—as if destined—a narrow crevice in the rocks just big enough for her to squeeze into. Without hesitation, she darted inside, her body scraping against the rough edges as she forced herself deeper into the tiny hiding place.

The Makara roared in frustration, his snout pressing against the entrance, but it was too small for him to reach her. His teeth clicked menacingly outside, the sound reverberating through the rocks as his body writhed with fury. Naida lay there, her body trembling, her heart racing. The darkness of the small cave pressed in around her, her only solace being that, for now, the Makara couldn't touch her. She closed her eyes, feeling the tears welling up as hopelessness settled over her. The sound of the Makara's taunts filled her ears, his voice cruel and mocking.

"You can hide, little hybrid, but not for long," he growled. "I will be waiting."

In the silence that followed, Naida's trembling acetic reached for the small fish still swimming beside her—her only companions in this lonely place. She whispered softly, her voice barely audible. "Father, please help me. I don't want to die here."

The cave grew still, the only sound her soft breath and the distant rumbling of the angry sea dragon. As she lay there, her eyes fluttered shut, exhaustion overtaking her. She whispered once more into the darkness, clinging to the hope that her father, Kalkisis, would hear her plea.

Benson Sr. stormed into Buckingham Palace, his fury palpable, driven by the boiling anger that had guided him all the way there. His presence was menacing, his fists clenched as he expected an immediate confrontation with Queen Emmary. Yet, as he paced through the marble halls, his face reddening with frustration, the Queen was nowhere to be found. Guards were posted at every entrance, their eyes keen but distant, offering no answers. Outside, tourists crowded the gates, their cameras flashing in unison, capturing every fleeting moment of the regal surroundings.

Fuming, Benson Sr. realized the futility of his unannounced arrival. With a growl of frustration, he stormed back to his hovered vehicle, slamming the door behind him as it lifted off the ground. Though the afternoon sun had begun its slow descent, casting an amber glow over the city, its warmth did little to temper his mood.

Meanwhile, Benson Jr., along with the vial in his pocket, had quietly asked Priya to leave the office early.

The guilt gnawed at him, and the office felt like a cage. Every moment he remained there increased his anxiety. As fate would have it, just as Benson Sr. returned, Benson Jr. had already left. His departure was swift and unnoticed. The Prime Minister, stepping into his office with his mind swirling with plans and accusations, was too late. His son—along with the vial—had already gone.

The Prime Minister furiously tapped away at his phone, sending text after text to his son. Each message was met with silence. The calls, too, went unanswered, each ring fueling his growing panic. His fingers shook as he tried once more, the final attempt ringing through to voicemail.

"Jr., call me back. Now!" His voice was tense. He could not afford to lose control over the situation, but the sinking feeling in his chest told him it was already spiraling out of his grasp. In a last-ditch attempt, he dialed Nava, but when her voicemail answered, he begged her to go to their estate. Benson Sr. only wished he had more time to clarify his role in their scheme. But the clock was clearly against him.

Moments earlier, outside, Benson Jr. had already fought his way through the mass of people. The streets were alive with noise—the shouts of protesters, the hum of hovercrafts passing by, and the steady murmur of tourists who were oblivious to the turmoil brewing just beneath the surface. He moved quickly, his heart pounding as he kept his head low, the vial hidden.

Equal Species members Alice and Willow, their expressions set with determination, exited soon after him, exchanging glances as they slipped into the thick of the crowd. They knew Linus would arrive soon at their hideout, and it was time to set their evening plan into motion.

Willow hailed a taxi, her voice sharp as the hover-vehicle descended just enough for them to climb inside. The sleek automobile rose again, lifting them above the commotion of the streets.

As they sped toward Kensington, Alice felt an unsettling chill run down her spine. She fidgeted in her seat, her gaze flickering toward the cityscape but unfocused. Something felt wrong—deeply wrong.

"Are you all right?" Willow asked, her voice steady, but her eyes betrayed a hint of concern as she watched her friend's unusual demeanor.

Alice hesitated before responding, her voice strained. "Have you ever just had a strange feeling something bad was about to happen?"

Willow rolled her eyes and huffed, brushing off the question with a smirk. "Oh, for heaven's sake, Alice. We know the risks. But it's for a cause much bigger than us. So what if we happen to be slaughtered or annihilated—one of us, whichever is the quickest on their feet, will live to tell the tale."

Her words were bold, even flippant, but they did little to ease Alice's nerves. Usually, she thrived in the rush of adventure, the thrill of rebellion, but today felt different. Stranger. The unsettling feeling clung to her like a shadow, whispering that something far worse than any of them anticipated was looming on the horizon.

Downstairs, in the dimly lit makeshift command center of their Kensington hideout, Willow and Alice settled in, the hum of their equipment filling the air as they made their final preparations. The sound of the doorbell echoed through the house, cutting through the low chatter. Andrew was engulfed in his video game and virtual reality streaming while their mom was at Bible study. The home was quiet.

Willow glanced at Alice, who shrugged before heading upstairs. When she returned, Piper followed close behind, her face scrunched in annoyance.

"Ugh, is no one else bothered by all these hover vehicles?" she grumbled, kicking off her boots as she entered. "It's like they speed right by you—but what if they fall? Then what? My motor insurance rates will skyrocket. Or worse, if I'm not in the car, I'm dead!"

Her disdain for the modern mode of transport was no secret.

"We rode in one here. They're not too bad, yeh," Willow said.

Piper, always the old-school rebel, had a deep love for traditional wheels—the kind you could feel gripping the road, not hovering through the air.

"Surely, it's just the palace's way of trying to justify its tax hikes. 'Oh look, you poor sobs, now you can afford your own version of luxury,'" she mocked.

Willow smirked, half amused but too focused to entertain Piper's rant.

"I miss those old days, yeh? When it was the rich and those wealthy bastards who could afford them. Let them turn their neighborhoods into The Judsons. Or when there were just a few—you know, a couple you could count. Why bring so many here? Our infrastructure isn't even built for the hovers."

Alice rolled her eyes, shifting her attention back to the screens in front of them, her mind still preoccupied with the bad feeling in her gut. But before they could change the subject, Piper blurted, "Oh, by the way, Max is coming with us tonight."

"No way," Willow protested, her eyes narrowing. "He's just a kid! He'll slow us down."

Alice crossed her arms, a frown deepening on her face. "I told you I had a bad feeling about this," she muttered, the unease in her voice evident.

Piper stood her ground, placing her hands on her hips. "The little con artist won't give up the badge unless he comes. Claims he needs closure for his brother."

Before they could argue further, the sound of footsteps signaled the arrival of the rest of their crew. Luckily, Andrew needed a snack break. Preston entered first, a cool expression on his face, followed by Linus, who gave a nod to the group.

"Why are you all so quiet now?" Linus teased.

"Piper is bringing the boy with us," Alice confessed. "I honestly can't bear to see his face. He took my watch."

Linus, consoling his girlfriend, rubbed her back softly before removing the day's weight from his shoulders and taking off his spring jacket. "I understand. But why does he have to come?"

"He won't give up the badge," Piper interrupted.

"Well, we bring him," Preston decided. "There's no use debating about it. He has the one thing we need to get inside."

"I agree," said Linus. "So, it's getting late. Are we ready with the Nuvi?"

The Nuvi, also known as the Neurovision Headband device, is a controversial yet powerful tool for memory recovery. Designed to fit over a person's head like a sleek, futuristic headband, the device taps directly into the brain's neural pathways, specifically targeting the hippocampus, where memories are stored. The Nuvi headband is made from a smooth, graphene-like material—flexible yet durable—and once activated, it projects the recovered memories as vivid, three-dimensional holograms in real time, viewable to everyone in the surrounding area.

These holograms appear above the user's head, floating like an interactive movie, where scenes from the user's mind play out in high definition, with perfect clarity for both sound and image. The projection process is immersive, with details so sharp that onlookers can witness even the most fleeting expressions or sounds captured in the memory.

It is because of this clarity that the Nuvi has caused widespread controversy. While initially lauded for its applications in therapy, criminal investigations, and archival purposes, public sentiment shifted as concerns about privacy grew—along with reports of memory loss. Many believe the technology exposes too many personal and intimate memories without proper control.

Now, the device is primarily used under strict legal regulations, with heavy government monitoring to ensure it's not misused. But the daughter of a Royal Guard, Alice had managed to find one long ago while deep cleaning their home for the holidays.

As Alice gently applied the headband to Linus's head, she smiled. "Are there any gals I should know about?" Her tone was playful.

Linus returned the gesture, laughing loudly. "You know better than that—as do I." The pair exchanged a sweet kiss.

Willow smiled warmly, her face alight as she basked in their affection. At five foot six, with 4C-textured hair cropped into a short, springy afro, she carried an easy wit and a natural charisma. A self-proclaimed lover girl, her style held the carefree spark of a millennial teenager—fun, expressive, and sometimes a touch quirky. Born to Haitian and Trinidadian immigrants who had made their home in Brockley in their twenties, Willow was the youngest of three, with two older brothers. The richness of her heritage shaped the brightness of her spirit, giving her both warmth and quiet grit.

They were all apart, each entangled in their own assigned duties, preparing notes from the projector images. Piper and Preston exchanged glances, rolling their eyes in mild disgust.

"Enough of that. Let's get a move on," Piper interrupted lightheartedly.

Willow shot her a teasing grin. "You're only jealous because you've yet to find a man to look at you like that."

Piper scoffed and quipped, "At this rate, I'm going to find a good, nice hybrid to marry—or at least kin. They seem to be the only breed of quality men."

"Now, now," Preston interjected.

The group chuckled, but the moment passed quickly. With their romantic interlude over, Alice stepped up to the control panel and flipped the switch to power on the Nuvi. Shortly thereafter, the device came to life. The room darkened slightly, and suddenly the flash of images burst into view—memories suspended in the air like moving paintings.

Alice deftly controlled the dial, rewinding through the haze of holographic memories, searching for the exact moment. The group leaned in, watching closely.

Within minutes, they confirmed it—the exact location of the bunker—identifying street signs and abandoned buildings in the surrounding neighborhoods. Their hearts quickened, realizing they were running out of time. The longer the Nuvi stayed connected to Linus, the more core memory he would lose.

Shutting it all down, they sprang into action. But just as they prepared to leave, everyone froze. The silence was sharp. Alice spoke, her voice uncertain.

"Where is Max?"

"Oh, that twerp!" Piper yelped.

VII.

THE USHU

The city of London buzzed with an anxious tension, as though all events were converging in unison. The Equal Species members lingered in restless anticipation, their patience for Max rapidly wearing thin, while Queen Emmary made her stately journey back to Westminster. Accompanied by a young Mary, Watson, and the King's Guards, she left Clara behind to speculate over their covert mission and its purpose.

The sun dipped toward the horizon, casting the cityscape in hues of fading light as Benson Jr. arrived home at his opulent Hampstead residence. There, a radiant and heavily pregnant Melissa waited to greet him proudly, eager to share her accomplishments. She had assisted the chambermaids in preparing their supper for the evening— an elaborate feast sprawled out in the grand dining room.

The platters were laid out, featuring dishes far beyond what was imaginable just a few centuries prior: hovering plates of tender seared Nebula prawns with micro-crystals of violent sea salt, a nutrient-enriched vegetable aspic in vibrant technicolor hues, and glazed lunar truffles paired with ancient grain bread made from rare harvest grown in controlled biomes. There was synthetically aged honey mead, thick and golden, served beside a deep, glassy dish of exotic marine gel—a delicacy for elite gatherings—adorned with edible diamond flecks.

Meanwhile, beneath the darkening waters, Naida called to her parents, her mind filled with longing as her voice echoed silently through the depths. She could picture them vividly, as though they might reach down to pull her from the murky abyss. The Makara waited, his restlessness mounting as the moon rose even higher, casting silver threads of light into the water and marking Naida's precious moments slipping away.

Max stumbled up to the house, his clothes torn at the sleeves and hems, dirt streaked across his cheeks, and his usually combed hair a mess of tangled curls. He wore a proud, defiant look, standing tall despite the haggard state he was in. Piper swung the front door open as they all seemed to emerge from the living room one by one, ready to pounce, their voices rising in a barrage of irritation and questions about why he was so late.

"Where have you been?" Alice demanded, crossing her arms. She was loud enough to be upset but quiet enough not to draw attention from the neighbors.

"Do you even know what's at stake?" Willow added, eyeing his appearance with both frustration and curiosity.

Max scoffed, shrugging them off, his lips curved into a tight, mocking smile. "None of your business," he replied. But Piper stepped forward, eyeing the young lad.

"Did those boys do this to you?" she asked with concern.

Silence settled over them as they exchanged wary glances, pity growing for the boy who stood in front of them, bruised yet stubbornly unbroken.

"Lowe it, man. Look, are we going or not?" he blurted. No one asked him another word. Without delay, they piled into Preston's wheeled truck. Preston cranked the ignition, his gaze lingering on the boy in the rearview mirror, though he refrained from saying anything. Linus took the passenger seat, ready to guide them through the backroads and hidden routes to reach the bunker undetected. The truck continued its rumble, and they were off—bound for the unknown, with Max quietly nursing his own mysteries.

Benson Jr. lingered outside his front door, drawing a slow, steadying breath as he prepared himself for what awaited him inside. The faint aroma of a home-cooked meal drifted through the doorway, its warmth wrapping around him, bittersweet against the guilt nibbling at his insides. He kept reminding himself: the sooner the monarchy got what they needed, the sooner he could go on to live a normal life. He repeated it like a mantra, but the weight of his mission pressed heavily on his shoulders.

"You're home early," Melissa said, her voice a mix of delight and surprise, but she didn't probe. She sensed the weariness etched into his face and busied herself with the little gestures that would ease his transition from the world outside. Gently, she helped him shed his coat and bag, relieving him of the day's burdens.

As she led him into the dining room, she gave a small, bashful smile and gestured to the table laid with an impressive spread.

"It's not quite finished," she admitted with a shy laugh. "I was expecting you a bit later, but I wanted everything to be just right."

The table was set with elegant precision, and Benson could see the care she'd put into every detail. Her hope shimmered in her eyes. She wanted him to be proud. And for a fleeting moment, he felt the pull of her love and hard work against the quiet ache of his secret.

He steeled himself, knowing the longer he delayed, the harder it would be to move forward. With a swift gesture, he motioned for the chambermaids to leave, and Melissa's smile brightened, mistaking his urgency for incoming tenderness. She beamed, thinking she'd delighted him so much that he was keen to share a private moment of gratitude. She puckered her lips in anticipation, but Benson's attention was elsewhere.

"Could you check the pot for me, love?" he asked, the strain barely hidden in his voice.

She obliged, turning away to fuss over the simmering pot, chatting about how much closer they'd become, how this was the marriage she'd always dreamed of.

"...I think we should start considering some baby names," she said, stirring the vegetables and meticulously adding her seasonings.

He reached for two glasses, steadying himself as he poured a generous helping of gin into his own and chilled orange juice into hers. His hand trembled slightly as he filled her glass, the faint tremor barely noticeable as his fingers moved quickly, uncapping the vial and emptying its contents into the cup. His heart pounded, and he forced his face into a neutral expression as she turned back, her eyes filled with warmth. She was blissfully unaware, trailing her fingers up and down his arm, reveling in the strength of his biceps, which only amplified her sense of closeness. Her affection was genuine, and so he lifted his own glass.

"Cheers," he said.

Melissa followed suit. "Cheers!" she chuckled. "To a wonderful family and a soon-to-be healthy baby to raise."

With that, they both tossed their respective drinks back. Benson looked on, bracing himself for what was to come.

As Queen Emmary, Watson, and a groggy Mary arrived at Westminster, the Queen showed no pity for the girl's fatigue or the obvious signs of hunger, giving her a quick nudge. Mary jolted awake, blinking at the towering historic architecture before them—the sprawling, fortress-like structure that loomed with a sense of foreboding.

In the meantime, deep within the heart of Dr. Astor's bunker, a completely different scene played out. The bunker was a fort unto itself, encased by thick concrete walls and reinforced steel doors, impossible to breach without high-level clearance. Guards patrolled every corner, their steps echoing through the cold, sterile hallways. Once past the main security checkpoint, the facility spread into multiple wings, each section designed with precision to house different stages of Astor's inhumane experiments.

In the main cell block, Modiri Mountain soldiers languished in containment cells, each prisoner trapped behind thick glass walls that allowed for constant surveillance. Their rooms were sparse, fitted only with the bare necessities, the walls a cold, industrial white. Past the cell block lay the experiment lab. Cases of strange vials lined the walls, their contents glowing faintly under the stark fluorescent lights. Metal tables sat in rows, covered in complex scientific instruments and specimen containers that emitted a soft hum. The air smelled faintly of antiseptic, masking the more pungent scent of various chemicals used in Dr. Astor's grim research.

Just beyond the lab was the cafeteria, dimly lit but buzzing with activity. Overseen by Beatrice, the cafeteria held an unsettling sense of order. Her appearance was even colder now: the right side of her head was shaved close to the scalp, a faint scar peeking through, marking the site of an older operation. She moved with robotic precision, clad in a spotless kitchen uniform, as she inspected each tray. She made her rounds meticulously, her gaze sharp as she observed each staff member and resident, ensuring they followed every protocol.

The floors of the bunker were a stark black and white, tile patterns designed to disorient the eye, and the walls out here were a clinical white with dull grey accents. The lights created a harsh, glaring atmosphere that seemed to amplify every noise—every scuff on the floor, every whisper—giving the place a tense, haunting silence.

The sleek black hover vehicle descended slightly at the bunker entrance, its reflective finish glinting under the harsh facility lights. Queen Emmary stepped out last, her heels clicking against the metal platform, followed closely by Mary, who looked nervously around the imposing structure. Watson joined them, using his keycard to grant access while keeping a watchful eye as they entered through the heavy, sliding doors that led to Dr. Astor's underground lair.

Inside, Dr. Astor stood waiting, his face alight with anticipation as he bowed slightly before the Queen. They exchanged a formal nod, and without delay, he ushered them down the stark white corridors lined with reinforced glass.

"Are we early?" Emmary inquired coolly. Mary, trying to keep pace, stumbled over herself more than once. But Watson, ever watchful, kept an eye on the young girl. Noticing her weariness, he interrupted,

"May we find something to eat for the Lady of Sambridge, Your Majesty?"

With a click of her tongue, Emmary quickly obliged.

"Oh, but of course. Let us make our way to the cafeteria, shall we?"

"That we shall," Astor replied.

Back in Hampstead, Benson Jr. sat at the head of the dining table, nervously glancing at Melissa, who was still enjoying the remnants of their meal. His gaze flickered to the untouched leftovers, and he found himself preoccupied, waiting for some visible sign that the vial's contents were taking effect. But as he pondered, a sudden look of pain crossed Melissa's face. She clutched her abdomen, a pained gasp escaping her lips. Within seconds, her discomfort grew into tortured cries, her hands digging into the table's edge as she trembled and writhed in agony.

"Oh my God, something is happening to me!" she bellowed. "Benson!"

The chambermaids, already stationed nearby as if following a silent order, sprang into action. With swift, practiced movements, they lifted Melissa from her chair, guiding her to the front door whilst supporting her body as she howled in agony.

"Stop!" she screamed. "Ah! This hurts so bad! Please, why are you taking me from my home? Call the doctor, please!"

Without a word, they began guiding her toward the transport vehicle waiting outside. Benson Jr., following in shock, felt the blood drain from his face.

"Benson!" she cried. "Why are you just standing there? Please! Do something. Where are they taking me? The baby!"

It was a cold, calculated process—almost robotic—and within minutes, Melissa was on her way to the bunker, the plan already in motion. Her cries faded as the transport doors closed tightly behind her.

Benson Jr. lingered alone in the empty house, the silence unsettling. He paced from room to room, fingers tapping against his thigh in restless frustration. The bottle of gin from the dinner table was now his only companion. Still underaged and inexperienced, he took deep, bitter gulps straight from the neck, coughing as each sip burned down his throat. Anger surged within him, though he wasn't even sure who it was directed at: the monarchy, his father, or himself. He couldn't pinpoint his feelings, but rage simmered and settled heavily, like lead in his stomach.

Miles away, the Equal Species had reached the outskirts of the bunker. With Linus's guidance, they chose not to park nearby, avoiding any risk of early detection. Instead, they left the truck behind and continued on foot, trudging through the dense underbrush, the cool evening air thick with tension. It was an unspoken agreement to stay silent, each of them wrestling with their own worry.

The faint moonlight flickered through the trees, casting shadows that stretched over the ground, and every step brought them closer to the daunting concrete structure.

Only Preston and Linus whispered now and then, their voices low as they strategized contingencies in case things went south. They exchanged glances, nodding in agreement as they sketched out an escape route and alternative plans, neither willing to leave anything to chance.

The group huddled tightly in the thicket, their breaths shallow as they lay in wait. From their hiding spot, they could see a large van arrive beside the bunker entrance. The van doors opened, and even over the hum of machinery, Melissa's screams pierced the night. Her cries were raw and tortured, each one ripping through the quiet like a blade. Her agony was almost too much to bear.

The chambermaids, led by Kora, climbed out one by one, their faces stoic and unfazed. Kora swiped a key card, and the steel door to the bunker whirred open, flooding the ground with a harsh light. The chambermaids moved with eerie coordination, their expressions indifferent to Melissa's tortured pleas, as though they'd been trained to ignore suffering. From the bushes, Linus's heart dropped at the sound of a woman's voice. Acting almost reflexively, he broke from the group.

"Linus!" Willow and Alice said quietly.

"Hey!" Preston whispered.

He crept silently around the van to peek inside. He gripped the rear handle and lifted his head just high enough to peer through the window. He recognized her—his niece. Melissa's face was twisted in pain, her hand clenching her swollen belly as her body writhed in discomfort. Linus felt an ache in his chest at the sight of her, his hand tightening into a fist as he resisted the urge to charge forward and pull her out. The others exchanged tense glances. Willow joined him and quietly pulled him back, whispering his name urgently, but she saw the look in his eyes: fierce and protective, almost animalistic.

Minutes later, as Kora and the other chambermaid entered the bunker with Melissa, they moved swiftly and with purpose towards the operating room. The heavy door swung shut behind them, sealing the entrance with a cold, metallic thud. The faint sound of Melissa's whimpers echoed briefly before silence settled once more.

Outside, Linus's face was twisted with rage. His fists clenched, and his voice erupted into the night. He shouted obscenities into the stillness, his anger raw and unreleased.

"She's lied to me my whole life! My whole life! And now, she disappears! Just gone! I don't even know who I really am. I know nothing."

His frustration simmered into desperation as he turned towards Alice. "Are you a spy or something?"

Appalled, she cried, "What! Me?"

"Yeh, how is it that I go from being a regular old schoolboy with a live-in mum to meeting you one fine day, and two years later, here we are! Your dad and my mum working with the monarchy—and then a niece? You can't blame me for thinking this is more than a mere coincidence, Alice."

"Oh, piss off!" she retorted.

"Guys!" Willow shouted. "This is not the answer. We can't turn on one another."

"This is the second time, innit, that I've had to see my niece in some van, here, at this stupid place—and I'm helpless. I can't do anything to save her. I can't even save myself. What are we doing here? I wanted answers, but it seems the answers are too big for me."

With a swift motion, Alice stepped up to him, gripping his cheeks, her forehead pressed against his as she tiptoed.

"I love you!" she said firmly. "I know these past few years haven't been easy, but we have to be strong for each other. Like you, my family was rattled also—but if not for you, then who?" she cried.

Linus sobbed out of frustration. "If I can't protect you and my family, then what good am I, Alice?" he whispered.

"You're so good." As she spoke, Linus looked away, but Alice refused to break eye contact. She needed to encourage him. Bringing his focus back to her, she said, "Your worth isn't determined by how you protect us, but by the passion and intention behind doing so. You are a remarkable and sensational human being, Linus Claymoore. The world would be nothing without you. Your niece needs you—and we are all willing to do whatever it takes, alongside you, to help you see your family on the other side of all this."

He received her message, their friends nodding in unison.

"Thank you," he stammered, fighting tears. "Thank you, all of you."

Linus lunged forward and, with a firm grip, pried the key card from Max, who offered no resistance, shocked by his intensity.

"It's all right. It's yours. No need to ask," Max said sarcastically.

Without a second thought, Linus marched towards the bunker's entrance, swiping the card and listening to the door's lock click open with a low beep. The rest of the Equal Species exchanged wary glances but followed close behind, united by the promise of unravelling the secrets hidden within those sterile walls.

As they slipped through the doorway and entered the dimly lit halls, none of them noticed the subtle red light blinking in the corner of each room they passed.

Every move, every whispered conversation, every hesitant glance was captured on surveillance cameras lining the corridors—their presence a silent witness to the impending confrontation.

Queen Emmary, Watson, Dr. Astor, and Lady Mary entered the cafeteria. The atmosphere was stark and sterile. Dr. Astor chuckled lightly as Emmary requested a "healthy meal for our Lady Mary of Sambridge."

"Of course, Your Majesty," he replied, his eyes glinting with irony. "I'll have Beatrice bring that over shortly."

Perfected by 2451, the memory loss procedure pioneered by Dr. Ruskin Peter Astor and his team was a marvel of medical technology. This slightly invasive method involved a bioelectric circlet worn around the temples and occipital lobe. It targeted specific regions associated with long-term memory through microcurrents and neural mapping, selectively erasing chosen memories without affecting cognitive function. The procedure left minimal scarring, caused no discomfort, and had a flawless success rate—ensuring a smooth "forgetting" experience.

Moments later, Beatrice entered the room with a tray balanced carefully in her hands. Watson's eyes widened in disbelief. Her kitchen aide uniform was spotless, though her new look—a portion of her hair shaved to signify her procedure—gave her an oddly clinical appearance.

"I thought you said the operation would be discreet?" Queen Emmary asked Astor as she and Lady Mary took a seat at the centre table in the now desolate room.

"Surely. However, there were some minor complications. Despite her age, she was quite the fighter," he teased.

Without a flicker of recognition, Beatrice set down the plates before Queen Emmary and Mary, each dish meticulously prepared and portioned.

"Thank you kindly," Mary said. She gazed blankly at Beatrice, oblivious to their shared past. Emmary watched her carefully, silently gauging if any spark of recognition remained. But there was none—Beatrice's gaze held only professional courtesy as she asked if they required anything else before she departed, her presence as emotionally detached as the sterile, white-walled cafeteria around them.

As Doctor Astor's handheld device buzzed, he glanced down, frowning as he absorbed the notification: Melissa had arrived, but security had detected intruders within the bunker perimeter. The soft glow of the screen reflected the gravity in his eyes, and he immediately responded to his security detail, signaling for discretion.

"Do not sound the alarm," he instructed, voice low and tense. "We can't risk disrupting the soldiers—they're still quite unpredictable." He narrowed his eyes. "Apprehend the intruders, but bring them down quietly to the lower level for questioning. As for Melissa, escort her directly to the operating room."

Turning to the Queen, Astor's expression softened as he informed her of Melissa's arrival, ensuring the process would be seamless. Emmary nodded, her expression betraying only a trace of impatience as she glanced over at Mary, who was calmly finishing her meal. Once Mary placed her silverware down, they all—except for Beatrice—followed Astor down to the operating room.

The cold, clinical light of the space cast a harsh glare over the young mother-to-be, who lay twisted in agony on the sterilized bed, clutching her abdomen as waves of searing pain surged through her. It was unnatural, as if something inside her was tearing her apart, inch by inch.

"Please make it stop!" Melissa wept. "I can't do this! Please! It hurts!"

Her breaths came in shallow, ragged gasps, and sweat pooled on her forehead as she thrashed, struggling to make sense of her surroundings. Two tall, imposing figures— pale-skinned men dressed in surgical masks, head covers, and gloves—entered the room, their faces obscured by layers of clean fabric.

Though she could barely comprehend it through the haze of pain, the gleaming array of instruments beside her made the purpose of their visit abundantly clear: a scalpel, forceps, retractors, and a small incubator, each one neatly arranged with chilling precision.

Melissa's eyes widened in despair, and she tried to lift herself, but another wave of agony forced her back down. She groaned, "I'm so sorry, but I can't do this—please!"

The chambermaids entered next, now donned in crisp scrubs, moving with an eerie calmness as they handed tools to the surgeons and adjusted the sterile drapes around her. Then, as if on cue, through her blurred vision, she caught a glimpse beyond the operating room window.

Her heart dropped.

Outside, as though they were spectators in a macabre theatre, Queen Emmary stood—serene and unblinking—with Mary by her side, her small hand tucked into the Queen's. They observed in silence, Emmary's expression betraying not one hint of emotion, as if she were watching an exhibit, not a woman in unimaginable torment.

"Mary," she whispered, Melissa's eyes now struggling to see. One nurse poked and prodded to get a line in for the administration of her epidural. But Melissa could not stay still. Pulling her arm away, her sister came into focus, and she cried, "Mary! Oh my God, Mary!" Melissa's face twisted, a silent plea for help that went unanswered as her body arched once more against the relentless pain. The scene felt like a nightmare she could not wake from, her mind clouded by pain and fear as the doctors and nurses maneuvered around her.

On the other side of the glass, Mary looked perturbed, her eyes rising to Queen Emmary.

"Why does she keep calling my name?"

Emmary and Watson exchanged a glance.

"Why, that's your sister, dear."

Shocked by her honesty, Watson scoffed.

"My sister?" Mary questioned innocently, searching her mind to recall the woman before her, but nothing came. She was drawing a blank—and it frightened her, momentarily. "I do not believe I've seen her before."

Melissa's eyes then locked onto Watson, remembering him from that day. Her brows knitted as she gritted her teeth in rage.

"Let me go!" she yelled, pulling away. But the nurse was stronger, tugging her back towards her. Others joined in to aid her. She was trapped—helpless and bound.

Far below the ocean's surface, Naida sat motionless, nestled within a deep, silent trance, allowing the ebb and flow of the ocean's ancient energy to fill her senses. The cool, vast darkness around her was alive, whispering through each ripple and gust of current, preparing her, urging her to stay centered. But just beyond, she felt its presence—the Makara—relentless in its pursuit. He clawed his way through rock and ruin, his hunger a dark pulse in the water. His violent approach told her he would offer no reprieve, only a merciless confrontation.

Then, at the very edge of her awareness, a sharp prick pierced Melissa's spine. The pain jolted her into a strange clarity, her scream rising to something altogether different—a piercing siren's call, raw and guttural. It burst from her, driven by mounting fear and bubbling rage, intensified by the pain from her unborn.

In the same instant, Naida's eyes snapped open, their former warmth replaced by a carbon grey that consumed every part of them—pupils, iris, and sclera. And just like that, her shadow vanished, leaving the Makara to halt in its tracks. Its body slithered aimlessly as her physical form remained in a settled position.

The Ushu had emerged.

VIII.

THE PERICULUM

The operating room was thrown into chaos as Melissa's siren call burst forth with a force that shattered every glass panel and instrument around her. Her scream cut through the air, sharp and wild, like the cry of a powerful hawk magnified a hundredfold, shaking the room to its very foundation. The glass exploded outward, fragments spinning like deadly shards of ice, slicing through anything in their path.

The doctors and nurses cried out as silver slivers embedded themselves in their skin. Dr. Astor staggered, clutching his neck as blood trickled through his fingers. Even Watson, momentarily frozen in horror, was thrust back into memories of Modiri Mountain, his mind caught between past and present. But instinct overtook him, and he sprang forward, shielding the Queen and Mary as the glass whipped around them.

Then, through the frenzy, a figure began to materialize—a vision against the shattered backdrop. Fiona had appeared, but not as a regular girl. She was something far more formidable: an Ushu. It was magnificent—a blend of human grace and mythical power. Her grey eyes, like a brewing tempest, locked onto Melissa, filled with both sorrow and fierce determination despite her temporary confusion. Her hair was a cascade of textured ash-brown waves trailing down to the small of her back, moving as if caught in an invisible wind. Her caramel complexion carried a flawless, warm undertone, minimized by the shadows encircling her.

Blue and grey feathers formed elegant bracelets around her wrists; her ankles and feet were similarly decorated, draped in priel—tail-converted shoes worn on land. Her acetics shimmered in sapphire and diamonds, as though nature itself had dressed her in regal ornaments.

Clothed in a sheer silk cloth that clung to her form, Fiona's presence exuded serenity and danger alike. Her petite frame hovered around the mayhem, watching Melissa with unblinking intensity, her gaze filled with a longing for her eldest sibling.

"Melissa?" she questioned. The Ushu's voice was haunting, imbued with an ancient resonance that vibrated through the very air. It was a voice drawn from the depths of the Earth and the open sky—an impossible blend of gentleness and severity. "Is it really you? What is this place? What are they doing to you?" Her words filled the room like an incantation, and even her pauses held weight.

Hearing the sound of someone else in the room, Queen Emmary fought her way from Watson's protection, eager to see for herself the voice of myths. She turned, placing her manicured nails and blemish-free hands neatly atop the glass, careful not to puncture herself. Her eyes peered from the bottom of the frame, and there she saw her—Fiona. Her voice was shaken as she whispered to herself,

"My dear God…"

Melissa leaned forward, trembling from shock as she looked her up and down, ignoring the groans of those around her.

"Fiona," she stammered, before fainting.

As Melissa's fear gripped her consciousness, her body succumbed to exhaustion, her mind slipping into darkness. In that very instant, Fiona's Ushu shadow was pulled back, vanishing from the operating room and returning to her physical form in the murky depths. Disoriented, Fiona—now Naida—lifted her lids to berry-blue eyes underwater, her gaze troubled and searching. She closed them once more, longing to return to Melissa's side, but each attempt proved futile.

Meanwhile, the Makara loomed above, massive and ominous, its scales shimmering faintly in the dim ocean light. But as Naida's fear transformed into unshakable resolve, she found herself no longer cowed by the creature's presence. Determined and fierce, she rose from hiding, extended an arm, clutching the Makara's massive head, her grip firm, her expression dark. She blinked. Her eyes, now a stormy shadow-grey, locked onto the Makara's gaze with an intensity that left it trembling. Her voice, low and guttural, cut through the water, reverberating like a growl:

"Go from me. You're making me angry."

The Makara, overwhelmed by a fear it had never known, whimpered as it backed away, its hulking body folding in retreat, scales flicking with anxiety. Just as the beast withdrew, the waters around Naida shifted with a sudden pressure—King Bao was approaching. Naida's pulse quickened, sensing the presence of another powerful force, but she remained unstirred, emboldened by her determination to make it back to land. Her need to return for Melissa ignited something within her.

Time seemed to warp, stretching what felt like hours into mere seconds. The injured nurses, staggering to the edges of the room, tended to their bleeding wounds as doctors emerged from their hiding places, their faces etched with shock. Amidst them, Dr. Astor rose, the wound on his neck eerily closed, leaving only a streak of dried blood as evidence. Silence gripped the room, thick with disbelief.

Meanwhile, in the lower levels, the Equal Species felt the tremors from the chaos above and instinctively ducked into cover. Slowly, they rose from their hiding places in the dimly lit soldiers' quarters, listening as the rumbling subsided. Max scrambled to his feet, pressing his face to each small window he passed, his eyes darting anxiously, searching for his brother. Linus, tense with determination, moved swiftly, checking the halls as he sought his mother's face among the shadows. Further back, Alice and Willow held their positions, keeping watch over the silent corridors, their eyes scanning for any sign of threat, while Preston and Piper resumed their careful inspection, ready for anything that might be waiting in the bunker's depths. The air was thick with anticipation, and every sound seemed amplified as they prepared themselves for what lay ahead.

Max's voice rang out through the long, shadowed corridors as he frantically called,

"Archie! Archie!"

His cries echoed down the narrow halls, stirring the few sleeping soldiers, who blinked awake, murmuring for him to lower his voice. Max's desperation seemed to drown their hushed pleas as he held onto hope of finding his kin.

Above, the aftermath of the siren's devastation still hung heavy in the air. Queen Emmary, Watson, and Lady Mary pushed themselves up from where they'd taken cover, dusting glass fragments from their clothes, their faces tight with shock. The Queen exchanged a grave look with Dr. Astor, who stood nearby with his hand pointing to his now-dried wound, signaling to the Queen that he had been right. The silence that followed was thick and tense.

"We will need to eradicate the Modiri. All of them," she confirmed after drawing a long sigh.

Watson almost felt vindicated, but knew he could never say it aloud.

"I will travel to America and meet with President Kirlin to discuss their aid in our mission."

"Your Majesty, if I may?" Dr. Astor interjected. "Please, let us not get ahead of ourselves. The Modiri are quite useful, if we can keep them at bay—"

"Bay? Did you not see what transpired here tonight? What was that that appeared in the room, and what kind of noise did she make that led it to happen?" She pointed to an unconscious Melissa. "We are no match for their kind in any war."

"War this and war that… what if we can avoid it altogether? That is my only proposal," he said cunningly. "We may never see a war, but I know that if we can properly prepare ourselves, we can be positioned to take on even the most challenging opponent. Your Majesty, we have the power," he chuckled. "We simply need to harness it—raise it as though it were a newborn child. An infant, if you may."

"You speak rubbish, born from your infatuation and clear signs of addiction to whatever it is you've been administering to yourself without proper supervision." Queen Emmary turned, locking eyes with a wearisome Lady Mary, who was well past her bedtime. She intended to end their conversation. "A megalomaniac is what you've become—with unlimited resources. The Crown's resources, I may add. And here I am, telling you—no, actually commanding you, to stop your madness and heed my orders. We will annihilate the Modiri from every corner of our waters. Do I make myself clear?"

Dr. Astor conceded.

"Yes, Your Majesty," he bowed. "What shall I do with the newborn that we are to extract tonight?" he questioned, extending an arm towards a sleeping Melissa, who had now been administered her spinal anesthesia.

"Kill it," the Queen commanded before taking her leave.

"B-but what of the Ember?" he stammered.

"Do you dare disobey me?" she bellowed.

"No, Your Majesty. I will do as ordered," he said quickly.

Dr. Astor's voice was low and urgent as he gestured down the corridor to the soldiers' ward, directing Queen Emmary, Watson, and Lady Mary towards an alternative exit route through the bunker. His decision weighed heavily on him: although he'd been ordered to terminate the foetus, a flicker of something stayed his hand at the last moment. Watson took the lead, ushering the Queen and Lady Mary down the narrow, winding staircase as Astor called into his security detail to prepare the Queen's transport outdoors. The rhythmic clanking of his armor echoed through the halls, a sound that drifted toward Alice and Willow, who were stationed nearby, alert to every shift.

Concurrently, Max's calls for his brother grew desperate. "Archie! Archie!" His shouts filled the corridor as he sprinted towards a door at the hall's centre, hearing a faint but insistent banging on the other side. Pressing his face to the small glass window, Max spotted Archie, who mouthed frantically, "The key card!" Whilst he turned his pockets inside out, dropping change, the watch from Alice, and some other miscellaneous items, he realized he was not in possession of it.

Completely forgetting that Linus had taken the card from him, Max bolted down the hall, his feet pounding as he begged the Equal Species member to hand it over. But a warning from Alice and Willow that someone was approaching rattled the group. Preston and Piper quickly motioned for everyone to retreat, but Max hesitated, fumbling with the key card now that Linus had returned it to him. Finally, he managed to prop the door open just enough, and with a loud click, Archie stumbled out, gripping Max's hand tightly as they both ran towards the exit.

The Equal Species moved with hushed precision, their figures blending into the dim shadows as they crept out of the bunker. Linus glanced back with a clenched jaw, disheartened that he hadn't been able to find his mother or Melissa in the maze of concrete and steel. Ahead of him, Max held onto Archie tightly, refusing to let go of his frail brother's bony shoulders. Archie's clothes hung loosely on his frame, his cheeks hollow and his skin pallid; he looked as fragile as if a gust of wind might topple him over. Max's relief was tainted by anger, seeing how his brother had been reduced to a ghost of himself.

Inside the bunker, Queen Emmary, Watson, and Mary strode confidently through the soldiers' ward. Emmary's gaze drifted over the soldiers, dismissing them as mere remnants of Astor's twisted experiments, barely worthy of her attention. Her chin lifted as she swept past without a second glance. Watson, however, stepped with more caution, feeling the pressure of every movement in the silent corridors.

Suddenly, his boot met something brittle, and a loud crunch reverberated through the hallway. He froze, looking down to see shards of broken glass glinting underfoot. His eyes darted to the open door, realization dawning as he inspected the room. The thought of an escaped science experiment sent a chill down his spine, though he steadied himself, unwilling to alarm the Queen or Mary.

Watson's gaze darted up and down the hall, his senses sharp, anticipating any lurking threat. Just as he was about to move forward, he felt a tug at his foot. Glancing down, he saw his boot caught on something small and metallic— an old watch, tarnished but unmistakably familiar. He crouched, reaching for it and lifting it to eye level, his fingers brushing off a layer of dust from the glass face. In the silence, he turned the watch over, inspecting it for clues. His breath caught as he noticed the faint inscription inside, etched with care: *"For you, Alice. Love, Dad."*

For a moment, the world around him seemed to blur, his chest tightening with a feeling he thought long buried. It was a link to a life he would no doubt die to protect— yet somehow, they were now crossed. The realization struck him like a cruel dream, one from which he was desperate to wake.

Watson straightened, swallowing hard, his fingers curling tightly around the watch as he slipped it into his pocket. Without a word, he continued onward, masking his expression as he led Queen Emmary and Mary to their car. Outside, a sleek hover vehicle awaited, and once inside, Mary fell into a deep slumber, her small frame nestled lovingly on his lap. He did not wake her.

Hours later, Dr. Astor stood alongside the surgical team, his eyes never straying from their diligent movements. His posture was tense, his hands clasped behind his back. The silence in the operating room was punctuated only by the soft hum of new medical equipment and the measured breathing of the surgeons, their hands precise as they sliced into Melissa. With each passing minute, Astor's impatience grew. The clock ticked with agonizing slowness in his mind. He watched every gesture, every adjustment of an instrument, his focus unwavering as if mere observation could hasten the process.

His gaze flicked briefly to the monitor, confirming they had been in surgery for two hours and thirty-four minutes. And then, at last, the moment came.

A small cry filled the sterile room, sharp and unmistakable, breaking the tension that had filled the air—until,

"A fin…" one nurse said, repulsed.

Astor's eyes widened ever so slightly as the newborn was lifted, her tiny form glowing under the lights.

"A girl. Oh, this is phenomenal." His hardened expression softened. "Finally."

The seven-pound Modiri was born with a faint maroon and white fin, splashed with muted hues. No scales—only slick discharge covering her tiny frame. Astor leaned forward, eyes narrowed as he examined the Modiri, a triumphant gleam flickering in his gaze.

"Shall we alert Her Majesty?" one nurse asked.

"No!" Astor retorted sharply. "I mean... no. I have plans for this little one."

Melissa began to stir, but only for a few seconds as she glimpsed the baby Modiri in the arms of the maniacal doctor.

"Give me... my... dau…" Her voice faded as her eyes shut once more.

The Equal Species members pulled up quietly to Alice's place, their steps heavy with exhaustion and the quiet aftermath of the night's mission. As they parked, Willow gave a soft, tired smile, leaning towards Preston from the back seat.

"After we get our things, would you mind dropping me home? I don't want to get in too late," she asked, her tone gentle but clearly eager to rest in her own bed.

"Yeh, of course," Preston replied. "I don't mind dropping you all home if you need me to—it's no problem."

"Thank you," Willow said.

Moments later, the group filtered down to the basement. Piper, Preston, and Willow packed up their things, murmuring to each other about how much sleep they'd need to shake off the night's events. They exchanged a quick wave before slipping out, leaving Alice and Linus behind. As they lingered in the basement, both too tired to talk much, Alice glanced toward the stairs.

"You think my mum left us anything in the fridge?"

Linus chuckled, shaking his head. "I'd say it's worth a look. I'll take anything at this point."

Meanwhile, Max and Archie, who had grown visibly more relaxed yet still appeared worn from their ordeal, lingered near the banister. Max shifted on his feet before glancing up at Alice.

"Would it be okay if we stayed here tonight? Just... I don't think Archie's up for going anywhere."

Alice and Linus exchanged a look. Archie did, in fact, look famished. The former Modiri Guard gave her a hopeful but exhausted smile. She softened, nodding immediately.

"Of course. There's plenty of room, and I can fetch you some blankets and pillows from the linen closet upstairs." But even with that, something gnawed at her. "Say, Archie, do you mind telling me what happened to you? If it's not too much, of course."

Archie stood at five feet nine. While his frame used to be muscular, he was now far more fragile and smaller in appearance.

"Sure," he said, clearing his throat. "You can ask me whatever you'd like."

Kind-hearted and selfless, Archie took after his mother's benevolent nature. As Alice slithered her way into a chair, she prepared herself for his responses.

"What happened to you down there?"

Linus and Max remained standing, guarding their emotions, hoping that if they weren't seen, they could better hide their expressions. And so, Archie began telling his story.

"Well, I wanted to do something that would help my mother—I'm the oldest, so it made sense, you know, as the man of the house, to protect and provide. But when I signed up for the Guardianship, I had no real clue what it entailed. We have destitute people here in London, and I never imagined it could get any lower. But the hybrids... they're considered literal gutter mice. And not because of the towns they inhabit—no—it's because of what they are, yeh know."

Alice interrupted him, noticing she hadn't offered him anything to drink.

"I'm going to fetch you some water. I apologize."

A few moments later, she returned with a glass, motioning for him to continue. Archie chuckled.

"I see a bit of myself in you—your attention to detail, hospitality, heck, even your generosity to let us stay the night," he chuckled nervously. "It's rare to meet people like you where we're from. Max and I—we grew up dealing with bullies all our lives, so never in a million years did I think it could get worse than that. I only believed it would get better."

"Does it not get better?" Alice questioned.

"No," he laughed. "There's no way up... or out. Once you're placed in the system where the system wants you to be, you stay there all your life. But they'll tease a better life, motivating you to take odd jobs—or in this case, sign up to become a science experiment without even knowing it, yeh."

"They experimented on you?" Linus asked.

"Not quite," Archie perked up, taking a long sip of his water. "After Modiri Mountain, we were taken to some facility—those of us who lived or weren't injured, of course."

"Modiri Mountain?" Alice asked.

"Yes," Archie took another sip. "It's this place up north—or somewhere. We were blindfolded, so I can't tell you where exactly. But the travel is painfully long, so I know it's nowhere near here," he began to tremble. "Recalling that day seems like something from a nightmare. There was a large bird and finned Modiri in tanks... and a woman was shot and killed. I watched it with my own eyes. The Royal Guards are not who you think they are—"

"Royal Guards?" Alice interrupted. "There were Royal Guards there?"

Archie, nodding his head profusely, as if eager to finally speak his truth, said, "Yes, there were plenty! They were the main ones, yeh know, trying to pump us young boys up for this mission. But it was a suicide mission. The monarchy is no match for these water creatures. But I see what they did now. They stripped them of their rights, identity—yeh know—so they would feel they were weaker or less than. But no... we almost all died that day."

He took another sip of water. Alice, noticing he was nearly out, signaled for Linus to refill the glass.

"The lady—he shot her straight in the head after the bird did the screech thing."

"Shot who?" Alice's eyes lit up with concern.

"The woman who went viral on the telly," he said.

Linus returned with more water for their guest.

He handed it to Archie.

"Telly?" he asked, hoping to catch up.

"Yeh, the one who went viral. Woman screaming about her kid getting taken."

Linus and Alice exchanged a look.

"I don't know her name—but what of her?" Linus asked.

"She was shot, yeh. The Royal Guard did it. They're all evil, the whole lot of them. You can't trust those people. Then they brought us to this bunker and fed us some super food. It's nasty. We threw up for days on end. That's why we lose so much weight. It's something in the food—it's depleting the nutrients but replacing them with something else."

"Wait, wait, back up," Linus said.

"Right, right, it's a lot," Alice agreed.

"Look, you guys, he's tired. Maybe after he gets some rest, we can have this talk," Max pleaded. But Archie silenced him.

"No. If I don't speak on it now, when will I? I'm not crazy. I know what I saw!"

"I'm not saying you're crazy, brother."

"Then what is it, Max?"

"Nothing," Max muttered, retreating to a corner in the basement.

Alice and Linus dared not interrupt, but they were both anxious to hear more, ignoring the growling in their stomachs and the headaches creeping in from not eating.

"Tell us about Modiri Mountain. Everything you remember," Linus instructed.

But Archie sighed. "There's no recollecting that place. I almost wanted it to have been a dream. For over two years, I convinced myself that it was. But today—the tremble, in the facility..." His lips began to quiver as if preparing to sob. "I was reminded, yeh. It happened. The Watson Guard—he shot that woman. And the bird—the loud bird who broke everything and—"

Alice gasped. "Go back. The Watson Guard? Who is that?"

"Surely. And what woman?" Linus pressed, growing impatient, though trying hard to keep his composure.

Archie, feeling attacked and visibly suffering from post-traumatic stress disorder, blurted, "Watson is the Royal Guard who shot the woman who went viral on the telly. Why is no one listening to me? He did it right in front of my face. It was the first time in my life I had a human brain splattered over me!"

"Enough! Lowe him, yeh!" Max yelled.

The weight of Archie's truth hit like a tidal wave, shattering the fragile stability Linus and Alice had tried to hold onto. Alice couldn't look at Linus—couldn't even breathe—as she staggered back, covering her mouth in a desperate attempt to stifle the sobs threatening to escape. Her mind reeled, memories colliding in jagged fragments: her father, the same man who tucked her in at night and smiled so easily, was responsible for the death of someone innocent. An image of Emaline flashed through her mind, and she could now barely reconcile it with the man she thought she knew.

Linus was silent, his face etched with tension, but his eyes betrayed a flicker of something deeper—a recognition that, despite his years of suspicion, he was still unsure of his mother's true connection to Emaline and to him. He stood stiffly, the reality crashing over him, yet he couldn't react. He could only watch Alice crumble, feeling her pain cut through him even as he wrestled with his own numbness and unanswered questions.

She remained frozen, her chest tight, a hollow ache spreading through her bones. The betrayal had sunk in— not just the truth of her father's involvement, but the terrible finality of it all. Alice would never look at him the same…ever again.

The hover vehicle glided silently through the dimly lit streets of London, coming to a stop before the gates of Buckingham Palace. Queen Emmary stepped out first, her posture elegant despite the exhaustion that threatened to topple her. Watson followed closely, a sleeping Mary in his arms, his armored boots echoing against the limestone entryway. The King's Guard flanked them in perfect formation, their solemn faces betraying nothing of the night's ordeal.

Inside, the Queen barely acknowledged the maids who scurried to greet her. Their curtsies were deep, but unnoticed, as she swept past them into the opulent halls of the London residence. Sleep tugged at her heavily, but fear clung tighter—fear of what might come, of the truths lurking in Scotland, of King Eldric's frail mortality now sealed by her grueling instructions to Dr. Astor.

She turned quickly to the head maid, her voice sharp. "Find Lady Mary new quarters," she ordered. "She will remain here in the main residence, close by me." The maids nodded and scattered, and Emmary's gaze flickered to Mary, whom Watson carefully handed off to Hazel. Emmary had plans for Lady Mary, convinced of one truth: King Eldric's days were numbered, and Amer's ascension to the throne was imminent.

Later, dismissed by Her Majesty, Watson gave a nod to his driver, the hum of the vehicle muffled as it pulled away from Buckingham Palace. He sat in silence, the watch rolling between his calloused fingers, the faint clinking of the chain breaking the stillness. His face was carved with a mixture of sadness and resignation, his stern features softened by the quiet grief only a father could feel. Alice knew his secret now. The unspoken tension between duty and love threatened to crush him, but the Crown's claim on him was ironclad. He had chosen his side long ago.

As the vehicle came to a halt before his home, Watson stepped out, his boots crunching softly against the gravel. Inside, the house was still, save for the faint creak of the old floorboards under his socks. The basement was silent, despite its occupants—Linus, Max, and Archie were sleeping soundly. Linus had volunteered to remain with them for Alice's peace of mind. Watson paused briefly, listening to the calm of the night before making his way upstairs, his towering frame careful not to disturb the quiet.

He stopped at Alice's door, pushing it open with deliberate care. The dim glow of the television bathed the room in flickering colors, cartoons playing to no audience but the slumbering girl beneath her sheets. Her chest rose and fell gently, the innocence of her sleep a stark contrast to the pain within him. He hesitated, his grip tightening on the watch before he crossed the room, placing it gently on her nightstand, the metal catching the light momentarily as he withdrew his hand. A pang of regret struck him, but he turned away.

In the master bedroom, his wife stirred at the sound of him entering. Watson moved quietly, his large hands methodically cleansing the remnants of the day from his face and body. When he finally slid into bed beside her, the mattress dipped under his weight. Her warmth greeted him as she instinctively turned towards him, her hand brushing against his chest. He wrapped his strong arms around her, pulling her close, seeking solace in the familiar embrace. She murmured something inaudible, her voice heavy with sleep, but her touch was enough.

For a moment, Watson allowed himself to forget the watch, the secrets, and the choices that now haunted him. There, in the stillness of the night, he was just a husband, holding the woman who grounded him and had found the strength in her heart to forgive him once before.

*

The river's chilly grip clung to Amer, each dive pulling him further into its dark depths. His muscles strained against the cold. The breaths he'd once taken had long since been forgotten, replaced by the burn in his chest. The farther he ventured, the heavier the water pressed against him, as though the river itself sought to claim him. His vision wavered, the edges blurring into the shadowy abyss, and queasiness crept in, threatening to undo his intention.

But he pressed on, driven by an intangible force—a fragile thread of optimism flickering in the corners of his mind. What hope? What purpose? He couldn't name it. It wasn't the castle that loomed in his memory, nor the faces that had once surrounded him. It was her. Fiona. Her eyes pulled him deeper into the water, as though the river were rooting for something greater—or his demise.

Above the surface, the sun dipped below the horizon, the fleeting golden glow replaced by the inky blue of night. The castle scurried in chaos, Mavis among them, her voice cutting through the air as she demanded answers to Amer's absence. Alarms blared, their sharp cries echoing through the castle grounds, warning of his disappearance. Panic rippled across the estate, but the waters Amer dove into remained silent, their secrets locked away.

As his strength began to falter, Amer's movements grew erratic. His lungs betrayed him, reflexively pulling in water as his body convulsed in desperation. His limbs twitched, and the darkness thickened around him. It was then, in the moment he teetered on the edge of surrender, that he collided with something solid—something alive.

But it was no mere fish. It was immense. A low, reverberating hum emanated from it, resonating through the water and into Amer's body. For a moment, the pressure eased, and he was cradled in an unfamiliar stillness. His senses flickered between consciousness and the void. He felt the creature shift beneath him, and as she spoke, a loud, thunderous ringing filled his ears.

"Human," she said, though his ears deceived him.

Acantha embodied the fierce beauty of the Periculum Kingdom, a vision of strength and allure born of the ocean's highest depths. Her dark, radiant skin shimmered with a soft light, catching the dim colors of the underwater world like polished onyx. Hazel eyes, as warm and entrancing as sunlight filtered through amber, held an intensity that spoke of wisdom and cunning honed by the trials of her kind. They were eyes that saw beneath the surface, reading the currents of both water and intent.

Her fin, an exquisite blend of cherry and dark-brown hues, unfurled like banners of war, gliding effortlessly as she inspected him. The brasloor was an intricate work of artistry, encrusted with ruby gemstones that shone against her skin. The ruby light seemed to pulse faintly, as though alive. Acantha's dark brown, textured hair cascaded down her back in flowing waves, reaching the length of her waist—free, yet wild in its grace. Adorning her skin were delicate, almost imperceptible quills, similar to those of a porcupine but finer, subtler. These quills protruded gently from her arms, toned abdomen, chest, and neck, like a natural armor forged by her lineage. They glistened faintly, adding an air of dangerous mystery to her feminine beauty without diminishing it.

She was the perfect marriage of beauty and menace; a reflection of the warrior spirit bred within their kingdom. Acantha and her sisters were not merely Lorelies, but daughters of Queen Ceto herself.

Amer strained to focus on the figure before him, her presence both alien and mesmerizing. Acantha hovered effortlessly in the water, her fin hypnotic and her eyes piercing, but readable—like a predator's gaze studying its prey. Her voice did not carry words to his ears. It was more like a haunting screech, a sound like nails dragged against metal—grating and unrelenting. Each syllable was a foreign vibration that rattled his bones, leaving him terrified.

"What—what are you?" he stammered, struggling to speak. Bubbles escaped his lips, leaving his body weaker, limp. His instincts screamed for survival as he recoiled from the siren figure, his heart pounding in his chest like a war drum. With a swift motion, Acantha spat into the palm of her right acetic. The saliva morphed into a shimmering, gel-like substance, which she carefully smeared over his nose and mouth—much to his disapproval. But she overpowered him. Immediately, his frantic gasps turned into steady, deep breaths as his lungs adapted to the surrounding water. Relief flooded his body, but the terror of her presence remained.

"What are you?" he asked again, the sound of his voice muffled.

"Acantha, the daughter of Queen Ceto, the Goddess of the Dangers of the Ocean."

"The dangers of the what?" he asked, confused; finally able to understand.

Amer flailed wildly, his limbs moving with no rhythm or control, as if trying to escape a nightmare. His eyes widened in sheer panic as he truly saw her for the first time and registered her words. It was all surreal, as if it were a bad dream. Letting out a desperate, howling scream, Amer pushed against the water, his arms and legs thrashing as he tried to flee.

He churned the water violently in his attempt to escape, propelling himself clumsily away from the enigmatic creature. But Acantha was faster than he could have imagined. With the grace of a predator and the speed of a spear slicing through the sea, she was beside him in an instant. Her proximity was a shock, her tail fluke brushing lightly against him as if to remind him that no matter how far or fast he swam, he was no match for her mastery of the ocean.

Her laughter echoed, but Amer found nothing amusing. He froze, the primal terror of her power washing over him, leaving him trembling and breathless once more. Acantha simply watched, her expression turning to delight as though deciding what to make of the strange, panicked creature floundering before her.

"What are you doing here?" she asked nicely, her voice low and raspy.

"I-I, um," Amer stuttered, his train of thought slipping away. "I-I can't remember, to be quite fair. But I'm terribly tired."

"Oh. Where are you from?"

"S-Sc-Scotland," he stammered, the gel-like substance moving freely around his mouth and nose.

"I am not familiar with that place," she admitted. "But you are the first human I have seen so far down here."

"What the heck are you?" he asked, hoping for a better answer.

Before she could respond, another Lorelie emerged—this one slightly longer, though they bore a strong resemblance. Hemera, one of the eldest of the Lorelie sisters.

"You're late for training, Acantha!" she yelled. The sound of her voice shifted Amer slightly.

Before departing, Acantha turned to him.

"Come with me. Meet my sisters."

Amer had no time to offer a proper response. She tugged at him, wrapping his torso firmly within her fin as she glided forward toward the kingdom.

The Periculum Kingdom, ruled by the fierce Goddess Ceto alongside her lady, Prissara, was a realm unlike any other in the northern seas. Where other underwater kingdoms gleamed with coral spires and shimmering domes, Periculum resembled a war-torn fortress perpetually braced for conflict. The kingdom stretched across a jagged seabed of dark volcanic rock, its terrain scarred by trenches and craters left by centuries of battle.

Massive skeletal remains of sea creatures, both ancient and modern, dotted the landscape, their bones woven into the architecture as grim reminders of past victories and the cost of survival. Towers made of blackened coral spiraled upward, their surfaces reinforced with metal plating scavenged from wrecked ships. They served not as ornamental structures but as watchtowers and defense posts, manned by Periculum warriors armed with what appeared to be seaweed—but which transformed into swords when drawn, and nets laced with venom.

The kingdom's centerpiece was Ceto's citadel, a colossal structure carved directly into an underwater mountain. Its walls were an ominous mix of basalt and red coral, bristling with natural defenses like sharp ridges and quill-like protrusions. A faint glow emanated from deep within, casting the surrounding waters in hues of crimson and shadow. This eerie light pulsed like a heartbeat whenever Ceto was present.

Periculum's citizens were as hardened as their environment. Their warriors patrolled in disciplined formations, their movements swift and calculated. Even their non-combatants—the Lorelies—bore the scars of a life lived under constant threat. Training grounds and armories took precedence over artefacts, and the sound of weapons clashing was as common as the flow of the currents. The kingdom's waters were dense and murky, often clouded by the sediment stirred by its relentless inhabitants. Large underwater geysers erupted sporadically, adding to the chaotic and volatile atmosphere. Predatory sea creatures prowled the outskirts, either tamed by the Periculum or daring to challenge them—only to meet a swift end.

Survival in the Periculum Kingdom was paramount, and weakness was not tolerated. They were physical marvels, their bodies sculpted by rigorous strength-based training. Their fins had adapted to exert a crushing power unmatched by any other aquatic beings. Thick and muscular, layered with ridges that gave them a vice-like grip, they were immensely strong—capable of coiling around prey or foes with the precision and power of a serpent contracting its victim. Even the Lorelie had honed their fins to serve as both weapons and tools. In combat, they could wrap their fins around large sea creatures or enemy combatants, immobilizing them with sheer force.

The fins' internal musculature allowed them to exert pressure equivalent to ten times their body weight, effectively crushing bones and suffocating their prey. This technique was a signature move, known as The Ceto Coil, named after their Goddess and taught to every warrior from a young age.

Training regimens in the Periculum Kingdom were grueling, designed to maximize both Lorelie's and the warriors' physical capabilities. They practiced lifting and manipulating heavy objects—such as massive boulders or the remains of sunken ships—using only their fins. Soldiers were often paired against one another in mock battles, their fins locked in a test of strength and endurance. The victor was determined by who could subdue the other first. These exercises not only built their physical strength but also enhanced their strategic thinking and precision.

In moments of attack, the Periculum could launch themselves through the water at explosive speed, using their fins to propel and ensnare their prey. Once locked onto their target, escape was impossible. Soldiers often followed this method with a swift strike from their seaweed sword to end the battle expeditiously. The Lorelie, on the other hand, could use this same technique to transport large loads of supplies—or even injured Mosquens—with ease. To face a Periculum soldier was to confront a force of nature.

IX.

THE IRIS

Acantha finned through the dark waters, transporting Amer through her home. The kingdom at night was an eerie silhouette of its daytime self.

"This is the safest time to rest," she advised, her tone carrying an unspoken warning. "My sister and I will train until we tire, but you may sleep."

Amer hesitated, his eyes narrowing as he tried to discern the contours of the alien landscape. He could barely see anything, his sense of direction scrambled by the disorienting vastness of the ocean night. The Lorelie led him to a cluster of chambers—rounded, stone-like pods carved into a towering coral structure. Their entrances were sealed with thick, kelp-like drapes that shimmered faintly.

Amer nodded reluctantly, his body heavy with exhaustion.

"Thank you," he mumbled, slipping into the chamber. But the moment Acantha's presence faded, his resolve hardened. He couldn't stay. He didn't belong here, and every instinct told him to leave while he still had the chance.

When he believed the coast was clear, Amer peeked out of the chamber. The kingdom was eerily silent, the currents carrying only the faint whispers of distant activity. The gel-like substance over his nose and mouth allowed him to breathe with ease, and he decided to take his chance. Kicking his legs furiously, he propelled himself upward, determined to find his way back to the surface.

The first rays of dawn began to filter through the water, casting a pale glow that illuminated the labyrinth of coral and rock. Amer used the light to guide himself, relying on the position of the rising sun and his memory of the river's direction to chart a course home. His chest tightened with every stroke, fear and determination warring within him as he pushed through the vast expanse of water.

Meanwhile, a sleepless Mavis paced anxiously in the castle courtyard, her frustration mounting with every passing hour. The guards had scoured the nearby rivers and forests throughout the night, their lightboxes cutting through the darkness, but Amer was nowhere to be found. The absence of any sign of him gnawed at her, and as the sky began to brighten, she knew she had to escalate their efforts.

"Contact the Queen and the General," she ordered one of the guards, her voice taut with urgency. The guard complied, but after multiple attempts to reach Queen Emmary and her companions, they were met with silence. Mavis clenched her fists, her jaw tightening. "Keep trying," she snapped.

As the sun rose higher, casting its warm light over the castle, Mavis stared out toward the horizon, her thoughts racing. Wherever Amer was, she prayed he was safe. But deep down, she knew there would be consequences—perhaps even the end of her life.

Watson stirred in his sleep, his usually stoic demeanor breaking as he tossed and turned against the soft sheets. The buzzing of his cellular phone on the bedside table became incessant, its screen glowing with a flood of emergency messages flashing one after the other. His bleary eyes struggled to adjust, but once he recognized the urgency, adrenaline took over. He bolted upright, the grogginess melting away as he scanned the alerts.

"The prince is missing."

The words jolted him like ice water. Without a second thought, he leapt from the bed. In a flurry of motion, Watson threw on his clothes, the sharp rustle of fabric filling the quiet room. He leaned over Bonnie, still peacefully asleep, and placed a firm but tender kiss on her forehead, murmuring, "I'll come back to you." She stirred faintly but did not awaken.

The heavy thuds of his feet echoed through the house as he descended the stairs, waking Alice from her sleep. She groggily turned in her bed, her mind still hazy with dreams, until her gaze fell upon the watch resting on her nightstand. Its presence—unexpected and unnerving—sent a chill racing down her spine. Her breath hitched, and her heart began to pound as her fingers hesitated to touch the object.

Downstairs, Watson was on a mission. His large frame moved with purpose as he grabbed his keys and headed out the door, his mind racing faster than his body. Clad in civilian clothing that concealed his authoritative air, he climbed into his vehicle and started the engine. The low growl of the car broke the early morning silence as he sped off toward the airport, his focus razor sharp.

The city blurred past him, the quiet streets giving way to the growing hum of a new day, but Watson didn't notice. All that mattered now was getting to the airport and addressing the emergency that demanded his attention.

Exactly two hours later, the hovercraft descended smoothly onto the landing pad. The soft hum of its engine faded as Watson stepped out to face the brisk Scottish air, its bite sharp against his cheeks. Already flushed from frustration and the exhausting journey, his large frame loomed over the vehicle as he waved impatiently for the driver to head toward the castle.

"No delays. Drive quickly," he barked.

Beneath the surface, Amer's desperate swim had finally brought him to the top, where sunlight fractured through the water in dancing beams. His chest heaved as he broke through, gulping in precious breaths of air. But his limbs, pushed beyond their limits, began to betray him. Exhaustion overtook him, and his arms fell limp at his sides. His body surrendered to the current, leaving him to float aimlessly on the water's surface like a leaf drifting along a stream.

The driver obeyed, zipping through the winding roads, the vehicle's sleek form weaving past rolling hills and towering trees. The iconic silhouette of the castle finally came into view. As they approached the gates, Watson's mood darkened further, his thoughts spiraling into anger at the lapse in vigilance that had led to this moment.

When the vehicle stopped, he wasted no time. He shoved the door open and stormed toward the castle grounds, making his entrance grand. His steps pounded against the stone path. His face was beet red, the fury coursing through his veins manifesting in clenched fists and the stiff set of his jaw. His cheeks, usually pale, were flushed with a fiery hue, and his eyes darted sharply across the courtyard as if daring anyone to stand in his way. His booming voice echoed through the entrance hall as he demanded to be brought up to speed.

Below, Acantha—realizing Amer had gone—scoured the underwater expanse within her home, calling out for her human companion.

"Human!" she cried, but to no avail.

Frustration and concern knitted her brow as her hazel eyes scanned the murky waters for any sign of him. Then she caught it—a faint trail, almost imperceptible, but enough for her senses to detect. His scent lingered in the water, leading her upward toward the surface. With a flick of her fin, Acantha surged toward the faint light above.

The castle halls rang with the sound of Watson's fury as he stormed through, but no one could provide him with any useful information. The staff's uncertainty only worsened his mood. Panic began to rise in his chest as he pushed through the back of the castle, making his way toward the river, believing Mavis was likely scouring the area. But as he neared the edge, something in the water caught his eye—a lifeless, pale form drifting in the current.

His heart skipped a beat. It was Amer.

Without a second thought, Watson tore down the lawn. Stripping down to nothing but his boxers, he didn't hesitate. Every fiber of his being screamed to get to the prince before it was too late. He dashed through the grass, water splashing up in all directions, his body pushing itself to the limit as he reached the water's edge. He dove headfirst, the cold shock of the river failing to slow him down as he swam toward the floating figure. With powerful strokes, Watson reached Amer, his heart pounding in his chest. Mavis, the maids, and the guards stood watch—astonished by his bravery.

Watson's hands gripped the prince's unconscious body, pulling him toward safety, each movement desperate as he dragged him from the water.

As he struggled to pull Amer ashore, a faint rustle of movement caught his attention. He turned, eyes narrowing in disbelief as he saw her—Acantha. Her body shimmered beneath the water's surface like a phantom. The Lorelie's hazel eyes locked with his, and for a brief moment, the world seemed to stand still. She observed him, her posture rigid, her expression unreadable. Watson didn't pause. He continued to drag Amer to the shore, his breath ragged as he tried to revive him.

After locking gazes with him for only a fleeting second, Acantha vanished beneath the water, her body disappearing into the depths as silently as she had arrived.

Watson laid Amer on the soft grass, his movements quick and urgent. The maids and guards raced down toward the river, blankets, pillows, and sheets whipping in the wind behind them. His hands trembled as he tore the gel-like substance from over Amer's nose and mouth, his fingers brushing against the seaweed and gel in a frantic effort to clear the prince's airway. Watson's breath came in short, harsh bursts, his own panic simmering beneath the surface—but he couldn't let it show. There was no time for delay.

Over in London, the Queen received the news. Both she and Mary began preparing for departure. Eerily so. Adjacent to Watson stood a terrified Mavis, hovering in disbelief, her hands above her head, her voice cracking with apology as she shouted frantic, incoherent pleas. Her words were lost on him. He tuned her out entirely. His focus was solely on Amer, his mind set on one thing: saving him.

He positioned his hands on the prince's chest, pushing down with force, his arms working tirelessly to perform CPR. The seconds stretched long—unbearable—and then, finally, the miracle he had been waiting for. Amer's body jerked—his chest rising and falling erratically as he fought for air—the gel-like seaweed having aided in saving his life.

Everyone around them seemed to hold their breath. Slowly, Watson exhaled in relief, wiping the sweat from his brow. But despite this, his fury had not faded. He didn't even spare Mavis a glance. As he lifted Amer's limp body into his arms, he growled, the words coming out like a venomous hiss.

"You will depart. Now," Watson spat. "Your suspension is imminent. The Queen will have her say on what comes to you." His eyes bore into her, filled with a mixture of frustration and disgust. He had no time for apologies or explanations—he had just fought to keep the future king alive, and all he could feel was raw rage.

As the first rays of dawn crept over the horizon, Queen Emmary moved through her chambers with a calm demeanor, but the fire beneath her expression was unmistakable. Her chambermaids fluttered around her in a well-practiced rhythm, readying her for what promised to be a momentous day.

The Queen chose her ensemble carefully. A copper-toned, knee-length pencil skirt hugged her figure, paired with a sleek black silk blouse that gleamed softly in the morning light. The blouse, long-sleeved and impeccably tucked, exuded quiet authority, complemented by the warm shimmer of andesine gemstones adorning her neck and ears.

Mary mirrored the Queen's composed exterior. She wore an auburn equestrian dress that flattered her slender frame, paired with pristine white stockings and polished leather loafers. Her red hair was pulled into a sleek bun, every strand perfectly in place.

After a quick bite to eat, they exited the royal residence and stepped into the hovering vehicle. The journey to Scotland was swift, the Queen remaining quiet, nefarious thoughts occupying every corner of her mind. The culprit who dared to harm the heir to the throne would soon face the full wrath of the Crown.

Alice had fallen back asleep after her father's departure, but the ticking of the watch on her nightstand woke her once more. Realizing now she had not been dreaming, a rush of adrenaline coursed through her veins as she scrambled out of bed. Barefoot and still dressed in her skull-patterned pajamas—oversized, with faded black cotton and frayed edges—she bolted out of her room. Her hair, messy from sleep, bounced wildly with each hurried step down the stairs.

Her descent was less than ladylike. She nearly tripped on the last step but caught herself on the railing before rushing into the basement. Inside, the dim light cast long shadows across the room. Linus was propped up on the old couch, scrolling aimlessly through his phone, his face illuminated by its cold glow. Nearby, Max and Archie remained sprawled on the makeshift bedding, their chests rising and falling in deep slumber.

Alice stormed in, her breathing labored. Without a word, she placed the watch down on the scratched coffee table in the centre of the room. Her hands trembled as she stepped back, her wide eyes locked onto the tiny object as if it might attack her.

"Linus," she whispered hoarsely, her voice quivering. "You need to see this."

Linus, sensing the urgency in her tone, looked up from his phone, confused.

"Good morning, sweetheart. Is everything good? What is it?" he asked with concern.

"It's my watch," she said, pointing. "Wake up Max!"

Max and his brother began to squirm.

"Pattern up, yeh. You have guests. What's all the commotion?" the young boy asked, outstretching his arms.

"What kind of sick game are you playing at?" Alice snapped.

Linus turned to face him as Archie began to open his eyes, unable to ignore the fussing.

"Game?" Max shouted. "What on earth are you mad about?"

"Eh," Linus interrupted, trying to mediate.

"The watch—it was on my nightstand this morning, broken. Did you come into my room?" she questioned him.

Shocked by the accusation, Max yelled, "No!"

"No need to shout," said Linus. "You need to think—when did you last have it?"

Max searched his mind, but everything was a blur. "I-I don't know." The room fell silent. "Maybe the bunker," he finally said.

"What about it?" Linus asked.

"I had it all day yesterday. It never left my pocket, and I can assure you it wasn't broken."

Alice began blinking profusely. A frightening thought entered her mind.

"No, it can't be," she whispered to herself.

"What?" Linus asked, overhearing her.

"Do you think it was my father?"

Linus scoffed. "No, there's no way."

Alice could feel her palms sweating from nerves. "But how else could we possibly explain it?"

He chuckled nervously.

"What does your father have to do with anything?" Max asked. But just then, without warning, Archie's body tensed abruptly, his limbs locking in place before shaking violently. The thin sheets covering him slipped off to the side as his convulsions intensified, revealing his malnourished frame trembling uncontrollably. His eyes rolled back, leaving only the whites visible, and his head jerked to the side as if in a silent, torturous protest.

"Archie!" Max screamed, his voice cracking as he threw himself to his brother's side, hands hovering helplessly over him, unsure of how to help. Linus stumbled backward, panic etched across his face, while Alice stood frozen for a split second, her breath hitching in her throat.

"Do something! Somebody help him!" Max cried.

Linus scrambled for his phone. "We need to call emergency!" he exclaimed.

"Wait!" Alice shouted. "What if they suspect something? He's a Modiri Guard—he isn't even supposed to be here."

"Well, we need to do something. We can't just let him stay like this!" Linus argued.

"Just call emergency," Max pleaded.

Upstairs, Bonnie stirred. She had grown accustomed to ignoring Alice's antics in the basement, but the sheer terror in the voices below cut through the quiet morning and past the floorboards. Throwing off the covers, she got to her feet and tossed a light robe over her night slip. Barefoot, she raced down the stairs.

Two flights later, Bonnie entered the basement, her wide eyes taking in the scene—a gaunt stranger convulsing violently on the floor, Alice panicked beside him, and Linus, along with an unfamiliar boy, was shouting at each other.

"What in heaven's name is going on down here?" she shrieked, her voice trembling with both anger and horror as she tried to make sense of the scene. Her gaze darted from Archie's seizure to Alice and Max, her maternal instincts warring with her fear.

"Turn him onto his side!" she instructed. "Quickly now!"

As Archie's body finally began to relax, the violent convulsions tapering off into shuddering spasms, a guttural retching sound erupted from his throat. His frame curled slightly to one side, his chest heaving as a surge of thick, moss-green vomit spilled from his mouth and onto the floor. The substance was unnatural, shimmering faintly in the dim light of the basement. Its gelatinous surface rippled as though something within it were writhing.

The grotesque movement sent a wave of terror through everyone present. Andrew now stood at the top of the steps, taking it all in.

"What the heck is that?" he bellowed.

Max recoiled instantly, his hands flying to his mouth as he gasped. "Someone help him!" he pleaded again, his voice breaking in alarm.

Alice stumbled backward, her skull-print pajamas brushing the edge of the puddle as she let out a strangled cry.

"It's—it's moving!" she screamed, her eyes wide in disgust.

Linus froze, transfixed by the vile mass, his voice quivering as he stammered, "Alice, get back here!" The vomit continued to churn, tiny, almost imperceptible shapes darting beneath the surface like microscopic eels or worms. A faint clicking sound emanated from it, as though the substance itself was protesting its expulsion. Bonnie stood by the staircase railing, clutching the banister.

"Kill it!" she shouted.

Everyone turned to her, bewildered.

"We have to kill it!" she repeated. But as she finished her sentence, Archie's body lay still, the life leaving his eyes—and with it, the substance began to dry. No one had an answer.

"Is he—?" Alice whimpered, her voice barely audible.

"No!" Max screamed, on his hands and knees, crawling to his brother. Archie was gone, just like that.

Alice whipped her body around, burying her face in Linus's chest, sobbing. He held her close, cradling her, while Bonnie ran upstairs in a state of shock she herself could not comprehend. In the kitchen, she stood over the sink, bawling. But before she could gather herself, Alice appeared. Standing in the doorway, she could no longer hold back her anger. She bit her lip in vexation.

"You forgave him, haven't you?"

Bonnie lifted her head, tilting it back before drawing a long sigh. "Your father and I have decided to move forward, yes."

"Move forward?" Alice echoed. "When? How? He lied to you and left us in a bunker with no care for what would happen to us."

"That was over two years ago, Alice. We have to move on. We have to forgive—"

"Oh? So what about this boy? There's a dead boy in our basement. Do you want to know how he got there?" she shouted.

"Lower your voice in this house, young lady."

"We had to break him out of that same bunker we were in two years ago. He's our age, Mother! He's young enough to be your child."

"In the bunker?" she stammered, stunned. "Why did you return there? What chaos are you all involving yourselves in?"

"It's not chaos. It's us trying to learn the truth about what's going on," she said. "The truth that you're complicit in, obviously."

Bonnie returned her daughter's stare. "Oh? And what truth is that?"

"That Father is—" Alice could feel her throat beginning to strain. "He's not a good man. He's killed someone." The tears spilled down her cheeks as she twisted her lips. "Father is not who we think he is, and that boy down there only further proves it."

The room was silent.

Bonnie, ever docile and domestic, fixed her hair before asking, "Would you all like breakfast?"

The first rays of sunlight kissed the icy peaks of the Snow Kingdom, casting a blue blush over the sprawling frozen expanse. The waters beneath, an otherworldly shade of aquamarine, danced with the light, reflecting the brilliance of the sun like shards of crystal.

Deeper below the surface, the Modiri stirred. Their fins unfurled as they woke, and their eyes, like polished gemstones, opened slowly, adjusting to the refracted light filtering through the depths. The sound of the current and the sea creatures formed a natural symphony to mark the start of a new day.

Inside the royal chambers, King Khione and Rudita moved around one another with an intimacy that spoke of centuries together. Their flowing forms intertwined momentarily before drifting apart again, the currents swirling gently in response. The King's presence was authoritative yet serene, and Rudita, with her glassy skin and eyes as deep as midnight, exuded grace. But there was a subtle tension in the water.

Their love was undeniable, but Rudita's heart bore the weight of unspoken resentment. She watched Khione with both admiration and frustration, her thoughts clouded by the unresolved rift between them. The Iris— the sacred relic they both longed to open—remained dormant. As Khione adjusted his ornate crown of frost-forged crystals, Rudita's voice broke the silence.

"My king," she began, her tone delicate yet laced with an edge of sorrow. "Do you not feel it? The Iris and the way it resists me? Us?"

Khione paused, his sharp eyes meeting hers with apathy.

"Hmph. The Iris will open when the time is right. We will not force its will."

"But it eludes me," she countered, her voice trembling. "Are you still vexed with me? Tell me, my tunt, does the fault lie within me? Or is it that you resist me as well, in ways you do not see—let alone I?"

Khione reached for her acetics, his touch cool yet steady. "You are the heart of this kingdom, Rudita. Do not let doubt cloud your strength."

"The only doubt I feel is that within these chambers," she said. "If you no longer vow to give me an Iris daughter, then simply admit it, so that I may remove the thought from my mind. Else it will devour me from the inside."

"The Iris is not controlled by me, nor by you."

"But it is your kingdom it serves, and your energy from which it feeds." Rudita slid her acetics from his, pulling herself away. She could feel her siren growing inside her, wanting to push its way out. "Please. I have been patient long enough. I no longer travel to the Timor waters, and I have accepted our loss."

Before long, Khione conceded, "I will venture to the Lamina Garden before nightfall." Despite his reassurance, Rudita's heart remained heavy. She turned away, gazing out through the translucent walls of the chambers toward the sleeping Iris. Its petals, encased in a protective aura of ice, seemed to mock her insecurities. She did not voice her fears again, but the questions lingered in her mind as she finned through the chambers. The frost-laden air rippled in her wake, betraying the storm raging within. As she approached the corridor, her gaze swept over the Snow Sentinels lining the crystalline walls. Their solemn expressions, etched as if by the ice itself, did little to comfort her.

Her sharp eyes caught Kaliope, the Healing Lorelie, finning toward her with an air of urgency. She paused and lowered herself into a curtsy, a gesture of respect for the Lady of the Snows.

"Kingdom Mother."

Rudita stopped abruptly, her chest heaving as if the gesture itself ridiculed her frustrations. She scoffed, her lips curling in disdain, her eyes gleaming with barely contained fury.

"Save your pleasantries," she hissed.

Without waiting for a reply, she let out a mournful siren call as she finned in the direction of the Lamina Garden's center. The sound resonated through the depths of the Snow Kingdom. The haunting wail echoed through the ice corridors, startling the Modiri within them. A wave of unease swept through the kingdom as heads turned.

Khione, seated on his throne, paused mid-thought as the cry reached his ears. He exhaled deeply, the weight of his Lady's sadness pulling at him.

"Rudita…" he muttered under his breath, though he made no move to follow her.

As the echoes of her cry began to fade, Kaliope hesitated only briefly before pressing forward into the Royal Chamber. She dipped her head as she entered. The Snows parted to allow her way.

"Father, I bring news."

Khione's eyes met hers. Lovingly, he said, "The sun kisses your face in all its glory. What is it?"

Kaliope blushed. Her father's love was undeniable.

"Thank you, Father," she bowed with a smile. "But it is the Modiri ashore. It appears the orb has awakened again. It's pulsating. I suppose they are losing Emars once more."

"I thought they had stopped," he mused.

"Yes, but these are younger—perhaps children," she informed him. "I cannot feel the ones from the mountain like before. But this one… I don't know. It feels different."

"Hmm. What is the obsession with our crystals for the land dwellers?"

"I do not know," she said, her eyes lowering as she braced herself to be reprimanded for her next request. "May we help them?"

Khione chuckled. "Why would we ever do such a thing?"

"They are not purebred, but they are still finned, which leaves them helpless."

Khione was many things, but never unfair.

"If it will warm your heart, I will hear of good reason," he instructed, to which Kaliope's eyes widened in merry disbelief. "Learn of the purpose behind the humans' desire for our minerals. And if it is a threat to our species, we will reclaim those who are ours."

Kaliope beamed, her smile large and her eyes cheerful.

"Oh, Father, thank you!" she said, wrapping her arms around his neck before planting a small kiss on his cheek.

On the other side of the kingdom, the Lamina Garden pulsed with the rhythm of Rudita's own thoughts. The faint hum of the altar's energy consumed her as she lay atop the ornate glass in its center, her body curved with grace yet stiff with unspoken torment. Her acetics, delicate yet purposeful, glided over the altar's surface, tracing the intricate patterns with almost ritualistic care. Rudita's touch was gentle—reverent, even—though her heart seethed.

The Iris altar at the Garden's center, a symbol of divine acceptance, remained sealed. Mocking her. Despite the ache of resentment brewing within, the Lady of the Snows maintained her composure. Tradition demanded it. To defy the altar openly, to let it feel the anger she harbored, would invoke her King's right to oversee her end. And Khione, though fair, was steadfast in his duties.

Lurking in the shadows of the garden, Fanira looked on. The witch, in her natural form, leaned against one of the towering crystalline laminae, her skin bleeding into the dim light. The eels that adorned her head moved lazily, twisting and curling with minds of their own, their glowing eyes adding a faint, ominous aura to her figure. Her eyes, like moonstones, lingered on the Kingdom Mother. There was no disdain in her gaze—only pity. She had witnessed this scene before, many times: Rudita on the altar, praying, pleading, hoping for the Iris to open and bestow its divine favor.

Fanira moved slightly, her eels flicking with irritation at the futility of it all.

"Cruel, isn't it?" she slithered. The Lady of the Snows was in no mood.

"Witch," she griped, acknowledging her presence.

"Shame that you're still no closer to your Iris… yet the hybrid is making progress in the East," she mocked.

Rudita lifted her head, her eyes tearing into Fanira. "She's not dead?"

"Dead? No. Why would you imagine it so?"

"It was you, wasn't it?" she growled.

"Me?" Fanira teased. "What on shells could I have done?"

"When they named you our Watch Witch, I simply knew you would have it out for me," Rudita snarled. "I was only a child, Fanira."

"You've always been quite temperamental. But as much as you like to blame me, I can assure you this is not my doing."

"Then who? Who must I blame for losing my one daughter and going without the chance for another?"

"Perhaps a mirror would help—"

"Don't be curt with me, witch."

Fanira continued to glide in circles around Rudita, whose head whipped from side to side so as not to lose her.

The witch scoffed. "You knew of the prophecy for this kingdom before you took your vows. We made sure of it. Your mother—"

"You dare speak on her?"

"…she asked for your acetics to Khione's, knowing the consequences that would ensue from your enmity for those unlike yourself."

The chamber fell silent.

"Leave me," Rudita whispered, as if she had experienced an epiphany. She needed to be alone. "Leave me!" she shouted when Fanira did not obey her.

Fanira lingered in the garden for a breath longer, her eyes locked onto Rudita's form atop the altar. The tension between them hung like a thick mist—unspoken, yet suffocating. She could see the silent storm in the Lady of the Snows' expression, a mix of hope and despair. Not wanting to aggravate her further, her sleek form began to retreat toward the edge of the sacred place.

"One final warning. You must brace yourself for the return of the girl."

Her words carried the weight of forewarning, each syllable heavy with implication. Fanira did not wait for Rudita's response. She merely slithered away, leaving the light of the garden behind her.

The kingdom was alive with the faint stirrings of its denizens. Though they gave her a wide berth as she passed, there was something about her presence that left everyone uneasy.

Finally, she reached the Royal Chamber, where she moved to her usual corner, curling herself into the shadows where the halo of light barely stretched. At its centre, Khione was sprawled across his throne, relaxed. In his large, clawed acetics, he toyed with a handful of small, smooth pebbles, tossing them idly into the air and catching them one by one. His eyes, the color of pale winter skies, were half-lidded, and a faint, sweet melody hummed from his throat, reverberating softly in the chamber's icy acoustics.

Fanira said nothing as she observed him from her corner. But his humming paused briefly as his eyes flicked to her, then back to his pebbles.

"Yes," he sang.

"Have you no update on the girl?"

"You mean whether or not she is alive?"

"No, that I can learn for myself. I mean, once she returns—where will your healer go?"

She spoke quickly, startling him out of his blissful comfort.

"My healer will remain here. The question is, where will your hybrid go?"

Fanira squinted. "What kind of malicious schemes are you plotting?"

"Schemes?"

"Ahvi. Your Lady of the Snows begs for an Iris, and you withhold one from her. And now, you believe that the hybrid will be gifted elsewhere?"

"Withhold," he sang. "Withhold, hmm. Such an interesting choice of words. Rudita has many children. She will need to be content."

"…And the hybrid?"

"What of her? She is in the East—training, learning. King Bao wants a bride, does he not?"

Fanira let out a shrieking laugh. "Is that your intention? Do you believe your proposition will bode well with the Kingdom Kings and Queens and our Sea God?"

"Ahvi," he said confidently. "Why would it not? Unless, like always, you know something I do not."

Fanira, from her corner, lifted her eyes to him. "When the time comes—because it will—you only need to allow it."

"Allow what?" he questioned.

But before Khione could muster another word, Fanira dissolved into the shadows, her form dissipating like smoke caught in a cold breeze. The silence she left behind was as heavy as the frost clinging to the chamber walls.

Khione, still lounging on his throne, let the smooth pebble he had been tossing fall into his palm. Whatever she had meant, it was now his burden to unravel.

X.

HOME SWEET HAMPSTEAD

The Scottish countryside lay eerily still, a pall of melancholy draped over the town as if the events of the early morning had seeped into the air itself. Even the birds, which usually welcomed the morning with a cheerful chorus, seemed subdued, their calls replaced by a chilling silence. Mist rolled languidly over the hills, the sunlight struggling to pierce the gloom.

Balmoral Castle loomed ahead, its grandeur softened by the heavy atmosphere. The arrival of Queen Emmary and Lady Mary sparked a flurry of movement as guards, chambermaids, and staff swarmed to greet them. Their hurried voices overlapped, each one desperate to provide updates and gain the Queen's attention. But Emmary, her presence commanding and her eyes alight with purpose, paid no heed to their chaotic chatter.

With a sharp click of her heels, she moved swiftly toward the winding staircase that led to Amer's quarters. The air of authority in her stride was enough to silence the staff. Lady Mary hesitated, watching Queen Emmary ascend the stairs with grace. She understood immediately that her place was not to follow.

Just then, a jubilant Clara appeared, her face lighting up at the sight of Mary.

"My dear Lady Mary, you've returned!" she exclaimed, clasping her hands together in delight.

With a warmth that melted the somber mood, Clara motioned for Mary to follow her to the kitchen. The spacious kitchen was a marvel of 2452 culinary innovation, gleaming with state-of-the-art appliances where the head chambermaid maneuvered with ease.

"I'll prepare your favourite," she said while gathering ingredients from the automated pantry. "Are you all right? You don't seem happy to be back. And how was your time with the Queen? Surely you must have learned a thing or two."

Mary wore a solemn look, unsure of how to formulate her thoughts into a question.

"Well, aren't you going to share?" Clara insisted.

Mary, sitting atop the island stool, her hands clasped perfectly in her lap, asked, "Do I have a sister?"

As Clara began crafting a luxurious dish known as the Risotto Luma, she hoped to change the subject.

"I am making your favourite risotto," she smiled. The dish was a masterpiece of the era.

As Mary watched Clara work, she asked again, "Miss Clara, do I have a family elsewhere?"

Clara did not want to engage. She had come to love Mary like a daughter, and the very question sparked some jealousy within her.

"I am not too sure. But I know you have family here, and we all love you very much."

"The Queen told me I had a sister, but she was in this strange place," Mary said. "She looked familiar—right—but I can't seem to remember."

"Her Majesty said this?" Clara looked to confirm.

"Yes, and it was the oddest thing. Her face—I recall bits and pieces, but nothing further."

The head chambermaid listened intently, but as the aroma of the dish began to fill the room, it momentarily lifted her spirits.

"Lady Mary, I am sure it was a mere slip of the tongue and nothing for you to worry over," she smiled. "I am adding a light concoction of fruits to help release the perfect balance of sweetness in this. I can't wait for you to taste it."

Mary curved her lips into an uncomfortable smile.

Meanwhile, Queen Emmary stepped into Amer's bedroom, the air thick with the sterile scent of medical treatment and lingering incense. The room now reflected the understated tastes of a teenager seeking individuality. The gilded moldings had been replaced with clean lines and muted colors. Along the dresser, a collection of carefully arranged action figures—no longer toys but treasured artifacts—stood proudly next to an array of neatly clipped newspaper headlines chronicling his accomplishments and interests.

Amer lay in the centre of the emperor-sized bed, his form dwarfed by its size. The navy-blue bedding was immaculately tucked around him, the royal crest embroidered on the corners of the fabric. His face was peaceful, free from the residue of the morning's horrors, but his stillness unsettled Emmary. She approached cautiously, her heels making soft clicks against the solid oak flooring until she paused by his bedside.

Her breath hitched as she gazed upon her child. Though the color had returned to his cheeks, the sight of him so vulnerable sent a pang of anguish through her chest. She reached out, her hand hovering just above his brow before withdrawing, unwilling to disturb him.

"You are the next King of England, my son," she whispered, as if to remind him, whilst running her manicured fingers gently through his perfectly trimmed hair.

From the doorframe, Watson stood at attention, his towering figure draped in freshly pressed civilian attire: an understated black jacket, a crisp white shirt, and boots polished to a shine. Though out of uniform, his posture remained disciplined, his presence commanding yet deferential.

Emmary slowly eased her way toward the balcony, where she overlooked the lawn and the river in the distance. Her eyes never moved to him. With hands clasped before her, she asked, "What happened?"

Watson lowered his head into a deep, respectful curtsy.

"Your Majesty, the guards say he went missing in the late hours of the night. They searched the grounds and the castle until morning," he paused. "But it wasn't until I arrived that I found him floating in the river. He was unconscious."

Emmary's rage was brewing.

"What of his Royal Guard?"

"Mavis, ma'am. She's been relieved of her duties, indefinitely."

"Is that it? Relieved?"

Watson cleared his throat. "Yes. I could do nothing more."

"Oh," Emmary sighed. "I suppose since keeping a watchful eye on our future king is not of grave importance to her, she no longer needs it."

"…Your Majesty?"

"I want to look straight into that eyeball. I want to see it for myself." Her voice began to rise. "Remove it from her skull and bring it to me."

Watson remained silent, for he knew of no proper response.

"Is there more?"

He contemplated his next words, but decided it best to disclose everything.

"There was a female hybrid—I believe it to have been—in the river when I retrieved him. It looked at me."

Emmary's heart sank. A fear washed over her.

"A hybrid?"

"Something was in there with him. We're still unsure if that's what caused the bruising—"

"Bruising?" she snapped.

Before he could finish, Emmary's heels stomped into the floorboards as she stormed back to Amer's bedside, stripping the sheets from his body and exposing him. His torso was wrapped in gauze, and his wrists and forearms were heavily bruised. She could see no further, as he wore only his white pajama trousers.

She let out a shrieking cry.

"My son! What have they done to you?"

Emmary began to seethe as she fell to her knees, cupping his hand into hers.

"I want them all to burn. Do you understand me?"

"Your Majesty, our prince is a fighter. If he was attacked—"

"If? What else do you suppose could have done this to him if not those devil creatures?" she wept. "Take to their towns. Bruise their children. They will soon learn to stay far away from mine!"

Her words became incoherent.

"What—what are they not getting? Do—do—do they believe we are incapable of ripping them apart, limb by limb? Do they think we are pitiable cowards and will not seek revenge? The rules are simple!"

She began to shout.

"Stay out of the water if you are a female hybrid. And only catch our food if you are male. It is not hard to grasp—and yet, they disobey us."

Watson nodded in agreement. "Take three of their hybrids, beat them to an inch of their lives, and return them." His eyes widened, but despite his apprehension, he agreed. As he curtsied and began making his way to the doorway, Emmary asked,

"Watson, what was Amer doing in the water in the first place? Was he bewitched?"

The Queen had grown vengeful, and so he lied. "I do not know, Your Majesty."

There was a questionable pause between them.

"You're dismissed."

The hours slipped by with a heavy stillness as Queen Emmary sat by Amer's bedside. Her gaze lingered on his face lovingly, searching for some sign of vitality beyond the shallow rise and fall of his chest. The clock ticked endlessly, but she paid it no mind. For her, time had stopped. She barely noticed the chambermaids who brought trays of tea and broth, which sat untouched on a nearby table.

Meanwhile, Watson, standing in the hallway, braced himself against the weight of his own actions. The guards he had dispatched were already on the move, carrying out his orders in the name of the Crown. His expression was stony, his jaw clenched, but the flicker of guilt in his eyes betrayed him. The memory of Amer's questions about Fiona—the curiosity, the spark of hope—gnawed at his conscient like a relentless tide.

If only he had stayed silent and kept Fiona's truth buried, the hybrids would still be safe from the Queen's wrath. Yet, his duty overshadowed his doubts. He could not allow himself to unravel—not now. Not when the survival of the monarchy demanded absolute loyalty and the sacrifice of all else, including his own humanity.

He exhaled sharply, forcing himself to refocus. Regret, after all, would not alter the course now set in motion. With a final glance at the door to Amer's room, he left to oversee the mission.

The Makara Kingdom was a masterpiece of underwater artistry, a realm draped in rich hues of aqua green, shimmering gold, deep navy blue, and bold accents of red. The colors intertwined seamlessly across the kingdom's architecture, creating a supernatural glow that pulsed with life. Towering structures shaped like great sea dragons stood as proud monuments representing the kingdom's lineage. Their intricate details—scales, whiskers, fins—were carved with such precision they seemed alive, ready to burst into motion.

At the heart of the kingdom stood its grand temple, a sprawling marvel resembling the Great Shaolin Temple, with pagoda-like tiers stacked high toward the ocean's surface. Each level bore carvings of legendary battles and ancient lore, the red accents symbolizing the bloodlines of their mighty rulers. The arches and doorways shimmered with inlaid pearls and luminous coral—evidence of the kingdom's wealth and pride.

But despite its grandeur, the Makara Kingdom was eerily quiet. Hundreds of Makaras glided gracefully through the waters, their scales catching the light and casting multicolored reflections on the seabed. The glow on their fins served as their identifiers, each shade a unique signature. Still, the kingdom's population was sparse, with only four Lorelie finning actively through the corridors, tending to the needs of their king. The empty seabed and hushed current felt like a monument to a fading legacy.

Naida's eyes fluttered open, greeted by the sweet, soothing aroma of ancient rosemary wafting through the dimly lit temple room. The space was serene, bathed in a soft golden glow. She lay still for a moment, her senses absorbing the opulence around her, before her fin stirred her into motion. The faint echo of rippling water accompanied her as she glided lightly toward the corridor, curiosity pulling her forward.

On the far side, a figure emerged, striking against the monarchical tones of the ancient kingdom. A Lorelie pulsed into view, her presence radiant yet understated. Her abyssal black hair, which seemed to swallow the light around it, was neatly pinned atop her head, not a strand out of place. Her skin, a vibrant pastel shade of orange, caught glimmers of gold that danced across the surrounding waters.

Her eyes, a striking cinnamon brown, were vivid and piercing, as if they held the secrets of the oceans themselves. Her curled fin shimmered with golden hues, unmarred by embellishments; its simplicity only amplified its natural beauty. The tail fluke—or dorsal fin placed to her rear, as was typical of the Lorelie Modiri in the East—matched the same golden luster that extended to her brasloor, plain yet resplendent.

The two girls exchanged a glance. Naida, unable to look away from her royal demeanor, curtsied.

"My Lady," she said respectfully.

Shocked, the Lorelie pulsed backward. "No, no, I am King Bao's daughter, Yvina," she smiled. "You are Naida, as I am told."

The Lorelies were propellers, the younger ones often losing their balance along the way—unlike their Kings, who were masters at propelling and needed no help with stability or steering.

Naida watched the Lorelie with intrigue.

Her voice soft. Pleasant.

"Yes, it is a pleasure to make your acquaintance," she hesitated.

"Our King awaits you in the master temple. He is meditating."

"What is this place?" Naida asked, taking a look around.

"This is the Makara Kingdom, ruled by the great King Bao, God of the Makaras."

"There's barely anyone here."

"Yes, our King is in need of a lady…" Yvina said, looking Naida up and down. The hybrid took notice and quickly decided to change the subject.

"How many Makaras are there?"

"Oh, there are thousands—some of whom live in other parts of the East, for that is where they can survive. The Shadows of the Grey, ruled by the great King Ryūmon, of The Shen Ryūmon, has many Makaras as well, whom he's trained. They are incredible creatures, really."

"Incredible?"

"Yes. They're warriors with magic of their own." As proudly as Yvina spoke, Naida still held her grudge against the Makara who had tried to have her for supper.

Around them were towering temples adorned with designs that told the rich history of the Makaras, and tall pagodas where fish swam in and out with ease. Yvina pulsed anxiously, pointing out key structures with a quiet pride. Her poised tone carried warmth and a tinge of relief—relief at finally seeing a Modiri outside of their realm, a potential Kingdom Mother.

"Tell me, what is it like where you are from?" she asked with excitement. She seemed to bloom in Naida's company, her voice lifting slightly as she spoke about the architecture, the rituals performed in their grand halls, and the role of the Makara dragons, revered like deities.

"I'm from a town called Sattle," Naida said politely. "It was a drab place. It rained a lot, and our family didn't have much. But we had one another."

"A family," Yvina said, disappointedly.

"Yes."

"Humans?"

"Not quite. My father was a hybrid, like myself, and my mother…" Naida paused.

"Oh, a hybrid… I see. You're the first hybrid we've seen here. To be quite fair, it's a tad disrespectful to the kingdom that King Khione would suggest your attendance. But I suppose our dear King remains hopeful—I dare not say desperate."

"Hopeful of what?"

"A Lady." Yvina smiled. Naida's face contorted.

"No, no. I am not in any way a lady to anyone," she said. "Why is that important anyway?"

"A Kingdom Mother is needed for all kingdoms. They are the nurturers—the ones the Lorelies and Mosquens fin to when they emerge from the Lamina plant."

But as Yvina continued, Naida found herself distracted. The marvel of the kingdom, the conversation of baby Modiri—all dimmed in her mind, eclipsed by the gnawing thought of Melissa. A knot tightened in her chest, her impatience growing with every passing moment. She wanted to interrupt Yvina, but the Lorelie was so elated, she couldn't dare interject. Her fin, however, twitched involuntarily, betraying her uneasiness.

"Are you feeling like yourself?" Yvina stopped to ask.

Drawing a long sigh, Naida felt it best to be truthful. "No. I would very much like to be with King Bao, to learn from him as quickly as I can so I may return ashore and aid my sister."

"Sister?"

"Yes. Her name is Melusine."

"Oh. Is she human?"

"She is a hybrid, like me."

"So why is she not here?"

Naida paused, trying to conjure up a clever response, but nothing came to mind. "She does not believe in the water, which is perfectly okay. She wanted to remain on land." Yvina could not hide her detest.

"That seems to be the pattern with you hybrids, or so I have heard."

"I do not denounce either side of my lineage. I embrace both, proudly," Naida corrected. "But sadly, I cannot be in two places at once."

"If that part were true, you would never have survived long enough to be here," Yvina said softly, offering Naida a small smile. "Please, I mean not to be so harsh. But I find it rather discomforting that anyone at all could know of our existence and their parallel to our bloodline and still reject us."

As they approached another temple, its golden spire piercing the water, Naida's hope began to fade.

"I never challenged it," she said, hoping to reassure her newfound friend. "But despite that, I cannot abandon my sister after what I've come to witness."

"What?"

Before she could respond, Naida's eyes drifted to the temple's entrance as a figure emerged from the shadows, his movement powerful and purposeful. It was Brimsey, a Periculum soldier, and his presence commanded attention. Like his sister, Acantha, short quills adorned his upper body, their subtle protrusion lending him an air of danger and intrigue. His fin, like dark molten hues infused with gold and silver, shimmered faintly in the filtered light, its elegance matched only by the seamless harmony it created with his lean, muscular torso.

Yvina, turning to look, lowered her eyes in admiration; Brimsey's appearance was strikingly unique. Wrapped neatly around his waist was a belt of vibrant green seaweed—an innocuous accessory at first glance. Yet with a swift motion, he could remove it, revealing its true nature: a majestic blade, gleaming and sharp enough to cut through ionsdaleite, the hardest material known in the oceanic world, rivaling even diamonds. This transformation alone spoke volumes of his skill and the Periculum Kingdom's mastery of both nature and weaponry.

His jet-black, kinky high-top fade was pristine, highlighting his angular jawline and perfectly symmetrical features. But it was his eyes—hazel pools that shimmered with hidden depths—that left both Naida and Yvina momentarily breathless. A handsome fellow, much like his brothers. His rugged appearance was balanced by a quiet confidence that was hard to ignore.

Naida's heart fluttered, a sensation she hadn't anticipated. Her thoughts of Melissa and urgency took a back seat as she found herself captivated by Brimsey's presence. He inclined his head slightly, his voice low and steady as he addressed Yvina with a soldier's deference, though his gaze lingered on Naida, a glimmer of curiosity evident.

Smitten, yet cautious, Naida could feel her cheeks flush—though whether from admiration or the unrelenting tension in her mind, she couldn't quite tell. The girls lingered for a moment, their hearts racing as they watched Brimsey make his way past them.

Naida had never been kissed before, but her mind betrayed her, imagining the press of his pink, plump lips against hers—a cool, electrifying embrace that left her breathless just at the thought. Her imagination ran wild, the strength of his presence etched into her thoughts even as he disappeared beyond the temple's entryway.

Yvina's soft voice broke the spell, her tone warm but firm as she placed an acetic gently on Naida's arm.

"Stay alive," she urged. "Make it through my father's tests so that you may know the Shadows."

Naida, snapping back to reality, nodded. Steeling herself, she turned toward the towering entrance of the temple, where the atmosphere seemed to shift as she finned closer. She glanced back at Yvina, who offered a small, reassuring smile before gesturing for her to continue. Naida squared her shoulders and finned inside, determination in her heart. She would endure whatever lay ahead—for herself and for Melusine.

Nava stirred awake in the soft embrace of one of the Hampstead residence's guest rooms, sunlight spilling gently through the lace curtains. The smell of bacon and waffles wafted through the air, wrapping her in a comforting haze that promised a morning of warmth, even if the circumstances of her visit were anything but.

Summoned by her son, Benson Jr., to soothe his nerves after the chaos surrounding Melissa's confinement to the bunker, she stretched languidly, preparing herself for what she hoped would be a peaceful day. After freshening up, Nava descended the grand staircase, her steps light but urgent, taking in the quiet elegance of the home. She moved through the corridors, the sound of her slippers brushing against the hardwood floor as she wandered in search of her son.

She found him in the study, a room bathed in muted morning light, its shelves stacked with books that remained unread but seemed to breathe intellect and history. Benson Jr., still clad in his plain pajamas, stood near the large bay window. A half-empty glass of apple juice rested atop his polished desk, forgotten. He gazed outside with an intensity that suggested he wasn't merely looking, but rather engaging in some silent, profound conversation with the world beyond the glass.

"Good morning," she said. Her presence startled him, his body giving a small jolt as he turned to face her. For a moment, his composure faltered, his eyes betraying a mixture of relief and apprehension. Nava offered him a knowing smile, her maternal instinct cutting through the tension like sunlight through morning mist.

"Morning," he replied. "How did you sleep, Mum?"

Nava hesitated before responding; there was something sinister in his eyes. "Um… well. This place is quite cozy." She entered the room fully, closing the door behind her to retain their privacy. "Are you all right? I could hear you moving about throughout the night."

"Hmph," he grunted. "I couldn't sleep."

"Do you wish to talk about it?"

His eyes darted to her. "Of course. I have many questions."

Nava felt it best to take a seat, and so she plopped herself into one of the upholstered chairs in front of the desk, crossing her legs.

"Ask me anything."

Benson Jr. remained standing. "Why did you and Father do this to me?"

"Do what?" she replied, startled.

"Place me in such a precarious position," he stated. "One minute, I feel like I owe him a duty, and the next, I resent you both. You've taken my young adult life from me, and for what?"

"For what?" she echoed, as if to throw the question back to him. "Your father made decisions without my knowing, and as a wife and mother, I stood in the shadows. I merely obeyed—submitting to his will, as it was said to be the best for you."

"Best for me?" he jerked. "Have you no knowledge of his cunning tricks?"

Nava lowered her eyes, embarrassed. "I am only the wife. I do not have a say. But I cannot divulge my truths unless I know we are discussing the same matters."

"What do you possibly mean, Mum? What other matters are there? Do you not see where you are seated? The silk garments that drape your body—did any of it come from me? My hard work or sacrifice?"

"You complain of being free of labor?"

"No, I complain of being emasculated, and asked to walk around as if it is normal."

Nava chuckled. "My dear son, you are merely privileged."

"…And so are my peers, yet none of them have been coerced into a premature marriage and asked to conceive with an alien for the greater good of their nation."

Nava clicked her tongue. "Ah, we are discussing the same matters," she said, nervously intertwining her fingers. "Your father committed himself not only to the people of our country, but to a larger force outside of even the monarchy."

"What does that have to do with me?"

"He had an affair," she replied, lowering her eyes in shame. "He believed the only way to protect you and me from public scrutiny and embarrassment was to go along with the Queen's request."

"An affair?" Benson Jr. questioned, holding her gaze. His heart sank at the news. "You never told me anything."

"Of course not. You were only a child—and in some ways, you still are. I just wanted you to retain your innocence. There was no need to involve you in adult matters."

"But I am involved," he retorted. "My life was altered because of his actions—and yours as well—and yet we do nothing?"

Nava laughed. "What do you suppose we do? We are mere pieces on a larger board of his life."

Benson Jr. grew agitated. "He's a drunk, a bad father, and now, a cheating husband. He's done nothing for this nation. There are protestors outside his office every morning, complaining about the inflation and tax hikes they've endured over the past few years, and instead of addressing them, he cowers in his office and drowns himself in alcohol—"

"Steady, son," she requested. "I know you are angry, but we must remain prudent and level-headed. Your wife is away—"

"Wife?" he asked, raising an eyebrow. "You mean the alien?"

"Enough now. I did not raise you to be disrespectful toward women—let alone the one carrying your child."

He paused. "…She isn't any longer."

"I beg your pardon."

"She was taken last night to the facility… I—I had no choice."

"What did you do?" she asked, her voice laced with worry.

"I did what Father wanted me to do, and now… now, I feel guilty. I feel useless. I feel ashamed. I feel like I've been betrayed by my own hero. It was a plan from the very beginning. The chambermaids all scurried away with her as if they had been a part of the plot all along. The only fool residing here was me."

"Do you not believe she, too, was blindsided?"

"No," he said with a steady tone, despite his eyes beginning to water. "You're the only one I trust. When I met her, those chambermaids resided with her in the flat, and then they relocated with us here. Why would I trust her? Or them? Or even Father? No one is honest."

Nava remained still, allowing his words to penetrate her.

"I assure you, son, she is innocent."

Benson Jr. paused, the tears dripping slowly from his eyes. "So, we're all just victims?"

"We are all just victims," she slowly confirmed.

Benson Jr.'s chin quivered, betraying the storm of emotions threatening to consume him. His fists clenched at his sides, his face twisted in anguish as he fought against the additional tears welling in his eyes. But the dam broke—not with sobs, but with a surge of fury.

In a single breath, he unleashed his wrath, thrusting books from the shelves with reckless abandon. Their spines thudded against the hardwood floor like heavy drumbeats, echoing his inner turmoil. Papers scattered like autumn leaves as he swept them violently from the desk— a chaos of ink and parchment. The half-empty glass of apple juice was next, hurled toward the window with a force that shattered both glass and silence. The sharp crash sent shards flying, the morning's tranquility obliterated.

Nava instinctively raised her arms, shielding herself from the splintered glass as she cowered in place, her heart pounding as she watched her son unravel. Benson Jr. was livid, his chest heaving as if every breath stoked the inferno within him. But then, in the midst of his outburst, something shifted.

His body froze mid-motion, his hands still raised as if to strike again, but his eyes grew distant. A realization seemed to dawn, silencing the storm. His rage ebbed like a receding tide, leaving him standing amidst the wreckage, his breath heavy, his expression hollowed by an epiphany that had halted his fury in its tracks.

"We need to get Father to resign and elect me to office," he said confidently.

Nava, stunned and still apprehensive about letting her guard down, turned to face her son, who stood behind her with a book in hand, preparing to toss it.

"He would never do such a thing."

"Well, we make him."

The last chambermaid, who had stayed behind, kept her ear to the door, eavesdropping. Upon overhearing their plan, she scuttled to the dining area to phone Dr. Astor.

XI.

THE EXTRACTION

Twenty-four hours later, morning came to greet Melissa—though time had lost all meaning in the windowless depths of the bunker. She awoke in yet another sterile operating room, strapped to a gurney with needles embedded in her arm and ankle. The shattered two-way mirror from the previous room remained untouched, a haunting reminder that Dr. Astor no longer cared for appearances and had no time to waste.

The infant Modiri she had borne was gone—sealed away in a distant grid room, suspended within a containment sphere tailored to its small form. Helpless, Melissa fought against the restraints, her cries piercing the silence as the heart monitor beside her blared faster with every panicked beat.

A chambermaid entered hesitantly, her steps faltering as she crossed the threshold. Though visibly shaken, she forced herself to meet Melissa's gaze.

"What are you looking at? Get me out of here!" Melissa demanded.

"I cannot," the chambermaid whispered, her voice trembling. "I'm sorry. I was only told to keep an eye on you."

Melissa gritted her teeth and thrashed, yanking at the machines with wild desperation. "Get me out of here!" she screamed.

The chambermaid recoiled, inching backward as fear spread across her face. "You're a monster. I will not come near you. You'd best stop that before you break those machines!"

But Melissa did not stop.

"A monster, you say?" she spat. "Fine. I'll be so. Once I break free, I'll snap your neck, and I'll take pleasure in watching the life leave your eyes."

The chambermaid's breath hitched. She turned and bolted, her terrified voice echoing down the corridor.

"Doctor!"

Moments later, Dr. Flynn entered. Draped in a long lab coat, he moved with a frailty that bordered on unnatural. His back was hunched, his fingers disturbingly long, the skin beneath his nails darkened as though stained. His eyes were vacant, drifting as if he weren't entirely certain where he stood. The slackness of his features unsettled Melissa deeply. He looked as unhinged as Dr. Astor had always behaved.

The crown of his head was bald, save for sparse patches of grey hair circling the perimeter like a forgotten wreath. Without a word, he retrieved a syringe of propofol from his coat, unscrewed the IV line, and attached it with mechanical precision. Slowly, he depressed the plunger, sending the liquid down into the drip.

Melissa's eyes widened in horror. Her legs thrashed violently against the restraints as she struggled to break free. "Why are you doing this? Please—I just want to go home!" Her voice cracked, raw with desperation. "Fiona!"

Her cry reverberated off the sterile walls, but Dr. Flynn didn't so much as look at her. When the injection was complete, he turned and walked out, shutting the door firmly behind him.

As the sedative pulled her under, Melissa whispered her sister's name, praying for just one more glimpse of her. Sleep swallowed her whole, soft and heavy, dragging her into dreams where reunion still felt possible.

Elsewhere, on the upper level of the compound, Cafeteria B pulsed with a muted energy. Dozens of men filed in, numbers embroidered onto the fronts of their plain scrub tops. Their steps were muffled by the tan non-slip socks issued in place of footwear; shoes and anything the doctors might deem a potential weapon were strictly forbidden.

The men shuffled into line, their movements precise, almost rehearsed, as Beatrice and her team stood behind the counter, sliding breakfasts onto paper plates divided neatly into three small sections. The air carried the faint scent of boiled oats and stale bread.

Low voices threaded through the silence, fragments of conversation that never quite broke it. From the corners of the room, uniformed sentinels stood watch—silent, armed, and unyielding. Their presence made clear this was no ordinary meal but a controlled ritual in a place that allowed no freedom.

One of the men lifted his gaze, locking eyes with a guard by the staircase exit. His lips moved, the words barely audible, almost swallowed by the hum of the cafeteria.

Nearby, a fellow experiment, Number 061, leaned toward him with a faint, cautious smile.

"Hey, man. Everything all right?"

Experiment 019 squinted, his expression caught between longing and despair.

"I want to go home…"

It was as if something inside him broke. His mind snapped back to that fateful day in Sattle, when he had raised his tranquilizer and brought down a hybrid caught violating the law. He had felt proud then, certain he had fulfilled his duty. The promise had been clear: he and his family would be rewarded, given a better life, more opportunities.

But it had all been a lie.

Years had passed, and nothing had changed. The walls stayed stark and white, the air sterile, the food strange and bitter—laced with the faint sting of medicine that offered little nourishment. Their bodies withered, muscle mass wasting away until they seemed to shrink in both flesh and spirit. Hollow eyes met his every day, their light dimming more with each sunrise. And Archie…

The weight of it crushed him. His hands trembled as his breakfast plate splattered onto the floor. The truth struck with the force of iron: they weren't soldiers anymore. They were test subjects.

"We're all going to die down here!" His voice cracked through the hushed cafeteria, loud and raw. "Free us!"

Around him, the others stirred. Once, they had been Modiri Guards—men promised the world while the monarchy scrambled to replace those who had fled beneath Kovo's tide. Now, they were nothing more than prisoners, stripped of the futures they had been assured.

The guards by the exits began closing in on Experiment 019. Some of the men could only watch, fear rooting them in place, while others tried to distract the guards by tossing bits of scrambled eggs in their direction, desperate to spare the boy. But he refused to be silenced.

"And Archie! Archie disappeared, and they aren't telling us anything. Where did he go?" His voice cracked as the cry tore through the cafeteria.

The guards seized him, but he broke free—if only for a moment. He bolted across the room, shoving tables aside to clear his path. Another experiment stepped forward to help, but a guard's fist connected with his cheek.

What happened next froze the room.

It was Experiment 028. Instead of collapsing, he stood tall, his expression unshaken. The guard, however, let out a piercing scream. He clutched his arm, eyes wide with terror, as the force of his own strike rebounded against him. The sickening crunch of bone filled the air as multiple fractures splintered through his hand. Tears streamed down his face as he howled in pain.

The other guards rushed forward, pushing past the line of experiments, but with a caution that betrayed their fear. None dared attempt another strike.

At the counter, Beatrice watched, her face stricken with shock and horror, her hands trembling as she realized the rules of this place had just shifted.

Startled, the guards retreated from the cafeteria, abandoning their plan to round up the experiments for escort. The moment they cleared the room, chaos erupted. Fists flew, tables toppled, and fights broke out—not only to test their strength, but to feed something darker, something far more sinister.

Experiment 019, already close to the door, slid down the wall, pressing his back against the cold surface. His eyes stayed fixed on the scene before him. The men battered each other with reckless abandon: a pot of eggs hurled here, a chair swung there, a face smashed into a table.

And still, nothing slowed them down. No bruises lingered. No fatigue took hold. They healed almost instantly, their bodies rebounding as though the violence fueled them.

They were a success.

Further down the hall, past several sharp corners, the air shifted. Here, men and women from across the country had gathered—educators, philosophers, doctors. Dr. Astor had recruited only the most skilled, but not for their credentials alone. He sought those willing to cast aside conscience, individuals as brilliant as they were ruthless. His experiments demanded it. Morality was a liability; immorality, a necessity. To succeed, one had to be callous, cold, indifferent—ready to sacrifice lives for what he deemed the greater good.

Astor's gaze lingered on the finned Modiri he had named Penelope. He watched her with an intensity that was both possessive and calculating.

The silence was fractured when a guard burst into the newly designed grid room. Breathless and wide-eyed, he stumbled forward, fear etched deep across his face.

"Dr. Astor, you need to come—quickly. The experiments, they... they're rebelling, and we cannot stop them."

Astor did not move. He dismissed the guard with a flick of his hand, as though swatting away an insect.

"Go from here."

"What about me and my men?" the guard demanded, his voice cracking under the strain. His fists clenched at his sides, trembling with a mix of fear and defiance. "We're no match for the things you're creating in here. We need reinforcements—backup—something to protect us."

Astor turned sharply. A thin, knowing grin curled his lips, though his eyes remained cold.

"Do you want what they're having?" he asked. The question dripped more menace than mockery.

The guard froze. His breath quickened, his chest rising and falling as the weight of Astor's words sank in. Step by step, he retreated, terror hollowing his features. Without another word, he fled, his boots pounding against the sterile floor until the sound faded into silence.

The room stilled once more. Then came a faint hum.

At the center of the chamber rested her sphere, no larger than a cradle, its surface smooth and luminous. Inside, the infant Modiri stirred, waking from the stillness of her slumber. Her delicate fin swayed gently, as though caught in a current only she could feel. The tiny fluke, a tender shade of pink, shimmered faintly in the sterile light.

Astor leaned closer, his breath steady despite the rush of excitement swelling in his chest. Perfect. She was perfect.

It had been years since he had last seen a finned Modiri so young. Something about her presence tugged at him—rare, extraordinary, perhaps even destined. His eyes devoured every detail while a whisper of triumph coiled in the back of his mind.

Then, as if by magic, small scales began to form across the fragile fin. They shimmered under the white light, the first sign of transformation.

He remembered from his studies the first finned Modiri birthed on land. It had not survived, gasping helplessly for oxygen until life slipped away. That tragedy had spurred the first trial: the creation of a machine to keep them alive outside the water. Thus, the Mizule was born. Crude in its earliest form, it delivered oxygen the moment the newborns emerged from the birthing canal.

When the Mizule proved successful, it was refined piece by piece until it became something larger, more complex—not only in size, but in brilliance. What began as a crude apparatus evolved into an intricate marvel of technology, designed not merely to ensure survival but to impose control.

Yet oxygen was not the only challenge. The finned Modiri's skin, delicate and iridescent, was never meant for the dry air of land. Without constant immersion in saltwater, their bodies began to wither. It was a slow, excruciating unraveling. Layers of skin peeled away as though shedding, but no new skin formed in their place. The process continued until nothing remained but fragile ash. The death was so cruel, so deliberate in its suffering, that even the scientists—cold and detached as they were—studied it with grim fascination.

To prevent this, the spheres were conceived. Seamlessly engineered to replicate the Modiri's natural environment, each sphere contained a carefully balanced chamber of saltwater. They preserved the creatures for a time—not out of mercy, but for the sake of knowledge. The Modiri were not allowed to thrive. They were kept alive only so the scientists could probe deeper, learn more, and push the limits of their creation.

Then, after some time, something miraculous occurred. The Modiri's scales—what the scientists first believed them to be—began to peel away. But these were no ordinary scales. Each fragment was larger, heavier, glowing faintly from within. They were not scales at all, but Embers. At first, they appeared rarely, scattered like accidents of nature. Yet their discovery marked the beginning of a new era: the extraction of Embers.

The process unfolded within sterile, gravity-controlled laboratories, where the air was crisp with the tang of antiseptic. At the center of each chamber loomed the Extractor, a towering biomechanical construct threaded with prismatic tendrils. These tendrils vibrated at exact molecular frequencies, coaxing the Ember from the Modiri's sphere. Slowly, almost reverently, the luminous fragment was drawn free, gleaming like a living flame suspended in crystal. It slid into an isolated chamber where no water could escape, severed from its host without disturbing the fragile balance of its sphere.

Once removed, the Ember was placed into the Hazmick, a containment unit engineered to regulate temperature and energy flux. Here, the scientists began the next phase. Through quantum resonance, the Ember was fractured into hundreds of micro-shards, each one preserving the same potent life-force as the original.

These shards were then dissolved into a bio-synthetic serum, producing a luminous liquid that radiated a faint, unnatural warmth. Robotic arms, guided with machine precision, siphoned the glowing solution into thousands of sterile vials, each no larger than a human thumb. Within every vial lay a fraction of the Ember's essence—enough to create Lith, a medicine unlike anything the world had ever seen.

Lith was a miracle wrapped in science.

Mainly administered intravenously, it worked within days, its potency adjusting to the severity of the illness. The compound threaded itself through the bloodstream, rewriting corrupted strands of DNA and awakening the body's dormant healing systems. For the first time in human history, diseases once thought fatal could not only be slowed but eradicated.

"Get me the General!" Dr. Astor's voice thundered across the lab, echoing against the steel walls. "Tell him— the King's cure is here."

Far from the sterile light of the laboratory, Watson lay in his bedchamber at Buckingham Palace, staring up at the ornate ceiling. The room, though modest by royal standards, had become his refuge—his sanctuary during long nights when he could not bring himself to return home.

The day before, he had spent hours carrying out the Queen's orders, and now an unfamiliar heaviness pressed down on him, settling deep in his chest. Before dawn, he had sought out the archbishop, hoping for counsel, perhaps even absolution for what had been done. But the weight remained. Prayer and guidance had offered no relief. What he needed now was neither.

What he needed was companionship. A friend.

With a groan, Watson rose from the bed, his broad frame unfolding as he stretched the stiffness from his shoulders and back. Crossing the chamber with steady strides, he reached the lavatory and splashed cold water onto his face. The chill grounded him. He changed into the civilian clothes he kept tucked away for moments like this, garments that allowed him to step out of the shadow of rank and duty, if only briefly.

Slipping quietly from the palace, he made his way to the rear of the estate where his car awaited. The engine rumbled to life, low and steady in the morning stillness, and Watson guided it through the empty streets toward Wellington Barracks.

He needed to see her.

More than that, he missed his comrade.

XII.

ENU

It had been twenty-five long years since Watson arrived at Wellington, beginning his service as a mere Guardsman. From there, he rose to Corporal, serving the monarchy alongside his trusted comrade, Bowie Benedict. When Benedict retired, Watson earned his favor, the veteran introducing him to the King. The King, impressed by his discipline and loyalty, appointed him Sergeant. Yet it was Prince Eldric's personal request that brought Watson back to Wellington—not as a guard, but as a mentor tasked with shaping the next generation of soldiers.

His ascent was steady and resolute.

From Guardsman to Corporal, Sergeant, and then Brigadier General, and now Major General, he climbed the ranks with humility. Still, Wellington never released its hold on him. The barracks had forged him, etched duty into his very bones, and he carried that weight with pride. Of all the cadets he trained, only one had ever earned his complete trust and respect: Brigadier Agha-Enu, the newly appointed officer Watson now entrusted with command of his brigade.

That morning, the air carried a faint chill, softened by dappled sunlight filtering through the branches above. Before the pale, neoclassical façade of Wellington

Barracks, a long row of soldiers stood in flawless formation. Silent and statuesque, every detail of their bearing reflected unwavering discipline. Their tall bearskin hats loomed above solemn faces, the brims casting shadows that concealed all trace of emotion. Clad in deep brown uniforms tailored to precise military standards, the men appeared less like mortals than figures carved from the very stone beneath their boots.

Making his way past the cadets and Sergeant Casper, Watson saluted him—firm, precise, honorable. Inside, he drew a deep breath, savoring the familiar scent of the barracks. Oh, how he had missed it. Without hesitation, he found the staircase and descended quickly, knowing exactly where to find Enu: their combat arena.

Brigadier Agha Enu was a force of nature from Dundee, Scotland—according to her paperwork. She was direct, fearless, and unflinchingly honest. At just thirty-three, she had become the youngest woman ever appointed Brigadier General, a title she wore with pride. Enu carried herself with a calm confidence that seemed to defy the chaos of the world around her. She was every inch a warrior forged from both flame and purpose. Her prominent dark brown eyes held a depth that could make even the boldest adversary reconsider a challenge. In her expression lived the memory of comrades lost—and the resolve of a woman who had risen from the ashes, stronger and unbroken.

When carrying out missions, her armor was both a weapon and a work of art. Forged from silvery steel burnished with weathered bronze, each plate bore intricate etchings of mythic beasts and ancestral sigils, as though her lineage had been hammered into the very metal. The breastplate, shaped for both protection and command, bore at its center a stylized emblem. Vines and talon-like ridges traced across her chest and ribs, their patterns shifting subtly in the light, like runes whispering secrets only she could interpret.

Her pauldrons arched like falcon wings, their edges flaring with the precision of ceremonial blades. Below them, her arms were shielded by segmented vambraces and gauntlets—strong yet flexible, crafted for speed without sacrificing defense. Every line of the armor spoke of efficiency; there was no excess, no vanity—only balance between elegance and lethal purpose.

Enu's stance radiated assurance, her hand never far from the hilt of her blade. A finely worked belt cinched her waist where the cuirass parted, revealing reinforced under-armor that allowed her to move as freely as she fought. Embossed greaves hugged the curve of her thighs, offering protection while preserving her grace. Even her earrings—sharp, metallic, almost talon-like—echoed her readiness. Her thick 4C coils, shoulder-length and springing like a lion's mane, crowned her head with unrestrained strength.

She was no woman to be pitied or coddled. She was something far rarer. She was a living blade.

Watson paused at the threshold of the arena, lingering in the hall before stepping fully inside. This was no ordinary training space. At Enu's request, the arena had been constructed with manual air pressure controls, allowing her to train under five to seven times Earth's gravity—sometimes even pushing it to ten. It was a gift only she could endure…until now.

Through the one-sided window, he watched her. Her thick curls had been pulled into a neat ponytail, yet the sheer volume left a halo-like afro fanning behind her head. Sweat darkened her t-shirt, clinging to her skin beneath a weighted vest. Dark leggings hugged her form, while wristbands absorbed the moisture dripping down her arms. Across from her stood her brother, Adi-Esam.

They moved like forces of nature colliding. Punches flew with no mercy, her strikes sharp and merciless. Each blow seemed to reverberate off the reinforced walls, the sound echoing through the arena. Esam ducked and weaved, desperate to stay ahead of her speed. For a moment, he gained the upper hand, driving a powerful drop kick into her chest. She staggered but did not fall.

Before he could retreat, Enu surged forward. Her right knee lifted with ferocious precision, striking him squarely and sending him sprawling onto the training mat.

Watson had seen enough. With a measured breath, he lowered the gravity controls, the heavy pressure in the room easing to something bearable. Then he stepped inside, leaving his sneakers in the hall. His hands came together in a steady clap that echoed across the arena as he walked onto the mat.

"Wow!" Watson exclaimed.

Esam, seeing his friend for the first time in months, broke into a wide grin and rushed forward. The two embraced in a long, firm hug, complete with heavy hand claps and hearty pats on the back.

"What's it like, yeh?" Esam asked brightly, his voice full of warmth.

Enu had slipped away to find water, her breath still coming in strong, measured gasps from the intense training. When she returned moments later, she caught sight of the men deep in conversation. Her gaze lingered on her younger brother.

"He's weak," she said flatly.

Watson and Esam exchanged a glance, both of their expressions tightening with quiet disappointment.

"Oh, come on, Enu," Watson urged gently. "Don't be so hard on him. He's come a long way—from transporting criminals to Officer Cadet."

"She's something straight out of space," Esam teased, shaking his head with an amused grin. Despite her words, the boy favored his sister deeply.

Esam's appearance carried its own striking presence. His skin, a rich, velvety brown, was one to envy. His face was sharply angular, with high cheekbones and a strong jawline softened only by the curve of his smirk. A neatly trimmed goatee framed his full lips, which parted as he spoke, revealing a glimmer of both charm and mischief. His eyes—dark, intelligent, and lively—held a glint that could shift between wit and warning, depending on who looked into them.

His hair was cropped into a neat high fade, the coils tightly formed, every detail immaculate.

Together, the trio left the arena. Enu and Esam laced up their sneakers as the lights dimmed behind them, the arena falling into darkness.

Just before stepping into the hall, Enu turned, her eyes narrowing on Watson.

"What are you doing here?" she asked.

"Well, that might be my cue to go," Esam joked, glancing at his bare wrist as though checking a watch that wasn't there. "She's getting too serious for me."

His voice trailed off as he pushed open the door at the rear of the hall, the sound of the staircase swallowing him as he left.

Watson turned back to Enu, attempting a lighter tone. "It wouldn't hurt if you smiled a bit more. For a Brit, you've got perfect teeth."

"General," she said coolly, ignoring the compliment. "What is it?" Her patience was thin.

He hesitated, shifting his weight. "Well, I needed a friend, is all…"

She scoffed, though a reluctant smile tugged at her lips. "A friend?"

"Oh, there it is—a smile!" The Major General beamed, the warmth in his voice softening the edges between them. Around her, his guard always seemed to lower. He was lighter, almost boyish, and his admiration for her was unmistakable.

"Listen," she began carefully, "I watch the news. And here, everyone talks. Nothing stays quiet for long."

Watson crossed his arms.

"True enough," he said. "Her Majesty requires a new Royal Guard for His Highness.

Her eyes narrowed. "Okay?"

"I've known you a long time, Enu. I'd be around a lot. You'd see more of the inner workings of the palace…"

Enu stepped back, a flicker of distaste crossing her face.

"I know it's an outrageous ask," he added quickly, hands raised slightly. "Of course I do. But you're the best in the class here. And Mavis, well… Her Majesty—"

"Mutilated her?" Enu cut in sharply. "Buckingham's orders get here quickly. Or did you forget?"

Watson's smile faded. "I never forget anything," he said, his tone suddenly grave.

"Oh… well." She looked away.

"You're needed at the Castle."

Her jaw tightened. "And if I refuse? Will Her Majesty take my head? Or would she have me cut it off for her?"

"I adore you like a sister, but tread lightly," he warned.

"I am a soldier, not a babysitter," she snapped. "You'll find someone else."

Her words stung, but he had to ask, "Is that your final decision?"

She met his eyes without flinching. "What do you believe?"

With that, Enu turned her back to him and strode toward the staircase, her steps echoing as she disappeared behind the steel door.

Her words lingered long after she had gone, pressing down on Watson like an unseen hand. For the first time in years, he questioned himself. Had he been humble in his service—or had blind loyalty chained him to the Crown? The doubt gnawed at him.

Just then, the vibration of his phone jolted him from his thoughts. He pulled it from his pocket and glanced at the screen. Bonnie. A knot formed in his chest. He answered too late; her call had already gone to voicemail.

Lifting the phone to his ear, he listened. Her voice spilled through the speaker, trembling with urgency. *"James, you need to come home. Quickly."*

A chill raced down his spine.

By dawn, before the birds had even stirred, the Equal Species had done the unthinkable. With Max leading the way, they buried Archie in the woods across from the bunker, the earth still damp and heavy beneath their shovels. The ground swallowed him whole, leaving only silence—and the aching question of what would come next.

The task was grueling, but no one faltered. Each carried their share of the burden, even when it meant swallowing back bile to avoid leaving so much as a trace of DNA. Their methods came from scraps of knowledge pieced together—snippets from social media, late-night true crime docu-series, even a stray WeTuber tutorial. It wasn't foolproof, but it was all they had.

To everyone's surprise, Preston was the calmest. His face betrayed no emotion as his shovel bit into the soil, the steady rhythm of his movements almost mechanical. His sister watched him in quiet disbelief, unable to reconcile the ease with which he worked against the horror of the act.

Alice and Linus had drawn the hardest task— preparing the body. With painstaking care, they checked every pocket, tightened every seam, and secured the bindings to ensure nothing would slip free. Their hands trembled only once, when the final knot was tied.

Though they reassured themselves that discovery was unlikely, they knew this was no ordinary mission. This was the kind of act that could never be undone.

When the last mound of earth was smoothed over, their shoes, hands, and fingernails were caked with dirt. No one spoke on the ride home. The silence pressed down on them all, heavier than the weight of the soil they had just laid.

Around noon, Alice had finished packing. A small suitcase sat by the door, its worn leather edges straining against the weight of hastily folded clothes. A few toiletries were tossed into a handbag, and a careful selection of shoes had been crammed into her backpack. She had no appetite—a rare and troubling sign for her—and her eyes carried the heaviness of a sleepless night.

Andrew argued with her in the cramped bedroom, his voice tight with desperation. "Alice, think about this. Where will you even go? Yes, Linus has a house, but it's his mother's. What happens after that?"

She refused to meet his gaze, her hands busying themselves with zippers and straps. Alice wanted only to reclaim her life, to be blissfully unaware, to work, to breathe without the shadow of deception at her heels.

Bonnie lingered in the corner, her silence louder than Andrew's pleas. She could not bring herself to beg or reason with Alice. Deep down, she understood. Alice didn't want promises or plans. She wanted parents she could trust. And in a world that seemed to shift beneath their very feet, their relationship had become a fragile dream, one that frightened Bonnie to her core.

A while later, the taxi pulled away, leaving Alice standing before the modest home in the quaint village just beyond the restless city of London. It was not a large house by any measure, but it was wide enough to shelter them all, offering a fragile sense of refuge. She lingered for a moment at the door, her eyes tracing the small garden out front, then stepped inside.

The air within was still, carrying faint traces of dust and old wood. Preston and Piper sat quietly at the dining table, their chairs angled toward one another, though neither spoke much. Linus waited at the bottom of the staircase, his posture uneasy, as if bracing for something yet to come. Max drifted through the living room, his eyes scanning every corner with careful scrutiny.

It was not the tenderness of a home he found, but the starkness of a place stripped of memory. The walls were bare of sentiment. Only a handful of photographs hung in the silence: one or two of Linus as a young boy, framed in thin glass. But there were none of Kovos, none from Beatrice's years in Sattle, and certainly nothing of her granddaughters. The absence spoke louder than any decoration could have, a quiet erasure of history.

At the far end of the house, near the sliding doors that opened to the back garden, Willow had claimed the den as their new meeting place. She had arranged it with a sense of authority, declaring it their headquarters before anyone could argue.

When Alice finally stepped inside, Linus tugging her suitcase across the worn floorboards, her eyes swept the room. The silence seemed to settle heavily on her shoulders, and though she said nothing at first, her expression betrayed the truth. She was not pleased.

"I don't think I can do this anymore…" Alice's voice was low and uneven, carrying the sharp edge of fear. Her hands trembled as she spoke, her gaze flicking toward Linus. He gave a small, steady nod, his expression firm with quiet support.

Across the table, however, Preston and Piper exchanged doubtful glances.

"There's no way," Piper said, leaning forward, her tone clipped with disbelief. "This is the kind of thrill you live for. You love the action, the excitement—venturing into the unknown. What's different now?"

Alice's eyes flashed, her voice rising in desperation. "What's different? It's too close to home! My family is being torn apart by this. Can you not see what's happening?"

The words rang through the room, silencing even the faint creak of the old house.

Preston shifted uncomfortably, but Piper pressed on. "It's not just you. Max's brother is dead, Alice. We're all in this."

"Yes," Alice cried, her hand flying to her head as though to hold herself together. "And we buried the body." Her voice cracked, breaking under the weight of the truth.

She stood there, the oversized concert shirt draping loosely over her frame, the faded print of a rock band's logo barely visible in the dim light. It made her seem smaller somehow, more fragile, a shadow of the girl who once embraced every risk with open arms.

Silence settled thickly over the room, heavy enough to choke. No one spoke. No one moved.

Max and Willow stepped into the living room, lingering just inside the threshold. The weight of the moment hung between them, pressing down like a storm about to break.

"I-I-I don't have a father anymore," Alice began, her voice trembling as though each word cost her strength. "And I'm not trying to take away from anyone else's pain in this room, but… he was a hero. He was my best… friend." Her voice cracked, and the tears finally spilled over, sliding down her cheeks faster than she could wipe them away. She shook her head, unable to contain the sobs pressing from her chest.

Max moved closer, his tone sharp with conviction. "This is what they want—for us to fall apart so they can break us down and brainwash us. We can't allow it, yeh!"

Piper straightened in her chair, eyes flashing as she pointed toward Preston. "Max is right. Even our mother—your mother—she's in on this. We know she knows more than she lets on. The deeper we go, the more everything in our family is going to change. Every single one of us has something to lose here. But think about the bigger picture. Think about our future. If this keeps going, our children's children won't even have lives to live. Their freedom will be stripped away. They'll be programmed to slave for pennies until they die."

"Jeez, Piper," Preston muttered, leaning back, his lips twisting in a grimace. He thought his sister's words bordered on dramatic, though the unease in his eyes betrayed his own fear.

Linus finally spoke, his voice calm but steady. "I still need to find my mother. And we still need to figure out what the Prime Minister and your mother are hiding." His gaze shifted to Piper, quiet but firm. "You're right, our work isn't done yet."

Linus rose from his seat and crossed the room to Alice, gathering her into a steady embrace. His warmth surrounded her, his gaze steady as it met hers. "I know you're scared. We are too. But we're not alone in this— that's the beauty of it. We have each other."

He turned toward the others, and one by one, his friends nodded in agreement.

Alice's eyes drifted to Max. Her voice wavered. "Max… what about your Mum and your brother? Aren't you worried about what else we might uncover?"

Max exhaled, running a hand through his hair before answering. "To be quite fair, my brother was gone for a long time. We'd already made peace with it, grieved as much as we could. I don't plan on reopening that wound for my mother. But as the new man of my house, I want to see the bastards who did this to my family pay. We deserve justice—just like everyone else."

The room fell into silence, though this time the air carried a different weight. Not despair, but resolve. Murmurs of agreement rippled through the group, a current of hope breaking through the heaviness.

"Okay, then." Alice straightened, her voice sharper now, her eyes scanning the room with renewed strength. "What's next?"

It was then that Willow slipped to the rear of the house, retrieving her laptop from the den. The glow of the screen revealed what she already suspected: the truth was waiting to be uncovered. When she returned to the front of the house, the mood had lightened. The others were smiling, reaching for food and cold drinks as though trying to reclaim a moment of normalcy.

Setting the laptop firmly on the table, Willow drew their attention. Her expression was steady, her voice calm but deliberate.

"So, Linus," she began, "I know we didn't find your Mum in the bunker. I wondered if maybe she had property elsewhere—a place you didn't know about—where she might be staying. But…" She paused, her eyes scanning the group. "In fact, she doesn't even own this home."

Silence settled. Willow tapped the screen, the document glowing in front of them. "According to the Land Registry, the deed lists Eugene Benson Sr. as the sole owner of this property."

XIII.

THE TEMPLE OF

XORRI

The air further East felt different—lighter, almost untouched—and the water shimmered with a clarity Naida had not seen elsewhere. In every other kingdom she had visited, there was a rigid uniformity. Outsiders would never find so much as a crevice to hide in or a stone to cower behind; every inch was carefully accounted for.

But the Makaras Kingdom was different.

Strangely different.

There were no Mosquens and only a few Lorelies—not even infants. Naida searched for the familiar scent of a Lamina Garden, yet found none. Instead, Makaras filled the waters, drifting and circling as though their presence was no more threatening than that of gentle, grazing beasts.

Gliding deeper, she entered an abyss where the light could not reach. The darkness was thick, almost suffocating, but her pupils adjusted. Slowly, shapes emerged below her: long rows of statues carved from the ocean floor. At first, they seemed still and lifeless, yet as she passed, each pair of eyes flared to life, glowing the color of molten gold.

The sight jolted her, a sharp fear rushing through her veins. She hadn't expected movement—especially not here, in the suffocating silence of this place. Then the glow began to shift, pulsing in rhythm, as though the statues were uniting in a single, dreadful harmony.

Each released a note, weaving together into a song that echoed through the abyss. To Naida's ears, it sounded like death itself—haunting, persistent, its vibrations carrying through the water like hymnals in a vast cathedral. The melody charged the very depths with energy, lingering in her mind long after the last note should have faded.

The great Temple of Xorri had stood for more than ten thousand years, resting over eleven thousand meters beneath the ocean's surface. It was a sight both breathtaking and perilous—one that inspired reverence and fear in equal measure. Should it ever be discovered, the temple would draw not only wonder but mass scrutiny, for reaching such depths was a venture that could easily claim a human life.

From the outside, it appeared like any other ancient temple, worn smooth by the weight of time and water. But within, the walls seemed alive. They had ears that listened and statues with eyes that watched—not to pry into secrets, but to warn those within of dangers yet unseen.

The temple's architecture unfolded like a maze. There were no doors, no separate rooms—only endless structure. Yet somehow, corners formed, shadows gathered, and hidden alcoves appeared where one could linger, temporarily forgotten. Around them, strands of seaweed drifted lazily with the current, indifferent to her presence, swaying as if they belonged to a world that had long since stopped noticing.

Upon reaching the temple's center, Naida drifted through open corridors where schools of fish glided lazily, weaving between sculpted columns and coral-cloaked ledges. Despite centuries of wear from the crushing depths, the temple and its pagodas still held a quiet, unyielding grandeur.

Then a voice called to her.

"Ushu."

The sound was faint, airy—almost a whisper. It carried none of the commanding strength she had come to expect from King Bao. A shiver ran down her spine. Some part of her wondered if it truly was him, but fear tightened in her chest. She had more questions than answers, and the uncertainty gnawed at her.

Another voice followed, this one unmistakable.

"Naida."

Her heart lurched. Kalkisis.

"Dad!" she cried, her voice trembling as the word left her lips. The sound seemed to vanish into the vast chamber, swallowed by the water around her. Panic fluttered inside her chest, and her fin moved faster, guiding her forward.

Just then, as if the temple itself had been listening, the statues began their melody once more. The haunting hymn surged through the water, vibrating in her bones. It startled her so violently that she almost lost her rhythm.

"Dad!" Naida cried again, this time finning desperately toward the rear of the temple, chasing both the voice and the hope it carried.

As Naida pushed farther into the temple, a shift in the water made her pause. From the top of the towering, multi-tiered pagoda, a figure emerged. The Great King Bao descended slowly, his presence materializing as if from the shadows themselves. To her naked eye, he seemed almost unreal—his form wavering like a penumbra, caught between light and darkness.

Then his voice boomed, the sound rolling through the chamber and startling her. Her gaze snapped to his frame as he hovered before her, his presence pressing down on her like the weight of the sea itself.

"The Moduuf sang their song," he declared, his tone resonant and dense. "You are a harbinger of something malignant."

"I-I don't understand," Naida stammered. Her voice trembled as fear coiled in her chest. She could not see him clearly; his shape seemed to resist the light, a figure meant only to be heard, not fully seen.

"Is it revenge you seek?" King Bao's voice lowered, each word deliberate, edged with danger.

He began to circle her, moving with a predatory grace. His upright form pulsed through the water, slow and insidious. Naida's head whipped around, desperate not to lose sight of him, while her fin and tail fluke thrashed nervously, stirring the shadows around her.

King Bao was never one to be blindsided, neither by friend nor foe. His Moduuf, though statues to spectators, were in truth spirits who held him in the highest regard.

They sang their hymn not for beauty, but for warning, each note carrying a message meant to distract and unsettle any intruder. Yet with Naida, the song carried something unprecedented—something even he had never heard before. Within the hymn, a confession pulsed like a hidden current.

"Does your king know of your vengeful heart?"

Before Naida could make sense of the words, a figure emerged above them both, cloaked in black and hidden among the shadows. Her eyes burned through the darkness, cold and unblinking, while eels slithered around her with a restless, unearthly grace.

"King Bao," Fanira hissed, her voice curling like smoke.

The King of the Makaras did not acknowledge her. His gaze remained fixed on Naida, heavy and merciless. At the sound of Fanira's voice, Naida recoiled, fear coursing through her as memories of the witch's cruelty from days past resurfaced like a wound torn open.

"Half-breed," King Bao thundered, his voice echoing through the temple. "Tell me of your vengeful heart!"

Naida froze. A part of her longed to deny him, to bury the truth deep where no one could ever touch it. But the thought had lain dormant for years, a secret she had sworn to carry silently, and now the song of the Moduuf threatened to unearth it.

King Bao turned fully toward her, his presence commanding, his aura shimmering with expectation. "Speak," he demanded, his voice low but edged with thunder. Naida's jaw tightened, the silence stretching thin between them.

From above, Fanira's voice cut through the tension. "Is it not your place?" she growled, her tone sharp and venomous.

Bao moved in an instant, his massive form materializing before Naida. His size dwarfed hers, the sheer force of his presence startling her into submission. "Tell me of your vengeful heart!"

The words erupted from him, thunderous, like lightning splitting the darkness. Naida felt her resolve shatter. She tried to resist, but the truth spilled from her lips as if torn from deep within her soul.

"I wish to avenge my father!"

The confession ripped through the temple, echoing like a curse. Naida's eyes widened in horror as the words left her mouth. It did not feel like her voice—more like something spoken through her, as if another version of herself floated just behind, pulling the strings.

"I'm so sorry!" she cried, clutching at her chest, her body trembling as fear consumed her. She felt as though the very act of speaking had sealed her fate, the weight of her confession pressing down like a final judgment.

Fanira broke the silence. "The prophecy must be fulfilled," she said. Her voice had shifted—pleased now, tender, almost eerily so.

King Bao did not answer, but displeasure burned in his mannerisms. A half-breed, chosen to duel one of their own—a purebred, born and bathed beneath the seas for centuries—in the name of destiny. The very thought unsettled him.

Perturbed, and rightfully so, he wrestled with the truth. Though a small part of him sensed there was more to the hybrids than the council had ever admitted, he held no desire to challenge the prophecy. Nor was he foolish enough to defy the Ahalty.

At last, with a heaviness that weighed on every word unspoken, Bao conceded.

Fanira did not need to hear the words spoken aloud; the truth was clear in his silence. "And so it shall be," she whispered before vanishing into the shadows.

Bao turned then, his towering frame facing Naida. She trembled, her eyes wide with disbelief, her body taut with dread. Slowly, he exposed his left acetic and swirled it with deliberate precision.

"Xomos Belginate," he intoned.

At once, Naida's body went rigid, her limbs growing weightless as she slipped into a trance. Suspended in the water, she drifted upward, her breathing shallow, her gaze unfocused.

And then it appeared.

The Ushu.

For the first time, Naida saw herself floating outside her own body. A piercing scream tore from her throat, the sound reverberating through the temple's endless expanse as terror claimed her.

From sunrise to sunset, Queen Emmary never left Prince Amer's side. The King's Guards and a contingent of Warrant Officers had doubled their watch around the castle, yet it brought her no comfort. To Emmary, their presence felt less like protection and more like mockery— by those creatures underseas and by her own companions within the castle walls.

Hopelessness gnawed at her, but her face betrayed nothing. As always, she wore composure like a crown, refusing to let the world glimpse the storm beneath. By the following noon, a spark of determination broke through her despair.

"Bring me Lady Mary," she commanded, her voice steady, edged with venom.

The chambermaid curtsied and hurried off, her skirts sweeping the marble floor behind her. Reaching Lady Mary's wing, she hesitated at the threshold, unable to cross into the noblewoman's quarters. Instead, she found Clara nearby and whispered the summons.

"The Queen requests Lady Mary to His Highness's sleeping chambers."

Clara frowned, unease tugging at her expression. Still, she gave no protest. With a silent nod, she slipped into Lady Mary's room, the command heavy in her heart.

Lady Mary's quarters were nothing short of exquisite. She lacked for nothing; her chamber filled with silks, polished wood, and the faint scent of lavender that lingered in the air. Clara moved quickly, dressing the young girl with careful hands until she was presentable enough to stand before the Queen. Within minutes, it was time.

With her hands clasped primly in front of her, Lady Mary stepped into the grand hallway, Clara trailing close behind. She walked with a confidence that belied her youth, her adolescent mind blissfully unaware of the gravity awaiting her.

The corridor led them to the Prince's wing, where Queen Emmary stood, smoothing the hem of her pencil skirt while instructing the guards to ready her vehicle. The

Queen's sharp eyes caught Lady Mary's approach, and a faint, cool smile touched her lips.

"Here lies your future King," Emmary said, her gaze locking onto Lady Mary's with unwavering intensity. She lowered her head slightly, though her authority filled every inch of the chamber. "You will remain at his side until he awakens. You will be the first face he sees."

From the back of the chamber, Clara released a quiet sigh of relief, though her hands trembled against her skirts.

"When he awakens," Emmary continued, her tone cutting as steel, "you will remind him of your loyalty—to him and to the Crown. That is your first order of duty. You would be wise not to disobey me."

Dozens of eyes lingered on the scene. Some guards swallowed hard, unsettled by the cold fire burning in the Queen's gaze.

And then, as swiftly as she had come in the morning, Emmary swept from the room, leaving only the echo of her words behind.

Timidly, Lady Mary glanced at Prince Amer. He looked peaceful, his chest rising and falling in a steady rhythm. Clara stepped closer, resting her hands gently on the girl's shoulders.

"I will be right here with you," she whispered. "Food, water—anything you need, I will fetch it."

Mary met her gaze with silent gratitude before crossing to the bedside. She sat upright on the stool, fingers laced tightly in her lap, and waited.

Elsewhere, Queen Emmary's thoughts churned. Flanked by officers, she slid into the waiting hover car, its doors sealing with a soft hiss. The vehicle lifted smoothly from the castle grounds, carrying her toward the private airfield and the flight that would soon deliver her to London—11 Downing Street.

London wore a dreary face that morning. The rain fell in a fine drizzle, dampening the streets as Queen Emmary's companions hurried to shield her with an umbrella. Her arrival was discreet, through the rear entrance of 11 Downing Street—a narrow lane once lined with small shops, now transformed into a private thoroughfare reserved for government officials and visiting heads of state.

The spaces bore little resemblance to its past. Prime Minister Benson Sr. had converted a section into modest sleeping quarters, his small cot evidence of long nights that too often ended in drink—and, more recently, in gambling losses he could scarcely afford. Nearby, the Shadow Chancellor of the Exchequer, Katie Eloise Porter, had claimed another portion, expanding her study to accommodate the endless demands of her post.

Porter herself carried the marks of strain. For months, her name had dominated headlines—filling £40 billion budget gaps one week, facing a £51 billion deficit the next. Yet beneath the weight of figures and scrutiny, she retained an almost ethereal beauty. Her golden-blonde hair, cut into a chin-length bob, framed her soft features with quiet elegance. The strands, parted neatly at the center, curled faintly at the ends, lending her a youthful air that belied the exhaustion in her eyes. Her complexion was fair, touched with a natural flush, and faint smile lines etched around her lips hinted at warmth seldom indulged.

When Queen Emmary entered, Porter straightened at once, her expression lighting briefly with delight. But as Her Majesty's cool gaze swept the room, the Shadow Chancellor's smile faltered. The Queen's presence demanded answers, not flattery, and Porter quickly folded back into composure, the warmth of her greeting left unreturned.

With two King's Guards posted outside the black rear door of the building, the shouts of protestors seeped faintly through from the other side, muffled but insistent. Inside, Queen Emmary released a long, disappointed sigh. The Chancellor's office was alive with activity—reporters, interns, and staff scurried about, each one pausing to curtsy or bow as she passed. Emmary moved quietly toward one of the newly added studies, seeking a moment's reprieve.

The office carried an old-world gravitas. At the back wall stood a heavy mahogany desk, its polished surface neat but well-used, flanked by an ornate glass-front cabinet that housed rows of leather-bound books and crystal decanters, silent witnesses to late-night brandy and whispered conversations. Beneath her custom-made four-inch heels, a richly patterned Persian carpet—or perhaps a clever imitation—muted footsteps, giving the space a hushed, deliberate atmosphere.

To the front, a deep brown leather armchair sat low and inviting, its tufted back softened by years of use. A matching couch stretched alongside it, facing a wooden coffee table cluttered with paperwork, a glossy magazine, and the remnants of a light breakfast: a white mug, a half-eaten croissant, and a red glass dish pushed aside without care.

The room's light came gently filtered, daylight streaming through tall windows veiled with sheer curtains that softened the sharp lines of the furniture. Paneled walls painted a muted beige, framed dark wood moldings, while a single leafy plant in the corner lent a quiet touch of life to the otherwise solemn space.

Once inside, Porter shut the door softly behind them, two additional King's Guards stationed just outside. She moved quickly through the room, fumbling with scattered papers and dishes as though tidying might steady her nerves. Her voice trembled.

"Your Majesty, please—sit. Anywhere you'd like."

Emmary obliged, brushing the chair with a swift flick of her hand before lowering herself onto the cushion.

Her gaze was sharp, her tone scathing.

"I come seeking answers."

Porter froze mid-step, a crystal decanter half-hidden behind her back. She turned with a strained smile.

"Of course. I'm happy to provide whatever information you require."

"Good." Emmary's reply cracked like a whip. "I want to know about the trade."

The Chancellor's face tightened. She hadn't expected this question, but lying was not an option—not with Emmary watching.

"Trade?" Porter's voice faltered. "Which one, Your Majesty?"

Emmary leaned forward, eyes narrowing. "Katie, we've known each other for years. You know better than anyone how I despise being deceived. Or should I say—patronized?"

"I…I truly don't know what you mean—"

"You're lying!" Emmary's voice rose, cutting her short.

Porter felt the heat of sweat prick her forehead despite the cool air of the room. Her throat tightened.

"Well…" Emmary's eyes bore into her, unrelenting. "On with it."

"Your Majesty, please forgive me, but I've been sworn to secrecy. If I speak, I could lose my—my life…" Porter stammered, her voice breaking under the weight of fear.

Emmary let out a sharp scoff, her lips curling into a bitter smile. "Sworn to secrecy? By whom?" She gestured behind her, as though pointing to a phantom. "Our king?"

Her eyes glinted with disdain. "Tell me, have you seen him lately? Do you believe he is of sound mind—peddling through the streets on a pushbike, handing out daisies like some harmless fool? His Majesty is as good as dead. And when the world learns of it, my son will ascend the throne."

Her voice dropped, heavy with menace. "I need answers, and I need them now."

There was no mistaking the shift in her tone. The air thickened, the shadows themselves seeming to lean closer. Emmary's loyalty was no longer to crown or country but to Amer, and she would stop at nothing—nothing—to protect him.

Katie hesitated, her pulse quickening. *The King? As good as dead?* The thought rattled her, but she dared not question Emmary further. Swallowing hard, she forced the truth out as she knew it.

"The Americans, along with several other nations, have purified their bloodlines. I only discovered the sale of Lith while working under my father before his passing. Once I was elected, I simply continued tracking the sales in our budget. The profits have been... enormous."

Emmary's gaze sharpened. "And where have the pounds gone?"

"That was never disclosed to me," Katie admitted. "I saw the figures, accounted for them, then transferred the funds to an undisclosed account. I don't know what the pounds are being used for."

Emmary's tone cut like glass. "So we may have been selling Lith harvested from our own Embers—an act that could lead to our ruin—and you never thought to question it?"

Katie's lips parted, but no excuse came. Finally, she whispered, "No."

"How much has gone to the account? And have there been any recent transfers?"

Katie moved cautiously to her desk. Her fingers trembled as she flipped open her portable laptop and sank into the chair as though she needed its support. Folder after folder appeared on the screen, passcode after passcode entered until finally, the figures glowed back at her.

"I can only access records from my time in office. The older books are archived... sealed." She glanced up nervously. "Accessible only by His Majesty."

"Sealed?" Emmary's voice was low, dangerous.

"Yes, Your Majesty." Katie's chest tightened. *What is the king hiding?*

"Six billion, two hundred nineteen million, two hundred sixty-seven thousand, six hundred British pounds," Katie said at last.

Emmary's breath caught. "Gone?"

"Not gone… transferred. To the account." Katie corrected. Her voice trailed off as she noticed the Queen's eyes drift toward the ornate Persian rug.

Emmary's head lifted slowly. "I want to know where every pound has gone. And as of this moment, you are no longer permitted to send another coin to that account. Do I make myself clear?"

Katie's throat closed. "Your Majesty, if I refuse, my family—"

"Do. I. Make. Myself. Clear?"

Sweat beaded across Katie's brow. She wiped it with a trembling hand, nodding quickly. "Yes."

As Emmary gathered herself to depart, Katie shot upright and offered a hurried curtsy. The Queen swept toward the door, exiting, her guards steady behind her.

For a moment, silence settled over the office. Then the curtains stirred, rippling as if touched by unseen hands. Katie's breath caught in her throat. She turned back to her desk just as a notification lit up the screen.

An email.

From Doctor Astor.

XIV.

LEAVE THE ALIEN

The door to the Queen's transport sealed with a quiet hiss, the absence of a motorcade lending her departure a calculated discretion. On the opposite side of the building, Benson Jr. stepped into the Prime Minister's office, a single envelope clutched firmly in his hand. It was a strange thing, realizing the boy he had been was gone. Not lost in the slow drift of years, but taken—snatched away the day his father decided his life for him.

Once, he had idolized the man. Prime Minister Benson Sr. had been larger than life, the figure every son wanted to become. But that hero had long since vanished, replaced by a man who reeked of liquor and squandered the dignity of his office with every careless choice. Benson Jr. had watched it happen in silence, too young then to stop it, but old enough now to know the damage it had done— to him, to his mother, to their country.

Speaking with her had brought the truth into focus. If anyone was going to protect her, protect what was left of their name, it had to be him. The thought of standing against his father was bitter, but the thought of letting things continue was worse.

Their conversation ended with his decision spoken aloud for the first time: he would no longer be Eugene

Benson Jr. He would run for Prime Minister as Noah Chambers—his second name and his mother's maiden name; his shield and his banner. It was more than a new identity. It was a break from the man who had cast such a long shadow over his life.

For the first time in years, he felt the ground steady beneath him. The boy his father had shaped was gone. In his place stood someone who would not be bent, someone willing to meet his father in open combat— political or otherwise—if that was what it took to reclaim what had been stolen.

Inside the building, Noah paused just beyond the threshold, his gaze sweeping the room in search of Priya. The place thrummed with a relentless urgency. Staff moved swiftly between workstations, holographic screens flickering with scrolling data, urgent transmissions flashing red. Voices overlapped as orders were relayed, messages recorded, and complaints filed in real time to every corner of the Commonwealth. Not a breath was left unclaimed. England teetered on the brink, and whispers from abroad had sharpened into open speculation.

Even within the Palace's own ranks, frustration simmered. The Prime Minister's refusal to deliver his already-prepared address was becoming more than a lapse in duty—it was an international embarrassment. Still, he kept his distance.

When Noah finally caught sight of Priya in his periphery, she was engrossed in her console, unaware of the tension coiled through him. His suit was immaculate, his presence unmistakable, yet he stood fixed in place, as if anchored by thoughts too heavy to shift. Only when she looked up and met his stillness did her brow crease.

"Is something the matter?" she asked, her voice sharp with disbelief at his sudden lack of urgency.

Noah cleared his throat, the sound low and uncertain, and extended the envelope toward her. His hands trembled, the weight of his decision still settling in his chest. Without a word, she snatched it from him and tore it open, her eyes darting over the lines with mounting irritation.

"Oh, for heaven's sake," she scoffed, lips curling in disdain. "Another entitled nepo child thinking they need some grand farewell. Just don't show up, would you?"

The sting of her words cut deep, but she didn't wait to see it land. Her four-inch heels struck the polished floor with sharp, deliberate clicks as she strode away, each step an exclamation point on her dismissal.

Noah drew a slow, steadying breath. This was it. The end of one chapter and the uneasy start of another. He pivoted on his heel, the air in the room suddenly thinner, and started for the door.

Behind him, Priya disappeared into the back office, pulling out her phone. Her fingers moved with urgent precision, firing off messages to her children—Preston and Piper. She needed them now.

Noah understood that winning the King's favor was essential if he ever hoped to be considered for the role of Prime Minister. But, as his father relied on Priya, he too would need an ally—someone to guide him through the labyrinth of politics. Finding that person would be a challenge of its own.

He walked for what felt like half an hour, thoughts churning with strategy and uncertainty, before sliding the key into the lock of his modest flat in Linden Gardens. The space was small, unremarkable, yet it carried the comfort of belonging—something rare in recent months.

Inside, he crossed to the table, picked up the phone, and began making calls. And just like that, the first threads of his campaign were set in motion.

Preston and Piper had always steered clear of politics, treating their mother's career—and her ties to the Prime Minister—as if it were a contagion they dared not catch. Still, Piper's compassion for her mother had a way of breaking through her resistance. With a reluctant sense of duty, she sent a brief text promising to come by the office later to help sort through the abandoned assignments Benson Jr. had left behind.

At the Barracks, the lunch bell rang, sending soldiers and cadets streaming toward the mess hall. Enu and her brother, Esam, moved down the line with trays in hand. She wasn't hungry, but discipline demanded she eat—fuel for longer, harder training sessions. Watson's proposition still pressed at her thoughts, and after a moment's hesitation, she decided to bring her brother into it. If anyone could help her decide, it was him.

"Esam, I need to ask you something," she said quietly.

He turned to her, startled. Enu rarely sought his counsel, and the chance to be useful lit something boyish in his expression. "Of course. Ask me anything."

"Watson wants me at the Castle. Guardsman for His Highness."

They slid small cartons of apple juice onto their trays. Esam's eyes widened with unguarded excitement. "That's perfect! Exactly what we've been waiting for. When do they put you on orders?"

"Slow down. I told him no."

The glow faded from his face. He tossed a few pieces of fruit onto his tray while she reached for salad. "Are you out of your mind? This is the opportunity." He leaned closer, voice low. "You need to be on the inside. We're wasting time here."

"We're not wasting anything," she replied, stepping away from the line. Esam followed, unwilling to let it drop.

"No, what are you avoiding?" he pressed, setting his tray down at one of the long dining tables.

Enu hesitated, her eyes flicking around the crowded hall. When she finally spoke, her voice was barely above a whisper. "My trident... it's starting to return."

Esam's gaze dropped, his voice shrinking with it. "Oh." He hesitated, almost recoiling from her. "I didn't want to say anything, but... mine's coming back too. And my eyes—they've started shifting on their own again."

Enu's nostrils flared. "Why am I only hearing about this now?" Her voice was low, but each word was clipped. "When did it start?"

"A couple of years ago," he admitted. "I was transporting an old woman from the Palace—she'd struck a guard and was sent to the cells. The moment she arrived in the marked car, it happened. Since then, I've been using the drops more often." He tried to soften his tone. "Listen, don't panic. We're going to be fine."

Enu speared a piece of salad, chewing slowly, eyes locked on him. When she swallowed, her decision was set. "We need to find the witch."

The noise of the chow hall swelled around them, yet for Enu and Esam, the world narrowed to a quiet bubble. They ate the rest of their meal in silence.

Over inside the bunker, Melissa lay asleep as she was carefully transported on a gurney toward the rear of the facility. There, she was loaded into the back of a cargo van, nearly identical to the one that had brought her. The Doctor had issued strict orders to the driver and her chambermaids: Melissa was not to leave her bedroom until Astor had personally visited their quarters.

Back at the house, small renovations had been made since her departure. Benson Jr. had been there during the changes but dared not question them. He had no intention of staying in the house any longer anyway. The rooms were unnervingly quiet and cloaked in shadow, corners swallowed by darkness. The head chambermaid entered first, followed by the driver, who assisted in bringing Melissa to the master bedroom.

The room felt hollow and unwelcoming. The plush pillows that once softened the bed had disappeared. The marble fireplace was sealed shut, and the French doors leading to the balcony were barricaded. Her wardrobe had been stripped bare except for a few essential garments and undergarments.

The delicate trinkets from the master bathroom—those small tokens that helped her feel feminine—were gone. Her beauty products, fragrances, and haircare items had vanished as well. The shelves, once lined with books, now stood empty. And perhaps most painfully, the crib that had occupied a quiet corner—a reminder of the *normal* life she had before—was gone too.

The hours dragged on, and Doctor Astor's tender gaze never left Penelope. He waited for the precise moment to extract her Ember, but for now, his attention was pulled by the chaos echoing near his labs. The test subjects were still restless, their movements loud and disorderly. Astor's lips curled into a cold smile as he stepped to the intercom, clipboard firm in his grasp. His voice, smooth and chilling, cut through the noise.

"I seem to be hearing quite a ruckus," he hissed with deliberate venom. "Let me remind you all: you belong to me. I am your God. Anyone who attempts to leave, or dares to taste food or water outside this facility, will be terminated. Your bodies are mine to command. Mutiny is not an option because it means certain death. Return to your cells immediately, await further orders, and continue fulfilling your designated duties."

The men halted, exchanging uneasy looks as they absorbed his words. They had battled fiercely all morning, yet none bore any visible wounds. Their resilience was unnerving, and still, there was no sign of surrender. Then a guard's voice rang out sharply, "Back to your rooms!"

Relieved, the guard stood straighter, no longer trembling. Slowly, the men filed back to their cells, their movements heavy but obedient. One cell door remained open—Archie's. As the men settled inside, the guards in the control room pressed the floor buttons. A loud buzzer blared, signaling the closing of the doors, and with a mechanical hiss, the metal barriers slid shut, sealing the experiments in once more.

The lab grew quiet again, but the tension lingered. Astor's eyes gleamed with dark satisfaction as he prepared for the next phase of his plan.

Hours later, Watson returned home. Despite the sun shining and the promise of clearer skies, the sorrow inside the house pressed against his family like a thick fog refusing to lift. Bonnie sat alone at the dining table, methodically eating a meal she had prepared out of obligation rather than desire. Her appetite had vanished, swallowed whole by a creeping depression that clung to her every breath.

As Watson turned the key in the lock, a sudden wish swept over him—that he hadn't come back just yet. His years as a soldier, combined with his service to the King and Queen, had trained him to lock away his feelings in neat, cold compartments. It wasn't that he lacked compassion; on the contrary, he had simply numbed himself to it, and that numbness frightened him now as he stepped inside.

Uncertain and uneasy, he hesitated. Should he offer a comforting embrace, speak false reassurances, or simply remain silent? The answer eluded him as he closed the door behind him.

Bonnie was different now. No longer lit up by his arrival, the simple sound of the front door closing sent a sharp pang through her chest. She was exhausted—her spirit drained beyond what she dared to admit aloud, though she knew Watson sensed it too. Her fingers brushed over Alice's broken watch, left shattered on the nightstand after her sudden departure. "What is happening to this family?" she finally asked, her voice barely steady as Watson stood silently in the dining room.

Watson cleared his throat. "I hope to be home more often…"

Bonnie's gaze met his, heavy and worn, the traces of recent tears still evident. He lowered himself into a chair, searching her face. "What's wrong?"

She bit her lip, then slid the watch across the table. "You tell me."

He studied it quietly, face unreadable, before drawing a slow breath. "Alice…"

"Alice," Bonnie interrupted sharply. "She's gone. She's moved in with her partner in the village."

Watson's brow knitted tightly.

"What?" he demanded.

She shook her head, her voice trembling. "I don't understand what's in your mind anymore. You're not really here—neither in body nor in spirit. You're married to the Crown, not me." A soft sniff broke her words.

"No," he said firmly. "I am here. I've made mistakes, yes. But I'm still the man you know, the man you love. I'll bring Alice back. I just need to talk to her."

Bonnie's anger burst forth. "Talk? A boy died in our basement, and you want to 'talk' to her?"

Watson's face drained of color, the blood seeming to vanish entirely. "A boy?" His voice cracked with disbelief. "He died?"

Bonnie sprang up, frustration igniting every word. "Yes. Whatever darkness festers in that Palace has crept to our doorstep." Her hands moved wildly, a storm barely contained. "He was a child. There's something you're not telling me—something you can't even protect us from."

"Bonnie… please, stop…"

"I won't." Her voice broke, fierce and raw. "Alice was right. As much as it hurts, I can't keep living like this. I've tried. I've been patient. But this—this is beyond endurance." Her cheeks flushed crimson as she battled the tears clawing to escape, her throat tightening with the effort. "I need to leave. We're not safe here."

Watson shook his head firmly. "No. This is the safest place. I'm a General. No one would dare threaten our home."

"Harm is already here. How can you not see that?" she demanded.

"What do you want me to do? You share nothing, yet expect me to have all the answers. Alice disappears on her own quests, Andrew hides behind his locked door—no one talks to me. But I will fix this!" he shouted, desperate to end the growing chasm between them.

"You complain about the children and their behavior, but whose fault is that, James?" Bonnie's voice was steadier now, more assertive.

She loved him deeply—more than anything—but her heart ached. She needed him to understand the truth, no matter how painful. Watson lowered his gaze, her words settling heavily on him. "I promise you, I will make this right," he whispered, barely able to meet her eyes.

Bonnie nodded, taking him at his word. "Your supper's in the oven. Feel free to warm it." Without another word, she turned and ascended the stairs, leaving Watson alone. His eyes lingered on the broken watch before he forced himself toward the basement door. He paused, then descended the stairs with cautious steps into the darkness below.

A prickling sensation crawled up the back of Watson's neck. The dim basement light flickered overhead, casting jagged shadows across a makeshift display on the wall. Photographs of Queen Emmary and His Majesty were tacked in a haphazard collage, interlaced with scraps of information about the royal bunker. Faded newspaper clippings fanned outward like a crime board, each headline whispering fragments of danger. And on the carpet, a brown stain—its origin uncertain, but enough to pull his stomach into a knot—spread like a silent accusation.

He stood frozen, the air heavy with the metallic scent of dust and age, his thoughts tangled. How was he meant to protect a family that seemed determined to suspect him; to fear both him and the monarchy he had sworn his life to defend? The question gnawed at him, strange and unshakable. There could be no choosing, he realized. Not family or monarchy. In the end, the only constant would have to be himself.

And with that, clarity struck. He had to find Alice— before whatever shadow was moving through their lives reached her first.

After work, Piper made her way to the Prime Minister's office. Behind a large desk, Priya was bent over her computer, fingers tapping a steady rhythm as she worked through the day's schedule. Outside, the last of the daylight bled into the streets, and the crowd of protestors that had swelled hours earlier was beginning to thin. Voices that had roared all afternoon were now muted, their owners retreating home with promises to return if no changes came.

Piper wasn't exactly eager to be here. But with Alice keeping to herself, and Linus trapped in a loop of anxiety, anger, and quiet despair, she decided it was better to be useful than idle. She slipped through the entrance, offering a quick, polite wave to the remaining staff before spotting her mother at the far end of the room, hunched over the keyboard.

Her exhaustion weighed heavily, blurring her vision. She hoped whatever tasks awaited would be light—filing a document, answering a couple of emails—anything that wouldn't demand too much of her dwindling focus.

"Mom," she called.

Priya kept typing, her eyes fixed on the glowing screen.

"Mom!" Piper tried again, sharper this time.

Without looking up, Priya spoke in a clipped tone. "Piper, hush. I'm in the middle of sending something important. Why don't you go to Benson's desk—third one on the right, near the entrance."

Piper bit back a reply and moved toward the desk. A sigh escaped her when she saw it: stacks of papers strewn carelessly across the surface, the sort of disarray that suggested no one had touched them in days.

It was a strange, unsettling thing—this quiet neglect from her mother. Piper could still remember when Priya had been the center of their home, a stay-at-home mother who always seemed to have time for her and her brother,

Preston. They had lived in a small but comfortable house, with their father working steady shifts as a train operator. Fifteen years on the job had made him a constant presence in their lives, dependable in a way Piper never questioned—until the day everything changed.

It happened without warning. One afternoon, he simply quit. No discussion, no farewell to the routine that had shaped their family. Soon after, he filed for a no-fault divorce. Priya hadn't seen it coming, and neither had the children. Their father assured them he would remain in their lives, but something had shifted. Preston and Piper both felt the fracture—not only the sting of betrayal, but the uneasy awareness that they might have to choose a side.

Their concern for their mother deepened as she became less patient, less nurturing. The warmth that had once filled their home cooled into a distant focus. Then, a few years ago, shortly after a Unification Day parade, Priya announced her decision to enter politics. She claimed the event had "awoken something" in her, a conviction that she no longer wanted to be just a housewife. She wanted to take part in shaping history—or at least stand beside those who did.

It had taken everyone by surprise—most of all her ex-husband. He hadn't known a thing until one afternoon, when the televised coverage of a public event showed her standing beside Prime Minister Benson Jr., clipboard in hand, looking as though she belonged there. She carried herself with a quiet satisfaction, a small sense of wholeness in serving someone with influence. With no husband to care for and her children nearly grown, she had been searching for something—or someone—that made her feel important again, wanted.

The years passed quickly, her position becoming second nature. Eventually, she urged her children to join her in the work, but they never saw it as a noble pursuit. To them, it was little more than an extended distraction from the heartache that had settled into her the day their father walked out. She had never truly faced that loss, never dared to confront the pain. It was still there, tucked away in some unlit corner of her heart.

"He just… quit. Old spoiled brat," she muttered over Piper's shoulder, watching her daughter sort documents into neat stacks and slide them into the desk drawer.

"Who?" Piper asked, deciding to indulge the remark. The office was quiet, the hum of the building muted in the evening stillness. Without her reply, it would have seemed as though Priya were simply speaking to herself.

"Who else?" Priya's voice dripped with sarcasm. "That boy couldn't tell his back from his front, yet he thinks he can just walk away. He's never known hardship." Her words faltered, the sharpness giving way to thought as she recalled a conversation she had overheard between Dr. Astor and Benson Sr.

Piper paused mid-shuffle. "What?"

"It's nothing," Priya said briskly, shutting the door on whatever thought had been creeping in. "Are you finished? I'd like to get home to my leftovers."

Piper wasn't finished, but she had no intention of admitting it. She wanted to leave as much as her mother did. She sifted through the remaining papers, flicking them aside with little care, until a small sticky note slipped from between the folds of a letter. The handwriting was cramped, almost unreadable: **LEAVE THE ALIEN**.

She frowned, eyes dropping to the letter beneath it. At first glance, it was harmless—an advertisement for baby formula. But the addressed names caught her attention: Eugene Benson Jr. and Melissa Benson. The name tugged at her memory. Could it be *that* Melissa? The one Linus had mentioned, the one whose name carried a quiet shadow in his voice?

Priya was already dimming the lights, her handbag swinging over her shoulder. Piper almost left the letter where it lay, telling herself it was nothing. But something—some unfamiliar voice within—urged her back.

Her mother's heels struck the concrete floor outside with an impatient rhythm. "Come now!"

Piper slid the letter and sticky note into her purse and followed her mother into the night, the darkness swallowing the last traces of the office.

The car moved steadily through the London streets, the low whirr of the engine blending with the muted rush of evening traffic. The windows were cracked open just enough for the night air to slip inside, carrying with it the faint scent of rain on stone. Piper sat in the passenger seat, her elbow resting against the door, phone balanced loosely in her hand. Streetlights flashed rhythmically across her face, alternating shadow and gold, while beside her, her mother drove in silence.

She tapped out a quick message to Linus, then hesitated before pressing send. For a moment she thought about deleting it—unsure if it even mattered anymore—but she sent it anyway. Somewhere across the city, he and

Alice were wrapped in the kind of stillness that comes after months of unrest. They were on the couch, limbs tangled, a blanket pulled haphazardly over them, the flickering light of a true-crime documentary dancing across their faces.

The fire that had once fueled them—the restless, unrelenting drive for Equal Species—had faded to embers. They knew the Prime Minister owned the home. They knew it could be taken from them without warning. They knew, perhaps better than anyone, that the future could turn in an instant. And yet, the urgency was gone.

Maybe they were tired. Maybe they'd given too much of themselves for too long. Maybe they'd been waiting for a sign, something undeniable that their fight could matter. But no sign had come. No call to arms, no lightning strike of purpose. And so they had settled into the kind of quiet that was almost dangerous—the kind that lulled you into thinking you had time.

Linus's phone vibrated against the coffee table. He reached for it lazily, glancing down at the screen. A photo from Piper. He opened it and saw the image: the advertisement she'd found earlier, now resting in her lap. Her knees were pulled together, the edges of the paper curling slightly under her fingers.

He stared at the picture longer than he meant to, sensing something in it—something unsaid. Linus shifted beneath the blanket, gently easing Alice off him, his gaze locked on the phone screen.

"What is it?" she asked, her voice caught between worry and irritation.

"It looks like… a letter," he said slowly. "Addressed to Melissa and the Prime Minister's son, Benson Jr."

Alice blinked, uncertain why that mattered. "Okay… and?"

"It's an advertisement for baby formula."

She frowned. "So? He's not a child. Maybe he and his partner are having a youngster. Honestly, it's a little intrusive that Piper sent this to you."

"Maybe," Linus said, rising to his feet. "But what are the chances this could be my Melissa?"

Alice didn't even hesitate. "Less than zero. Your niece is a hybrid. There's no way."

He ignored the certainty in her tone and began firing off a string of texts to Piper. Why had she sent this? What made her think it was connected to him? Moments later, her reply came—not just a message, but a photo. The sticky note.

Linus stared at the words scrawled across it: **LEAVE THE ALIEN**. Piper followed with a longer explanation. Her mother told her that Benson Jr. had abruptly resigned that morning, which was why she'd been called to the office to help. The letter and sticky note had been sitting on his desk.

Why would Benson Jr. call anyone an alien?

Linus didn't need more convincing. "We're getting Piper, and we're going to the address on that letter. I need to be sure." His voice carried a quiet finality that left no room for debate.

Alice let out a long, weary sigh.

The upper maisonette in Hampstead Village, hidden among the quiet turns of Thurlow Road, looked like the sort of place where nothing bad could ever happen. The lawn was a perfect sweep of green, not a blade out of place.

The bricks gleamed, scrubbed and polished until they looked almost new. Doors shone with fresh paint, windows reflected the sky without a blemish. It was the sort of home that whispered wealth, influence, and control. But inside, control had curdled into something darker.

Melissa came awake slowly, surfacing from a heavy, drugged sleep. Her head felt thick, her mouth dry. The air in the room was stale and faintly sweet, like flowers left too long in water. Somewhere beyond the locked French doors came the faint shuffle of shoes, the swish of skirts, and the murmur of women's voices. Four of them—she recognized their tones, the clipped precision of chambermaids accustomed to following orders.

She lay still, letting the sound seep into her awareness. They were stationed outside. Watching. Guarding. The orders, she already knew, would be simple: keep her in until the doctor arrived. When that would be, no one had told her. Perhaps no one cared. Perhaps they were hoping she wouldn't last that long.

The thought made her heart pound harder. She tried to move, but pain knifed through her wrists and ankles. She gasped, then hissed between her teeth as she reached down and felt the damage for herself. The skin was raw and ridged where something had dug into it. She traced the soreness with trembling fingers, as though touching it could make sense of what had been done.

"Ow," she whispered, the sound almost swallowed by the thick dark.

A thin line of gold shone under the door, the only proof she wasn't entirely cut off from the world. It felt like a mockery—light she couldn't reach, voices she couldn't join.

Melissa closed her eyes, forcing her breath steady. Panic would be useless here. She needed her mind clear, sharper than the fear that gnawed at her. Somewhere beyond that light was the key to the door. Somewhere beyond those women's murmurs was the answer to why she was here—and just what they intended to do with her.

A low current of unease rippled among the chambermaids. The youngest had just finished recounting what had happened in the bunker, including Melissa's threat, and the memory had left them uneasy. They took some comfort in knowing the locks had been changed—Melissa could no longer leave the room without help—but the risk of relaxing was too great. They decided on shifts, ensuring at least one set of eyes would remain on the door at all times.

Inside, Melissa groped along the nightstand until her fingers brushed the cool metal of a lamp switch. The soft glow that filled the room was feeble but enough to draw the attention of those beyond the door. Nora, the eldest maid, lifted her chin toward one of the others.

"Go to the study and ring the doctor. Tell him she's awake."

The girl obeyed without question, her steps fading down the corridor.

Melissa swung her legs over the side of the bed, wincing as her feet met the floor. Pain flared in her ankles, sharp enough to pull a hiss from her lips. She eased herself upright, the hem of her linen gown whispering over the wood as she moved.

The room felt stripped bare. Her clothes were practically gone. Personal belongings—vanished. Every trace of the life she had built had been swept away, as though she were being erased piece by piece.

She kept walking, searching for something familiar, but it was the empty corner where the crib had once stood that broke her. Her knees weakened, and she pressed her face into her sleeve, stifling the sound of her sobs.

Her hair hung in tangled strands, her body heavy with exhaustion, yet the absence in that corner weighed the most of all. Melissa's spirit felt hollow, disconnected from anything that might have anchored her. The ache in her chest seemed to seep into the very walls, a faint tremor whispering through the old foundation. Outside her locked doors, the chambermaids spoke over one another, their voices tinged with unease yet dismissed with casual remarks about an approaching storm.

She let herself grieve—just for a breath—the child who was gone from her arms. But grief quickly gave way to a sharper, burning fear. The thought of someone, anyone… or *him* harming her child sliced through her, and in an instant, she was on her feet.

Her gaze swept the stripped room as she moved toward the balcony. She wrenched the curtains aside, only to find rough wooden planks nailed across the doors, blotting out the world beyond.

"I'm in prison," she whispered, the words tasting of disbelief and rage.

She strode to the bedroom doors, pounding against them with the flat of her fists. "Let me out!" she shouted, the force of her voice ricocheting off the walls.

Chairs scraped and clattered beyond the door as the chambermaids scattered, their footsteps retreating quickly down the stairs. Then silence.

Melissa's fury swelled in the void they left behind. She tore through the room, searching for anything she could use to force the doors open, but every drawer was empty, every corner bare.

Everything was gone.

Alice had taken the wheel—though Linus had adjusted the seat—picking up Piper on the way. The drive into Hampstead was short—only about fifteen minutes—but the tension in the car stretched far beyond the miles. Piper sat in the backseat, leaning forward with her arms resting on the headrests, her voice dripping with sarcasm.

"Sorry to interrupt movie night," she quipped, eyes flicking to Alice, who remained unreadable behind the wheel. The coldness hadn't softened since Piper had first stepped inside. Linus had mentioned they were watching documentaries, something heavy.

"I tried to give you all space," Piper continued, her voice barely concealing frustration. "But what else was I supposed to do? Just ignore all this?"

Alice's sigh was quiet but weighted. "It's not about space, Piper. We're… drowning here. It's more than we can handle right now."

Piper's brow furrowed as she pressed on, "You're going back and forth, Alice. Either you're still part of Equal Species, or you're not. Make up your mind."

Linus's voice cut through the rising tension, calm but firm. "Let's not argue. It won't help anyone. We can ease back in—careful steps, not a headlong plunge."

Piper exhaled, settling back into her seat. "I guess that makes sense." She glanced at her phone and then back to the road ahead. "Oh, and Preston asked me to remind you to text him, Linus."

"Yeah, I will. He's still practicing, right?" Linus replied with a hint of dry humor.

Piper nodded silently, eyes fixed on the motorway as the car moved steadily forward, the hum of the engine filling the quiet spaces between them.

Melissa lay in her bedroom, surrendering slowly to a sense of defeat. She was just a girl, adrift in a world far beyond her understanding, trapped in a place too vast and cold for someone so young. The weight of helplessness pressed down on her, and for a moment, the thought of death felt like an escape—a way to be reunited with her mother and father once more.

Faint memories drifted through her mind: Emaline's warm smile, the steady, deep voice of Kovos calming the chaos whenever the girls' laughter threatened to spill over. A single tear traced a cold path down her cheek. She was utterly alone.

Just as sleep began to pull her under again, a faint sound stirred in the stillness, subtle but insistent. Her eyes snapped open. Rising to her feet, she scanned the room, sensing a presence where none should be.

Then it struck her—the bathtub. It seemed almost absurd, but desperation had no room for doubt. The last time she and Fiona had been near it, something magical transpired.

The bathroom itself was a study in contrast. Once lavishly adorned, it now felt stripped and empty, the luxury reduced to a cold cast-iron tub standing like a silent sentinel. Neither she nor Benson Jr. had ever used it, both preferring the shower, but now it was the one thing that might offer a way forward.

With a deep breath, Melissa moved toward it, hope stirring quietly beneath her despair. Outside, Alice, Piper, and Linus arrived, the tension thinning. Linus pulled out his phone, carefully confirming the address, then double-checked to be certain. "This has to be it," he said quietly. From Alice's small car parked across the street, they studied the large house. Lights glowed steadily throughout, the calm facade giving no hint of the turmoil inside.

Upstairs, Melissa released the pipe, water gushing into the tub. Her eyes widened as a faint smile touched her lips, recalling moments shared with Fiona. As the water swelled, so did her determination. She knew she had to escape, to save her daughter—and this might be her only chance.

She glanced long and hard at her reflection in the mirror. Her soft grey eyes met jet-black, textured hair framing delicate features. Pressing her hand to the glass, she seemed to say a silent goodbye to herself and the life she once knew. Turning back to the bathtub, she eased her right leg in first, then the left, lowering herself carefully as the water reached its brim. One final look around the room, a deep breath, and she closed her eyes before submerging beneath the surface.

The chambermaids bustled nervously, readying the house for nightfall, when one of them caught sight of Linus and Piper approaching the front door. "Nora!" she called out sharply. "There's someone coming this way."

Upstairs, Melissa's transformation was unfolding with slow intensity. The cramped tub barely contained her shifting form. Her Modiri body grew larger, more muscular, and powerful. She felt the familiar tingling as her hands webbed together, her hair lengthened and thickened from the roots, and her skin deepened to a rich tan. Her legs merged, reshaping into a strong sapphire fin studded with shimmering silver gemstones. This time, the change carried a subtle maturity—a sign of the years she had lived as a human. Slowly, her brasloor began to take shape. The tub cracked under the strain, water leaking through the fractures.

Downstairs, Linus hesitated at the door before finally summoning the courage to ring the bell. A sharp voice answered from a nearby window. "Who are you?"

Linus turned to face the chambermaid, his voice steady but polite. "My name is Linus Claymoore. I'm looking for my niece, Melissa. I believe she may be here."

"Do you see the hour, boy?" she snapped.

"I do, and I apologize for coming so late." Before he could say more, Nora appeared, pulling the chambermaid back from the window. Her voice cut through the air. "Go. Now."

Piper rolled her eyes. "Well, she's certainly rude."

The cast-iron tub groaned beneath the sudden force, its edges cracking as the water surged over the sides. Melissa's fin pressed hard against the brittle porcelain, muscles flexing instinctively. Her eyes snapped open— deep, berry blue, glowing faintly in the dim light. With a flick born of muscle memory, she lashed her powerful tail through the water, the force shattering the tub entirely.

The thrash was deafening as she crashed through the ceiling, shards of plaster and wood raining down into the kitchen below. The impact shook the house, rattling windows and sending dust swirling in the sudden draft. Water gushed from broken pipes, flooding the floor, mingling with the debris.

Piper and Linus froze, their breath caught in their throats. The quiet retreat they had been preparing for was swept away in an instant. The sheer force of Melissa's arrival filled the room with a heavy, raw energy.

Melissa lay there for a moment, the shock of the fall fading as she flexed her limbs, feeling the unfamiliar power coursing through her. The fin, now fully formed and gleaming, curved beneath her like a weapon forged by the sea itself.

The chambermaids' screams pierced the night, one flinging open the front door before sprinting down the road, her voice carrying a single terrified word: "Alien!"

Alice sat upright in her car, heart quickening with sudden curiosity. She turned toward the house, trying to make sense of the commotion. Piper and Linus exchanged wary glances before stepping carefully inside, the remaining chambermaids retreating hastily, fleeing on foot in the opposite direction. Their fearful shouts echoed faintly through the quiet streets, sending a ripple of unease through the neighborhood. The word "Alien" trailed after them, slicing through the darkness like a warning.

Inside, the house lay in ruins.

The destruction stretched from the master bedroom through the kitchen—walls shattered, furniture overturned, debris scattered everywhere. Amid the chaos,

Melissa crouched under a stream of cold water gushing from broken pipes. Her skin was umber and trembling, the shock of her transformation slowly fading. She was bare, vulnerable, the chill cutting into her like a blade.

Linus's gaze locked on her fragile form. Without hesitation, he pulled off his shirt and gathered blankets nearby, wrapping them gently around her trembling shoulders. Piper moved quickly to help, draping the fabric over Melissa with careful hands, shielding her from the cold and the chaos alike.

Suddenly, lights flickered on all along the street, neighbors drawn awake by the noise. Alice hurried to the front door, her breath catching as she watched Linus, Piper, and Melissa step out from beneath the cascading water and wreckage.

Her voice trembled with disbelief and hope, "Oh my dear… it was really her. What is happening…?"

XV.

OBI

Linus fought to hold back his tears, overwhelmed by a rush of emotion. Part of it was selfish—he wasn't alone anymore. With Beatrice gone, finding even one surviving family member brought an unexpected sense of relief. But another part of him ached with responsibility. His brother had been cast into poverty for being born different, while Linus had lived his life believing lies. Helping his brother's children felt like the smallest reparation he could offer.

He held Melissa tightly. She was drowsy from the transformation—this time without pain, yet the lingering effects still weighed on her. Summoning the strength to speak, she whispered, "Please… take me to the water."

Linus's gaze darted to Alice, who looked to Piper.

"Water? As in the river?" Piper asked.

He nodded, certain they all thought the same. He hoped Melissa recognized him; though she never said it, he was sure she did. His resemblance to her father was undeniable. But she had more pressing matters to tend to. She needed to find Kaliope—and from there, her daughter.

In the backseat of the compact car, Linus sat with Melissa leaning against his shoulder, her breath shallow and uneven. Piper and Alice occupied the front, their voices overlapping in a tense debate.

"We need to get her to the emergency room," Alice insisted.

"What? She'd need a hybrid band. Do you want us all arrested for treason?" Piper snapped.

"Calm down—it was just a suggestion. But she fell out of a ceiling, for heaven's sake."

Linus leaned forward, his voice steady but urgent. "We don't know what her life is like under the water. Maybe we should do as she asked. Maybe someone there can help her."

Alice waved him off. "She's human at the end of the day. Look at her—she can't even keep her head up."

"I'm with Linus," Piper said quietly. "We take her to the water."

Alice let out a long, frustrated sigh. "What river is even near here?"

"The closest I can think of is Dover Port," Linus replied.

Both women turned to him with identical grimaces.

"No way!" Alice exclaimed. "Two hours? Are you mad?"

"No, Alice. Please. She's my family. I just want her to be alright."

Piper stayed silent, her eyes fixed on Melissa, as if searching her tanned, drawn face for answers none of them yet had.

Alice agreed, though reluctance tugged at every part of her. It wasn't a choice made from desire, but from necessity—her life offered no rewards grand enough to grant her the luxury of refusal. She would not return home, and the thought of living under the same roof with a man who would inevitably grow to resent her was unbearable.

Night stretched into the small hours, the motorway carrying them deeper into the dark. Piper rested her head against the window frame, the glass lowered so the wind could tangle freely through her hair. Linus glanced at Melissa now and then, reassured each time her breathing was steady. Relief settled over him; she was here, safe.

He understood his duty now. Their journey as the Equal Species had to continue, and her protection on land was his to bear. When she was not in the water, she was his charge, a responsibility he accepted without hesitation. Quietly, he vowed to uncover the shadow lurking within the Monarchy and to find a way for their kind and the Modiri to coexist in true harmony.

They had all tried to fight the pull of sleep, but the steady rhythm of the road and the uneventful night had eventually claimed them—everyone except Alice. She remained awake, her hands steady on the wheel, eyes fixed ahead while her thoughts drifted far from the road. She saw her father's face in her mind, her mother's quiet composure. *Were they thinking of her now? What had her father said when he realized she was gone?* She didn't ask herself these questions in search of answers; she knew none would come. It was more a quiet defiance, a wish that her absence might make them see what they were losing, that it might push them to mend whatever had been splintering at home.

When the first traces of light brushed the horizon— soft and pale against the lingering night—the car slowed to a gentle stop. Only thirty miles from France. Turning in her seat, Alice reached out and touched her friends' shoulders one by one, her voice low and warm as she roused them. Melissa stirred last, her eyes fluttering open to the quiet announcement of their arrival.

Dover Port lay beneath the looming majesty of the White Cliffs, their pale faces stark even in the darkness. The town's waterfront stretched ahead, the promenade drawing the eye toward the still, turquoise sweep of the harbor. At night, it was a haunting sight—quiet, vast, and shadowed by the cliffs above.

To the left, a tall flagpole carried the Union Jack, its fabric stirring faintly in the sea breeze. Clusters of modern waterfront buildings and a lone hotel stood close to the water's edge, dwarfed by the sheer chalk walls that rose behind them, streaked here and there with stubborn green where vegetation clung to the rock. High on the hilltop, Dover Castle kept its ancient watch over the coastline. The piers and breakwaters of the port reached out into the black water like steady arms, guiding unseen vessels home.

Melissa walked barefoot along the cool concrete of the promenade, her steps quickening as she drew closer to the harbor's edge. Piper, Alice, and Linus followed at a measured pace. The breeze caught Melissa's dark hair, lifting it gently as she leaned over the water, dipping one foot in as though testing the temperature before a dive.

"Are you okay?" Alice asked quietly, resting a hand at the small of Linus's back.

Melissa turned to face them, a soft smile lighting her features. "Thank you, Linus."

"Uncle," Alice corrected with a knowing glance, her voice warm. She had seen the lengths he had gone to find Melissa and understood how much this moment meant to him.

Melissa crossed the few steps back to him and wrapped her arms around his torso.

Welcoming her embrace, he said, "I love you." The sound of his voice was firm but tender. "And I promise that while I'm here, I'll do everything I can to make sure that when you return, you'll be safe—and you'll have a home to come back to."

Linus smiled, his eyes glistening.

"Thank you, Uncle Linus," she repeated before turning to Piper and Alice with a final nod of gratitude. Then she stepped away, her bare feet whispering against the concrete. At the edge, she paused only a heartbeat before slipping soundlessly into the cold, dark waters.

They crept to the water's edge, their breath held, each silently wishing for one last glimpse of her. Melusine did not disappoint. In a sudden, fluid motion, her body shifted—skin shimmering as her legs dissolved into a sweeping sapphire fin, its surface scattered with silver gemstones that glinted like fragments of starlight. The transformation sent a surge of water splashing against the rocks, misting their faces.

Beneath the rising sun, her fin arched high above the waves, catching the light in a perfect, fleeting moment. Piper and Alice dropped to their knees, overcome by the beauty before them. Melusine surfaced, her gaze meeting theirs, eyes a luminous berry-blue that seemed almost unreal. She was changed entirely—otherworldly now, her skin catching the dawn in faint, glittering tones.

Linus's breath caught in his throat. And then, as if pulled by an unseen tide, Melusine slipped beneath the surface, her fin slicing downward into the shadowed depths until nothing remained but the ripples.

In the far reaches of the East, south in the Temple of Xorri, the silence was torn apart by a sound so harrowing it seemed to claw at the soul—a piercing, relentless cry. It was the wailing of the Ushu, a voice that did not simply echo through the temple's halls but bled into the bones of all who heard it.

But the story had begun long before that night. It began in the era when the Kingdom now called The Shadows of the Grey bore another name: the Nukeya Kingdom. Once, it had thrived under the reign of King Fufuhani, the Ether God—a sovereign as feared as he was revered. The warriors of Nukeya were unmatched. They wielded not only the strength of their bodies, but the depth of their spirits and the sharpened edge of their minds.

Fufuhani ruled with a will as unyielding as stone. Mercy was not a quality he prized; instead, he forged leaders through rivalry and trial. Among his most trusted Mosquens, loyalty was tested in blood. He often summoned them to the arena, forcing them to fight until the air itself tasted of iron. To the victor went honor, but to the king went the certainty that only the strongest would rise to lead after he ascended to the Ahalty—the realm of Gods.

Of all his Mosquens, there were four whose names were carried on the wind like a prophecy: Kewo, whose silence masked a mind as sharp as obsidian; Riko, whose sword struck as swiftly as a falcon dives; Hichi, whose laughter could unsettle even the bravest foe; and Ryūmon, whose gaze held the gravity of unspoken truths. The king watched them closely, knowing that one day, one of these four would inherit not only his throne but the fate of an entire kingdom.

Ryūmon had spent years watching his brothers with the patience of a hunter, studying every flaw, every lapse in judgment. He learned which tempers flared quickly, which cravings could be exploited. A well-timed bribe—an elaborate dish prepared to their taste—or a rare fish traded for a weapon they prized was enough to win a sliver of trust. They were stronger, faster, and in Riko's case, merciless in combat, but Ryūmon understood that brute force alone was not the only path to victory.

The Modiri of the East were never celebrated for their strength. Their renown came from a magic that others coveted, a gift passed through generations like an heirloom. Yet King Fufuhani, their father, craved something beyond enchantment. He hungered for dominance on the battlefield, for warriors whose name would stir fear in distant lands. He spoke often of the duels in the North—ritual combats where skill and savagery were tested before roaring crowds—and his eyes would gleam with longing.

Ryūmon listened. And while his brothers trained their bodies to exhaustion, he honed his mind into a blade sharper than any steel. He set them against one another with a quiet, calculated precision, weaving suspicion into every word he spoke. A jest became an insult, an idle comment a seed of mistrust. Soon, each believed that eliminating the others was the surest way to earn their father's favor.

One by one, they fell—sometimes in the arena, sometimes in the shadows, but always by the design of Ryūmon's hand. In the end, the proud warriors lay silent, their ambitions extinguished. He alone remained, gliding in the stillness that follows a storm, the taste of victory both intoxicating and bitter on his tongue.

Although Ryūmon had secured his claim to the throne and the rightful seat over the Nukeya Kingdom, a shadow clung to him still. Years of an unnatural plague had stripped him of his sight, yet that was not the cruelest punishment. In the darkness, he saw them—his brothers—haunting him. Their silhouettes drifted at the edges of his mind, lingering like uninvited phantoms, mourning him as much as he mourned them. Their spirits, unclaimed by the Mortis God, remained tethered to him, unwilling to cross into whatever lay beyond.

The renaming of the kingdom came not from Ryūmon's decree, but from a moment he could neither predict nor control: the first Ushu manifested. It did not emerge through him, but through his Iris daughter, Ramiel. And the shadow that had claimed her was none other than Hichi, his brother, desperate for another chance to fin among the living.

For the love of his daughter, Ryūmon devoted himself to mastering the ancient Wor Modiri magic, determined to free her from the Ushu that clung to her shadow. Yet, as the years passed, even his deepest incantations could not prevail. The will of his deceased brother—driven by a relentless desire to rise again—proved stronger than any spell.

Decades later, another Modiri had risen in the South, claimed by Kewo. Many revered them as creatures of legend, majestic wanderers from the East. But Ryūmon knew the truth. Failing to protect his kind from his brother's vengeance had eroded his mind, leaving him weakened, his strength hollowed by relentless guilt.

In the end, Ryūmon fell.

Drawn into the very darkness he had once sought to control, he became a silent architect of ruin. His eyes, the color of storm-tossed seas, reflected the grief that consumed him. His once-proud features had hardened, carved deep by sorrow. The kingdom he had sworn to protect stood barren, steeped in the echo of regrets too heavy to name.

While Ryūmon locked his fears deep within himself, his last brother roamed in the unseen realm, praying for those trapped within the confines of their own nightmares—people too frightened to move, too hesitant to live, too unwilling to face those who had wronged them.

For centuries, Riko had waited for his chance. And then… Naida appeared.

Riko—now an Ushu—hovered in the water before King Bao, its form coiled with rage. From the moment he saw the grey gleam in Naida's eyes, he knew. One of the lost Nukeya warriors had found her.

Ryūmon, his brother in the old kingdom, had never been willing to face such a shadow. But Bao was not Ryūmon. He did not cower.

"Stop your bellowing," he roared.

The Ushu froze, its gaze narrowing.

"What is your name?" he demanded, his voice a deep rumble. His towering form dwarfed the specter, whose features mirrored the young hybrid drifting cautiously at its side.

The Ushu's lips curled. "Ah…eh…Ushu," it replied, mocking him.

Bao's eyes darkened. "What is your name?" he asked again, his tone colder, sharper.

"Ah…eh…Ushu."

Slower this time. More deliberate.

"You are a shadow of the undead. What is your name?"

It feigned a pause, its mouth shaping the syllables as though to taunt him. "Ushu."

"Why do you not claim your Obi?"

"There is no Obi," it hissed. "That is a human. Look at it."

"She is your Obi," Bao said, unflinching. "And you will claim her."

The Ushu sneered. "You going to make me?"

Bao's gaze was steady. "If you will not claim your Obi, what shall I call you?"

A slow smile crept across its face. "Riko. The Nukeya warrior."

"That kingdom no longer exists," Bao replied. "You are here because you refuse to release your fin. But she is only a girl. You will not harm her."

The water shivered with its low growl. "Hmm."

King Bao knew the task before him was grave. Riko was a combat Mosquen, and as Naida's Ushu, his Sila'rum could easily prove dangerous to the young girl. Yet what troubled Bao most was the question that gnawed at him—what had frightened her so deeply that she had unconsciously summoned one of the most malevolent Ushu's to her shadow?

Naida drifted further into her trance, her expression distant and unseeing. Bao's unseen gaze returned to Riko, and he recognized instantly that no mere Wor Magic could tame him—Riko's power moved far beyond it.

With a decisive motion, Bao forced the Ushu out of the temple, past the Moduuf statues, straight downward. It plummeted to the seabed, striking the sand with a violent thud. Grains spiraled upward in a murky cloud, scattering sea creatures in frantic bursts of motion. The Ushu lifted its gaze, eyes blazing with unbridled fury.

"Find your way back to your Obi if you wish to live," Bao commanded from inside. His voice carried no hint of mercy, only the finality of judgment.

As dawn touched the edges of England and its people stirred in their beds, Melusine pressed onward through the deep. She did not know how far she had drifted from the Snow Kingdom, nor where her path would lead, yet determination urged her on.

Seconds later, the first sting came without warning—a sharp slice against her skin as she finned, her great tail sweeping behind her like a banner unfurled in a silent current. Another strike followed, quick and unseen. Crimson spiraled into the water, curling in the pale morning light.

Then came the laughter. Low at first, then circling her like the attacks themselves. She froze, suspended in the water, heart thundering. Twisting sharply, she swept her fin through the current, the silver-colored scales on her brasloor catching the sun, gleaming even as blood swirled in slow ribbons around her.

Again, something darted past—too swift to catch. She turned left, and the next blow came from the right.

"Who is there?" she called, her voice carrying into the gloom.

Only the sea creatures drifted by, unaware of her dread. But then came another blow. And another. She saw no one in the murky waters around her.

A voice slid into her ear like a serpent through water.

"Filthy hybrid. You will meet your demise here."

Melusine's breath caught.

"No… I am not—"

The words died on her tongue as a Philosopher struck her into silence.

The Philosophers of Leucothea were bound to the Nwala Kingdom. These Modiri, though fascinating, never grew beyond four feet in length even in adulthood. They hunted in packs, fangs and talons as razor-sharp as a piranha's bite. To see one meant others were already nearby. Their size was their only disadvantage—what they lacked in stature, they reclaimed in cunning. Their voices could cut deeper than their claws, weaving manipulations that broke the mind before the body.

Among them were the Lorelies and the Mosquens, both deceptively beautiful. Their delicate fins and brasloor shimmered in a pale pink hue known as puce. Childlike in form, with bright eyes and vivid markings, they were as deadly as they were alluring. Aquamarine gemstones glittered along their fins; Lorelies bore faintly pink tail flukes, while the Mosquens carried the deep blue of zaffre.

The Philosophers of Leucothea bore Melusine toward their domain, working in a tight, whispering formation. Small bodies, quick wrists, clever minds: they moved like a single thought, slipping silk cords of eelgrass beneath her shoulders and waist, guiding her through the dim water with sharp, efficient tugs. Song fish clustered at the edges of their procession, a glittering escort that kept to the periphery, circling but never touching.

Blood feathered from the shallow cuts along Melusine's flank, thinning into pink threads that dissolved in the current. Her sapphire tail hung slack, the silver flecks dulled by shadow. The Philosophers barely spoke to outsiders; when they did, it was in soft, needling tones that turned more to deliberation than comfort. Limestone spires loomed and fell away. Kelp parted. Caverns opened like mouths and closed again behind them.

The sea accepted its offering.

Far above, Balmoral Castle breathed in quiet dread. Guards lined the walls, boots planted, eyes fixed. Curtains stirred in a draft no one felt. By the bed, Lady Mary sat perfectly still, fingers interlaced in her lap, listening for a sound she had not heard in days.

It came as the smallest grunt. Amer's lashes fluttered, and a hushed ripple moved through the room as if someone had dropped a stone into a still pond. Relief rose in Mary, quick and bright, only to falter; she feared the moment his gaze found her. Would he send her away? Would he remember the last words he spoke?

The door eased open. Clara slid inside with the stealth of someone who had been waiting just beyond the threshold, cheeks flushed, eyes alight. She stopped a pace behind Mary, eager to witness the prince's first look— eager to see whom he would reach for.

Amer drew a breath that sounded almost human again. The guards leaned forward without moving. Mary steadied herself, lifted her chin, and waited for the truth of his waking to settle the room.

Amer's gaze swept the chamber. His attire had been changed, his skin scrubbed clean. Clearing his throat, he turned to Lady Mary.

"My mother placed you here, did she not?"

Lady Mary squinted, her eyes drifting to Clara as if seeking guidance. The chambermaid stepped forward and bowed with practiced grace.

"That she did, Your Highness—so that you might see your lady has been obedient, waiting patiently for your return."

"Can she not speak for herself?" he asked sharply.

Clara exchanged a weary glance with Lady Mary, then stepped back, gesturing for the young woman to answer.

"Her Majesty did," Lady Mary said quietly.

"Do you not wish another life for yourself?" he asked.

"No. I am only here for His Highness."

Amer drew in a slow breath. "You need a personality. Alright."

Perplexed, Lady Mary simply nodded, agreeing without question as he closed his eyes once more.

Buckingham Palace stirred with its familiar rhythm as dawn lifted over the city. Watson rose from bed, stretching his arms as though trying to shake the unrest from his body. Today, his first duty was clear: he needed to find Her Majesty. News of the young boy's death left him feeling burdened, and though he could not yet untangle the full truth, he longed for reassurance that his family remained safe—safe from what, he still could not entirely say.

He chose his attire with deliberate simplicity: a khaki button-down shirt tucked neatly into dark trousers, polished dress shoes, and his insignia pinned with quiet pride. When he opened the door, he nearly faltered.

Enu stood before him.

She saluted smartly, though her smile betrayed a hint of unease. "Good morning."

Caught off guard, Watson recoiled slightly. "Morning. How did you know I was here?"

"You ask the right questions, you get the right answers," she replied, tilting her head. "But the real question is—what are you doing here?"

Watson exhaled, weighing whether he should unburden his truth to her. "Why've you come?"

Her expression softened. "Change of heart. But not the kind you're thinking." She stepped aside, allowing him space to leave the room.

She was neatly dressed herself: navy-blue trousers, a peach-colored polo, her dark hair drawn into a sleek ponytail twisted into a bun at the back. Everything about her appearance suggested readiness, though the flicker in her eyes hinted at something unusual.

The difference in their heights was impossible to ignore. Enu often kept her gaze fixed ahead when they spoke, sparing herself the strain of looking upward for long.

"I thought about your invitation," she said as they moved through the Palace corridors. Watson led the way toward the lower level, intent on retrieving documents before locating the Queen's companions to inquire about her whereabouts.

"Oh?"

"Yes. I am interested. But if I may—" she lifted her eyes briefly to him, "I'd like to make a suggestion."

Watson slowed his pace.

"Esam," she said. "He'd make a fine replacement for Mavis. As for me, I belong at your side. Your right hand. I have the training, the knowledge, and—if we're honest—I've bested you in combat more times than you realize. Except, of course, for the times I let you win." Her lips curved in the faintest smile, half jest, half-truth.

Watson exhaled heavily. He wasn't amused by her boast, though he couldn't deny the sense in her reasoning. In these uncertain times, he needed someone of her caliber close. Together, they were stronger than any pairing the

Guard could offer. If another Kovos emerged, he trusted no one more than her to face *it* beside him.

"You'll have it," he said at last, his voice low but firm.

Enu felt relief stir within her, though her face revealed nothing. In the dim basement, Watson moved deliberately through shelves and cabinets, pulling together a stack of documents—intelligence briefings, readiness reports, operational orders. He instructed her to keep close, his voice carrying the finality of command.

She had intended to return to the barracks to share her news with Esam, who she knew would be waiting for her, but Watson's plans quickly eclipsed her own.

"We will find Her Majesty," he said firmly. "There are matters that require discussion."

Their carefully laid scheme, the one she and her brother had labored over, was beginning to unravel before it had the chance to take shape. Orders rarely shifted so suddenly; changes of this kind usually demanded the approval of several high-ranking officers. Yet here, Watson's word alone seemed to carry the authority of decree.

It went against every protocol she had been trained to uphold, but she dared not question him. As they stepped onto the top floor of the Palace, a uniformed guard approached, his boots clicking sharply against the marble. He stopped before them and saluted.

"Good morning, Major General Watson. Good morning, Brigadier General Enu." His gaze returned to Watson with a hint of unease. "Sir, a Doctor Astor has been ringing and sending messages for you without pause."

Watson's expression did not shift. "And Her Majesty?"

The guard straightened. "Her Majesty has requested a quiet day, sir."

Queen Emmary lingered within the Palace, though the thought of retreating to the Sampalk House in Norfolk had crossed her mind more than once. The vast country estate promised rolling fields and air free of London's ceaseless rhythm, yet she resisted the urge to flee. What she craved was not distance, but stillness—a place where her mind could unspool and her body could move unobserved. She chose a secluded quarter of Buckingham Palace instead, tucked away from the echo of footsteps and the shuffle of attendants.

This wing, seldom visited, had the comfort of a private residence. Its modest kitchen smelled faintly of bread she had warmed earlier, and the adjoining dining room was softened by pale drapery that stirred with the draft. From the tall windows, she could study the city below, the slate rooftops glistening with the sheen of morning rain. It was sanctuary enough: a retreat within her own walls, close yet apart, where the crown did not press so heavily.

Her hair, freshly washed, spilled in dark waves past her shoulders, freed from pins and sprays. Her skin carried the warmth of her shower, softened by fragrant oils, and the simple linen gown she chose brushed against the polished wooden floors with a whisper. She moved without haste, each step unburdened, her bare feet leaving the faintest sound in the silence. Here, away from the endless choreography of her public life, she was unadorned, almost anonymous.

Watson, unaware of her refuge, assumed she had withdrawn to Norfolk. With Enu steady at his side, he directed their course toward Kensington to answer the call from Doctor Astor.

XVI.

EXPERIMENT 002

The sky pressed down, swollen with rain, thunder growling across the horizon like an omen. Kensington held its beauty still, its clean avenues and polished facades betraying nothing of the quiet schemes woven within the town.

Children in raincoats hurried from their play as the first drops scattered across the pavement, their laughter swallowed by the sudden shift in weather. Windows shut, doors closed, and the streets emptied beneath the weight of the storm.

Inside the car, Watson and Enu rode without a word. The soft whirl of the engine filled the silence, steady and unbroken. Enu's eyes moved over the city beyond the glass, tracing the familiar lines of a place that felt strangely distant. She had not ventured far from Buckingham Palace in years, not since her departure from Scotland. The barracks had been her world—rigid, confining, unchanging—and Kensington, with its restless life, seemed almost foreign to her now.

Just beside her, Watson tried to push the thoughts away, but his mind betrayed him. Images of his wife and children surfaced unbidden, threading through the silence of the ride like an intruder slipping through an unlocked door. Kensington was vast, and they were nowhere near his neighborhood, yet unease gnawed at him. Each day, the pieces fit more tightly together—his daughter's watch turning up in the bunker, the story of a dead boy in his basement. None of it was a coincidence.

He had no desire to heed Astor's call.

Today was about answers, and if necessary, confrontation. The car slowed to a stop, its lights casting pale streaks across the damp pavement. Enu was the first to step out. She straightened her top and whispered under her breath, relieved that the rain had come as scattered droplets rather than a full storm. Still, she glanced at the clouds and hoped they would be back at the barracks before the downpour gathered force.

Watson joined her a moment later. He strode past, jaw tight, and rapped his fist against the front door, pressing the bell immediately after. The seconds dragged on, heavy with impatience, as no sound of footsteps came from within.

"Where is he?" Watson growled, his voice carrying more demand than question.

Enu's gaze lifted toward the house. "There's a woman at the window…"

She was right. A figure lingered behind the glass before slipping away. Moments later, the door creaked open, revealing Doctor Astor's assistant. She was a delicate young woman, her frame so slight it seemed the door itself shielded her. She kept most of her body hidden, her voice fragile, almost mournful.

"You're here for the Doctor?" she asked softly.

"Yes," Watson answered, his tone clipped with impatience.

"He hasn't been here for quite some time. He's in the other unit."

Watson's eyes narrowed. "Other unit? The bunker?"

"I assume so," she murmured, her gaze falling to the pavement as though ashamed of her own words. When she finally looked up, her expression shifted toward the sky. Dark clouds were gathering, the first hints of storm pressing low over the rooftops. Her plea was barely audible. "Please… will you go now?"

Enu and Watson exchanged a questioning look. Without a word, they turned away, and the door closed gently behind them.

Inside the car again, Enu frowned, curiosity breaking through her usually steady composure. "What's a bunker? Like a safety center?"

Watson's reply came low, steady. "It's not for everyone. I'll explain later."

And with that, the vehicle pulled back into motion, carrying them toward a different storm.

Back at the barracks, Esam's nerves frayed with every passing minute. He had not heard from his sister, and the silence gnawed at him like a slow fire. Behind the mess hall—where they had promised to meet after her talk with Watson—he paced restlessly, his sneakers scraping against the polished hallway floors. The fitted tracksuit clung to him, but it was not the clothes that were antagonizing. It was the burning mark carved into his skin.

The trident.

Hybrids carried it from birth, etched into them as naturally as a vein or a heartbeat. For most, it was not a torment but a truth: no pain, no discomfort, only the quiet reminder of what they were. Yet the removal—and its return—was another matter entirely. Now it seared as if it meant to brand him all over again, every pulse of fire whispering that he was running out of time. He needed the witch. Without her, there was no stopping its return.

Esam checked his watch. The barracks had grown quiet; most of the soldiers were already in the dorms or scattered across the recreational wings. The training grounds stood abandoned, the field house's indoor pool dark. Perfect for secrecy, but far from reassuring. Enu was supposed to be watching his back, and her absence hollowed him with unease.

He forced himself to keep pacing, though his chest tightened with every step. Fear was dangerous here. If someone caught him wandering—if someone saw the way his skin burned—they would know. His heart slammed against his ribs, begging for her to appear.

Once the vehicle merged onto the motorway, Enu sat stiffly in the passenger seat, a coil of discomfort tightening in her stomach. Morning traffic thinned as they left the heart of the city, the skyline shrinking behind them until only the wide stretch of road and the distant district remained.

"What is this bunker?" she asked again, her voice sharper now, as if repetition would force a straight answer.

Watson's grip tightened on the wheel. "You need to be sworn to secrecy," he said at last. "This world I'm bringing you into—it isn't the one you think you know.

Everything you've been told about those wretched hybrids, about harmony and unity, about society coexisting as one—it's a lie. A story crafted to keep our citizens calm, to keep the world from looking too closely."

Enu turned toward him, her brow furrowed.

"The truth," Watson continued, "is that rebellion has been stirring beneath the surface for years. The King knew. He always knew."

Her throat tightened. "Is this about his cure?"

"The cure we've failed to produce?" His eyes flicked toward her, then back to the road. "Perhaps."

"And the Lith?"

He hesitated. "We don't have it."

Enu snapped her head toward him, disbelief flashing across her face. "You mean to tell me that all this time— all these years—there's been nothing?"

"What do you mean, nothing?" he asked carefully.

She bit down on the words threatening to spill out, realizing too late she was skirting dangerous ground. If she revealed too much, she'd never get the answers she needed.

Watson's brow lifted. "What do you mean, Enu?"

"I mean…" she faltered, steadying her breath. "I understand Her Majesty has stepped in as acting King, but we've been told—no, promised—that he's improving. That his recovery is steady." Her voice broke with frustration. "You're telling me none of it is true?"

"Yes," Watson said firmly, his tone leaving no room for doubt.

She shook her head, a hollow laugh escaping her lips. "This is a problem. A very big problem. We have allies—

powerful ones. National leaders who believe our King is regaining his strength, and others oblivious to his health entirely. And now you're saying there's been no progress? Nothing at all?"

"This is the new world you're stepping into, Enu," Watson replied quietly. "And before we go any further, I need to know I can trust you."

The vehicle hummed as it cut through the motorway, tires whispering against the asphalt. Watson's hand rested cautiously on the wheel, every movement measured. Enu's gaze drifted from the hard line of his jaw to the blur of trees rushing past her window, but her thoughts slipped to Esam. She looked down, staring at her shoes against the mat, fighting the pull of fear that threatened to drag her under.

Fear prickled along his spine, but Esam forced himself forward, descending into the indoor pool house with cautious steps. His eyes flicked over his shoulders, sweeping every corner, though the grounds were nearly deserted. Only a handful of soldiers drifted through the corridors, wandering aimlessly rather than lingering in their dorms.

Inside, he flicked on the lights. The vast field house glowed to life, revealing an indoor pool designed with a stately, almost ceremonial precision. The water stretched in a narrow rectangle the length of the hall, its surface a flawless mirror that caught the glow from above.

Tall arched windows lined the walls, pulling daylight into the space and softening it with a golden clarity. Overhead, fixtures hung high from the rafters, lending the room both grandeur and austerity. The tiled floor was polished to an immaculate shine, every line and angle reinforcing a sense of order. The symmetry of the architecture—the windows, the pool's exacting shape, the disciplined glow of the lights—gave the place a solemnity that bordered on ritual. Swimming here was less a pastime than a tradition.

Esam began peeling away his garments when his phone vibrated against his palm. The screen lit with Enu's name.

We have a problem…

His thumbs fumbled across the screen, letters scattering out of order. Nerves muddled his fingers without her steadying presence. He typed fast:

Where are you!

In a vehicle with the Major, heading to a… bunker. But we need to find the witch now. You cannot wait for me.

His breath quickened. *What's happening?*

I'll explain when I see you. But you must also ask her about the Emars. I need to know what's happened to them.

A sudden slam cracked through the silence. Esam jerked his head up, heart hammering. The sound echoed off the high walls. No one entered—the disturbance came from the far end of the pool, beyond his sightline.

Beneath the waters of the Makara Kingdom, silence held dominion inside the Temple of Xorri. King Bao hovered in place, his body gently pulsing as he meditated, each movement deliberate, as though the sea itself bent to his rhythm. Nearby, Naida floated in a trance, her form suspended in the dim glow filtering through the carved stone arches of the temple. Her body was still, but within her mind a storm raged—fragments of memory clawing their way forward, threatening to consume her from the inside. Bao did not stir at her torment. Her suffering was of no consequence to him.

Yet beyond the sanctity of the temple, shadows gathered. At the base of a jagged reef, the Ushu known as Riko perched upon a rock, his sharp teeth bared in a grotesque grin. A fish darted past, and in one swift snap, he split it in two, swallowing the pieces with savage delight. The taste ignited something primal in him, a reminder of pleasures long denied.

Naida's survival meant little to him. Her human legs marked her as flawed, a grotesque twist of nature. What mattered was himself. Riko knew becoming an Ushu was a chance that came only once, a gift that would never pass his way again. So he devoured without restraint, tearing into every morsel the sea offered. Each bite was a stolen luxury, a fleeting ecstasy after centuries of hunger.

And as he fed, his laughter rippled through the water, dark and low, carrying the promise of danger that waited just beyond the temple walls.

But Riko's gluttony had not gone unnoticed. Far beyond the Makara Kingdom, in the realm where shadows breathed and shifted like living things, King Ryūmon stirred. The God of the Shadows of the Grey had felt the disturbance, the pull of energy that flowed across the currents, and he was already cutting through the deep on his way toward Bao's temple.

Unlike his brother-king, Ryūmon wore no conical crown to mark his sovereignty. His presence alone was enough to command reverence. His skin gleamed like smoke quartz under fractured beams of light, his jet-black hair bound high by unseen magic. From his back unfurled a great prehensile fin, its sheen a brooding sardonyx laced with streaks of metallic silver, sharp as fractured blades.

His jade kimono clung to his tall frame, the fabric whispering with each measured pulse of movement, as though the sea itself parted in obedience. The water around him darkened when he passed, currents folding over him until he was nearly indistinguishable from the shadows he ruled.

He was menace incarnate; a God sculpted of silence and dread. Torture lived in his gaze, as though every soul he had claimed still writhed somewhere within his depths. He moved without hesitation, cutting through leagues of ocean with unyielding focus.

His quarry was already decided.

Riko.

Fanira located the God of the Shadows of the Grey.

She pressed forward through the thrumming currents, her lithe eel form cutting through the water with urgent grace. She sought the vengeful king, a figure who had not spoken in centuries, his silence as black as the depths he ruled. Every beat of her fins was an effort against the weight of the water and the dread that pressed upon her.

"You cannot interfere," she pleaded, her voice straining to pierce the quiet that surrounded him. Unlike most Modiri, whose fins swished rhythmically against the current, the kings of the East moved differently when pressed for speed, their bodies thrusting side by side to part the waters before them, ascetics hidden beneath flowing garments.

But King Ryūmon did not waver. His gaze was fixed ahead—unblinking, unkind, lethal.

"It has been written and cannot be altered. If you slay your brother, the Ahalty will hear of it. They will show you no mercy," Fanira called again, forcing words past the rising panic. She felt the chill of the depths press against her as she struggled to be heard.

Ryūmon's lips did not move, yet his power pulsed outward. He had mastered his sorcery, each spell honed over decades, each movement studied. He was ready for vengeance, for punishment, for death itself, should it come.

"Think of the future of the East," Fanira cried, desperation sharpening her tone. "Where will you all lie if you disobey the ancestors?"

The currents trembled around him, the very waters seeming to recoil from the shadow of his wrath. Ryūmon advanced, silent, unstoppable, the dark pulse of his intent radiating outward like a storm about to break.

Meanwhile, back at the barracks, Esam prepared himself for the plunge into the pool, every movement measured, every breath steady. Time was slipping through his fingers, and he could not afford hesitation. He lowered himself first by the legs, then let his torso follow, arching his back as his upper body dipped beneath the water. His shoulders and head disappeared last, the cool liquid enveloping him in a tense embrace. The pool stretched ten feet below him, demanding he kneel briefly before the transformation began, a wave of energy coursing through his body. Scales shimmered faintly beneath the surface, muscles tightening, reshaping. The air above was forgotten as his form melded with the water around him, becoming something both human and more.

Meanwhile, Fanira realized her entreaties to King Ryūmon were futile. The shadows clung to him, his heart stubborn. With a quiet resignation, she abandoned her attempts and slithered herself forward, her eel form slicing through the currents before twisting, elongating into a sleek Billfish. She would never outpace the King, yet she pressed on regardless, convinced that arriving in time— even at the very last second—was infinitely better than not arriving at all. The water roared around her as she surged onward, a streak of determination against the relentless pull of the sea.

Esam, now fully transformed into his Modiri form, bore eyes the color of ripe blueberries, sharp and alert beneath his brow. His 4B-textured hair, which on land resembled a dark Caesar cut, had grown nearly four inches, rising in the shape of a high-top fade. Every inch of his upper body thrummed with strength—muscles deepened, abs etched like sculpted stone, and forearms thickened with raw power.

As his body extended, the beginnings of his fin emerged, slicing through the water with a majestic weight, while his boxers slipped silently to the pool's floor. The fin itself glimmered a dark denim hue, flecked with sapphire-colored gems that caught and refracted the light, and his tail fluke shimmered with a subtle, lighter denim glow. Along his right forearm ran the metallic gleam of gold-plated armor, smooth and seamless against the scales beneath.

He was no longer just Esam. He was a Snow, a being of lineage and legacy, a predator and protector fused into one living form, and the pool seemed to shrink around him as his presence claimed the water.

Far beyond the ocean's hidden depths, Fanira could feel him—Eratos. His presence radiated urgency, a silent plea threading through the currents. He needed her, but she was drawn elsewhere. Naida's plight demanded her attention, and she could not falter. As she surged forward, her peripheral vision caught the shadow of King Ryūmon, gliding closer to the Makara Kingdom. Each powerful stroke of his movement stirred tremors in her heart, a whisper of dread she could not ignore.

Back in the indoor pool, Esam floated in still water, body tense yet restrained. His instincts screamed for action, for his fin to flap and propel him through the water, but his mind held firm. Reaching out telepathically, he sent his thoughts to Fanira, hoping she would hear him. *"Eriph and I are in need. The trident symbol appears once more."* His arms stretched across his chest, ascetics clinging to the opposite shoulder, muscles taut beneath the surface.

Fanira caught the call, felt the urgency thrumming in his voice, but she refused to respond. Her anger burned hot and rigid, a fire she could not extinguish. She pressed on, knowing that every moment mattered, and that some battles demanded patience, even in the face of need.

The Makara Kingdom lay serene, the water shimmering in soft currents as the Lorelies frolicked among the giant Makaras, who glided through the depths without concern. Riko drifted alongside them, his curiosity of the world centuries later, outweighing any thought of

Bao's commands. The world around him was a rare glimpse of peace, and for a moment, he allowed himself to explore, savoring the freedom. Yet, beneath the surface of that calm, a faint urgency lingered. Naida's body floated helplessly within the Temple of Xorri, fragile and unprotected.

A low rumble vibrated through the water, echoing along the ocean floor. His brother had arrived. But Riko did not tremble with fear, nor simmer with anger. Instead, a cold certainty settled over him. He would confront Ryūmon, and he would do so here, at Naida's expense if he had to. The moment had come.

Fanira had returned to her original form, and King Bao remained unmoving within the temple, lost in deep meditation, unwilling—or perhaps unable—to intervene. Then, a sound rippled through the depths: the haunting, resonant singing of the Moduuf. Its echoes carried far and wide, signaling Fanira's arrival and drawing all attention toward the confrontation that was about to unfold. Two brothers, poised and relentless, faced each other on the ocean floor, while Naida's fate hung between them like a fragile thread.

Esam continued his fight to maintain control over his Modiri form, his fin thrashing quietly within the water with slow force. Each movement sent ripples cascading across the surface, droplets splashing against the tiled edges, the room echoing faintly with the sound of rushing liquid. He willed Fanira to respond, to guide him toward the young hybrid she had chosen as her vessel, but there was only silence. Not a flicker of movement, not a murmur of direction—nothing but the water pressing around him.

Beneath the surface, Naida stirred, though her movements were not connected to the struggle in the pool. She felt Melusine's presence somewhere distant yet undeniable, a pull in the depths of her mind. Above her, King Bao's pulse moved steadily toward the temple entrance. The subtle shift in the currents, the faint disturbance of the water around him, signaled that he could no longer ignore the commotion beyond the walls of the Temple of Xorri. Lowering his head, his eyes locked on the scene below: the Ushu, Riko, and his kingdom brother facing one another, tension radiating like a storm gathering on the horizon.

He pulsed downward with relentless speed, the water parting in shimmering currents around him. Fanira glided above, her black cloak billowing like smoke in the darkness, her cat-like eyes piercing the depths below. Sunlight hardly reached this far, leaving the ocean floor in shadowed gloom.

Startled by his sudden presence, King Bao lowered himself just enough to remain parallel to the Mistos, his form tense, muscles coiled like a spring.

"Order your Kingdom Brother to stand down," Fanira hissed, still feeling the tug of Esam's call through the currents.

"He seeks vengeance…" Bao's voice was low, steady, weighted with inevitability.

"Against a child hybrid?"

"That is no child, no mere hybrid," Bao corrected.

"What are you saying? You no longer concede?"

"I have… but will he?" Bao's eyes darkened beneath his conical hat, locking onto his kingdom brother below.

There, Riko had returned to the ocean floor, his sharp gaze meeting King Ryūmon's with a mixture of anticipation and defiance, the tension between them thick enough to stir the surrounding waters.

Far beyond the city, on the outskirts of London, Enu and Watson arrived at the bunker. Its imposing façade offered no comfort, and fear settled in her chest like a weight. Questions pressed against her mind. *If the Emars were the key to maintaining peace between humans and Modiri, why was the king still unwell? Where was the cure everyone whispered about?*

Watson swiped a badge she had never seen before, the scanner beeping approval as the gate lifted, revealing the roof parking lot. Moments later, they walked in silence, the distance stretching like a mile, until they reached a nondescript elevator. Once inside, Watson swiped the badge again, and the lift descended smoothly, carrying them down to the ground floor, deeper into the hidden heart of the bunker. Enu's pulse quickened with each floor they passed, her fear mingling with the anticipation of what awaited.

"Well, well, well. If it isn't my cunning little brother," Riko murmured. His tone began as teasing, almost playful, but hardened into something menacing. "I hope after all these moons, you've sharpened that little magic of yours."

As Riko advanced, Fanira's gaze stayed fixed on King Bao, silently pleading for reason. "…if this continues, your Kingdom will suffer more than it already has. It cannot thrive under one acetic alone."

"It was never meant to be—Toyleri…" King Bao began.

"Yes," Fanira cut in, her voice firm. "But she is gone. Traditions exist for a reason. They cannot be altered on a whim. What was, was. What shall be, shall be. You must stop him."

King Bao's eyes lingered on her, weighing each word carefully.

Riko's grey eyes narrowed. "Did you come here to slay me?" His voice was calm, unnervingly measured, but his presence radiated menace. The Ushu mirrored Naida in form, yet every ounce of his posture, his tone, and his intent was her opposite.

Slowly, King Ryūmon's right acetic moved to appear from within his kimono. Riko mirrored the motion, extending his own acetics with deliberate precision. His legs parted, feet pressing into the sandy ocean floor as he readied himself, muscles coiled, posture commanding. The ritual was familiar yet foreign, each movement carrying the weight of centuries, the tension of inevitability.

He was ready.

King Bao descended steadily through the water, carrying the authority of his realm. He had waited long enough; it was time to intervene.

King Ryūmon, eyes closed, began drawing upon his abolishment spell, the currents around him darkening with the weight of his power. But before the incantation could take form, Bao materialized, his presence cutting through the water like a blade.

The Ushu hovered not far behind, sleek and menacing, its stance primed for combat. A thin flick of its tongue traced over sharp teeth, an almost predatory anticipation gleaming in its eyes. It welcomed the coming clash.

"Kingdom Brother," Bao's voice carried clearly through the water, resonating in the vastness of the Makara Kingdom.

King Ryūmon opened his eyes slowly, brows knitting together, lips curling in a low growl. Shadows swirled behind him, whispering in tongues older than the seas, urging a single command: Move. Yet his lips did not part. Bao held his posture, unflinching.

"If you strike the Ushu," Bao warned, his tone cold, yet cautious, "you will strike the hybrid as well."

Shadows swirled and churned around the Makara King, black tendrils consuming the water with whispered commands that echoed from every corner: *Move*. Yet King Bao remained unshaken, immune to such feeble manipulations. He adjusted his conical hat, its polished surface catching the very faint shimmer of light that penetrated the depths, and fixed his gaze on his kingdom brother. "Enough of this," he intoned, his voice cutting through the current.

The shadows hissed in defiance, writhing with a will of their own. "It is my responsibility to purge these waters of the evil I have birthed," they murmured, voices layered and discordant.

"No," Bao countered, steady and resolute. "It is not your duty. The kingdoms we protect require obedience to the Ahalty to flourish, as they do in the North. Riko is now the responsibility of the hybrid."

"…And if trouble arises?"

"There will be none. I have conceded to train it," Bao replied, his tone carrying both certainty and a weight of foresight.

"Why, Kingdom Brother?" the shadows pressed, seeking to undermine his resolve.

Bao exhaled slowly, the current carrying the sound of his thoughtfulness. "I have seen the prophecy. The hybrid is the key to our elevation."

"He will kill it," the voice whispered, venomous and urgent.

Bao's eyes darkened, a silence stretching through the waters before he spoke. "He will not."

Fanira felt a rare sense of satisfaction, convinced her presence in the Makara Kingdom was no longer required. Yet she knew she could never remain physically close to the hybrid siblings in London. Retreating into a shadowed cave nearby, she let the darkness cloak her form, her mind reaching outward to scan the area around Buckingham Palace.

She searched tirelessly for any trace of a hybrid child, but the currents of magic offered nothing. Frustration flickered across her features as she redirected her focus to Eriph, only to find that the girl was not in London at all. She was somewhere distant, somewhere foreign, a place whose energy was faint and disorienting. Fanira's Mistos senses narrowed, her brows knitting in concentration.

Inside the pool, Esam emerged with a splash, water cascading relentlessly down his sculpted body. His effort to reach the witch had failed, leaving a sting of frustration in its wake. He hauled himself onto the edge of the pool, muscles trembling from exertion, and waited as the transformation reversed. Slowly, his Modiri form receded. In minutes, he shrank back into his human body, curled in a fetal position on the wet tiles, vulnerable and exhausted, every droplet of water glinting against his skin.

Beneath the surface of distant waters, Fanira's anger simmered. Eriph had ventured too far from London, slipping beyond the reach of her senses. The distance made communication impossible, and the lack of connection ignited a fierce urgency within her. With a powerful flick of her limbs, she cut through the currents, turning her path northward.

The Mistos's thoughts drifted restlessly as she cut through the sea. She once believed the God of the Shadows could be trusted, that he would not turn his malice toward the hybrid child. Yet much to her surprise, his hatred ran deeper than any allegiance to prophecy. His vengeance had no end; he would burn himself to ashes if it meant striking at those he despised.

The sea around her whispered of unrest. Schools of fish scattered at her passing, silver bodies flashing like shards of broken glass. The prophecy was meant to bind them together, to ensure balance.

Her heart pounded against the swell of the tide. If his fury could not be tempered, then neither the hybrid nor the kingdoms of the East would stand unscathed. Fanira's resolve hardened. She surged faster, her body breaking into the form of a sailfish, a blade of living light against the ocean's dark expanse.

Far behind her, King Bao pulsed with authority, his energy radiating like a beacon through the waters. Across from him, Riko—the Ushu warrior—stood poised in a stance of defiance, talons flexed and ready to rend. The sheer silk that once veiled it had vanished, leaving its tall frame unshrouded. Against the dark expanse of the deep, it was a living silhouette, carved in sharp relief by the faint glimmers of bioluminescence.

Its hair billowed around it like strands of black fire, caught in unseen currents. Its body was then clad in a second skin of armor, its surface black as obsidian yet traced with molten-gold veins across its chest and torso. The glowing accents shimmered like buried lava, lending it the aura of a warrior forged in both shadow and flame.

The Ushu's face remained half-hidden in darkness, but what the light revealed was unsettling in its allure: a slow, knowing smile that curved across its lips, and eyes that glowed with a predatory brightness. It radiated beauty and menace in equal measure, an apex hunter born of the abyss, entirely at home in its dominion.

"You will go to your Obi," King Bao said at last, his voice steady.

Across from him, King Ryūmon recoiled and thrust himself backward, departing in silence. The Ushu did not falter in strength, only in posture. Its defenses loosened.

The bunker was cold, a damp, unnecessary chill that clung to the skin. Enu shivered as they moved deeper into its concrete corridors. Watson walked with uncanny precision, his steps confident, his hand darting to panels and buttons as if he had memorized the layout long ago. The familiarity unsettled her, but she concealed it, her face an unreadable mask. She kept close enough not to draw suspicion, yet far enough to take in every detail of the space.

Doctor Astor's new office and the extraction room built for Penelope lay to the west of the complex. To reach them, they would have to cross the cafeteria and slip past several operating rooms. The air smelled faintly of antiseptic and something metallic, as if the walls themselves had absorbed years of blood and machinery.

"What goes on here?" she asked quietly, her pace matching his.

Before Watson could respond, the sharp chime of an elevator echoed down the hall. Doors parted, spilling chaos—boots striking hard against the floor, voices raised in panic. Enu and Watson froze as the commotion swept toward them. A young woman burst past, her hair damp with sweat, her movements frantic. Guards closed in behind her, their weapons ready, yet they seemed not to notice the two figures lingering beside them.

At the room's doorway, the woman halted, breath ragged. "We've located Experiment 002, Doctor," she said, her voice trembling. "He's been buried behind the building."

XVII.

LAY CLAIM

Her words ignited a commotion that swept through the bunker like a high tide, voices rising until Doctor Astor finally appeared. His gaze slid to Watson and Enu waiting in the hall.

Watson met his eyes with open contempt, irritation etched across his face, while Enu regarded him with quiet astonishment. The man looked frail, almost brittle, yet somehow he had engineered a system so intricate it rivaled the mind of a machine.

"We need to talk," Watson muttered, voice low and clipped.

"Of course," Astor replied. He gestured toward the grid room. "Go on ahead. I'll return shortly. The body requires examination." The words left him with a peculiar eagerness, as though the thought of cutting into Archie filled him with a perverse delight.

Watson and Enu stepped into the chamber. The other doctors glanced at them with disdain, their expressions sharp and unwelcoming, as though the pair had trespassed into a sanctum.

Enu began to pace, her eyes drawn not to the glowing screens or the extractor machines, but to the sphere at the room's center. Inside, Penelope drifted in suspension, serene as if caught in a dream. It had been years since Enu had laid eyes on an infant finned Modiri. Something inside her stilled. She moved forward, almost entranced, her steps carrying her closer and closer until a voice cut through the air.

"Stop!"

The command jolted her back to herself. She flinched, retreating a half step.

Watson hurried to her side. "What was that? Are you alright? This place is saturated with chemicals—watch what you touch."

Enu spun toward him, anger sharpening her voice.

"For the last time, Major, what is this place? What do they do here?"

Watson held her stare for a moment, weighing her fury against his duty. She meant well—he knew that much—and so he spoke, revealing only what he dared. He began with the memory of Sattle, the day his orders had come to track down Lady Mary.

"Lady Mary of Sambridge?" Enu interrupted, disbelief flickering in her tone. "A hybrid bloodline?"

"Correct," Watson answered, his voice flat.

He shifted into a stance of discipline, heels aligned, hands clasped tightly behind his back. His gaze never wavered as he studied the infant Modiri drifting in its chamber, suspended in calm ignorance of the fate already decided for it. The sight pressed against him, stirring the memory of the Queen's decree. His brows drew together.

"Did Her Majesty not order the termination of this creature?" he asked, his tone cutting into the silence.

The doctors stiffened. Their eyes darted from one to another, none brave enough to speak. The hush that followed carried more dread than words could.

Then the sound of a door sliding open broke it. Doctor Astor strode back inside, peeling off bloodstained gloves as if shedding a second skin. Without looking at anyone, he flung them into the disposal chute, the snap of latex against metal punctuating the air like a gunshot.

"Oh!" Astor brightened, a smile stretching thinly across his lips. "You've stayed. Good."

"Nothing is good," Watson snapped. "You've disobeyed Her Majesty—again!"

Astor's chuckle was low, dismissive. "Now, now. Don't be so quick to anger, Major. Fury will wear a man down." He circled Watson with a casual grace, drifting toward the great sphere. Beneath its pale glow, he knelt, retrieving seven slim vials from a plastic case sealed with rubber stoppers. Holding them aloft, he admired the liquid within as though it were treasure.

"These," he declared, pride swelling in his voice, "are the new and improved Lith. No large Ember this time— only a fragment—but enough. Hours upon hours of labor, and we have done it." His smile widened as though expecting applause.

Watson's face remained granite.

"The Queen's orders…"

"Her Majesty will be pleased when she learns of our success," Astor cut in, thrusting the vials closer to Watson's line of sight. "Do you not see? This is the cure. This is salvation."

Watson faltered, his stance loosening. "And what happens now?"

"Now," Astor said softly, savoring the word, "we see that it reaches His Majesty. That, Major, is where you come in."

"Me?"

"Yes. You will deliver these to the castle. Place them in the King's quarters. His servants must introduce the Lith into his IV twice a day. Before breakfast. Before supper. Without fail."

Watson recoiled, disbelief flashing in his eyes. "You ask me to betray the Queen's command?"

Astor leaned close, his voice sharpening. "No. I ask you to help restore our King."

Enu stood silent, her eyes darting frantically between the two men, as if the air itself might shatter from their clash.

Watson remained frozen for a moment, caught between duty and conviction. He could neither fully agree nor outright refuse Astor's request. Delivering the Lith was exactly what their mission had called for, what they had anticipated all along. To ignore this moment would be to betray the King and his reign. Yet a quiet vindication stirred within him as he remembered the Queen's earlier orders—she had finally glimpsed what he had warned her of years before. He had tried to prepare her, to guide her, but his words had fallen short.

His gaze drifted to the vials, each one glinting faintly in the harsh fluorescent light. He pictured the King, restored, strong, the corridors alive once more with his voice issuing commands that shaped their great country. A flicker of hope surged through him, mingled with the weight of responsibility pressing against his chest.

At the rear of the room, Doctor Astor leaned over his surveillance screens, eyes scanning every camera feed with meticulous precision. He muttered to himself, hunting the figure he blamed for Archie's escape. The room's tension thickened, pressing against Watson from every angle.

Enu fumbled for her phone, fingers trembling as she tried to reach Esam, only to find the signal dead. Static silence swallowed her attempts. Her worry sharpened, crawling through her veins like icy water.

Then, almost imperceptibly at first, the sphere shivered. A thin line of fracture crept along the glass, jagged and delicate. Penelope stirred within, her fin trembling, eyes fluttering open. A subtle, eerie light from inside the sphere cast dancing reflections across the walls, illuminating the room in fractured patterns. Time slowed as Watson, Enu, and Astor each registered the small but monumental sign: the Modiri was waking.

Watson's hand clenched at his side, muscles taut, as he watched the hairline crack spiderweb across the glass. Doctor Astor lingered behind them, his expression unreadable, but there was a flicker of something darker—anticipation, hunger, perhaps. The room held its silence, broken only by the faint drip of condensation from the ceiling, until Penelope moved again, this time more purposeful, pushing against the water, testing the boundaries of her confinement.

*

The Nwala Kingdom lay hidden beneath the English Channel, a secret realm only miles from the French coast. Its beauty was painstaking, unnaturally so, as though the ocean itself had sculpted a dream into stone and water. Gardens of coral and seaweed stretched across the seafloor, swaying with the current like dancers in a shadowed ballroom. Jagged cliffs and coral-crusted ridges rose sharply, alive with darting schools of fish that glittered before vanishing into dark crevices.

At the kingdom's heart, an impossible waterfall poured upward—a cascade of bubbles spiraling endlessly toward the surface. Light fractured across the streams, scattering in a thousand glinting threads that lit the gardens and rocky spires like trails of liquid fire. Pastel-hued rivers wound through the terrain, their currents carrying plankton that shimmered like drifting stardust.

Above the falls, a soft mist curled into the water, blending with suspended sediment. Sunlight filtered down in broken beams, striking the haze and scattering into shifting rays that danced across the landscape. Towering rock formations crowned the horizon, their weathered surfaces teeming with marine life. Some loomed like statues—ancient guardians of the realm—while others stretched upward like coral towers, their spires reaching for the faraway surface.

Every current, every shifting light, carried intention, as if the sea itself were breathing life into its masterpiece. Normally, the Nwala Kingdom was not merely a place but a living panorama, a sanctuary of motion and gaudy color suspended in the deep—its brilliance bordering on excess, yet impossible to dismiss—where beauty cloaked a sly power, one easy to overlook beneath faces that resembled children, innocent only at first glance.

But this day was different.

The Philosophers Queen, Leucothea, was never one to question the commands of the High Sea Gods. She carried out their orders with precision, swift and unquestioning. Yet the peculiar life of this hybrid stirred something within her, a curiosity that surpassed duty.

As the little Lorelies and Mosquens released Melusine into the kingdom, she struck. In an instant, with shocking speed and precision, she seized the hybrid, her movements sharp and painful. Unlike her kingdom brothers and sisters, Leucothea bore a strikingly distinct presence. There was a subtle menace in her posture, a cunning in her gaze. Her skin was a warm caramel beige, her monolid-shaped eyes deep indigo, glimmering with intelligence and cruelty.

Yet what unsettled observers most was her form. She resembled a child, barely five feet tall, with a slender frame that belied her true strength. From her shoulder blades sprouted wings of delicate, intricate design, the kind that made her appear almost angelic. Dark blonde hair framed her face, and her fin shimmered a bold rouge, dotted with peach-colored gemstones that stole the light with every slight movement.

Her brasloor, ornate and strapless, accentuated her lithe form, leaving nothing to hint at the power coiled beneath. She did not look dangerous. That was the most terrifying truth of all. Every element of her appearance— the small stature, the gentle wings, the vibrant fin— masked a lethal cunning. Leucothea was beauty and menace intertwined, a predator disguised as a youngster, and the waters themselves seemed to withdraw in apprehension at her presence.

The only Queen to rule her kingdom without a mate, Leucothea carried magnificence in every movement, every glance. Her scales shimmered with a rare fusion of Mosquen and Lorelie, a testament to her lineage, and her Lamina Garden flourished effortlessly under her care, producing offspring for the kingdom without challenge.

Her royal chambers were a marvel—an entire mini-city suspended beneath the waves, hovering above cloud-like formations that stretched endlessly below. The stone beneath it was sharp as a needle, a lethal foundation that she could command to crush anything on the seabed beneath her, should she wish. The space was open, exposed to scrutiny, yet no one dared traverse it without her leave.

Melusine could feel the weight of Leucothea's arm coiled tightly around her throat, each second pressing the air from her lungs. With a sudden, violent motion, she was thrust into the heart of the Royal Chamber. Darkness swallowed her, broken only by the glint of the Queen's fangs. Melusine's shoulders were pierced by Leucothea's wings, each puncture driving a spurt of deep, mahogany-colored blood into the water, staining the chamber with slow, spreading streaks.

Leucothea moved with unhurried precision, drinking every drop as Melusine screamed for mercy, her cries echoing and reverberating through the suspended city. The chamber itself seemed alive with the tension, the water thickening with the scent of blood and the raw, merciless dominance of the Queen.

The Philosophers circled the edges of the chamber, their eyes alight with anticipation, each waiting for the moment they might tear Melusine apart, limb by limb. The hybrid trembled violently, her screams echoing and rebounding against the suspended structures above, until the effort and fear finally drained her. Her body slumped, collapsing into unconsciousness, her teenage form trembling even in stillness.

Leucothea did not pause. The sound of her fangs tearing through flesh, the wet, unforgiving slurps, filled the water, relentless and adamant. She sank her talons into Melusine with brutal force, holding the young girl's skin in a vice-like grip to prevent the regenerative shimmer from sparking to life.

The water around them darkened as Melusine's fin beat sluggishly at first, then weaker, until it ceased altogether. Silence fell, heavy and suffocating, broken only by the Queen's methodical, almost ritualistic consumption, and the quiet, ecstatic murmur of the chamber's witnesses.

The London rain fell in uninterrupted sheets as Priya turned the key to the Prime Minister's office, each droplet hammering the streets outside with a muted fury. Relief washed over her for a moment—no protestors in sight—but it faded the instant she stepped inside. The office lay in ghostly silence. Computers hummed quietly, phones sat like forgotten relics, and stacks of papers teetered precariously across every desk, waiting for attention that would not come.

Frustration tightened her jaw, warmth rising in her cheeks as she shook her umbrella violently, letting the water sluice into the bin by the door. She shrugged off her raincoat and hung it neatly nearby, the damp fabric still carrying the scent of wet pavement. Fingers trailing through her hair, she straightened a stray strand, trying to impose order on the chaos around her.

Her hands moved rapidly over the phone keyboard, firing off emails to staff and interns, demanding explanations for their absence. The soft clatter of her shoes against the polished floor sounded unnervingly loud in the empty space. The faint scent of coffee lingered, mingling with the damp, earthy odor of rain seeping in through the doorframe.

As she paced, a subtle shuffle at the rear of the office made her freeze. The sound was tentative, almost apologetic, but it was there—a presence, alive and breathing, moving cautiously behind another door. Her pulse quickened. The echo of rain against the windows, the hum of the computers, even the drip of her umbrella seemed amplified in the stillness. Every instinct urged her to turn, to confront the intruder, yet she lingered, straining to hear over the symphony of the storm.

"Sir, Prime Minister," Priya called, her voice low but edged with tension. Inside, she prayed it was him; outside, her instincts warned her to bolt if it was not. The grunting grew louder with each step she took, her phone tucked hurriedly into her pant pocket as she approached the rear of the hall.

She paused, hand hovering over the door, took a steadying breath, and knocked. Slowly, she pushed it open. There he was—slumped on the floor in a pair of white knickers, his posture slumped, utterly unguarded. The sight made her recoil, an involuntary shiver running down her spine.

"Oh, for heaven's sake. Gather yourself!" she snapped, voice carrying a mixture of exasperation and command. Her gaze darted to the corners of the room, hands raised instinctively as if to shield herself from further chaos.

Benson Sr. shifted unsteadily, the remnants of a late-night drunken escapade dragging at his movements. He fumbled for his garments, eyes squinting as he located an oversized shirt. Socks and suspenders clung awkwardly to him as he finally stumbled behind his desk, trying in vain to reclaim some shred of composure.

"I'm fine," he grumbled, his words low and ragged, more an excuse to himself than to her.

Priya lowered her arms, planting her feet firmly. She needed to anchor herself against his inertia. "You are not fine! This—this is not fine! It is irresponsible at best and negligent at worst. You are the Prime Minister of this country. The people are demanding answers. The staff here needs a leader besides me. And, to be honest, your son needs a proper scolding. He just up and quit!"

Benson Sr. listened—or as much as he could muster—fingers interlaced, his eyes glazing as though the very thought of water might be more interesting than her words.

He grunted. "Quit then."

"I beg your pardon?"

"Not because you're incompetent," he said slowly, deliberately, "but because I am."

Priya's eyes narrowed, sharp and scolding. "I need you to tell me exactly what is going on here. Every detail."

Benson Sr. tilted his head, drew a long, weary sigh, and admitted, "The King is unwell."

Priya pressed further, leaning forward. "And…?"

"And… he needed an Ember," he replied, voice heavy, almost reluctant.

"And!" Priya nearly shouted, her pulse quickening.

"I volunteered my child," he said, arms flailing in frustration, "to wed an alien… to get the King his… Ember."

Priya blinked, disbelief and shock rippling across her face. "I don't understand. An alien? An Ember? What…? You owe me more than this explanation." Her voice sharpened, commanding clarity. She was done being left in the dark.

"The Lith," he began, his tone measured now, "it comes from the Embers that the finned Modiri supply. Without them…"

Priya cut in, incredulous. "Lith? We have none left?"

"No. It's been this way for years," he said, shrugging as if shrugging could erase the years of shortage.

Her eyes widened, the weight of realization settling. "So, citizens have had no access to Lith this whole time?"

Benson Sr. offered a half-hearted shrug, the faintest trace of guilt—or perhaps apathy—etching his features.

"No, no, no! You don't get to do that," Priya's voice cracked, sharp and insistent, echoing off the cold walls of the office. "I need an answer. What is going on? Where has all the tax sterling gone?"

Benson Sr. shrugged again, a motion so slight it seemed almost automatic. His thin lips pressed together, and his eyes, heavy and half-lidded, betrayed exhaustion— or indifference, Priya couldn't tell which. He looked every bit the man who had spent too many nights lost to drink and lethargy.

"Prime Minister, get a hold of yourself!" she snapped, her hands clenching at her sides. "The people need answers. What is happening?"

He exhaled slowly, as if weighing each word against some invisible ledger of conscience. "Her Majesty... she has been running the country without disclosure. Modiri Mountain stopped producing Embers, and the medicine—the Lith—is no longer being made."

"Just like that?" Priya's voice rose, disbelief cutting through the room. "How? How was there nothing in reserve?"

Benson Sr. shrugged once more, a hollow gesture devoid of guidance or explanation. He truly did not know. Though he and King Eldric had maintained a professional relationship, much of the king's intentions, his methods, and his actions had never been shared. "King Eldric holds all the answers," he said finally, voice low, almost a whisper. "And right now... whether we like it or not, his best days are behind him and his future days are numbered."

Priya recoiled, her voice trembling with disbelief. "Lies. We were told—administrators, officers—all of us told that he was improving. That Lith was being administered daily, that he would return any day. A mere cold. That we only had to hold on. The citizens... they would never need to know. Are you saying… none of that was true?"

Benson Sr. leaned back, eyes heavy, letting the weight of her words settle in the room like smoke. "Amer will ascend the throne. Soon." He drew another long, deliberate sigh before fishing the morning paper from the bottom drawer, squinting with one eye to read clearly.

"In the meantime," he said, letting the paper land with a soft thud that echoed louder than it should have in the silence, "my son, who now goes by, Noah Chambers, is challenging me for the role."

Priya's breath caught. Her fingers clenched at the edge of the desk, knuckles whitening as she stared at the page. Noah's photo glared back at her, bold letters beneath it declaring: **NOAH CHAMBERS**. Campaign promises, intentions to run for Prime Minister—each word a dagger twisting deeper into her disbelief.

The office seemed to shrink around her, and she could almost feel the weight of the city's eyes, the trust of every citizen, and the lies that had shrouded them all, settling like a shroud in the room.

Her mind raced. How had she been so blind? Every calculated move, every directive she had followed without question, now seemed meaningless.

Priya felt betrayed. Yet, she would need to make a choice; a tangible force demanding allegiance. On one side stood the young, ambitious politician, sharp and purposeful, a symbol of change and promise. On the other hand, the inebriated, sloppy, and careless figure of Benson Sr., the very face of a government she had long learned to fear and despise. Her stomach twisted with frustration and uncertainty.

She stepped back, giving him enough room to slump deeper into his chair. His eyelids fluttered, then closed, the sound of his snores filling the office like a persistent drum. Each rasp grated against her nerves, scraping raw her patience and sense of propriety. Her fingers tightened around the paper, crumpling the edges ever so slightly. The burden of truth and responsibility was nearly unbearable.

She turned away, closing the office door behind her with a muted click, the echo swallowing the stench of alcohol and neglect that clung to the room. In the main room, she paused, letting the faint hum of the empty office settle around her, before spreading the paper open across a vacant desk. Her eyes scanned every line, every image, eager to unravel the story, desperate to understand the implications and the path that would demand her loyalty. Outside, the city carried on, oblivious to the quiet rage inside its walls.

By noon, the dining table was buried beneath scattered papers. A second cup of coffee brewed in the corner, its steam curling into the air, while the scent of waffles and fresh apple juice lingered in the cottage. The Equal Species had gathered once again in the little village, their curiosity far outweighing their hunger.

Piper and Alice, brimming with excitement, recounted their encounter with Melissa to Willow and Preston, who exchanged doubtful glances. To them, it sounded like something pulled from a children's film— too fanciful to be real. Yet Alice refused to let their skepticism silence her. Her passion, once dulled, now flickered back to life, bringing a glow of joy to her expression.

Linus sat apart from the others, quietly brooding over his phone. He had already decided he wouldn't return to work—not for a while. The thought of explaining his sudden absence to his employers no longer bothered him. He had enough saved to rent a modest flat in Oxford, should the need arise.

Alice paced the length of the room, her voice quickening as she relived the moment.

"You both should have seen it! She was beautiful. We hear about sirens on the telly, but nothing compares to seeing one in person. Her eyes changed, her skin shifted, bronzed… she became someone else—something else— right in front of us. She wasn't ordinary. She wasn't even human."

Piper nodded eagerly. "It was incredible!"

At the kitchen threshold, Willow and Preston lingered, arms crossed. Their eyes drifted to Linus, still absorbed in the unsent email on his screen.

"If you're going to do it, just do it," Willow said, her tone firm but not unkind.

"We'll be fine," Alice added softly.

Linus drew a breath, pressed send, and shut the phone with finality. Clapping his hands, he looked up at the group, a fresh resolve sparking in his eyes.

"Alright," he said. "What do we know?"

Everyone sat in a thick silence until Willow finally moved. She leaned over the table, her fingers sifting through the scattered sheets until she found the article she was searching for. The headline glared back at her: a sharp increase in hover mobiles, paired with yet another tax hike. Her brow furrowed as she scanned the words.

"Who's behind this?" she muttered, almost to herself. "We're already being squeezed dry."

Alice leaned forward, her voice edged with bitterness. "It's never enough for them. They keep taking more, and now they're rewriting the rules on our medical insurance. Denials are about to skyrocket."

Across the table, Piper's eyes caught on something else—a small, easily overlooked advertisement nestled in the corner of the page. She stilled. It was the same one Priya had seen earlier that day.

"Hey…" Piper whispered, drawing the others' attention. Her fingertip pressed against the grainy image of a young man. "He looks painfully familiar. Though the name doesn't ring a bell. Does anyone know who this is?"

The name beneath the photo read Noah Chambers. Everyone leaned in, confusion spreading across their faces. No one answered.

"Well, it's an ad for a campaign manager," Linus muttered, holding the crumpled page as though it might disintegrate in his hands. "Strangest thing I've ever seen. Never heard of some half-baked political posting like this. Must be from a commoner. Either way, he's aiming for a governor's chair."

Alice drifted closer. She plucked the ad from his grip and studied it, her brow arching. "Odd is an understatement. Announcements like this don't just appear out of thin air. Something's off."

While the others crowded around, Willow slipped into a chair at the edge of the room, her laptop already open. Fingers moved swiftly over the keys, curiosity pushing her faster. Within seconds, the screen flooded with headlines, articles, and official statements. Her eyes widened. "He's the Prime Minister's son…" Her voice trailed off before she looked up, astonished. "But he's just begun using this name. A press release went out only days ago. I don't understand. Is he actually planning to challenge his father for the seat?"

Alice let out a low laugh, her lips curling with amusement. "That would be absurd."

"Would it?" Willow pressed. Her tone had sharpened, but beneath it was an undeniable note of excitement. "Think about what's happening—the strikes, the scandals, the economic hikes. Maybe he's seen something, heard something, that made him decide to step in. Maybe he wants to be the one to change it."

Alice shook her head. "You think the Prime Minister's son is some righteous leader in the making? I doubt it."

"Righteous?" Willow's eyes glimmered as she leaned back in her chair. "Perhaps not. But we won't know until we find out."

The group exchanged uneasy glances before Linus finally asked, "And what exactly are you proposing?"

Willow snapped the laptop shut with quiet resolve. "I'll apply for the position. If he's really behind this, I can learn more from the inside."

"That's my girl," Piper said, her sarcasm cutting through the air. Then, with a grin, "No, seriously—she's always the first to throw herself into the fire for us."

Preston, who had been silent until now, shifted forward. Concern etched his face. "What if it's not safe?"

For a moment, Willow hesitated, her gaze lowering to him. She admired Preston more than she often admitted—even to herself—and the softness in his question stirred something unspoken between them. She offered a small, almost shy smile. "I'll be fine," she said quietly.

It was discreet at first—her feelings for Preston. A passing glance here, a lingering thought there, until they threaded themselves into the fabric of her days. Willow never dared to voice it; words seemed too fragile, too dangerous, to hold something so delicate. Yet Preston knew. He carried the knowledge in the spaces between their conversations, in the way his eyes lingered a fraction too long.

It wasn't fear that kept him from addressing it, not exactly. It was the uncertainty of what she might say if pressed. Their bond had never been spoken of, only felt, and to name it aloud risked shattering the balance they both quietly nurtured.

"Well," Preston said, breaking the tension with an easy calm, "if you need a ride to the flat for the interview, I'll be happy to take you. Just say when."

He rose from his chair, moving with a purposeful stride toward the staircase, his hand brushing against the banister as he disappeared.

"You two are insufferable," Alice teased, her voice low, almost a whisper. Willow flushed and looked away.

"Stop it, Alice," she muttered, though the faint smile tugging at her lips betrayed her.

As the day unfolded, plans were made. Max, however, remained distant. He had retreated home, locked in the quiet sorrow of his brother's death. The grief had taken time to sink in, but now that it had, it pressed heavily against him. The thought of company was unfathomable. He needed silence. He needed space. However, Noah Chambers, unaware of the storm gathering around him, would soon hear from Willow Weathers.

Far from their small circle of lives, the sea stretched endlessly beneath the late-morning sun. A restless blue sheet, it shimmered as though dusted with molten light. Along the English Channel, waves curled and whispered against the southern coast before sweeping outward, carrying their pulse northward. The waters deepened with each mile—green shifting to sapphire, sapphire to indigo—until the swells rolled dark and glassy, catching the light in sharp, jeweled fragments.

By the time the ocean reached the Arctic, the rhythm shifted. With the seasons changing, the sea no longer whispered; it roared. Waves struck with jagged force, their crests flinging high before collapsing in curtains of mist. Against this backdrop lay the Snow Kingdom, its surface scattered with sharp fields of ice that gleamed with charm, joy spreading like sunlight across a frozen plain. Yet behind the pastel shimmer of its beauty, a quieter presence lingered—something shadowed, waiting.

Kaliope and her sisters played across the ice, their laughter ringing bright above the churning sea. They chased one another in a game of Arctic Dash, their movements swift, mirrored in every ripple of water below. Seraldine, no longer the child she once was, moved with a new grace. Her hair, once loose, now hung in small plaits that had begun to knot into long ropes, adorned with seashells she had collected along the seabed. They brushed against the lower part of her fin when she moved, swaying like pendants of the sea itself. Her beauty was striking, her gaze low and steady—eyes that seemed to pull others in, hypnotic and unblinking.

"You're not playing fair!" the youngest Lorelie cried, tears streaking her cheeks as Kaliope once again triumphed with ease. The little one's protests only widened her elder sister's smile, a playful tease hidden in her expression as she secured yet another victory.

Kaliope looked unchanged by the passage of years. The flower from Kalkisis still nestled in her hair, its petals vivid against her dark tresses, lending her an aura of radiance. She glowed—more than a healer, she had become a symbol of hope for those around her, a quiet pride that carried through every gesture.

King Khione adored all of his children. Yet their mother, Rudita, remained curiously detached, her indifference echoing through the halls of the kingdom. Too often the Lorelies and Mosquens drifted into distant corners of the realm, seeking refuge far from the Lamina Garden, where the hush of faint suckling and swaying petals was never enough to mask the sound of Rudita's cries.

Though Kaliope never let bitterness take root, there lingered a subtle sting in her heart—a quiet sense of betrayal, as if their kingdom were never enough for their mother. She never spoke of it, but in her silence she bore a responsibility that was not hers to carry. Shielding her siblings from the sting of abandonment had become her calling, one she upheld with dignity and devotion, even when it pressed heavily on her spirit.

"I'll let you all win this time," Kaliope teased, her voice carrying like a song across the cold expanse. The water shimmered around her as her fin unfurled in a graceful sweep, scattering ribbons of light through the crystalline blue. Her laughter mingled with the rippling currents, a moment of warmth against the vast, unending sea.

But the joy faltered. A sudden sting tore into her ear, sharp and merciless, slicing through her playfulness like a hidden blade. The pain surged—piercing, unfamiliar—until her smile collapsed, replaced by a trembling gasp. Her cries broke loose, raw and ragged, a sound so strange that it startled those nearby.

The younger Lorelies darted to her side, fins flashing with urgency. One of them, eyes wide with worry, whispered, "Are you alright, sister?"

Kaliope could not answer. Her throat caught against the cry, her body seized with the ache. Pressing her acetics hard against her ears, she tried to muffle the noise that clawed at her from within. It was no use. The sound pressed deeper, gnawing without mercy, drowning her in its persistence.

Desperate, she spun in the water, driving herself downward, her fin slicing through the depths. The light dimmed as she plunged, fleeing toward the sanctuary of the healing chamber carved into the bedrock of the kingdom. Shadows bent and curled around her, but she did not pause. Somewhere within that chamber lay the answers, and she knew she would not find peace until she uncovered them.

Within the royal chambers, King Khione busied himself with a pastime that few would expect of a ruler—coral crafting. The chamber smelled faintly of brine and polished shell, its shelves lined with delicate pieces he had shaped with his sharp talons: spirals, blades, and miniature beasts, all frozen in their moment of creation. At the center of the room, he bent low over his work, acetics steady as he carved a shard of coral into the likeness of a sword, meant to be placed in the grip of one of his ice-bound figurines.

The gate shuddered open, and Rudita slid into the chamber, her presence cutting through the quiet. Her eyes glimmered with disdain, sharp and merciless.

"You are no King," she hissed, her voice low.

Khione did not look up. He had grown accustomed to her venom, so much so that her words no longer pierced the way they once had. It was not indifference that kept him silent, but an understanding: reason was not what she sought. She wanted an adversary, a surface on which to cast her fury, and he allowed himself to be that surface. Better him than their offspring, whose loyalty and stability could not afford to fracture.

The coral flaked softly under his left acetic. He turned the piece, refining the edge of the blade, as though her words were nothing more than distant waves against stone.

"Do you hear me?" Rudita's voice cut through the quiet of the chamber as she circled him, her movements cautious, like a predator sizing up its quarry. "You are no

King. No true ruler would leave his waters without an Iris. Yet you care nothing for my despair, nothing for the longing that burns in me—for the one thing you ripped from me!" Her cry rang against the coral walls, sharp as a breaking shell.

Khione did not look up.

His task demanded patience, control. Even the smallest slip of his strength would shatter it.

"Why?" Rudita pressed, her tone fraying. "Why do you hate me so?"

"I do not hate you," he answered evenly.

The words stunned her. For a moment, silence hovered between them. She faltered, torn between swallowing her fury or pressing on, desperate for another reply.

"With no Iris daughter, we will never be honored," she finally declared, her voice trembling with defiance. "The High Sea Gods will not appoint us. Without her, our kingdom will remain beneath all others."

"Beneath whom?" Khione's gaze lifted at last, his eyes cool as winter seas. "What matters is strength. Loyalty. That we already hold."

He set the coral aside, its half-formed edge glinting faintly in the dim light. "The Periculum and the Snows are without adversaries. No one dares challenge us. Not the South and, even the Western Modiri are no threat—they bury themselves in cowardice and call it survival. The hybrids and the land finned, as I've heard it, are gone, their legends kept alive only by the Mistos and Western storytellers who peddle myths to whoever will listen.

Respect," he said, leaning forward, "is a hollow prize. Power is not."

Kaliope withdrew into her healing chamber, desperate for relief from the strange discomfort gnawing at her. The chamber's stillness pressed close, broken only by the low purr of the center orb. As she approached, the piercing ringing in her ear softened, as though the sphere itself drank the sound away.

She set her acetics atop the massive globe, its surface pulsing faintly with light. The moment her skin brushed its energy, a vision burst through her mind with such force she flinched backward. Terror clawed at her chest. What she had seen lingered like a shadow too vast to name—something foreign, something that reeked of a darkness she had never known.

Her fin carried her swiftly from the chamber, heart hammering so violently it drowned her thoughts. Fear, dread, disbelief—emotions collided within her until she could hardly tell them apart. She needed her King. Only he might understand, only he could act. Clutching to that hope, she fled toward the royal chambers, whispering silent prayers that her warning would not go unheard.

Inside, Rudita floated before King Khione, her gaze hollow, her voice stripped of fight. He lay motionless, acetics resting idly on his coral craft, the figure of a ruler who had long since laid down his fin.

"You've changed. You will never venture to the Lamina Garden… will you?" Rudita's words fell heavy, more resignation than accusation.

Khione gave no answer. His silence was not born of ignorance; he understood the gravity of what was at stake—the birthright of an Iris daughter, the balance of their kingdom. But fear bound him, colder than any ice he could conjure. Fear of judgment, of the laws that forbade leniency toward the Lady of the Snows. To defy them was not seen as mercy, but betrayal. And so he remained still, the weight of duty and fear pressing down upon him, while the kingdom's fate trembled in the silence between them.

The tension that had settled in the royal chambers shattered the moment Kaliope entered the long hallway. Her presence was a subtle wave of authority and warmth, sensed immediately by both Rudita and King Khione. The Snows themselves seemed to part, allowing her passage as though acknowledging her quiet command. Khione did not rise to meet her; he remained sprawled across the royal floor, his head turned toward the entrance, an acetic resting gently along his jawline, holding his chin aloft with unforced dignity.

Rudita's eyes widened, her nostrils flaring as the faint scent of Kaliope's healing aura filled the air. A wave of revulsion passed over her; she recoiled instinctively, hissing under her breath. The sight of the young Lorelie—so radiant, so calm—offended her senses. She had no wish to see the girl, let alone claim her as anything resembling kin.

Kaliope's fin cut gracefully through the water as she approached, her gaze falling first on her father, languid yet commanding, and then on Rudita. It was Rudita's eyes that unnerved her most, sharp and rigid, brimming with scorn.

"Come, come, my daughter. Do not be afraid," King Khione called softly, motioning to her with a slow wave of his acetic.

"I-I come with a request… Father…" Kaliope stammered, her voice betraying the urgency in her heart. Rudita's stare seemed to intimidate her.

"What is it, my dear?" Khione's voice was patient, gentle, like sunlight on still water.

"It is the hybrid, Melusine," Kaliope whispered. At the name, Rudita flinched violently, fins whipping the water into rippling waves as she vanished from the chamber in a flurry of indignant motion. Her shrill cries echoed faintly down the halls, sharp as glass. She would not hear of any hybrids.

"Do not mind her… your Kingdom Mother… is… well…" Khione's voice trailed off, wary of Rudita's wrath.

"Father…" Kaliope pressed, her tone urgent, her fins slicing the water in measured, careful strokes.

"What do we care for the hybrid? She fled, did she not?" Khione asked, his words heavy with detached authority.

"Yes, Father. They were only girls… and now… it is Queen Leucothea. She is mutilating her… I beg you, Father, intervene!" Kaliope descended closer, her fin brushing solemnly against the current, her body tense with fear for the child's life.

Khione's expression remained stoic, his deep, resonant fin flapping with a slow, unstoppable rhythm, a wall of calm resolve. "And so… my Kingdom Sister follows the orders of our Sea God, Poseidon. I will not interfere." His tone was flat, final, the weight of the ocean itself behind his refusal.

"No, Father, please! I beg you! She is only a child… please!" Kaliope's voice trembled, carrying both desperation and defiance.

Khione's gaze softened, the faintest flicker of warmth reaching his eyes. All his children stirred a deep affection in him, but Kaliope—she was the Lorelie whose wishes he could never deny.

"Must we lay claim?" he murmured, a question more to himself than to her.

Her eyes blazed with hope. She pressed her acetics gently against his, her expression sorrowful, raw in a way that tore through the stoicism he had cultivated over decades.

"Fine," he said finally. The word slow and thoughtful, carrying the weight of both leadership and reluctant surrender. Khione's voice resonated calmly throughout the royal chamber: "Deimos."

The Snow entered almost instantly, moving with a predator's precision. Kaliope pressed herself closer to her father, seeking safety behind his powerful frame. The Snows were imposing, towering figures whose presence alone seemed to bend the water around them. Some wore intricate armor across their chests, forearms sheathed in gold-plated guards that gleamed beneath the filtered light, the metal offset by the deep black of flowing silk. Their fins, sharp and powerful, moved with a blend of gold and white, evidence of both training status and heritage.

Others, Khione's elite guards who wielded the magic of his trident, shimmered in dark denim tones flecked with sapphire-colored gemstones, their movements fluid yet deadly. Deimos, the king's right hand and trainer of the

Snows, was a figure who commanded awe when he glided into a space. His hair defied gravity, swept high, dark as midnight waves, and his skin glowed like melted dark chocolate under the chamber lights. He radiated power— not just in appearance, but in the raw, lethal precision that seemed to trail his every motion. Handsome, yes, but deadly in equal measure.

Khione's eyes did not waver from his daughter, following the gentle arcs of her fin as she slipped quietly to his rear, hidden in his shadow. The silence stretched, taut as a drawn net, until the king finally spoke: "Venture to the Nwala Kingdom. Lay claim to the hybrid, Melusine. Bring her here."

The charge was simple, yet absolute, carrying the authority of the ocean itself. Deimos inclined his head, a faint, satisfied smile curling at the edge of his lips. There was no hesitation in his movements—obedience flowed from him as naturally as the tides, and he would carry out the king's will with ruthless efficiency.

XVIII.

VENGEANCE

The journey was far from gentle. The Modiri moved with a speed that defied nature, slicing through the water at nearly ninety miles per hour without the aid of magic. Waves erupted around him, frothing and sparkling as Deimos finned with powerful accuracy, his body undulating like a dolphin cutting through currents. At times he rode beside them, spear in hand, a living shadow of lethal intent as he pressed toward Queen Leucothea's domain.

Elsewhere, Naida could not remain still. Her body trembled with urgency, a tug-of-war between instinct and restraint. Her sister was in danger, and every fiber of her being screamed to dive into the chaos, to intervene. But beneath that desperate drive, something darker stirred. Riko, the Ushu, waited within the depths of her subconscious, a silent sentinel with impossible strength. He would not allow her passage.

The water around her seemed to thicken, resistance coiling like a living thing, and Naida's mind fought a bitter war. She could almost hear the echo of her sister's struggle, feel it reverberate through her very bones. Naida had always been haunted by visions, though in her youth they came as wonders rather than burdens. As a child, she carried within her an imagination so wild it felt endless, shaping dreams that lifted her beyond the confines of the waking world. Night after night, she returned to a secret place: a field of flowers that seemed to float in the sky, suspended above everything and untouched by time. There she could wander freely, the air sweet with impossible blooms, the horizon stretching forever into a vast and endless blue.

Sometimes she would creep to the field's edge, peering down at the world far below. The people seemed like shadows in motion, lives so small and distant compared to the expanse of her dreamscape. She was not merely a visitor there; she was its maker, the architect of every petal, every cloud, every curve of light. It was her creation, her sanctuary, a place she guarded with the fierce possessiveness only a child could hold.

Bedtime was never a punishment for her, nor was naptime. They were invitations, a passageway back into the realm she built with her imagination. She longed for sleep, knowing it meant stepping once again into the world of her design. When dreams were interrupted, it stirred a fury in her chest, an ache to return, to reclaim the fragments she had left unfinished.

But as the years pressed forward, something changed. The field began to wither, its edges fraying as though torn by unseen hands. No matter how she tried, Naida could no longer shape the world as she once had. The visions slipped from her grasp, growing faint, elusive. What had once been her private kingdom now seemed beyond her reach, and the loss unsettled her in ways she could not name.

For the first time, a deep fear took root. Without the power to design her escape, she felt the encroaching presence of a life she had not chosen. A life not sculpted by her creativity but imposed upon her. The terror of being bound to it—trapped in a reality where her hand had no sway—lingered in the corners of her mind, heavier than any nightmare.

The young hybrid returned to that hidden place, hoping—foolishly—to glimpse her parents. Their faces, once vivid, now dissolved at the edges, thinning into the haze of her subconscious. Something darker pressed into the space they left behind, eager to take root.

Riko lingered there as well, restless and resentful. He despised the bond to Naida, his Obi. She was the vessel; he was only the shadow that clung to her spirit. What seemed harmless in theory proved suffocating in practice, like sharing a body with another mind that stretched thought too far and sharpened it to pain.

Among the Modiri, the mind burned within its limits. An Ushu pushed beyond them, trading endurance for speed and instinct. Riko had never crossed blades with his brother, yet his hold on Naida drained her all the same, pulling her trance down into heavy sleep. He entered it without resistance.

Inside her dream, he found her standing in the field she had designed as a child, a sanctuary where blossoms once crowned the air. Now darkness smothered every petal. The place had become a grave—not of earth, but of memory—where her parents lay beyond reach, sealed in the silence she could no longer break.

Naida did not turn to face him. She remained still, her gaze fixed on the emptiness around her. Her hair billowed in the unseen current, and her storm-grey eyes glistened as the silhouette of Riko studied her with unrelenting intent.

"I need to go to my sister," she said quietly.

Riko hissed, his voice sharp and serpentine. "No."

Naida could not fathom Riko, nor the Ushu, nor the unsettling presence that lived within her body. Yet she felt his pull—the way his power slid over her choices, shaping her will as though it were clay in his grasp. She longed for Melusine; she could feel her even now. Blood-curdling screams echoed through Naida's core, each cry rattling her bones and making her body tremble. But unlike before, Riko did not yield. His refusal was not merely disobedience. It was something colder, a disinterest born of loathing for the very form she carried—the Obi he found repulsive.

When Naida finally turned to face him, it was like looking into a mirror warped by shadows. A reflection of herself, but darker, more sinister. He wore her body's outline—her arms, her legs, her hair, her eyes—but his skin was black as obsidian, encased in armor she had never seen nor imagined. Even she recoiled at the sight. And when he spoke again, the voice was not her own. That, above all, made the air turn colder.

"Not again," he said, his voice low, almost petulant.

"What are you?" she whispered.

"I am you."

Her lips parted, disbelief trembling on her tongue. "No… you only look like me. You can't be me."

"Flesh was stripped from me many moons ago," he explained, his tone bitter yet enlightening. "I was destined to take the form of the one whose shadow I sought to claim."

"Why me?"

"Why me?" he echoed, throwing the question back at her.

The two stood locked in silence, studying one another as though the answer might be carved into their faces. Above them, the dark clouds from her dreams churned and spread like an endless storm. The suspended rock beneath them glowed faintly, its surface charred and black.

"I don't understand…" Naida murmured.

"Your soul called for retribution. But it is the heart in need of protection."

"You're here to protect me?"

Riko's eyes lingered on her. He knew the truth but kept it pressed against his tongue, unwilling to give it shape.

"That depends," he said slowly. "What is it you seek protection from?"

Naida's chest tightened. "I'm… not quite sure."

His gaze sharpened, cutting into her like a blade. "You're lying."

He vanished into the darkness as though swallowed by it, his shadow slithering along the edges of the space, circling her. His voice echoed, deep and unsettling, reverberating as if it came from every direction at once.

"I am your thoughts. I am your heartbeat. I am your fears. I am your vengeance. I am a combat Ushu. You called for your revenge."

The words slithered over her skin like serpents. Naida spun, searching for his silhouette, chasing the sound as it leapt from shadow to shadow.

"I… I don't know anymore," she whispered, her voice trembling. "At first, yes—because of what she did to my father. But she trained me, raised me, gave me a place when I had none. For a time, she was kind… I know I will never see him again, but I have no home ashore. And if I strike at my Kingdom Mother, the sea itself may turn against me. King Khione… he would…"

Her throat closed around the words. Tears threatened, but she swallowed them down, her heart torn between fury and forgiveness.

"Come, child," Riko's voice urged, soft and serpentine. "Speak your woes."

"I am not the child I once was," Naida replied, lifting her chin though her voice wavered.

"Surely not. Yet you called, and I answered. Do not pretend it was for nothing."

In that moment, Naida realized the truth she had buried for years could no longer be denied. She still resented Rudita, though time had dulled the sting. The Lady of the Snows did not deserve death—not by Naida's hand—but punishment was long overdue. Rudita had never shown remorse, never sought forgiveness. Each year in the Lamina Garden had only hardened her, feeding a bitterness born of failed ambition. She had trained the hybrid only to gain access to the Iris's energy, and when that promise collapsed, her hatred deepened.

A storm churned in Naida's chest, and Riko felt it stir.

"What happens if I refuse?" she asked, her voice breaking.

"We are bound by the Ahalty," he said. "You, the Obi—Naida. And I, the Ushu—Riko."

Her lips trembled. "…And if we are not victorious?"

"We die." His reply was sharp, immediate.

Naida gasped, her breath stolen. "I don't want to die. She is too powerful—we won't survive her."

"But she is not content," Riko warned, his tone hardening.

Naida's brow furrowed. "What do you mean? We get along…"

"She longs for an Iris daughter."

"She will have one," Naida pressed. "She swore my training would earn her passage to the Iris's center once again."

Riko's form flickered against the storm above. "…And yet, I am here."

Her pulse quickened. "Am I in danger, Ushu?"

"You waver between vengeance and healing. I care for neither. I will emerge and conquer—every single time."

Naida wanted to believe he was lying. She wanted to believe Rudita had changed, that her heart had softened, that she no longer looked at her with cold detachment. But Riko's words cut too close to the truth she had always feared: while Naida dreamed of peace, her Kingdom Mother's quiet hatred would never cease to grow.

Her heart raced, though all she longed for was harmony. The loss of her parents had hollowed her, leaving her spirit to cry out for the Ushu, the one who carried the burden of her heart as if it were his own. Yet in her yearning, she remained blind to the hearts of others.

She turned to him, her storm-grey eyes brimming with a quiet plea. "Will you be my protector?" Her voice was soft, almost regal in its resolve, though she had never realized until now how deeply she needed one.

"Vengeance will be ours." Riko lowered himself in a formal bow, his tone carrying both promise and power. "I am Riko, the Nukeya warrior—tu ahvi, Naida, deh Ushu."

The words reverberated through the vast silence of the Temple of Xorri. King Bao, pulsing in meditation, lowered his conical hat as the echo reached him. His gaze fixed on Naida, for she had begun to change.

The hybrid's brasloor shimmered, its surface darkening to obsidian glass as fine threads of light wove across it like veins of molten silver. The transformation spread, shaping itself into armor that linked seamlessly to her fin, curving upward in a structure that framed her face like a living helm. Her fin followed, black as midnight, scattered with diamond-like sparks that gleamed in the temple's gloom.

Her ash-brown hair lengthened, rippling in the water as it curled gently at the ends. Her frame stretched, gaining form and strength, as if the current itself was sculpting her anew. For a suspended moment, she hovered, radiant and ironclad in the vastness of the temple.

Then her fin flared, the force of it stirring the still water around her. Her eyes snapped open—swirls of storm-grey and deep berry blue blazing within them. Power coursed through her veins, the bond of her Ushu alive in every breath, every motion, every thought.

King Bao allowed the faintest smirk to curl his lips. "Hmm," he rumbled, voice low and resonant. The Ushu had, in fact, found his way back to his Obi.

"It is time you learn your magic."

Naida's head snapped toward him. Her body felt heavier, though not with weariness—Riko's presence pressed against her bones, his will intertwining with hers. They moved as one now. She could feel him in the smallest motions, controlling threads of her body, and she did not resist. With him, she feared nothing.

Throughout the five kingdoms of the North, the currents themselves seemed to shiver. Waves shifted, tides quickened, and the very waters whispered of a presence moving through them. From their distant thrones, the rulers of the North sensed it all. Queen Ceto, Goddess of the Dangers of the Ocean, tilted her head, eyes narrowing at the sudden surge in her domain. King Khione, God of the Snow Sea, felt the chill of his northern waters ripple unnaturally. King Palaemon, God of the Sailors' Sea, frowned as the waves shifted under his gaze. Queen Leucothea, Goddess of the Nwala River, paused mid-motion, sensing the pulse of foreign energy. Even King Glaucus, the Fishermen Sea God, leaned closer to the surface, drawn by the tremor in the tides.

For the first time in recorded history, an Ushu had entered the North. The balance of the seas, long held steady by the kingdoms, trembled at the arrival of this singular force.

Far away in the Nwala Kingdom, Melusine was drawing her final breaths. The small Philosophers gathered, circling like carrion birds, their bodies twitching, their sharp talons restless. Their murmurs were a chorus of mindless chittering, their eyes fixed on the weakening hybrid. They waited for their Kingdom Mother to cast the corpse to them like scraps.

Then Deimos arrived. His presence was felt before it was seen, a shift in the water that made the Philosophers recoil. He descended through the vast chamber, the Royal Halls of Nwala—a place few ever entered, and fewer still left alive. He hovered just above the open throne space, looking down upon the scene: Queen Leucothea clutching Melusine's limp form, the hybrid's body battered, her pulse faint.

The Queen's wings unfurled, their edges glistening as she released her prey. Melusine dangled in the current, too weak to resist. Leucothea's frame was small beside her victim's, but her hunger made her monstrous.

"Well, if it isn't the little Snow Mosquen," she hissed, eyes never leaving Melusine. "What brings you here?"

Deimos's voice filled the chamber, deep and commanding, echoing with the weight of his father's lineage. The Philosophers hissed and clicked, but none dared advance; they knew better than to challenge a Snow.

"By order of King Khione," Deimos said, gripping his spear, "I lay claim to the hybrid, Melusine."

"By order of the Sea God, Poseidon," Leucothea countered, wiping blood from her lips with the back of her acetic, "the hybrids are mine to devour."

"I will not repeat my orders." His tone sharpened.

Leucothea's grin widened, her eyes glittering like shards of rose quartz. "Is that so?"

"Ahvi."

"You are brave, Snow Mosquen, to venture toward death," she spat, her voice a serrated edge.

"You are wrong," Deimos replied coldly. "It will be your head or mine that returns to the King. And I assure you—it will not be mine."

The Philosophers surged closer, their whispers rising to shrill excitement. Leucothea spun toward him, her iris swirling like spun sugar, pink and furious. "You dare threaten me, Mosquen?"

"I merely advise," he said, spear gleaming in his hand. "Release her. Your Kingdom Brother has laid claim. These are our laws."

"And if I refuse…"

The words had not left her mouth before the water bristled. In an instant, hundreds of shards formed—glass and ice shaped into jagged icicles, all pointing directly at her and her creatures. The chamber held its breath.

Deimos's fin beat once, hard, the force scattering the fish in the brightly lit corridors. He twirled his spear, the water hissing around its edge.

Leucothea's snarl broke, and at last she flung Melusine's body aside. "She's as good as dead. She will not make the journey."

Deimos did not flinch. Orders were orders. Dead or alive, Melusine would leave with him. He swept forward, catching her limp form with one arm, lifting her onto his shoulder. She looked small against his frame, broken but not yet gone.

Without another word, he turned from the Queen and her beasts. His silhouette cut through the chamber's despair as he carried her away, the spear gleaming like a warning in the kingdom.

Deimos cut through the ocean with uncanny speed, his form a blur beneath the surface. The strength of his lineage propelled him forward, each powerful fin stroke sending arcs of light trailing behind him. He twisted and curved around coral reefs, kelp forests, and shoals of startled fish, avoiding anything that might slow his relentless pace. Even the fastest predators of the sea could not hope to keep up.

The Kingdom leaders waited in quiet anticipation, knowing it was only a matter of time before their Sea God, Poseidon, would summon them. Yet the call did not come as quickly as expected. Poseidon required precision. He needed certainty. After a private consultation with the Mortis God, his decision was final: only two calls would be made—Queen Ceto and King Khione.

From parallel corners of the ocean, the two deities began their journeys toward the center, each moving with a purpose that reflected their dominion.

Ceto's large fin sliced through the water with relentless force. Its dark molten hues resembled waves streaked with fiery red-orange veins, as if magma flowed beneath her scales. The edges of her fin rippled with scorching heat, like smoldering embers clinging to volcanic rock. Along its length, sharp quills jutted outward, absent only from the boned tail fluke, adding an air of lethal elegance to her movement.

King Khione no longer wore the black silk, nor the gold-plated bands that had once encircled his forearms— armor that had marked him beside Rudita. His abdominal scales gleamed like polished obsidian—beneath his shoulder armor—each edged with fine threads of molten gold and silver that shimmered with the ocean's movement. His fin, once entirely gold, had darkened as his power deepened, now scattered with sparse sapphire diamonds that caught the light like trapped starlight. Below, his boned tail fluke spread wide and regal, its metallic lining casting fractured glimmers through the water. It was no longer ornament or protection, but a crown shaped by the unexplored depths of the sea itself.

Despite their magnificence, neither Ceto nor Khione revealed the full measure of their strength. Each moved with the quiet restraint of the most powerful rulers of their realms, the true weight of their power hinted at only in the way the currents parted, and the water seemed to acknowledge their presence.

After a journey through the sun-dappled currents, King Khione and Queen Ceto arrived at the center of the ocean. They approached one another with measured grace, each offering a respectful curtsy that acknowledged the other's power and dominion. Together, they entered the grand hall of Poseidon's palace, a cavernous space where sunlight fractured through the crystalline waters, scattering prisms of light across polished coral floors and towering shell columns.

At the center, Poseidon hovered with quiet authority, his eyes scanning the vast hall before settling on the immense glass tank that dominated the chamber. Within, white sharks glided smoothly, their movements hypnotic, a serene ballet of aquatic precision. The Sea God's acetics rested carefully atop one another behind him, a subtle display of discipline and ritual.

Both Khione and Ceto lowered themselves in a deep, formal curtsy, yet Poseidon did not turn to face them.

"Greetings," he intoned, his voice low and steady.

"Good day, my God," Khione replied, his tone measured, while Ceto inclined her head in agreement.

"I have called you here because an Ushu has appeared in these realms," Poseidon rumbled, the weight of his words pressing through the water like a current.

"An Ushu?" Ceto's question cut through the hall.

"Does King Ryūmon, the Shen Ryūmon, know of this shift in history?" Khione asked, tension threading his words.

"Ahvi," Poseidon replied, shaking his head in confirmation before finally turning to face them. He finned gracefully to his throne, curling his massive fin beneath him as he seated himself. His acetics rested neatly atop the polished sea glass armrests, a picture of calm control.

"And what of it?" Khione pressed, his voice tighter now.

"King Ryūmon, acting under orders from King Bao, has conceded," Poseidon revealed.

A sharp gasp escaped both Ceto and Khione.

"Why?" Khione's scales seemed to bristle. "We know the Ushu is dangerous. Who is it?"

Poseidon paused, allowing the gravity of his next words to sink in. "Your hybrid."

Ceto's eyes snapped toward Khione, wide with disbelief.

"The hybrid?" Khione's voice carried a mix of shock and fury. "Impossible. It is not a purebred. Why would an Ushu attach to its shadow? Its unrest stems from its fin, not malice. Fear of releasing it and seeking counsel from our Mortis God, surely!"

"Calm yourself, my son. I understand," Poseidon's voice held a measured steadiness that only slightly eased Khione's rising panic.

"Is she cursed?" Khione's tone was sharp.

"No. It appears not to be intentional. It is a cry for vengeance."

A lump rose in Khione's throat. The thought of a hybrid seeking revenge against his Queen ignited a storm of fury and anxiety within him. "She will die before she can challenge my Lady of the Snows," he declared, his loyalty to Rudita unwavering, even tempered by her defiance. An Iris daughter, he reminded himself, would come only once Rudita's lesson was learned, and Naida's training with King Bao concluded. Judgment aside.

"The Ushu has marked the hybrid with your drapery," Poseidon continued. "She is bound to your domain in perpetuity. There cannot be two Majestic Lorelies within the same kingdom."

The blood seemed to drain from Khione's face. *Kaliope*, he thought, his jaw tightening. "This is not the order I intended," he muttered through clenched teeth.

"Yes. But it is the order. The hybrid must now venture to Ceto to complete her training. Will you allow it?"

"And if I choose to reject these orders?" Khione's voice was taut with defiance.

"Disobedience," Poseidon replied.

"What is its name?" Khione pressed.

"The combat Ushu. The rest is unknown."

Ceto's gaze never left Khione. She saw the conflict etched across his features, the turmoil of a king torn between duty, loyalty, and the unpredictable tides of fate. Then, a memory surfaced—Fanira, the prophecy. Perhaps this path had always been destined. With a slow, steady nod, Khione conceded.

"I'll allow it," he said, the words heavy with reluctant acceptance.

"And so it shall be," Poseidon declared, the water around them humming with the certainty of divine decree.

XIX.

RUDITA

Departing the Sea God's kingdom, Khione seethed with fury. Naida had been deemed a danger to their ocean, and now she would be delivered to Ceto. The thought hollowed him, a gnawing fear rising with every stroke of his fins. *Why had he ever allowed the hybrid into their realm? Why had he listened to Fanira's whispering counsel?* His decisions pressed on him with a weight that would not lift, each choice coiling tighter around his chest.

He surged forward, but the urgency that had once driven him was gone. Instead, he let the waters guide him, breaking through to the surface where the late afternoon sun spilled across his skin in warm, rippling sheets. His head bobbed with the rhythm of the waves, eyes closed, surrendering to the hush of the sea. With a flick of his wrist, he fastened his trident to his back. It clung there, firmly, an extension of himself that never left his side. For a moment, he let himself drift—caught between duty and the simple desire to breathe.

Miles away in London, Noah was tidying his small flat in Linden Gardens. The address had been printed in a newspaper ad, a call for applicants to a campaign manager position, instructing them to arrive promptly at 12:30 p.m.

It was hardly a professional posting: a domestic residence instead of an office, a photograph of the Prime Minister's son beside a name no one recognized, and a listing buried in a paper that few bothered to read. To the world, it might look like a scam.

But it was all Noah could afford on his dwindling, almost vanished budget. Still, he clung to optimism, even something close to delusion, convincing himself that twenty eager applicants might walk through his door. Young men and women ready to serve, ready to help him restore a vision of the country he loved. At the very least, one had answered. Willow was already on her way. And so, when the appointed hour came, Noah waited— hopeful, restless, alone.

By one o'clock, the young boy had given up. The packets of policy drafts he had printed at the local library now sat in a heap at his feet. With a sharp exhale, he scooped them up and shoved them into the trash can by the door.

"What a bunch of rubbish," he muttered, the words tasting bitter on his tongue.

He retreated to the kitchen, poured himself a cold glass of milk, and leaned against the counter in defeat. That was when the knock came.

Noah froze. At first, he thought it might have been for the neighbor, but the sound echoed again, this time unmistakably against his own door. He set the glass aside and, with sudden urgency, dug the discarded packets back out of the trash. He flattened the pages against his thigh, smoothing the crumples until they resembled order, then stacked them neatly on the small dining table where they might appear purposeful rather than abandoned.

His suit was far from impressive—cheap fabric with seams that tugged if he moved too quickly—but he adjusted the lapels and hoped it would pass. For today, it had to.

At the third knock, he crossed the room, every step heavy with hesitation. On the other side of the door, Willow shifted, checking the address on her folded slip of paper for the second time, her impatience mounting.

Finally, Noah opened the door.

"Hello," her voice rang warm and cheerful from the hall.

"Yes—yes, hello…" Noah began, his throat tightening as the moment rushed in on him. "Please, um, do come in."

Noah stepped aside, allowing her to pass. Willow froze for a moment, stunned by the sight before her. He was destitute. The Prime Minister's son, living as if he were no more than a drifter.

She shifted her crossbody bag from behind her hip to the front, clutching it tightly in case this pale, ragged version of Benson Jr. tried anything reckless. His hollow eyes and disheveled appearance made him look less like royalty and more like a man pretending at poverty.

She squinted, then spoke. "Noah Chambers?"

"Yes, yes, that's me." His voice carried an odd eagerness. "And your name?"

"Willow… Willow Weathers." She hesitated, then pressed on. "I saw your ad and wanted to interview for the position. May I ask, is it paid? The notice didn't say."

"Well," Noah began, rubbing his hands together as he crossed the room, "I was hoping to find volunteers for now. I'm a new politician, just starting out. But I could... speak to my mum and see if we can sort out something for snacks and travel."

Willow prayed she had misheard him. Her face betrayed her disbelief. "Um... sure. Where would you like to interview me?"

"Ah, yes. Interview." He moved quickly to the dining table, pulling out a chair at the far end and gesturing for her to sit. He then lowered himself into the opposite seat, the distance between them like a gulf.

Willow folded her hands in her lap, weighing her time against the risk of honesty. At last, she leaned forward. "Listen—my name is Willow, as I said before." She gave a nervous laugh. "The truth is, I came because I'm part of a group investigating the corruption inside the palace... and the hybrids."

Noah's eyes widened, his breath quickening. "The hybrids?" His voice cracked. Suspicion flooded his face. "Are you some kind of spy? Did my father send you? Get out!"

Willow shot upright, panic jolting through her chest. Her hands lifted instinctively, palms open in a desperate attempt to calm him.

"No, no, please," she pleaded, her voice trembling. "I just—I think we're on the same side. We could help one another, that's all."

"Help?" His voice cracked sharply with suspicion. "A team? Do I look like a fool to you? If you came here to rob me, you're wasting your time. Everything worth anything is with my mum. Best leave now before I call the law."

His outburst rattled her, but she scrambled through her bag, heart thundering, until her fingers found the scrap of paper Piper had discovered. The sticky note, creased and nearly smudged from wear. She thrust it out toward him.

"You wrote this, didn't you? Leave the Alien. Well, we found her. My friends helped her return to the ocean. She had a child. Yours, I assume." Her eyes locked on his. "You should want to work with us."

The words seemed to puncture his anger. Noah fell silent, gaze fixed on the note. His shoulders stiffened as though he were bracing against a memory he didn't want.

"Listen," he said at last, his voice lower, measured. "I only ever wanted a normal life. I didn't choose any of this. It was my father—he forced it. That's why I'm running against him now. He's reckless. Selfish. The kind of man who destroys both his family and his country without blinking. No offense to you, but hybrids aren't meant for this world. Not mine, not yours."

Willow's breath caught. "How can you say that? You were with one of them."

"Against my will."

"She bore your child," she pressed. "How much against your will could it have been?"

The fire in her tone made him flinch, but he didn't answer. Instead, he exhaled, long and weary.

"You need to leave," he said quietly, opening the door.

Her fingers fumbled for a pen. She scribbled her name and number on the bottom of the note, tearing the ink across the crumpled surface. She pressed it back into his hand.

"If you change your mind…"

He held the door for her. No more threats, no more raised voice. Only silence as she stepped into the dim hall. The door closed firmly behind her, cutting the connection like a final breath.

The slamming of his car door carried an anger Enu had never seen in him before. Her friend, her mentor, her trainer—Watson was unraveling. Beads of sweat gathered at his brow, and though his face remained hard, she saw the tremor in his hands. He wasn't shaken by Doctor Astor's demand that the Lith be delivered to the King. It was Penelope's movements inside the sphere that haunted him.

Enu recognized the signs: the silent torment of a man battling shadows no one else could see. He hid it well, burying the truth beneath a mask of command, afraid that admitting weakness would brand him incompetent. Without a word, he leaned across her, opened the glove compartment, and pulled out a small pill bottle labeled Hybernol. Two white tablets disappeared down his throat, swallowed dry in a gesture both practiced and desperate.

"Why are you so jumpy? Is everything alright?" Enu asked carefully.

Watson's eyes flicked toward her, cold and unreadable. He didn't answer. Instead, he dropped the black bag into her lap—the one that held the vials.

"I'm fine. We're going to Balmoral."

The words sounded casual, but Enu felt her chest tighten, panic clawing its way upward. Her fingers moved quickly over her phone: *The Major and I are going to see the King. There is more to discuss. There's a place… hidden. A finned Modiri is there. Any word from the witch?*

But Esam was occupied with an adventure of his own. He had strayed far from the barracks and wandered into the winding streets of town, his steps purposeful yet uncertain. More than ten years had passed since he and Enu last sought *medicine* from the witch—the one who carried no memorable name, yet was remembered by all who had ever needed her.

He walked endlessly, scanning the crowds, hoping against reason that someone—anyone—might approach him. In his mind's eye, he imagined a young hybrid slipping out of the city's flow, a thin band on their wrist marking them as other, their bag filled not with groceries or trinkets, but with what he required. Something hidden, something forbidden, delivered with a glance and gone in a heartbeat. Yet the streets gave him nothing. No stranger. No sign. Only the restless surge of London moving past him, indifferent to his need.

Far from the city, Fanira pressed northward. Her form shifted with the waters, transforming into the fastest mammal the ocean could provide, each change calculated to keep her unnoticed. Too often she had been spotted before—hailed as a rarity, a curiosity, a prize for hunters and fishermen. Each time had nearly cost her freedom. Now, she swam with caution, her speed masked by the tides, weaving through open stretches where the sea seemed endless, trusting the currents to conceal her voyage.

Elsewhere, Naida's gaze lingered on King Bao, who pulsed in meditation, his stillness so absolute it seemed he had merged with the stone around him. He did not look toward her, nor offer guidance, as though, once again, her presence was of no importance. Too fearful to break the silence with a question, she tried instead to imitate his posture.

It was far from simple. Her tail fluke, no longer the fragile limb of her youth, had fused with her fin. Bone and muscle had thickened, transforming it into something formidable—an anchor and a weapon, like the one King Khione wielded with ease. The sheer heaviness of it made stillness unbearable. Every small shift rippled through her body until, at last, King Bao's voice thundered through the chamber.

"Hybrid."

Naida flinched. "I am so sorry!" Her words tumbled out, trembling with shame. "I... I was only trying to do as you do."

"Remain without movement. Concentrate."

"On what?" Her voice was fragile, almost childlike.

"The mageía."

Her brow furrowed. "But what is that?"

"It is the art of turning what is awake into slumber."

Naida's eyes brightened with recognition. "Oh, like my father... Kaliope told me."

"Then you understand," he replied. "Concentrate."

She tried, but her body betrayed her. A sudden growl rose from her stomach, loud in the chamber's stillness. Heat rushed to her face as she pressed a hand to her belly.

Riko's voice pierced her thoughts, high-pitched and impatient. *I'm bored. And hungry.*

Her eyes widened, flicking nervously to King Bao. Surely he had heard. But no—his features remained composed, unbroken by the intrusion. Relief washed over her as she realized the truth: only she could hear Riko, the Ushu bound to her.

"Please, shush," Naida whispered, her voice breaking under the strain.

King Bao's conical hat tilted toward her, the shadow of its brim cutting across his severe features. "Is it disobedience?" His words were cold, sharp enough to slice through the chamber's stillness. The threat of punishment lingered behind every syllable.

Naida froze. Memories of his discipline haunted her, enough to coil fear tight in her chest. She would do anything to avoid his anger—anything to keep his conical hat from lowering in her direction. "No, please," she blurted, her acetics trembling. "It is the Ushu. He will not hush."

"Master it," Bao commanded, his voice carrying the weight of an absolute decree.

"I-I do not know how," she admitted softly, shame pressing her head low.

"It starts here," Bao slipped his right acetic from the sleeve of his Ao Tac, lifting it with an unhurried grace until it touched the crown of his hat. "The Crown Chakra-Zen."

A quiet hum seemed to resonate in the chamber, then faded as he slowly returned the acetic to its place.

"I will do my best," Naida whispered, her body quaking with the effort of restraint.

"Silence." The word cracked like thunder. His presence seemed to expand, a mountain pressing down upon her. "You must do the shadow work."

Her breath hitched. "What is that?" she asked, her voice barely audible.

"Govern your darker self and achieve lightness," Bao said, his tone unyielding, more teacher than comforter.

"But how?"

No answer came. The chamber held its silence, a silence more suffocating than sound. And far away, in the Snow Kingdom, Deimos arrived with Melusine.

The Snow Kingdom lay draped in its usual serenity, the waters hushed and gleaming, but that harmony faltered the moment Deimos crossed its threshold. His arrival was slow, melancholy, each stroke of his fin carrying the weight of what he bore. Over his shoulder rested Melusine—her body slack, her pulse faint, her beauty dimmed to a fragile version of itself.

He moved through the crystalline halls until he reached the healing chamber, only to find it empty. Kaliope was nowhere to be seen. A flicker of unease passed over his face. It was not in Deimos's nature to worry, yet he lingered, lowering Melusine carefully onto a cot of woven seaweed designed to cradle the wounded. His acetic lingered for a moment, not from affection, but from something deeper, something rarer: a desire for her survival.

Away, laughter echoed faintly through the waters. Kaliope and her sisters were at play, darting across the surface in a spirited race of Arctic Dash, their voices carrying like bells above the icy waters. When Deimos turned to the other Lorelies, his questions were curt, edged with command. They gestured upward, toward the shimmer of the surface.

Without hesitation, he seized his spear and surged toward the light. Breaking through the waves, he cut a stark figure against the horizon, water streaming from his shoulders. The sight froze Kaliope mid-dash. Snows never ventured here—never broke their stillness for play or joy—so if Deimos had come, it could only mean danger.

Her heart stammered in her chest, an involuntary quickening that was half dread, half recognition. Though part of her was thrilled at the thought of Melusine, one look into Deimos's piercing, berry-blue eyes told her the truth: something was terribly wrong.

She abandoned the game, slicing back into the depths with urgent speed, but she could not keep pace. Deimos pressed forward without hesitation, cutting through the water toward the King's chambers. Kaliope was left behind, her path diverging from his. Alone, she turned toward her own quarters, where she would find Melusine waiting, brittle and near the edge of life.

Kaliope drifted into her chamber with hesitant strokes, her chest tight, her vision blurring before the tears could even form. What she saw stole the breath from her lungs. Melusine lay upon the seaweed cot in a state unlike anything Kaliope had ever imagined.

Her sisters followed behind, their movements subdued, the usual lilt of their presence replaced by an oppressive silence. They hovered at the edges of the room, their gazes caught between sorrow and disbelief, while Kaliope's own grief spilled silently into the water. The tears were indistinguishable from the sea around her, yet she felt every drop as it burned.

She finned closer, her heart pounding, and the small flower from Kalkisis still nestled in her hair brushed gently against her cheek—a reminder of hope, fragile but memorable. Determination hardened inside her. If her own life was the cost of saving Melusine, she would surrender it without hesitation.

Bending her fin, Kaliope sank to her knees before the cot. Her acetics stretched forward, trembling with urgency as she summoned her power. A soft glow radiated outward, bathing the ruined body of the young hybrid.

The sight was almost unbearable. Melusine's upper torso was torn open to the bone, her right eye gone, her left acetic ravaged, her fin shredded to ribbons. Deep gashes marred her flesh, her body broken and chewed, her tail fluke mangled nearly beyond recognition. And these horrors, Kaliope knew, were only the beginning of the visible surface of injuries that reached far deeper.

Still, she pressed her acetics to the wounds, her magic sparking against the torn flesh, her breath catching in prayer. She would not allow death to claim Melusine. Not while she still drew breath.

Kaliope bent lower, whispering into Melusine's ear, her voice breaking though her resolve held firm. "I will not allow you to leave this world prematurely as your father did. I will fight until my last breath to see you whole again. I love you, and I pray you will fight with me."

To her astonishment, Melusine's remaining eye shifted toward her. A single tear slipped free, gliding down her scarred cheek. She could not speak—her body too broken, her voice stolen by trauma—but the tear was answer enough. Kaliope's heart jolted, startled yet uplifted, for it was a sign to press on.

Strength surged through her. She straightened, her acetics trembling with purpose, and called out to her sisters. "Prepare several plates of Maridella."

Her voice carried through the chamber, echoing like a vow. Rudita lingered nearby, listening in silence. With King Khione away at Poseidon's summons, she turned from the chamber and drifted toward the Lamina Garden. Shadows clung to her heart as she went.

LONG AGO…

A subtropical summer pressed down upon the Atlantic, its waters glinting beneath a merciless sun. A cargo ship carved a steady path south, its massive hull groaning against the tide. Then, with a shudder that shattered the morning calm, an entire column of shipping containers broke loose and plunged into the sea. Steel struck water with a thunderous crash, and beneath the surface schools of fish scattered in frantic bursts of silver. The ocean itself seemed to recoil, quivering as if weary of yet another trespass.

For centuries, those waters had carried the arrogance of humankind—rubbish, weapons, stolen cargo, even the bodies of the unwanted. To the sea, it had never been a question of what would fall, only when.

Far beneath, in the abyss where minimal sunlight reached, another world endured. Hidden from human sight lay five kingdoms that stretched like silent empires along the coasts of Africa—realms of legend and power, bound by currents and guarded by gods.

King Ajama, Kasadi of Ajama, God of the Marrowshades, ruled over spectral depths where skeletons whispered secrets. King Jendali, Gaheli of Jendali, God of the Vipers, commanded swiftness and venom; his legions feared for their silent strikes. Queen Chira, the Chira-Chira of Chira, God of the Achira Sculptures, held dominion over brilliance itself, her people shimmering with artistry and allure. Queen Njoni, Khari of Njoni, God of the Egyptian City, reigned with the wisdom of dynasties long past, her court alive with ceremony and tradition. And King Bubar, Saila of Bubar, God of the Stone Siren, his kingdom as enduring as the tides themselves.

Together they formed a force beyond the world's notice, ancient and watchful, and something deep within them had begun to stir.

"Has she gone again?" King Bubar's growl rolled through the cavernous hall, a sound as deep and resonant as the ocean floor itself.

The Stone Siren Kingdom stretched for more than three thousand meters, a vast realm of quiet splendor hidden beneath miles of shifting current. Lorelies drifted gracefully through its coral-lined passages, their amber fins flashing like molten glass. Tiny linen-colored gemstones freckled their tails, catching what little light filtered from above.

Their skin held the rich shade of dark-roasted coffee, smooth and luminous beneath the wavering glow of bioluminescent coral. They adorned themselves with intricate jewelry—oversized rings looped through their nostrils and chained delicately to the ornaments woven into their hair. Some wore towering six-inch updos; others wrapped their springy 4C coils between spiraling plates of beaten gold. Their deep-green eyes, the color of olives, gleamed like polished stone, warm and arresting.

The Lorelies embodied a quiet grace. Their voices floated through the water in murmurs so light they seemed like the breath of the sea—words scarcely more than whispers. They were the sirens of the Stone Sea, keepers of a beauty both gentle and formidable.

At the heart of their kingdom rose its namesake: the Stone Siren. Carved from the rarest gold, the colossal figure shimmered in the shifting light, her presence both guardian and overseer. The currents carried her brilliance across the kingdom like a silent blessing, a reminder that the Lorelies were never truly alone.

King Bubar was known as a ruler of laughter, a monarch whose wit could send ripples of joy across the Stone Siren Kingdom. His booming jokes and easy charm left his people radiant with delight, their days buoyed by the warmth of his humor. Yet one Lorelie alone could turn his thoughts into restless currents—Rudita, his Iris daughter.

Brilliant and brimming with curiosity, Rudita's mind wandered toward questions that unsettled even the most patient heart. She challenged her father's decisions with a quiet persistence and wondered aloud about worlds beyond their own. *Where did the objects that sank into their depths come from? Who were the humans who cast them down? Did those creatures above mean harm, or did they even know the Lorelies existed?* Her inquiries came like sudden bursts of light in the deep, leaving Bubar both proud and perpetually wary.

Rudita spoke freely, yet of late she had become more elusive, drawn to someone whose presence eclipsed her usual chatter.

Zaila—the lady of the kingdom—was a vision of unearthly beauty. Her skin held the warm glow of caramel, dappled with tiny freckles that dusted her cheeks and neck like constellations. Eyes bright as distant stars seemed to hold entire galaxies of secrets. Her crimson fin shimmered with amber crystals, each one catching the faintest glimmer of light. Soft, light-brown hair framed her face in loose, silken curls, moving like ribbons underwater with every turn of her head.

King Bubar found himself spellbound by her, time and again. Compliments rose to his lips as naturally as the tide, and her ready smile never dimmed—he would never allow it to fade. He often joked about his own looks with a disarming grin, calling himself a grotesque Modiri: skin marked with imperfections, features too delicate for his broad frame, and an umber colored fin larger than any in his court. He blamed his bulk on the heavy armor he wore rather than the stolen morsels of surface meat he sometimes devoured on long, sleepless nights. Beneath the jest, though, lingered a quiet affection for the very people whose admiration he claimed not to seek.

"Oh, my tunt…" Zaila's voice, low and velvety, carried a natural flirtation, especially when she addressed her king.

"No, no." King Bubar waved a dismissive acetic, his tone firm. "You cannot defend her today."

"I do not wish to defend," Zaila replied, dipping her head in a subtle bow. "Only to offer counsel."

Bubar's dark brows drew together. "Counsel about what? The Snow Prince?"

"My dear," she said softly, "were we not once young ourselves?"

"The same? No." He gave a short, scornful laugh and sank deeper into his throne. "The vivonation is a cruel tradition."

"Why do you call it cruel?" Zaila's voice sharpened, a quick snap in the quiet chamber.

"She is the only Iris we have," Bubar said.

"As a ruler, you never worry," Zaila answered gently, "but as a father, you love her. Then tell me, ruler—why the furrowed brows?"

"He is far too young. Arrogant. He wields his spear as though it were a swordfish. It is graceless, a mockery of our Ahalty."

"He is young, yes," she conceded. "But once a Snow and now a future King—should we not grant him mercy?"

Bubar's gaze darkened. "His father, King Forios—"

"Ahh, yes. Will he claim a seat upon the throne?"

"Ahvi," Bubar muttered.

Zaila's lips curved in a sly half-smile. "Well… one day… will you accept it?"

Before he could answer, the great stones of the royal chamber groaned open. A Saila entered, spear in hand, posture rigid, fin angled downward in a soldier's salute.

"I bring urgent news," he said.

Bubar's eyes shifted past his lady, and Zaila too turned toward the messenger.

"Deliver it," the king commanded.

"It is the witches, my King," the Saila declared, his voice carrying a chill through the chamber. "They are preparing for war."

Oblivious to the catastrophe brewing in the South, Rudita and her sister Ruqama reached the far North after a journey that stretched across two long days. The distance felt endless, the waters heavy with the hush of deep currents. Rudita would have traveled alone, as she had many times before, but Ruqama had insisted on coming. Between their steady strokes, they paused to rest in small seabed caves where faint ribbons of bioluminescent coral flickered like distant stars, casting pale light over their tired faces.

Rudita's thoughts often wandered to the summons her father had received: her vivonation, the sacred rite that would mark her passage, awaited after 6,138 moons. The time drew near.

Far to the North, Prince Khione had only just begun his training as heir to the Snow Kingdom, his ascent to be sanctioned both by the Ahalty and by his father, King Forios, who had at last accepted a seat among the ruling ancestors.

The Ahalty—the Iris spirits of the sea—were the silent architects of all ocean kingdoms. Twenty sovereigns formed their council, each granted a choice: to be turned to living stone and sleep within the Ancient Modiri Gardens, or to remain enthroned and hold vigil until the deepest wish of their heart came to pass. Many, after decades or even centuries of patient longing, surrendered to the stillness of stone.

Yet some refused the quiet. Among them sat King Fufuhani, the Ether God, who waited with an endurance that unsettled even his peers. No one knew the desire that kept him wakeful. His rule inspired immediate obedience—no questions, no resistance, only the blank, unwavering gaze of those who shared the throne and dared not speak his name above a whisper.

The Snow Kingdom pulsed with life, its underwater corridors alive with the movement of Lorelies and Mosquens. Rudita and Ruqama remained hidden in the shadows, hearts quickened by the thrumming energy around them. Rudita's eyes swept frantically over the crowds, desperate to find him.

But Prince Khione was not among the bustling Lorelies. He was in the Duel Chamber, locked in combat alongside his father and the other Snows. The matches were grueling and relentless, testing both strength and spirit, unforgiving of any misstep. The mighty clash of a trident against spears and the resonance of powers filled the chamber like a storm trapped beneath icy walls.

Outside, the Lamina Garden hummed with a softer energy, a contrast of harmony and patience. The garden rarely produced an Iris Mosquen, and when it did, it was understood by all that this child would one day ascend to the throne. From the moment of his birth, Khione's siblings had instinctively recognized his calling. The knowledge of his destiny clung to him, as inevitable as the tides.

With no Iris daughter in the kingdom to assume such a role, another would need to come from afar. And so, as he grew and began to understand the weight of his destiny, Khione's thoughts often drifted toward the future—toward the lady who might one day fin beside him.

Rudita's gaze continued its careful sweep, and disappointment crept slowly across her features. She longed to see him, needed to, yet she remained patient, cloaked in the quiet anticipation that stretched between the bustling masses. They waited, hearts tethered to the hope of a single moment, a single glance.

After a long pause, as if by fate, the gates of the Duel Chamber lifted, their heavy creak rolling through the surrounding seas. Sea creatures drifted lazily, indifferent to the disturbance, weaving through the currents with quiet grace. Rudita pressed her acetic against the back of a passing mammal, peeking above its fin. A wide smile lit her face, and her hair flowed around her, straighter and smoother than her sisters', though still textured, catching the faint glow of the deep.

Her eyes shone with exhilaration.

"Come! Come see for yourself!" she called to Ruqama, voice bright and trembling with anticipation.

Her sister finned forward, the mammal steady beneath them as if it understood their playfulness, allowing them a safe vantage.

Khione emerged from the chamber, unarmored, his chest bare. His dark denim colored fin cut through the water with quiet elegance, the adolescent tail fluke smooth and lightly shimmering against the dim sea light. His hair, bound at the back by a live squid that held each strand obediently, trailed behind him like a living bobble. He rested, surveying the kingdom he would soon rule with eyes that had once known only the innocence of youth. Mosquen had yielded to the crown, and even the waters seemed to acquiesce to his nascent sovereignty, bending and swirling with subtle reverence, as though the currents themselves sensed the rise of his reign.

Rudita shuddered. Her heart raced with a strange, consuming emotion—a love she had never known but welcomed without question. She hovered, frozen in awe.

Khione's gaze shifted, subtle and slow, as if drawn to something he could not yet understand. Rudita felt it even before she saw him look her way—a brief flicker of recognition, a faint awareness that stretched across the currents between them. Her cheeks warmed, though the sea carried no heat.

"He's as handsome as they say," Ruqama whispered, but Rudita could not hear. Her eyes remained locked on him, admiration pulling her downward as she drifted slowly toward the seabed, lost in the rush of emotions she had no words for.

"I will be his queen very soon," she murmured, voice soft, reverent. "I will touch him with the rise of the sun and the rise of the moon. Moon after moon, sun after sun, for all eternity."

Khione, now fully aware of the presence of the young Iris, paused mid-fin, a faint shift in his posture betraying curiosity. There was something about her—the bold, bright spirit that mirrored the tides themselves.

"Rudita, snap out of it," Ruqama chided, breaking the spell with a teasing nudge.

"I can't…" Rudita admitted, her voice high and childlike, as she traced the smooth back of an icefish, lost in the dizzying, exhilarating awareness of him.

Ruqama rolled her eyes, half-amused, half-exasperated, as the currents carried Khione farther away, leaving Rudita suspended in a world that had suddenly become his entirely.

King Bubar sirened for his daughter, and even her whimsical trance could not resist its pull. Rudita and Ruqama finned urgently, cutting through the currents toward home, their movements precise and obedient.

Inside the Stone Siren Kingdom, a weighty seriousness had fallen over the waters. Three Mistos witches had arrived, their black cloaks swaying like shadows through the currents. King Bubar and Zaila emerged from the royal chambers, their presence commanding the attention of all. The entrance to the kingdom was fortified with statues and stones, a barrier that had never before been breached. Yet the witches moved within as if granted passage by forces unseen.

"State your duty," King Bubar bellowed, the authority in his voice rippling across the gathering. On one side, the three Mistos; on the other, the entire kingdom behind Bubar and his Sailas. Spears glinted, muscles coiled, every Mosquen prepared to obey the first command.

One of the Mistos approached. Eels writhed atop her head like living crowns, twisting and hissing in the currents. Her voice was low, raspy, almost malevolent.

"Fear not," she whispered.

King Bubar recoiled. "Fear? I know not such things."

"Your fear does not come from what lies beneath," the witch rasped, "but from the troubles yet to come."

"What are you speaking of?" Bubar demanded.

"There is a war on the horizon."

"Whose war?"

"A conflict that will alter our waters forever."

Bubar laughed harshly, disbelief etched into his features. "No such thing. Many wars have risen and fallen; we endure, unchanged...except for the mutilations."

"This war is unlike any before. It is not of man or Modiri. It is of a creation. It is mutiny."

"Mutiny against whom?"

"Against them all."

King Bubar's grip tightened on his trident. "Our Sea God, Poseidon—does he know of this?"

"He has been in counsel," the Mistos answered.

"And?"

"We wait," she replied.

"Then you waste your time here?"

"No. It is the Iris…"

The name struck him like a thunderclap. King Bubar's eyes widened with fury. "You dare speak of my Iris?"

"You dare disregard my words?" she hissed, her voice a blade through the water.

"Speak plainly," King Bubar commanded, his tone cold and measured.

"The vivonation... do not proceed."

The words barely left her lips before another Mistos swayed forward, whispering something unseen. She inclined her head in silent agreement, but Bubar's gaze hardened, displeasure flaring like a storm in his eyes.

"What are you hiding?" he demanded.

"We conceal nothing," the first Mistos replied. "Our purpose is to spread the prophecy."

"Then spread it!" His voice thundered through the Stone Siren Kingdom. "And what of my Iris?"

"Enmity," the witch said, each syllable curling through the currents like smoke.

"Your prophecy is false," Bubar roared, the water around him vibrating with the force of his words. "My Iris bears no bitterness. She cannot. Her smile outshines the stars themselves. You will leave these waters at once." He lifted his trident, the tip glinting sharply, poised as if to strike.

In perfect synchrony, the three Mistos revealed their eyes—yellow, feline, glowing with an otherworldly fire. Even those behind him shivered, a chill creeping along their spines. Yet King Bubar remained unmoved. Stronger, wiser, faster, he could have ended them in an instant with the force of his powers, but he restrained himself, hoping they would simply withdraw.

"We are done here," he confirmed, voice steady, final.

The Mistos vanished into the depths, their dark cloaks dissolving like shades in the current, the kingdom slowly resumed its rhythm. The hum of moving fins and murmured chatter filled the waters once more, a fragile normalcy returning after the storm of prophecy. Zaila finned toward her king, her movements hesitant, eyes wide with unspoken worry.

"It was I… I requested Rudita's acetics to Khione's. Was I wrong? Must we fear?" she asked, her voice trembling beneath the weight of the question.

King Bubar's gaze swept over the surrounding waters, ensuring their privacy before answering. "No. This is no fault of yours. Rudita is your Iris. You sought only to honor her vivonation, to safeguard her legacy. You acted as any Kingdom Mother would, protecting both her future and the esteem of our people."

Zaila shivered, a quiver running through her fins. "But I have heard it before… of my… of my Iris…" Her eyes glistened with unshed tears, and she struggled to meet his gaze.

"Heard what?" Bubar asked gently, though the edge in his voice betrayed his concern.

"I would lose her… to some… to some…"

King Bubar's jaw tightened. "Enough," he said, boldly. "She will be safe. She is our Iris. Soon, she will rise as the Lady of the Snows. I once opposed it, yet it is a high honor. You did not fail us. In times such as these, courage is our only path forward."

Zaila inhaled as she lingered near him, drawing strength from his steady presence, the streams around them carrying the quiet authority of a king who would not be shaken.

Rudita outpaced her sister with ease.

What was meant to be a journey of two full days, she conquered in barely thirty-six hours, driven by the distant call of her father's summons. Yet when the familiar spires of the Stone Siren Kingdom came into view, a heaviness settled over her like a shadow of the deep. The waters felt muted—currents that once sang with quiet joy now drifted in subdued silence.

She searched for her mother, the one soul to whom her heart was bound with unshakable closeness. Gliding through the echoing corridors of stone and coral, she finally found her in the Lamina Garden. Zaila floated just above the great Iris, its altar alive with a soft, pulsing glow that bathed the chamber in hues of violet and pearl.

"Where did you go?" Zaila asked, her voice low, almost a murmur that trembled with more than simple curiosity.

Rudita eased forward, her movements suddenly careful. "North," she admitted. "I only wished to see him again."

"I cannot fault you," Zaila said, turning to her with a smile that flickered like the distant shimmer of light above the surface. "He is a fine young Mosquen—gentle, honorable, respectful." Her eyes softened, but there was a tension beneath her words. "You are so young, my Iris. So innocent. So cherished."

Rudita's brow furrowed. "Is something wrong? Ruqama and I heard Father's siren."

Zaila's tail folded beneath her as she drew closer, her gaze intent. "Promise me something."

"Anything," Rudita replied, edging nearer until the faint warmth of her mother's presence wrapped around her like a tide.

"You will follow your heart—always—but never the rush of impulse."

Rudita tilted her head. "What if what lives in my heart is the very thing that drives me to act?"

A small, rueful smile touched Zaila's lips. "I should have known you would question me. Yet listen well: give yourself time to feel before you decide to move. A reaction is not always the answer."

"A reaction is always required, Mother," Rudita whispered, the quiet certainty of youth glinting in her tone.

Zaila raised her acetic and rested it against her daughter's cheek, her touch tender and cool. "Then choose the right one," she pleaded softly. "Whatever the tide brings, choose wisely. And remember—I will always love you."

Rudita pressed her own acetic over her mother's, holding it close, her heart drumming to the rhythm of that eternal promise.

Then Zaila began to hum—a siren's lullaby that had carried Rudita into sleep since childhood. The melody wound through the gardens, a sound older than the stone and softer than the seafoam. Rudita nestled against her mother and upon the Iris altar, surrendered to the melody's embrace. The weariness of her journey pulled her into slumber, while Zaila cradled her with a quiet, unspoken dread etched across her sorrowful face.

XX.

LITH FOR THE KING

Arriving in Scotland carried a quiet ache. Enu and Watson stepped from the private cabin onto the secluded runway, the late-afternoon light cold and silvery across the tarmac. Memories of home seemed to thin a little more each day, like mist dispersing over water. She suspected—as did Esam—that the chow-hall meals were to blame, laced with something meant to dull recollection. Yet she clung to the fragile hope that her hybrid blood would not betray her, that the faces of her family would not fade completely.

Today, something felt altered. Perhaps it was the sharp Highland air, or the way the body remembers what the mind forgets, but her mother's stories stirred with sudden clarity: tales of Instru and Lisser, the ancestors who crossed into Scotland generations ago and, as part of an ancient treaty, became the first of twelve Lorelie to walk the land as hybrids.

A breeze lifted from the runway, carrying dust that coiled about her like an unseen presence. She imagined their touch—ancestral warmth, ancestral warning—before a faint pressure, almost a shove, urged her back from the sleek black hovercar waiting nearby. But she had nowhere else to turn. Ignoring the spectral caution, she slid into the vehicle.

Watson followed in silence, his posture tight, his thoughts still snagged on the morning's events. Enu sensed the tension and decided to break it.

"Will there be food at the castle?" she asked, her tone light.

He blinked at her, surprised, then gave a dry scoff. "We can ask Clara for a bite. She'll oblige."

"Good. Will Her Majesty be there?"

"I am unsure. We shall see. Are you nervous yet? Do you feel it?"

"The reason you asked me here?"

A low hum of assent.

"I suppose I do. Well, aren't you going to explain?"

Watson's gaze sharpened. "Is your curiosity about the bunker because no one ever briefed you on its existence— let alone its location—or do you truly want to know why it was needed in the first place? The dangers waiting for us?"

"As a high-ranking officer, I deserve both answers."

"High-ranking, yes," he said evenly. "Trustworthy? We will see."

Enu narrowed her eyes in disbelief and settled back against the seat, spine stiff. Whatever lay ahead, she would be ready to defend herself. For Watson, the drive stretched on like a slow exhale. He kept the bag of vials clutched to his chest, fingers locked around the strap as though it were the last thing tethering him to safety. The hover vehicle glided along the mountainous road at an almost deliberate crawl, its navigation AI breaking the silence with a smooth, synthetic voice: *Would you like music?*

Before Watson could decline, Enu leaned forward with a mischievous grin. "Yes, please—hard rock and roll."

The speakers came alive with a sudden crackle, then a surge of sound: a sharp electric guitar riff, bass pounding like a racing heart, drums that rattled the cabin. Enu bobbed her head to the rhythm, her face scrunching whenever the beat seemed to shake her bones.

Watson barely noticed at first. His thoughts strayed to his family—faces he hadn't seen in far too long. Were they safe? Had his absence left them exposed? The questions dragged the minutes into something heavier, stretching the ride into what felt like hours.

Enu's impromptu concert grew wilder. She mimed an invisible guitar, arms swinging with playful precision, and then called out, "Louder!"

The AI obliged. The music swelled, a wall of sound that rattled the windows. Her head snapped with the beat, hair whipping across her cheek.

Something in the drummer's relentless pulse finally broke through Watson's haze. His shoulders began to twitch, almost involuntarily, until the rhythm took him completely. He closed his eyes, letting the vibration sink into his skin, and for the first time that day a grin cracked across his face.

"Yeah!" he shouted over the music, surprising them both.

For a brief, exhilarating stretch, time ceased to matter. Enu and Watson moved in unison, caught in the surge of sound and the shared release of unspoken tension.

Then the hover vehicle braked hard.

The music cut off mid-riff, leaving only the echo of their laughter as the sudden silence closed in.

A hush of unease clung to the halls of Balmoral Castle, as if the royal residence were harboring something sinister inside. Amer sat upright on the edge of his bed, a tray balanced across his knees, while Mary—small, pale, and visibly nervous—fed him spoonfuls of warm porridge.

Yet his mind wandered far from the room. He could not stop thinking about the figure beneath the water. If it truly was a woman—and if that was what Fiona had become—the thought pressed like a cold stone against his chest. The possibility that the love of his life had taken on such a monstrous form threatened to splinter something inside him.

He was young, but he understood the gravity of love, and now more than ever he grasped its power to wound. He needed to see Fiona himself, to know whether the girl he once cherished had vanished into legend or nightmare. Until then, he could not imagine giving his heart to anyone else.

Mary's gentle presence tugged him back. She blew across each spoonful to cool it before guiding it to his lips, her eyes wide with both care and unspoken fear. There was a soft innocence in her that rattled him. This—her tending to him, her quiet devotion—felt somehow wrong.

Where were her parents? Why had he never met them if she was meant to be his future queen? His mother would know, yet she remained absent. More than once he imagined the sharp click of her heels striking the flagstone floors, announcing her approach. But it was never her—only the distant clatter of guards' armor echoing through the corridors.

All except Watson. A sliver of him missed the man's steady presence, though he would never say it aloud. He let his thoughts drift while Mary raised another spoonful toward him. She was lovely—radiant, even—but heartbreakingly young. The tension in the room thickened until the sound of approaching footsteps stirred the silence, pulling Amer from his thoughts and setting his pulse quickening.

The sudden arrival of Watson and Enu caused Amer to sit further upright, a sharp ache lancing his ribs as he moved too quickly. He barely noticed the pain. The sight of Watson at the threshold filled him with a fierce, inexplicable certainty: this man had saved him. He could not have explained how he knew—only that something deep within whispered it as fact.

Before Watson and Enu could bow or offer a formal greeting, Amer pushed aside the tray balanced across his knees and swung his legs from the bed. Mary darted back in alarm, nearly upsetting the porridge bowl.

"Watson," Amer said, his face breaking into a smile. He crossed the room in a rush, his unsteady stride drawing anxious glances from every corner.

"Your Highness…" Watson's voice caught as he quickly shifted the strap of a weather-worn bag across his shoulder. He bent to meet the prince's embrace, stiff at first, then yielding with a reluctant warmth.

Enu watched in silence, her gaze sharp, while the guards at the doorway exchanged wary looks. Clara appeared quietly to gather the half-finished tray from Mary's trembling hands.

Then Watson's eyes found the young girl.

The moment fractured. In a heartbeat the room's walls vanished, swept away by the brutal memory of Kovos. The roar of the tide filled his ears, the brine of seawater mingled with the iron scent of blood. He saw the man—Mary's father—surging through the dark surf, eyes lit with lethal purpose. A silvered spray caught the moonlight as Watson lost his footing, the weight of the sea dragging him down while bruises bloomed across his body.

His chest tightened; the old wound throbbed as if reopened. For a brief moment he could not breathe. He tore himself from Amer's embrace as though burned and turned sharply, pretending to adjust the bag's strap once more. He would not look at Mary again.

The girl, unaware of the storm she had conjured, followed Clara out, her soft footfalls fading down the corridor. Enu noticed what the others missed—the quick recoil, the flicker of fear beneath Watson's practiced composure. Her brow furrowed. Threads of unease began to weave together in her mind, each movement in the room feeding a suspicion she could no longer ignore.

Amer's mind churned with questions he could no longer keep to himself. He dismissed the guards with a single flick of his hand, keeping only Watson. Enu waited just beyond the locked door; her quiet presence lingered like a held breath in the corridor.

Watson remained standing as Amer limped back to the bed. The bandages were gone, his color improved, and even his voice carried new steadiness.

"Why will you not let yourself relax, Watson?" Amer asked, settling onto the edge of the mattress.

"Your Highness, I am still on duty."

"You're dressed casually for a man on duty."

"Still on duty," Watson repeated, his tone clipped.

Amer tipped his head toward the door. "And the woman outside—will she replace Mavis?"

"No." Watson's eyes flickered. "Esam will assume Mavis's post as Royal Guard. Enu is a Brigadier General. She will work alongside me from now on."

Amer lowered his gaze, disappointment shadowing his features. "Alongside you on what? Do not bother lying. I have seen them."

"Seen what?"

Amer clicked his tongue in irritation. "Stop treating me like a child. Be honest. There are creatures in the water. The woman I love… she could be one of them—or worse, held captive by one."

"I highly doubt that is the case, Your Highness."

"That?" Amer's eyes narrowed. "But you do not deny there are monsters beneath our seas?"

Watson's silence stretched. Memories stirred—hybrid villages, the Queen's secret orders, the faces of those who should never have been seen.

"Why will you not answer me?"

"I apologize, Your Highness."

"I don't need apologies to my title. I need truth. If what I've overheard is real, the throne will be mine sooner than anyone expects. I must know what threatens this kingdom before I am crowned. If you will not be honest, who will? I thought we were friends."

Watson's jaw tightened. "I have the utmost respect for His Highness."

Amer heard the evasion in every word. "I will be your king soon. I need your trust if I am to help you."

Watson's gaze shifted to the floor. A slow breath escaped him; he knew Amer's destiny was not to inherit the throne at this time, but to stand beside King Eldric in battles yet to come.

"Your Highness," he said at last, voice low, "I am glad to see you well. But I must take my leave. Esam will receive orders to relocate here at 06:00 tomorrow."

He inclined his head briefly. "Please forgive my abrupt departure."

Without another word, Watson turned and strode into the corridor, his footsteps carrying him toward the King's wing before the prince could summon another plea.

"Enu!" Watson's voice carried down the hall, sharp enough to echo off the decorative ceiling. He didn't look back. His eyes burned, the threat of tears pricking their corners, yet he kept moving—stride firm, shoulders squared. Enu followed without a word, her presence steady at his back.

In the chamber they'd left behind, Amer shut his eyes and drew a slow breath, willing the dull ache in his ribs to ease.

"Jarvis!" he later called, the sound startling against the quiet.

The door opened and a young guard stepped in, posture stiff. "Yes, Your Highness."

"I need a boat. Small, with paddles."

Jarvis hesitated. "I… I'm not sure such things exist, Your Highness."

Amer arched a brow. "I'm younger than you and even I know they exist. Learn your history. They existed once; they exist still. Find one. Discreetly. Tell no one. When it arrives, you report to me and me alone."

The guard swallowed. "Ye—yes, Your Highness."

He backed away in a hurry, the clatter of his armor rattling down the corridor like a startled drum.

On the far side of the castle, deep in the Royal Quarters, Watson and Enu entered the King's chambers. A faint scent of lavender and damp washing hung in the air. Matilda bent over a basin, wringing out a length of fresh linen, her sleeves rolled to the elbow. Beyond her, on the balcony that overlooked the inner courtyard, King Eldric sat slouched in a heavy wheelchair.

The late afternoon light gilded the courtyard below, but the man it touched seemed already half withdrawn from the world. He wore soft nightclothes, his frame dwarfed by the fabric. Skin once robust had thinned to parchment; faint spots mottled his arms where the flesh seemed to be failing. His head tilted to the right as if his neck could no longer bear its own weight.

Watson and Enu bowed. "Good afternoon, Your Majesty," Watson said quietly.

The words caught in his throat. From behind, the King looked diminished—his body a mere shadow of the ruler Watson once knew. When Eldric shifted slightly, the change in profile struck harder: jaundiced eyes, their whites mottled with yellow and pinpoints of cloudy white; cheeks hollowed into sharp angles; lips pale as old marble. What hair remained clung in fragile tufts, and when the breeze stirred, a few strands lifted away like smoke.

A chill rippled through Watson, cold as the northern sea. Enu stood beside him, silent, unable to reconcile the frail figure before her with the monarch whose voice had once commanded their nation.

The room was still, silent except for the faint hum of the castle beyond its walls. Watson's hands trembled as he turned toward Matilda and Enu, his gaze a silent command: this was the moment where loyalty would be tested, trust would be proven. Enu's eyes met his, steady and unflinching, a quiet acknowledgment passing between them without a word. She felt the weight of the task pressing down, the sight of their king—so diminished, so fragile—threatening to pull tears from her eyes. But she straightened her back, shoulders rigid, a pillar of composure. Honor, discipline, restraint—these were the codes she would not break.

Watson lifted the bag of vials and handed it to Matilda, who froze, the damp linen slipping from her fingers. Her confusion was evident; the air around her seemed to thicken.

"This is vital," Watson said, his voice low but firm. "Two doses a day into his IV, every day. One before breakfast, the other before dinner. The full vial each time."

Matilda's eyes widened, a spark igniting within her. "I—I don't understand. Is this... the Lith?"

"It is," Watson affirmed. "Our king needs it. No—our nation needs it. To bring him back to us."

Tears welled in Matilda's eyes, spilling freely down her cheeks. "Of course! My God... of course! I can't believe we have it!" Her voice shook with exhilaration, hope radiating from her every movement.

But Watson's tone shifted. "However..."

The light in Matilda's eyes dimmed. "What?"

"Her Majesty cannot know."

A shadow of fear crossed her face. "Oh dear no," she whispered, shoving the bag back toward him. "I cannot defy her. She would have me killed. I... I cannot."

"Matilda," Watson's voice tightened, pulling her close. The sudden intensity made her flinch. "Listen to me. We need this. He needs this. If you do not act now, he will die. Be discreet. Do what must be done."

Her hands trembled as she clutched her rosary, lips moving in a silent plea. "Oh, my God... oh, my God..." Her voice cracked under the weight of the decision, tears streaking her cheeks. Finally, she exhaled sharply. "Okay. I... I will do it."

Enu watched quietly from the side, her expression unreadable, absorbing the seriousness of the moment.

Later, once their agreement was sealed and Matilda's help confirmed, Watson and Enu slipped from the chamber. The corridor stretched before them, silent except for their measured steps. Watson turned toward Enu, his gaze steady. "Do you think you're ready now... to handle what I need to tell you?"

"Yes…" she began, her voice tentative, but before the words could fully form, a high-pitched announcement cut through the air.

"The Queen has arrived!"

The house fell into an expectant hush, every footstep and whisper fading as all attention turned toward the foyer. Queen Emmary had entered.

The days that followed drifted by in a haze. Despite his mother's constant encouragement, Noah found himself swallowed by discouragement, adrift without direction. Each day blurred into the next. He lingered in his apartment, subsisting on takeout and immersing himself in endless reruns of his favorite shows. The phone remained silent, the campaign stagnant. Ideas for new policies flickered through his mind, only to vanish before he could commit them to paper. He felt stalled, a failure hovering at the precipice of possibility, unable to summon the inspiration to move forward.

He wandered aimlessly through the rooms, his thoughts settling repeatedly on one person—Willow. Perhaps she, *with her resourceful little team, could offer guidance*, he thought. With a final sigh, he scraped the remnants of a pint of cookies-and-cream ice cream and reached for his phone. Hesitation lingered for a heartbeat before he dialed her number, a flicker of hope stirring amid the inertia.

Piper stepped into the Prime Minister's office and was immediately struck by how small she felt. The place pulsed with quiet industry: interns hunched over laptops, staff secretaries gliding from desk to desk with folders tucked neatly beneath their arms. Their unforced rhythm made her own presence seem clumsy, like a misplaced note in a well-rehearsed symphony.

Priya had arrived long before the others, her punctuality carrying a tension that hinted at something unspoken. When her eyes found Piper, an urgency flashed through them. At home Priya's life had narrowed to shadows—hours spent in solitude, a glass of wine to dull the ache, the occasional tablet to ease the tightness in her muscles. She told herself it was only to cope, yet the absence of Lith—the king's critical treatment—gnawed at her. Where, she wondered, had the taxes truly gone? If not to preserve the monarch's life, then what purpose swallowed so much of the nation's wealth? And what role, if any, did the aliens play in this quiet siphoning?

Piper had just set her bag on Benson Jr.'s old desk when her mother rounded the corner, her movements brisk and calculated. Without a word, Priya hooked her arm through her daughter's and steered her toward the back of the room, past the low murmur of voices and the hiss of the coffee machine. The warm aroma of freshly brewed beans followed them as they slipped into the narrow supply closet near the kitchen. Priya shut the door and turned the lock with a quiet click.

Piper leveled her gaze at her mother, her arms folded tight across her chest. The silence between them carried a brittle edge. Resentment pricked at her—a low burn that had been building for days while Priya shut herself away at home. Piper and Preston had been left adrift, guessing at the reason behind their mother's retreat and finding no answers.

"Oh, don't give me that look," Priya said, her voice softer than her daughter expected.

"Well, you've ignored us for days and now you drag me in here without a word of explanation." Piper's tone was sharper than she intended, but she didn't pull it back.

Priya's eyes flicked to the door, as though she wanted to be certain no one lingered outside. "I'm glad you came," she murmured at last.

"I just—there are…new developments. I needed time to think before I could even speak of them."

Piper's irritation cooled into curiosity.

She straightened slightly, the weight of her mother's words stirring something urgent inside her. This might be the very lead the Equal Species had been waiting for.

"The King," Priya continued, the words heavy. "There is no Lith left. And his health—" she hesitated, her voice thinning to a whisper, "—his health is failing fast."

Piper blinked. "What do you mean?"

"My dear daughter…" Priya's shoulders sagged. "We haven't announced anything to the public because the truth is too bitter. Our king is in a state of rapid decline."

"That can't be right. We've always had medicine. No one here stays sick—terminal illness is something we've only read about in books."

"I'm afraid this is different."

Piper felt a chill trace the back of her neck. "Are you saying the King is dying?"

"…Or he may have already," Priya admitted. The words seemed to hang in the small space like a sudden drop in air pressure.

Priya lowered her voice until it was scarcely more than breath. "The Prime Minister and Her Majesty devised a desperate plan: they wanted Benson Jr. to wed an alien, hoping an Ember child would reignite the production of Lith and save the King. But from what I've learned…" Her eyes dimmed with resignation. "It all fell apart. And Benson—" she broke off, her silence more telling than any conclusion.

"So…the King is dead?" Piper's arms slipped from their tight fold, her fingers curling open as if the words themselves had loosened her grip. A rush of images flooded her mind—ceremonies, balcony waves, carefully staged appearances. Had every glimpse of the monarch been an elaborate performance?

"We believed they were just kidnapping the hybrid children…" The thought tumbled from her lips before she could stop it.

Priya's brow knit. "Kidnapping? Hybrid children? I don't follow."

"Mom," Piper said, her voice steadier now, edged with a grim clarity. "They've been lying to us—every one of them. Something far bigger is at work here."

Priya stepped closer, confusion shadowing her face. "Whatever do you mean?"

"The King. The hybrids. Melissa…" Piper shook her head as the pieces began to align with unnerving precision. "It all makes a terrible kind of sense now."

She turned on her heel, the decision already made. "I have to go."

"Piper! No, wait!" Priya's plea echoed after her, but her daughter was already through the door.

Seconds later, the heavy black door of 10 Downing Street swung shut with a sharp, resonant thud that silenced the corridor behind her. Outside, the morning air carried a cool dampness, the faint scent of rain clinging to the cobblestones. A crowd of protesters had gathered at the edge of the street—placards raised, voices beginning to swell in a restless chorus.

Piper halted just long enough for their chant to reach her, her pulse quickening with their rising anger. She cupped her hands to her mouth and called out, her voice slicing through the din. "You're wasting your time here! Take your voices to the gates of Buckingham Palace! Let the Queen answer for her deception!"

The shouts faltered for a breath, the crowd turning toward her as if a sudden wind had shifted their course. But Piper kept her head down, the noise of the protesters thinning as she moved farther from Downing Street. She quickened her pace toward the waiting car, her phone trembling in her hand as she scrolled to Alice's name. The screen blurred for an instant—tears she refused to shed.

She pressed call.

One ring. Two. Straight to voicemail.

"Alice, call me. It's urgent." Her voice cracked under the strain. "I just left my mother's office. The King is dead—terminal illness. This is so frightening. What if cancer returns? What if…" Her throat tightened until the words almost choked her. "…people start to die from sickness again? I'm heading to the cottage."

She ended the call with a shaky exhale, the quiet click of the phone unnervingly loud.

Across the city, in a handsome Victorian house on a quiet street in Brockley, London, Willow readied herself for work. The pre-lunch light poured through tall sash windows, spilling over the polished wood floors and softening the edges of the framed photographs along the hallway. Her phone buzzed against the countertop.

An unfamiliar number.

She frowned, brushed it aside, and reached for her jacket. A text followed immediately, the screen lighting the dim room.

I'm here. —Preston.

Willow's mouth curved into an unguarded smile. Those late-night calls had become a quiet constant, their long talks about a future that seemed almost close enough to touch. She called a quick goodbye to her parents and slipped outside.

Walking toward the car, she redialed the unfamiliar number. Two rings. A faint crackle, then a low voice: "Yes, who may I ask is this?"

She hesitated. "This is Willow… who's speaking?"

"Noah," he said, his tone certain. "Do you remember me?"

She froze for half a breath, then slid into the passenger seat as Preston held the door. "Yes. How are you?" The question left her lips while her gaze caught Preston's.

At the edge of the countryside, in a moss-framed cottage, Alice and Linus lay unemployed and tangled in the soft folds of a faded quilt. Morning light filtered through the curtains in pale ribbons. Alice stirred first, stretching before reaching for her phone.

She tapped play on the newest voicemail and set it on speaker. Piper's strained voice filled the quiet.

Linus blinked awake, propping himself on an elbow.

"Terminal illness?" he echoed, disbelief roughening his tone.

"That's impossible," Alice whispered, sitting upright as if an invisible hand had yanked her from the bed.

Alice pressed her phone to her ear, the roar of London traffic filling the pauses as she waited for Piper's voice. Across the city, Piper sat behind the wheel, the muted wail of sirens and the hiss of passing buses bleeding through the line.

Their words came quick and sharp. Piper poured out her fears—if terminal illness had returned, then the nation's most guarded secret, the production of Lith, might have faltered. That would explain the whispers of hybrid children vanishing, though the mechanics of it all remained maddeningly unclear.

For decades, universal healthcare had kept long-term sickness at bay. Taxes had dropped as disease faded into rumor, but recently the rates had begun to climb again, stirring public outrage. It raised a single, stubborn question: *where was the sterling going?*

Meanwhile, habits had shifted. Fast food chains cut corners, corporations stripped meals of nutrition, and the public indulged, confident that Lith could cure anything. For years it had—until now. Something fundamental was slipping. And it was happening fast.

XXI.

THE MAGEÍA

Naida struggled. It was not the tension between her and Riko, the Ushu, that weighed heaviest, but the relentless fog of her own fear—an invisible barrier keeping her from embracing the full scope of her power. She forced herself to focus, closing her eyes and retreating into tranquility, yet every so often she was allowed brief reprieves: the simple joy of fresh greens and fish, prepared carefully by Yvina. The Lorelie moved with quiet grace, her voice soft and steady, eyes wide with admiration as she witnessed the hybrid's transformation. She could feel the subtle shift of her aura, yet even that was not enough to free her from her father's grasp.

Moon after moon passed in the Lorelies' den. Naida pressed herself tirelessly, thinking of her father, Kalkisis, and her mother, Emaline, but their faces could not spark the magic she sought. Gently, she would rest her acetic against the finning fish, lulling them into a peaceful slumber, but the larger, more powerful creatures remained impervious. Her abilities faltered precisely where she needed them most.

One morning, Brimsey returned to the Temple of Xorri, King Bao leaving Naida to her meditation, which had begun to feel tedious, even stifling. Adolescence stirred restlessly within her—an appetite for mischief, for movement, for anything beyond the quiet repetition of her practice. She drifted away from the silent blue and sought Brimsey amid the drowned pagodas, their tiered roofs veiled in drifting silt. He was engrossed in his own work, honing the terrifying precision of his gift: the ability to turn any living thing to stone. Naida watched for a moment, a spark of rebellion flickering in her chest, and wondered if it was time to test her limits in ways she had never dared before.

As she finned closer, Naida felt a tremor deep within her, a subtle shift that made her chest tighten. Brimsey's back was to her, his focus absolute on the massive Makaras gliding below. Beneath them, small schools of fish hung frozen, petrified in the water, sinking slowly toward the seabed. Her heart seized as the realization hit—each tiny life was vanishing, one by one.

"Stop! Why are you hurting them?" she shouted, her voice slicing through the currents, but Brimsey remained motionless, unmoved, almost indifferent.

Naida's gaze lingered on him, monitoring, struggling to intervene—and then it began. The vanishing. First, the memory of her father. His face, once vivid and reassuring, blurred at the edges, fading into the emptiness of her mind. Her sister's laughter, her home ashore, the sunlit corridors where she had once played—they all began to dissolve, as if they had never existed.

A cold panic gripped her. Her acetics pressed against her small ears as her head shook violently, trying to stave off the erasure.

"Dad!" she cried, her voice cracking, bubbles scattering from her lips into the cool water.

Brimsey did not flinch.

Naida thrashed around him, fins slicing the currents, powerless to stop the theft of her reality. Riku surfaced, struggling to reach her, but even he could not stem the tide. Memories—her life, her family, her very sense of self—slipped away like grains of sand through clenched fingers. She wept, each sob echoing through the water, helpless against the uninterrupted tide consuming her world.

King Bao hovered just above the young hybrid and the Mosquen, his presence radiating a quiet sense of authority. From the shadowed depths of the Periculum Kingdom, he summoned Brimsey with a single thought. His orders were precise: unmake the mind of the hybrid. She must be stripped of what she clung to, cleansed until only the heart of her true nature remained.

The hybrid's resistance was evident, the remnants of her past life resting heavily on her. She had been too hesitant to embrace change willingly, so he would force it. Her memories, the love she had known, the family that had shaped her, would be burned away before she could step fully into the waters of her destiny. It was cruel, merciless, but Bao believed it necessary.

Naida's sobs echoed through the currents, her heart aching as faces and places slipped into the void, fading as though they had never existed. She struggled, thrashing, clawing at the water, but Brimsey was ruthless. His power was trained, precise, absolute. The Periculum Mosquen never moved a fin, never blinked. A still pool of hazel eyes deepened into smoky amethyst, fixed forward. She fought harder, summoning every ounce of strength, but the void encroached faster than her will.

Moments later, Naida gave in, letting her body sink slowly to the seabed. The sand rose in delicate clouds around her as she settled, the gentle flicker of grains reflecting the dim light filtering from above. She felt hollow, as though everything she had ever held dear had been wrenched from her without consent. Desperately, she tried to summon their return—but nothing.

Her eyes snapped open, piercing berry blue in the shadowed waters, and she saw Riko hovering nearby. He searched her mind, seeking the memories she had once carried, only to find them gone. For a moment, he hesitated, and then decided against further torment. She was suffering enough. She wanted to give up entirely, to lie there and surrender to the emptiness. What purpose remained if she could no longer remember, no longer feel?

Above her, King Bao hovered, a pitiful look etched across his concealed face. Brimsey's powers were far more than the petrifying display she had witnessed. His true gift lay in stealing memories, reshaping them, erasing the very essence of a being.

Though it seemed all was lost, Brimsey's assault was only temporary. Naida faced a stark choice—she would either confront her shadow, release the fears that bound her, and reclaim her inner strength, or she would perish. There was no middle ground.

The longer Naida lay there, squeezing her eyes shut in desperate hope, the faster tears welled, stinging and blurring her vision. She whispered into the heavy silence, "Please… be there…" But nothing answered. The memories she sought—her father laughing in the living room, tickling her as she shrieked with joy—had vanished, leaving only a blank, cold void where warmth once lingered. Panic clawed sharply at her chest.

Rising with trembling bravado, she finned toward Brimsey, who remained unnervingly still. His gaze seemed to pass through her, untouched by her presence or pleas. Clenching her teeth, she shouted, "Give them back to me!" The words echoed across the water, but he did not respond, did not move, as though her voice were swallowed by the sea itself.

"I said, give them back!" she wailed, her desperation erupting into the currents around her. The kingdom beneath the waves carried on its rhythm, indifferent to her torment. Her cries felt insignificant, her suffering reduced to the tantrum of a child.

Yet as she surged closer, she saw a shift in Brimsey's eyes. They narrowed, fixed on her, a cold intent to petrify her body. But Riko, the Ushu, felt the tension in her muscles and countered it, a subtle force holding her in place. Naida's body hummed with heat, her berry-blue eyes glowing brighter, defiant, bold. The two powers clashed in a silent standoff across the water.

"Give them back to me..." she growled, her voice low and feral.

"Give them back!" Naida screamed, her fangs bared, glinting as her voice tore through the water. Her eyes squeezed shut, arms flailing wildly, acetics curled as if mirroring the chaos inside her. The kingdom had fallen into a deep, unnatural slumber. Brimsey floated motionless, Yvina and the other Lorelies drifted silently, and even the fish and Makara glided through the water like statues, suspended in eerie calm.

King Bao hovered above, watching her struggle with detached authority. Seconds later, he thrust Naida into the depths of another trance, the currents around her thickening with unseen weight.

"Xomos Belginate," he intoned, the words vibrating through the water like a distant drum, commanding and inexorable.

Riko tore himself free from Naida, his shadow and sleek form lingering nearby, tense and alert.

"Why?" he demanded, his voice a low ripple in the water. "Is this not what you wanted?"

King Bao offered no answer. Instead, he restored the kingdom around them. The fish shimmered back to life, the Makaras regained their gentle glide, and the Lorelies stirred ever so slightly. Yet Naida remained adrift, suspended in sleep, her mind trapped between memory and void, powerless beneath the weight of his command.

King Bao propelled himself backward through the currents as he embarked on the journey to his brother's domain: King Takao, the Fènguā to Takao, God of the Ancient Kingdom. Every pulse of his body left ripples in the deep, marking his passage through the shadowed expanse of their magical realm.

Meanwhile, after moons of slumber and quiet restoration, Melusine's eyes fluttered open. Her body was slowly knitting itself back together, cells regenerating with the precision of tides. Kaliope had departed moments before, her work complete, leaving the hybrid's healing to unfold naturally. It was now no secret within the kingdom:

Melusine had been claimed by their King, a permanent part of the realm, and her presence stirred whispers among the Lorelies. Some clung to old grievances, unwilling to forgive the once loud, brash hybrid. Others, however, welcomed her with gentle smiles and cautious warmth.

As her strength returned, Melusine moved among the Lorelies, bowing subtly, offering words of thanks for their hospitality. Gratitude lingered in her chest for others she dared not approach—especially the royal chambers, where power and scrutiny met every visitor. She was guided by Harpercy, a shy but kind Lorelie whose soft giggles brought ease to Melusine's nerves. Harpercy delighted in her role, taking pleasure in showing her new sister the ways of their home. Melusine followed, careful to match her small, steady pace.

Suddenly, Kaliope appeared, moving with urgency that cut through the calm of the bitter, chilly waters. "Melusine, we must go to the King," she urged, her voice a mixture of command and concern. Even from afar, Kaliope sensed the piercing gaze of her Kingdom Mother upon Melusine, watching every movement as she emerged from the chamber. Time was short—Kaliope knew that Rudita would soon approach the hybrid if they delayed. Without hesitation, she pressed forward, guiding Melusine toward the audience with their leader.

Inside the Royal Chamber, King Khione's talons chiseled a new sculpture. The gentle sway of the water atop the ocean's surface had stirred something within him, an inspiration that made the cold marble beneath his acetics feel almost alive. He carved small, precise circles into the stone, each meant to mirror the golden stars scattered across the night sky. Though the marble reflected only the pure white of snow, the shapes seemed to shimmer with a hidden light.

Deimos glided forward, his presence forceful as he moved among the rows of Snows lined along the icy walls. Beyond them, the seaweed floated like silk in the currents, a soft, undulating curtain leading toward Khione's throne. Melusine and Kaliope approached slowly, careful to respect the silent order of the chamber. The Snows parted gracefully, forming a path for the two to pass.

Melusine faltered, her gaze locking on Deimos. His massive frame dwarfed hers, yet she recognized the protector who had saved her life. A mixture of awe and gratitude coursed through her as she lowered herself into a slight bow. She whispered, almost hoping he would hear her despite his rigid posture, "Thank you for saving my life."

The Snow Mosquen's eyes flicked downward briefly, acknowledgment and restraint evident in his tone. "Ahvi," he replied, each syllable succinct. The stoicism of the Snows—their disciplined presence—puzzled her. Turning to Kaliope, she allowed a small giggle to escape, the tension leaving her shoulders.

"Are they all like this?"

Kaliope covered her mouth shyly with her acetic, a soft laugh escaping. "Yes," she said. "Best enjoy the playfulness of the little Mosquens while you can. Once they come of age—and Deimos gets his hold of them— you'll never see them smile again." Her tone carried both amusement and a subtle warning.

"Oh no, that's just awful!" Melusine recoiled, her eyes widening as a wave of sadness washed over her.

Kaliope's expression softened, a small smile tugging at her lips. "Perhaps we should visit Father now. You might feel more comfortable sharing your thoughts with him."

"Yes, of course!" Melusine replied, nodding, and the two of them finned quietly through the currents toward King Khione's quarters. They drifted slowly past his throne, letting the swaying seaweed and gentle glow of bioluminescent coral guide their path to the rear of the sanctuary.

"Oh, Father," Kaliope called in a sing-song voice, her tone playful yet reverent. "Oh, my seashells, what are those covering your eyes?"

King Khione turned his massive frame toward her, catching a glimpse of Melusine in his peripheral vision. The hybrid froze slightly, startled by the sheer size of him. His presence was unlike anything she had ever seen, yet there was a gentleness in the curve of his lips, the warmth in his eyes that contradicted his formidable appearance.

"They're spectacles. Aren't they neat?" he said proudly, lifting his acetics to display the small, glimmering objects he had carved.

Melusine inclined her head politely, her voice soft. "You mean glasses?"

"Is that what you humans call it?" Khione asked, a hint of curiosity threading through his deep tone.

"Yes," she murmured.

"Ah," he said, and for a moment, the chamber was filled with a quiet, light laughter that seemed to ripple through the water. The tension that had gripped Melusine's chest began to ease, her fears slowly dissipating in the cold currents.

Just then, a shrill cry echoed through the sanctuary, startling both Melusine and Kaliope. Rudita's voice cut sharply through the gentle hum of the water, a jarring contrast to the serenity of the chamber.

"Do not mind her," Khione reassured them, his voice calm and steady, carrying a quiet authority that seemed to absorb the chaos.

"Father," Kaliope's voice broke the quiet, reverent in its timbre as she finned closer toward him.

"Yes, my dear Kaliope," King Khione replied, his tone calm, yet layered with authority that made the water around him feel heavier, more present.

Kaliope glanced at Melusine, her eyes gentle as she gestured with a subtle flick of her acetic. "Melusine would like to say something…" She moved slightly, ushering the hybrid to fin closer.

Melusine hesitated, then edged next to Kaliope, her acetic curling nervously. "Yes… thank you… for your mercy on my life," she murmured, her voice almost swallowed by the currents.

King Khione's gaze softened for a heartbeat. "Ahvi. Welcome home," he said, the words warm but fleeting. His expression hardened almost immediately, and his voice deepened with gravity. "Do you carry vengeance in your heart?"

The sudden shift jolted her. She recoiled slightly, unable to fathom such a notion. "No," she stammered, her words trembling. "I carry gratitude... more than anything. I know... in the past—"

Kaliope's acetic squeezed hers gently. "We must not revisit it," she interjected, eyes pleading, urging calm.

Before the moment could settle, Rudita stormed into the chamber, her movements sharp, slicing through the quiet. Her voice rang curt and accusatory. "The hybrid will have no place here. That would mark one too many."

King Khione's eyes snapped toward her, a flash of reprimand in their depths. "Rudita, darling—"

"No!" Rudita cut him off, her words like shards of ice in the frosty space.

"Daughters, please..." Khione's tone carried the gentleness of a father as he motioned for them to leave the chamber.

Kaliope tightened her hold on Melusine's acetic, guiding her slowly and cautiously toward the exit. Fear clung to her with every fin stroke as Rudita's gaze burned into her back. They moved past the swaying Snows, the vast expanse of the kingdom stretching outward, light shimmering on the water around them.

Once they were farther away, Melusine's voice trembled as she asked, "Kaliope... is it possible... that you may help me find my daughter?"

The Healing Lorelie froze, her eyes widening in surprise, a soft gasp escaping her. "Daughter? Why... of course..."

The Modiri child grew increasingly restless. Inside the glass sphere, the water pulsed as the infant twisted and turned, her tiny fin flicking in sudden, impatient motions. Each soft cackle of the sphere, each subtle shift of its currents, made Astor's heart leap despite all the resolve he had built around his work. He told himself he had accepted the risks of these experiments, their inevitable decline—but still his pulse quickened every time the child stirred.

What future awaited them? The question haunted him as he composed yet another urgent message to the chancellor, requesting an additional infusion of sterling to keep his research alive. She would not delay; she understood the consequences of hesitation all too well.

Progress with the Lith was steady. Soon it would be ready for shipment to the Americans. Yet today, there was more than scientific advancement to occupy his thoughts. His team had finally pinned the location of the ones responsible for Archie's daring escape. Astor's eyes narrowed, a hard glint catching the sterile light of the laboratory. "Bring them to me," he ordered his security detail, his voice a quiet blade in the buzzing air.

Balmoral Castle lay beneath a hush so deep it felt almost unnatural. Only the kitchen broke the stillness: the ring of metal on metal, the low murmur of servants moving between gleaming counters.

Matilda kept her promise, bringing the king's medicine under a veil of discretion. By morning, a faint renewal had settled over him—his skin held a softer glow, the faintest trace of youth—yet the transformation remained slight, scarcely visible to the casual eye.

But it was not the king that Queen Emmary yearned for. Her heart was fixed on their son. Amer's chambers had been sealed, a single royal guard permitted to deliver meals. Emmary kept to the adjoining suite, unwilling to be more than a few paces from him.

They had fashioned a quiet rhythm within those walls: breakfasts shared on the stone balcony where mist clung to the hills, evenings spent side by side with books and whispered debates about the nation's fragile politics. On rare nights she let her hair fall loose and challenged him to chess, mother and son leaning over the board while the distant forests darkened.

Esam, meanwhile, limped through his duties, the drag of his injured foot drawing wary glances from fellow guards. He roamed the grounds with patient precision, tracing every path along the perimeter. The river that edged the estate drew his gaze again and again, as if fate had set him to watch over water. He memorized the schedule of the sentries, the pattern of shift changes, the hidden corners beyond the reach of the cameras.

Though he had yet to stand before the queen or her son, Esam worked with quiet purpose, determined that his time at Balmoral would count for more than mere routine.

Enu's body ached from the incessant rotation—Scotland to London, four hours of sleep, Buckingham Palace, back to Scotland, then once again to the Palace. Now, as dusk deepened over Balmoral, she returned to the castle beside Watson, who moved with the same brisk energy as when the day began. Fatigue never seemed to touch him; the punishing schedule might have been routine to him by now.

She had met the other guards in passing, offering the polite introductions her rank required, but like her brother, she had yet to stand before the Queen. That changed on the third day.

Queen Emmary emerged from the prince's chambers as if stepping onto a stage. A charcoal pencil skirt hugged her frame just below the knees; a pearl-tinted satin blouse caught the natural light. Her dark hair, twisted into a neat chignon, revealed a complexion that looked freshly renewed. Even her nails—short and polished, a soft bubblegum pink—spoke of quiet refinement. Yet behind the youthful glow, her eyes carried little warmth.

She surveyed the corridor and the new faces it held with an edge of distaste. The younger guards struck her as clumsy, unseasoned. Her gaze lingered on Watson as though his presence alone steadied the air.

Both he and Enu wore their off-duty uniforms, the dark fabric softening their military lines. The click of the Queen's heels echoed sharply on the marble as she approached.

"Where did you find these uncoordinated misfits?" Her voice cut through the hall like glass.

Watson's mouth curved in the barest suggestion of a grin. "Uncoordinated?" he said lightly, matching her stride down the corridor. Enu followed a respectful pace behind, hands clasped neatly at the small of her back.

The Queen stopped without warning.

Enu nearly collided with her.

"And who are you?" Emmary demanded, turning the full weight of her scrutiny on the newcomer.

Enu straightened, heel taps clicking together in instinctive salute. "Brigadier General Agha Enu, Your Majesty. Here on special orders with the Major General."

"Special orders?" The Queen's gaze slid to Watson, her tone sharpening into quiet inquiry.

"Yes, Your Majesty. A spectator and nothing more," Watson confirmed, his gaze locking sharply on Enu's. It was a silent command, a cue for her to echo his words.

"Correct, Your Majesty," Enu said, steadying her voice.

"Well, it is good to meet you," Queen Emmary replied. Enu stepped forward, extending her hand—a touch of nerves tightening her fingers. But before the handshake could land, the Queen pivoted smoothly on her heel and continued down the corridor. The abrupt dismissal left Enu's hand suspended for a fraction too long, the air suddenly cool where the gesture had been refused.

"We will travel to America in the morning," the Queen announced without looking back.

Watson's brow arched. "Morning?"

"Yes. Will that be a problem? President Kirlin is expecting us. There is much to discuss."

"Understood. Of course."

Enu's breath caught. America—by morning? Her mind reeled at the thought. When would there be time to rest, to train? The schedule felt like a persistent punishment, a new order landing before she could recover from the last.

Elsewhere in the castle, Esam stood stationed outside Amer's door. He had seen the Queen earlier, yet she passed him as if he were part of the marble columns. The silence around him deepened until the door creaked open and Amer emerged, his expression unreadable. He scanned the hall with a slow, deliberate glance before motioning for Jarvis.

"Inside," Amer murmured.

Jarvis obeyed, slipping into the chamber and drawing the door shut with a careful click. Esam tilted his head, uncertainty flickering across his face. By rank, he stood above Jarvis; anything His Highness had to say to the younger guard could—and should—be said to him. After a brief hesitation, Esam placed his hand on the latch and let himself in.

Appalled by the intrusion, Amer swung toward the door, his dark eyes narrowing. Jarvis stiffened where he stood, confusion flickering across his face like a sudden draft.

"Why are you in here?" Amer's voice cut through the chamber, low and sharp.

Esam nonchalantly stepped forward.

"Your Highness, with respect, I am your newly appointed guard. It is my duty to oversee your safety— wherever you are, and no matter who is present."

Amer's shoulders rose and fell in a quiet shrug.

"Fine. Close the door."

The heavy oak groaned as Esam obeyed, the latch clicking shut with a sound that settled uneasily in the silence.

"Well," Amer turned back to Jarvis, his tone softening only slightly, "any news on the boat?"

"Yes—yes, Your Highness," Jarvis stammered. "I found one with paddles, as ordered. It's anchored at the rear of the grounds."

"Good."

A crease formed between Esam's brows. "Boat?" he asked, the single word edged with suspicion.

Amer's gaze snapped to him, cold and unsettling. "That is not your concern. You were not invited to this council for a reason. And now, I fear I must swear you to secrecy."

"There is no need," Esam replied evenly. "As I said, my purpose is your safety. Whatever your plans, I will accompany His Highness."

A flicker of amusement passed over Amer's face. He chuckled, the sound dry as paper. "You will do no such thing. I will never share my intentions with you. You will not know when I leave, nor when I return—much less why I embark on this journey."

"As you wish," Esam said quietly. Yet behind his composed expression, he held a secret. He'd come to know the castle grounds better than any of his peers. Amer would not slip from his sight. Not for a single moment.

The Queen, flanked by Watson and Enu, strolled through the castle grounds while a small detail of guards followed at a respectful distance. The gardens, washed in early-afternoon light, were a quiet marvel of emerald lawns and sculpted hedges. Queen Emmary slowed, drinking it in; she had almost forgotten how striking the place could be.

Her gaze settled on a narrow trail edging the rose beds—the very path she once walked with her husband as he weakened, the wheels of his chair whispering over the gravel. Memory pressed against her chest, heavy yet strangely calm. She turned to Watson, eyes composed, a quiet acceptance in their depths.

"Preparations for His Majesty's final days will need to be put in order."

Watson and Enu exchanged a fleeting look of unease.

"Have you not been to see him?" Watson asked carefully.

"What for? So his last breath can be drawn in my presence? I will not allow it. I know his fate and have accepted it."

"Do you?" Watson's voice softened, but the question lingered like a subtle challenge. He paused, wary of crossing a line. His respect for the King was unshaken, and a faint sense of betrayal stirred within him at the Queen's detachment.

"Is there knowledge I am missing?" she asked, arching a brow.

"No. I suppose not."

"I understand your allegiance to my husband, our great King," she said, her tone cool but measured. "Yet we must move forward. A terrible illness has taken hold of him, and while he is past the point of recovery, there are others whose futures must now be safeguarded."

"But the Lith," Watson ventured, "you advised Dr. Astor to rid the lab of the finned Modiri."

"Finned Modiri? Hmph. Either way, yes, I was there. I remember." Her voice sharpened, the faintest edge of sarcasm in it. "Is there a problem? You seem… different since my return."

"No," Watson replied at once. "Only seeking to know how best I can be of service. My loyalty to Her Majesty does not waver."

"Phenomenal." A brief, knowing smile curved her lips. "Then we begin preparations for his quietus—and perhaps even hasten the process." A soft, almost careless chuckle followed. "Our young Amer and I have spoken. Though young, he is ready."

"I understand," Watson said, though his jaw tightened.

Queen Emmary turned and started back down the gravel path toward the castle, the summer breeze lifting a stray wisp of her hair. Their conversation was at an end.

Inside, her voice rang across the marbled hall. "Guards! Fetch the chambermaid. Lady Mary must be readied for our departure in the morning."

XXII.

THE CAMPAIGN

By late afternoon, Willow closed her laptop and gathered her things, the soft click of drawers and the rustle of papers marking the end of her workday. She slipped through the quiet corridors and out toward the office parking lot where Preston waited, their schedules syncing as if by unspoken agreement. It had been decided earlier: the Equal Species would meet at the cottage, with Willow bringing Noah into their evening plans.

Piper, meanwhile, had taken a different route after leaving the Prime Minister's office. Drawn by an old curiosity, she turned toward the city's stone-front library, the kind of place where dust and history mingled in the air. She searched the dim stacks for slender volumes chronicling the nation's forgotten illnesses—afflictions once common but now the stuff of legend. Breast cancer, strokes, diabetes…all diseases erased since the Lith had entered their society, as if plucked clean from the human story.

Elsewhere, Alice and Linus strolled through the narrow aisles of a neighborhood market, filling a basket with bread, cheese, and fruit. They expected the night to stretch long and wanted something hearty to share. Max remained unreachable, but no one pressed for an explanation.

By the time their separate paths converged at the cottage, the sky had begun to darken. Low clouds rolled across the horizon, and a sudden rumble warned of rain. Piper, Preston, and Willow quickened their pace, dashing toward the door as the first drops spattered against the windows, eager to escape the downpour gathering above.

"Come on, hurry now!" Alice called, holding the door wide as they tumbled inside. The air smelled of wet earth and the faint sweetness of the bread Linus had left warming in the oven. Willow set her bag on the bench and brushed a few stray raindrops from her hair. They removed damp cardigans and squeaky shoes.

"Thanks, Alice," she said, breathless.

Piper's lips curled into a sly smile. "Well, well, well… if it isn't the secret lovebirds," she teased, lifting a hand in mock accusation. "Don't bother denying it. I saw them arrive together—holding hands, no less. Tried to pull apart before I noticed, but I'm far too quick for that."

"Oh, Piper…" Willow groaned, cheeks flushing.

"What's the big secret? My best friend, possibly about to become my sister-in-law? That's headline news."

"See, now you're getting ahead of yourself," Willow said, half laughing, half flustered.

In the kitchen, Preston and Linus busied themselves with clinking dishes and the low hiss of the kettle.

"Proud of you for finally saying something," Linus murmured to Preston as he passed him a mug.

"Ah, stop. It was bound to happen," Preston replied with a quiet chuckle, tapping his friend's shoulder before crossing back to the living room.

He helped Piper stack the books she had carried in, their covers spotted with rain. "Heavy load," he said, eyeing the titles.

"I went to the library," Piper replied, her teasing gone. "You all… this is frightening. What are we going to do?"

Willow frowned and flipped through one of the damp-edged books. "Why is this suddenly so urgent?"

Piper drew a sharp breath. "The King is dead."

The room fell still. Even the kettle's hiss seemed to fade. The weight of the words settled like a sudden frost.

"Rubbish," Willow said at last. "No way. There's nothing on the news?"

"It's a cover-up," Piper insisted, her voice tightening. She pointed to the open pages in front of her. "These diseases, these plagues—what if they're coming back? And no one's warning us. They've been lying for years, hiding the truth in silence. Even our taxes are built on their deception."

A slow unease seeped into the room, as though the storm outside had found its echo in every quiet heartbeat.

"But even if any of that is true, we have no proof," Willow said, her voice steady but low. "There's no sense in riling people on speculation alone. We're already living in a pressure cooker. One wrong spark and no one knows how the public might react. Truth or not, it would end badly."

"She's right," Linus agreed, leaning forward with his elbows on his knees. "And even if something needs to be said, it can't come from us."

Willow exhaled slowly, her gaze sweeping across the group. "I invited Noah here," she admitted at last. "Before you all get worked up—he called this morning. He wants to work with me on the campaign."

"Campaign?" Alice asked, blinking in confusion. "And who is Noah?"

"The Benson boy," Piper reminded her. "Prime Minister's son."

"Oh!" Alice's eyes widened. "He's coming here?"

"Yes. I told him we'd all be here tonight."

A small smile broke across Alice's face as she glanced at Linus. "Good thing we went shopping after all."

"If he's willing," Willow continued, her voice carrying a quiet urgency, "maybe he can help bring the truth to light—no more lies, no more careful omissions. If people knew the true state of the King, they'd demand answers. No one wants those diseases to return. We're talking about our children, our entire civilization."

The idea hung in the air like a fragile promise. Even Piper, who often met tension with a quip, remained silent.

From outside came a low, unfamiliar hum. It started faintly, like the vibration of distant thunder, and grew until it resonated against the windows. Alice stiffened.

Piper crossed to the curtain and pulled it back a fraction. Her breath caught. "There's... something out there," she whispered.

A sleek, black hover vehicle floated just beyond the garden. It didn't move. It only hovered, a dark silhouette against the deepening sky—as if watching, listening, waiting.

No one spoke. The quiet inside the cottage deepened until even the ticking of the kitchen clock sounded too loud.

"Should someone go out and say something?" Alice asked, her voice barely above a whisper.

"No," Linus replied, keeping his gaze fixed on the window. "It's probably just someone lost. We ignore it, they'll leave… hopefully. Or—" he turned toward Willow, his brow furrowed, "could it be Noah?"

Willow gave a helpless shrug. "No clue."

They clustered near the narrow cottage window, their faces caught in the faint glow of the outdoor light. Outside, the black hover vehicle remained motionless. No flicker of movement inside the tinted glass.

None of them knew the truth—that the craft carried no driver at all. It was an extension of Dr. Astor's lab, a silent predator disguised as a car. Inside its metallic frame, a surveillance core thrummed, beaming a live feed straight back to the underground bunker miles away.

On a wall of monitors, their images bloomed into view one by one: Willow leaning against the sill, Linus and Preston both tense behind her, Piper and Alice drawn into the uneasy vigil. The vehicle's headlamps pulsed faintly, doubling as high-grade biometric scanners. Within seconds, data streamed across Astor's screens: names, ages, family histories, occupations—every secret distilled into lines of cold text.

Astor's eyes narrowed when a familiar name appeared. Alice Watson. His fingers drummed the console as he flipped through the scanned files, the light from the monitors sharpening the creases around his eyes. A slow, calculating smile tugged at the corner of his mouth.

Without a word, he keyed in a final command. The hover vehicle, obedient as a trained hound, disengaged from its silent watch. With a low, mechanical hum, it pivoted in midair and drifted back into the stillness, returning to the hidden lab that had sent it.

Inside the cottage, the group stayed frozen at the window long after the sound faded, the evening pressing in heavy and still. None of them sensed the quiet invasion that had already begun.

Dr. Astor's bunker pulsed with the sound of machinery feeding on energy and ambition. Banks of monitors flickered, reflecting off steel counters cluttered with glass tubes and neatly labeled vials. At the center of it all, more Embers bled like molten stars into the extraction device. The infant stirred now and then, a soft shiver beneath the halo of light, but nothing that would interrupt Astor's work.

He moved like a man possessed, adjusting the microscope with a surgeon's precision. His experiments had begun to outgrow their original purpose, branching into something far greater—something only he understood.

The quiet was broken by the measured click of heels on the polished floor. Chancellor Katie Porter emerged from the elevator, her navy suit sharp against the sterile glow. Hair pinned in a sleek knot, she carried the brisk confidence of someone accustomed to command. She had arrived in a private car, careful to avoid attention; her visit was meant to be brief.

Katie halted at the upper platform, her eyes catching on the massive screen stretched across the west wall. Two faces stared back at her in frozen high definition: Alice and Linus. Their profiles were magnified until every feature was uncomfortably clear.

"I should have come sooner," she murmured, exhaling as though releasing a burden. Her hand hovered near the railing, but she avoided contact, as if the very surfaces of the lab were tainted. She never trusted Astor.

"Why?" His voice floated up without turning. He remained bent over his work, sliding a sliver of specimen beneath the magnifying lens.

"The Queen came to see me," Katie said. "She's given me instructions."

Astor's hand paused, the fine instruments trembling slightly. "Is that so?"

"Yes. I'm to cease funding for whatever it is you and King Eldric have demanded of me."

At that, Astor finally turned. The cold blue of his eyes locked on hers like a sudden blade. "You will do no such thing," he said, his words low and sharp.

"And why not? According to Her Majesty, the King is as good as dead. Why must we continue?"

Astor's composure cracked. His voice burst through the lab with such force that technicians at distant workstations froze mid-task. "He is not dead!" The sound echoed off the steel walls. "You will not question my genius!"

Katie took a step back, her pulse quickening. She glanced over her shoulder toward the elevator, gauging the distance to a quick escape. "You're losing your mind."

Astor straightened, his lab coat settling across his shoulders with willful care. His voice dropped to a hiss, each syllable carrying the chill of a promise. "And you will lose your life if you disobey us. Do as you were told. Leave."

With that, he bent again over the magnifying glass, as if nothing at all had transpired, the steady purr of the machines swallowing the last echo of his threat.

By nightfall, the cottage had settled into a gentle warmth. Linus's bread—still faintly fragrant of rosemary—lay in thick slices on a wooden board. The tea steamed in mismatched mugs, carrying the faint scent of honey and chamomile. Conversation had rolled easily through the evening, but as the hours stretched on, a quiet restlessness began to settle over the group. Piper stifled a yawn, blinking at the flicker of the light above.

"Where is this guy?" she asked, rubbing her arms against the growing chill.

Willow, already checking her phone, tapped a quick message to Noah. His reply appeared almost before she'd set the phone down: *Arriving shortly.*

"He's on his way," she announced, the slight tremor in her voice betraying her nerves. "Am I the only one who's anxious?"

"Nope," Alice shot back without hesitation. "And inviting him here might be the dumbest idea we've had. No one should know about this place."

Willow raised a brow. "Well, where else was I supposed to meet him? My parents' house? Piper and Preston live with their mother—hardly ideal."

Alice tilted her head toward Linus with a teasing grin. "Sounds like we're the orphans, babe."

"Stop it," Willow said with a halfhearted laugh, but the playful mood snapped at the crunch of tires on gravel.

The sound cut through the stillness. Everyone froze.

It wasn't the low whine of a hover vehicle—thankfully—but the softer purr of a traditional engine. Outside, headlights washed the hedgerows in pale gold as a car eased to a stop.

A figure stepped out. Noah, dressed down in a dark tracksuit and a baseball cap, scanned the property with a quick, cautious sweep of his eyes. There was something about the home that stirred an odd flicker of recognition in him.

Alice, never one to hesitate, pulled the door open before he could knock.

"Come in," she said, her voice bright, almost too bright.

Inside, the brightness from the kitchen lights softened the wooden beams overhead. Linus, lounging on the bottom step of the staircase, rose and extended his hand.

"Linus."

"Noah." His grip was firm, his glance searching the room until it settled on Willow.

She stepped forward, her smile both inviting and cautious. Behind her, Preston and Piper called their greetings from their seats, earning only a small, weary wave from the newcomer.

"So…" he began, the word hanging in the warm air.

"Right," Willow said quickly. "I take it you've given more thought to our earlier discussion?"

"I have."

"Oh—where are my manners?" Alice cut in, reaching for the teapot. "Water? Tea? We've even got fresh bread."

Willow couldn't tell if her tone leaned toward sarcasm or genuine hospitality. Either way, she gestured to the table.

"No, I'm fine, thank you," Noah replied, his eyes still moving, still weighing the space as if the walls themselves held secrets. "Sorry if I'm looking everywhere," Noah said with a faint, almost sheepish smile. His gaze wandered over the timbered beams and the ivy-framed windows as though each detail tugged at some memory just out of reach. "This place feels... oddly familiar, though I can't say why."

Willow tilted her head, studying him. "That's all right. But..." She drew a slow breath, forcing her voice into something steady. "I suppose we should get down to business."

"Of course."

Noah straightened, the shift in his posture subtle but intentional. He shrugged off his tracksuit jacket, revealing a crisp white V-neck. The soft fabric clung to his frame, the simple gesture carrying the quiet confidence of someone ready to speak with purpose. He draped the jacket across the back of a chair and settled his focus fully on Willow, the easy smile fading into something more determined. The hiss of the kettle and the faint creak of the old floorboards filled the pause, a fragile hush before the conversation truly began.

In the wee hours of the night, the Arctic roared like a living beast. Thunder rolled across the horizon in long, metallic rumbles that shivered through the black water. Rain fell in hard, hissing sheets, each drop striking the ocean's skin with a sound like a thousand tiny drumbeats. The surface quivered beneath the assault, a silvered lattice of ripples that caught what little light remained. The rain was no gentle drizzle—its frozen needles would have scorched human flesh, leaving skin mottled and blistered within moments.

Above, the heavens offered no reprieve. A dense quilt of storm clouds smothered the stars and the moon, turning the night into a vault of ink. Yet far below that smothered darkness, the ocean kept its quiet rituals. Tiny synnett fish drifted through the black like wandering sparks, their luminous bodies pulsing with a soft white glow. They glided in perfect harmony with the current, as though summoned to appear only when the sea reached its deepest shade.

The Modiri, with eyes evolved to pierce any darkness, watched the procession without strain. But even they sensed the solemn purpose of the synnett's glow. The little creatures carried their light like a secret offering, and their flicker threaded through the Lorelie's chamber in slow, liquid ribbons.

Within, Melusine stirred restlessly. Her fin brushed the swaying seaweed, parting the fronds in slow, calculated motions. The luminous fish wove around her like drifting stars, and for a breathless moment the chamber seemed a cathedral of quiet, the storm's fury above reduced to a distant, muffled hymn.

Alone in the quiet drift of the Lorelies' halls, Melusine glided toward the royal chamber, her pulse quickening with each slow sweep of her tail. She longed for another glimpse of him—just a moment's exchange, a trace of his voice—anything to ease the restless curiosity that had carried her through the night. She would not arrive empty-handed. From the pouch nestled against her side, she drew the small cluster of berries Kaliope had pressed into her acetic before their slumber. Their faint, briny sweetness perfumed the water, a simple gift and, perhaps, a quiet invitation to speak.

The passage narrowed into the corridor of the Snows. Rows of them lined the icy walls like statues carved from frost, their forms catching the pastel shimmer that filtered from the distant synnett fish. They slept upright in their sentinel stance, as tradition demanded, each taking turns to guard while the others drifted in a warrior's trance. Only one pair of eyes remained open—his.

Melusine slowed, her movements measured and fluid so as not to break the hush. The spear in his grasp gleamed faintly, its point a pale echo of the frozen stone. His gaze lowered as she approached, and for an instant, the hush of the chamber deepened until even the soft sway of seaweed seemed to still.

"Good night," she whispered, her voice barely more than the ripple of a current. They were near the King's throne now, the gate to his chamber lifted long ago on Rudita's unexplained orders.

Melusine drew back the flap of her pouch, revealing the berries nestled like tiny fish eggs in the dim light. "I brought you something," she said softly, offering the fragile cluster to Deimos.

The senior Snow did not answer. His eyes, half-shadowed, lingered on her gift in silence, the surrounding waters holding their breath as if waiting for the night itself to speak.

"It's all right if you're not one for initiating conversation," Melusine said gently. "My name is Melusine. I hear yours is Deimos. That's a beautiful name."

The Snow Soldier remained motionless. He gave no sign that he'd heard her until she spoke again.

"Where I come from," she continued, her voice soft but insistent, "silence in the middle of a dialogue is usually taken as disinterest."

At last, Deimos moved. He extended his acetic, taking the cluster of berries with a slow, intentional grace, then pointed toward the chamber's exit.

"You will return to your slumber now," he said, his tone a quiet command.

"Yes," Melusine replied with a quick smile. She turned to go, her heart thrumming. Warmth crept across her cheeks and the smile lingered, unshakable—until the shadows ahead shifted.

Rudita materialized without warning, her immense form blotting out the faint glow of the corridor. Eyes gleamed like wet obsidian, and as her fangs slid into view, the dim light caught their sharp curve.

Melusine's breath hitched. Her smile vanished, and a tremor coursed through her chest. "I-I-I'm so sorry," she stammered, her fins faltering as she dipped in a hasty bow. She thought she might have drifted into the matriarch's path.

But Rudita only watched, silent and unblinking. With a slow sweep of her massive fin, she turned away, leaving the young hybrid to gather herself and hurry back into the Lorelies' halls.

In the east, King Bao had arrived. As the sun sank toward the horizon, a final ribbon of light shimmered across the sea, setting the waters aglow. The sunset poured a warm sheen over the surface where Orbital Relay Operators and Ocean Recovery Crews worked in quiet coordination aboard their mid-sized vessels. Overhead, satellites and drifting stations took on the next leg of their task—catching, storing, and launching cargo pods toward precise coordinates. Most struck their targets without error. A few, however, missed with unnerving regularity. Whether by chance or design, no one could say.

The Unagi circled King Bao in slow, fluid arcs as he advanced, their fins flashing silver in the dying light. Far below, King Takao—the Fènguā to Takao, God of the Ancient Kingdom—waited like a vision few mortals had ever glimpsed. Suspended in the blue as though the ocean itself had shaped it, the being known as the Weeping Orb of Zan Zian glowed like a living jewel.

It appeared to be a crystalline heart, grown from coral roots and laced with veins of red luminescence. Threaded through its mass were filaments of some unknown substance, neither plant nor mineral. The colossal sphere seemed to breathe, swelling and contracting in a slow rhythm that made the surrounding water tremble. At its core, a lattice of pale geometry pulsed like the beat of a vast, hidden heart, each flicker sending a faint wash of light through the tangle of coral and stone.

No fish strayed near. Recovery crews spoke of an invisible current that pushed them back, and some swore they heard faint hymns rise from within—a music that lingered long after they returned to shore, driving a few to restless madness.

Legends claimed the orb was the last relic of a sorcerer's bargain with the heavens. Some said it held the ocean's strength to shield the world from catastrophe. Others feared it was a prison, binding something too immense to release. Whatever the truth, it shone in the deep like a fragment of another realm, a beacon of wonder and quiet dread in the heart of the Eastern waters.

King Bao inclined his head in a measured bow. When he spoke, his voice carried like a low, resonant tide, each word steeped in ceremony.

"Kingdom Brother."

The vast sphere before him glimmered, as though roused from an age-long sleep. No form emerged—no Modiri shape to inhabit the sound—only the voice of King Takao. It rolled from the orb with the weight of stone fracturing, a tremor running beneath the deep, regal timbre.

"Kingdom Brother."

Bao straightened. "I come on behalf of the Attanga."

A pause—an audible ripple through the surrounding water. "Oh?" Takao's reply rumbled like distant thunder. "I know not of what you speak."

"A hybrid."

"No." The single word struck like a closing gate.

"Kingdom Brother," Bao pressed, the faint shimmer of his acetics hidden. "Is it not tradition?"

"Not for an outsider."

"But this union is of the Attanga... and an Ushu."

Silence stretched until the depths themselves seemed to hold their breath. Then Takao's voice sharpened, a sudden surge of power. "Ushu!"

"Ahvi," Bao said carefully.

"How can that be?" Takao's voice grew rough, nearly a growl. "What of the Ahalty? What say they?"

"Tradition must be upheld," Bao answered. "I have yet to see the Ahalty or our Sea God Poseidon, but I have seen the hybrid. She is ancient—her legend demands to unfold."

"You would concede to such folly?"

"Ahvi," Bao countered softly, "I seek the stone. The one destined to be bound to it."

"I will not release it. Show it to me," Takao ordered.

The orb's glow deepened, red veins brightening like heated metal. Though without shape or face, Takao's presence pressed against the water, immense and undeniable—the mightiest of the Eastern rulers. The ocean seemed to tighten around them as Bao held his position, motionless, while the sphere's ancient consciousness reached inward, probing the hidden corners of his mind.

Naida's subconscious churned, a storm within itself, yet something had shifted. This time, she would not be dictated to. This time, she was in control. She muttered to herself as she paced the dreamscape, the shadows stretching and folding around her.

"They just keep taking them from me!" she bellowed, the words echoing against the vast emptiness. Her chest tightened, tears threatening to spill, but she pressed them back. "No more crying, Naida. No more fear. Find them."

She lowered herself to the ground, legs crossed, arms resting at her sides, eyes shutting as she had watched King Bao do countless times. She had never taken him entirely seriously, yet emulating his poise brought a strange steadiness. Now, it mattered less what he embodied and more what she would find within herself. "Find them…" she whispered.

In the void of her mind, she searched, pressing her eyes together as the emptiness stretched endlessly, a blackened ocean that seemed to grow with every heartbeat. She lingered, tracing unseen contours, until at last, she let go.

Her shadow was no longer an enemy but a forgotten twin—a keeper of buried wounds, locked-away fears, and the silent rage she dared not show. To fin alongside her shadow was not to conquer it but to bow before it, to light a lantern in the silence that had taken root.

Naida's shadow work demanded surrender: the release of masks, of false crowns, of the brittle need to appear unbroken. It required courage, not to fight, but to feel—to sit with the ache of memory, to trace anger to its source, to weep where she had once pretended strength.

The control she relinquished was not weakness. It was liberation: freedom from the tyranny of image, from the endless performance of being "strong to be accepted".

She no longer fled from the darkness within. Instead, she embraced it, weaving night and day into the same living thread, feeling the full spectrum of herself, unafraid and wholly present.

Within the temple, Riko could feel the shift. His shadow receded, flowing back into Naida's vessel as if returning home. She was him, and he was her—but not as before. This time, she emerged as an Obi, a true Obi, commanding presence and power. Riko could no longer slip away at will; she was the authority now, the guiding force. The darkness that had once constricted her began to crumble, its walls dissolving as she faced the grief she had long buried. Slowly, she allowed herself to feel it all.

And then he appeared, exactly as he had always been. A sly smirk curved his lips, a glint danced in his eyes, and though his Modiri form appeared slightly smaller than the purebreds she had seen, it was enough. With her eyes closed and her heart wide open, she whispered, "Dad…"

"Fiona," he murmured in return.

The sound of his voice shattered the final dam within her. Years of restraint, of tears thought lost forever, poured forth. "I miss you so much," she cried. In response, Kalkisis's form wholly materialized before her like an apparition, his arms encircling her shoulders, grounding her. She could feel the press of his hands against her skin—human hands, solid and real—no acetics, no Modiri distance, just a father embracing his daughter.

"You don't have to be strong," he said gently.

"But I do. I have to—for Mary and Melissa, for you, for Mummy," she sobbed, her body trembling.

"No, no, Fiona," he insisted, voice steady, eyes full of unbending care. "You do not."

"They keep taking you all from me…" Naida's voice trembled, a fragile thread stretching across the emptiness of her mind.

"They cannot take anything. We will never leave you," he said, his tone steady, anchoring her through the storm of her grief. Slowly, her chest rose and fell, a deep sigh escaping as she struggled to regain composure. "I want our memories back," she whispered, longing heavy in her words.

"Then bring us back," he said with a soft smile, the kind that seemed to light the shadows around her. "You've grown so much."

Naida chuckled, warmth spreading through her cheeks, a blush creeping across her face. "How are you here?"

"The Mortis God… she is kind," he replied.

"Oh! Will I meet her?"

"I pray it will not be any day soon," he said, a hint of gentle caution threading through his voice.

Naida's gaze fell, tracing the abyss around her as more color began to seep into the darkness. The flowers she had nurtured began to bloom again, petals unfurling like sparks of hope. Her eyes shone with renewed light, twinkling with the possibility of reunion. "When will I see you again?"

"Anytime you need me. I will come," he assured her, a presence as steady as the tide, yet untouchable.

"I will not allow anyone to take you from me ever again," she declared, her voice fierce, carrying across the void she had built around herself.

"I trust you…" Kalkisis murmured, his form beginning to dissolve into the shimmering shadows of the world she had created. His voice drifted like a fragile echo over a cliff into the nothingness, tender yet distant. "I love you, Fiona."

And with that, he faded, leaving her in the quiet afterglow of their reunion, a warmth lingering where his presence had been, a reminder that some bonds could never be broken.

The world of her subconscious shifted, transforming into a riot of color and life. Flowers continued to bloom in vibrant swathes, clouds shed their grey weight, and the suspended stone returned to its natural hue. Naida, relying on no one but herself, decided it was time to wake. Slowly, she opened her eyes in the Makara Kingdom, suspended in the water before Brimsey, who stared, astonishment frozen across his features. She rose upright, posture steady, ready to face him.

Reactively, Brimsey drew his seaweed weapon, preparing to strike, his fear mirrored in the sharp tension of his muscles. Naida raised her arm instinctively, trembling as she shielded her face. A flash of movement— Riko broke free, barely, his shadow coiling around her, intercepting what would have been a fatal blow to her skull.

"Stop!" Yvina's voice rang, cutting through the tension. Startled by both the intervention and the sound of Yvina's command, Brimsey hesitated, then lowered his weapon.

"Why is she awake?" he bellowed, addressing the Lorelie.

Naida's gaze turned icy, her eyes a piercing berry blue. "You took my family from me!" she seethed.

"No, you will both stop!" Yvina interposed, finning swiftly to position herself between the two.

Brimsey scowled, anger flashing in his gaze. "And how did she… do that?"

But Naida's attention was elsewhere—on Riko. His voice boomed inside her mind, a thunderous echo vibrating through her skull.

"Listen here, hybrid! If you perish, we both do. I did not endure in limbo all these centuries, escape the prisons of my brother's realms, only to be annihilated by some worthless adversary!"

"Stop yelling at me!" Naida shouted, but from Brimsey and Yvina's perspective, it seemed as though she were arguing with herself. "How was I supposed to know he was going to hit me?!" she demanded.

"Hit? Hit! He was going to kill us!" Riko's shadow hissed through her consciousness.

"Then what do I do now?" she asked, panic lacing her words.

"Summon me, defend us, but do not do nothing!" Riko's voice thundered one last time.

"Oh… well, how do I summon you?" she asked, eyes darting through the swirling currents around her.

"Figure it out!" he snapped, then fell silent.

"Ushu? Ushu! Hey, where did you go?"

Back in the Ancient Kingdom, King Takao had seen enough. The waters around them began to tremble, small ripples rising into larger swells as a vein from the massive crystalline sphere extended outward. Suspended in the water before King Bao was a tiny statue—Kutoka.

Like Aiolos, Kutoka was a sea creature for the Attanga. He was a colossal black polar bear, his body covered not in fur but in scales that sparkled like the surface of a deep ocean. Instead of ordinary paws, his limbs ended in webbed claws and pads, perfect for slicing through water with devastating speed and precision.

Perched atop his head was a crown of burnished gold, intricately wrought, fitted with small sapphire diamonds that gleamed like stars in the dark sea. The crown was a symbol not only of his might but of his dominion over the depths and land. Even in miniature form, the aura of authority radiating from Kutoka was undeniable.

"It bears a crown?" King Bao asked, his gaze fixed on the statue.

"Destiny determined it," King Takao rumbled.

XXIII.

AMERICA

In the morning, Kaliope sensed the lighthearted energy spilling from Melusine—a girl wrapped in the thrill of new affection. She combed her long hair with a whalebone, teasing out each knot before weaving in tiny, lost seashells. In the reflection of the icy sculptures, she practiced a soft, lilting "baby" voice, as if rehearsing a spell meant only for Deimos.

She longed for him to notice her.

Deimos was everything she had once dreamed of for a companion: strong, disciplined, kind. Yet before she could surrender to such thoughts, her heart remained tethered to a single mission—finding the daughter who had been taken from her. In her mind, Deimos might one day be the perfect figure for the child to look up to.

Melusine hummed a gentle tune as she readied, but the melody faltered when Rudita's furious cries pierced the quiet. From the royal chambers came the sharp cadence of anger—accusations hurled at King Khione. Rudita's voice was edged with impatience and a simmering disgust at his sudden kindness toward the hybrid.

The other Lorelies exchanged knowing glances, their eyes cutting toward Melusine like polished shards of ice.

She kept her head bowed, but Kaliope felt the ripple of unease and gave a reassuring tug at her arm.

"Come with me," Kaliope whispered.

Melusine followed, her fin trailing in a slow, solemn sweep. Inside the private alcove, Kaliope arched a brow.

"Do not let their quarrels trouble you. Kingdom Mother only needs time to adjust."

"I understand," Melusine said, her voice low. "But the past makes it hard not to be afraid."

"She will bring you no harm. Father and I will see to that," Kaliope promised.

Melusine's eyes searched hers. "Did you ever promise my father the same?"

A pause settled between them like the hush before a storm. Kaliope's gaze shifted, her voice softening as she chose a different path.

"Some time ago, I sensed the presence of an infant—a child of Modiri blood—and the faint stir of its Emars," she said. "I told Father, and he believes if we can understand the purpose of these Emars for humans, we might help them in their struggle against mankind."

"Emars?" Melusine tilted her head. "Do you mean Embers?"

"I suppose. Sea stones born of our scales."

Melusine's throat tightened. "I believe… perhaps I was used for that purpose. They took my daughter the moment she was born."

"Was she a hybrid?"

"I don't know," Melusine said softly. "Beneath my skin, I felt her—small movements, gentle insistence. I spoke it aloud even while doubting myself. Part of me wanted her to be human, so we could be ordinary."

"If she were, then perhaps she is not the one I felt," Kaliope said. "But if she carries a fin, then it may well have been her. If you allow me, I will need to speak through your heart."

Inside the healing chamber, the orb glistened like liquid moonstone, its soft glow spilling across the walls in shifting ribbons of light. Kaliope extended her right acetic, the translucent appendage catching the orb's gleam as she laid it gently on Melusine's chest. They both closed their eyes, letting the hush of the chamber settle over them like a second skin.

A sudden wave of unease cut through Kaliope's calm. Her eyes snapped open, and a warning slipped from her lips before she could stop it. "Melusine, if we are to find this infant, her Emars may weaken. If that happens, she could be in danger."

"You mean—if she cannot produce Embers, she will die?"

Kaliope's gaze softened. She lowered her acetic from Melusine's chest and gave a slow, heavy nod.

"No, continue," the hybrid said firmly, a quiet strength anchoring her voice. "I am her mother. I will not allow harm to touch her. If I must fight, I will."

Kaliope held her eyes for a heartbeat, then lifted the acetic once more. The two began to float, their fins barely stirring the still water as they surrendered to the ritual. Eyes closed, hearts open, they sank into a deep current of shared thought.

Images unfurled inside Kaliope's mind like a reel of moving light—snatches of memory and fragments of Melusine's life flickered past, each moment sharper than the last. The chamber thrummed with the force of their joined energy. The orb's glow deepened, pulsing in time with their hearts, its surface shimmering as if alive.

Then, without warning, Kaliope's breath caught. A sharp gasp escaped her and echoed through the chamber. Outside, her sisters stirred, their fins trailing slow circles, drawn by a pull they could not name, curiosity brightening their eyes.

"Naida!" Kaliope's cry rang through the chamber like a sudden crack of lightning. The vision of Naida's Ushu in Melusine's subconscious had jolted her.

"You saw her?" Melusine asked at once, eyes bright with hope.

But Kaliope's expression carried no trace of joy. Worry shadowed her features.

"Naida… when you saw her, she was not—"

"Yes, she was there," Melusine interrupted, her voice eager and trembling. "Only for a moment. Is she all right? Tell me." She guided Kaliope's acetic back toward her chest, urging her to continue.

Kaliope pulled away, the movement sharp. "That was not truly your sister. She is an Ushu. What you glimpsed was only an echo of her presence."

Melusine frowned, disbelief flickering across her face. "An echo? No. I know my sister. She was there. Different, yes, but it was her." Her voice wavered, softening into something more fragile. "I'm certain of it."

Kaliope did not answer. Instead, she turned and swept from the chamber, leaving Melusine alone with her racing thoughts.

She cut through the corridors of ice, her fins slicing the water in swift, urgent strokes. The cold grew sharper as she approached the royal chamber where Deimos and the Snows stood guard, their bronzed forms unmoving.

"Deimos, I must speak with Father," she said, breath tight with urgency.

The guards remained still, their silence like stone.

"Deimos!" Her voice sharpened, carrying a note of panic.

From within, the King's deep rumble broke the hush. "Let her through."

The Snows parted. Kaliope swept past, flashing Deimos a quick, triumphant grin and a teasing flick of her tongue before gliding toward the throne.

"Father…" Kaliope's voice came like a wave through the hush of the royal chamber. She glided in a slow circle around his throne, her tone low and careful.

"Ahvi," King Khione acknowledged, his gaze fixed on the faint glow of the frozen pillars.

"It is Naida," she pressed.

At the name, his expression tightened, the warmth in his eyes hardening to ice as if he already knew what question would follow.

"She is…" Kaliope hesitated, her chest rising and falling with a quick, nervous breath. "She is a legendary Ushu?"

"Ahvi." The single word rumbled from him like a warning.

"Father, how can you be so calm?" Her voice sharpened. "She may be a danger to us all—" She broke off, her own words striking her like a sudden blow. "No…"

Khione said nothing. His silence carried more weight than any answer.

"You allowed it?" Kaliope's plea wavered, her eyes searching his face for a denial.

He met her gaze with the quiet sorrow of a father who has already counted the cost.

"She will be slaughtered," Kaliope whispered, the words trembling. "She is only a child."

"She is a child no more," Khione replied, his tone solemn.

"Queen Ceto will show her no mercy. She will not return to our kingdom."

"It is not your burden to carry."

"After all this time, has she not forgiven us? Do you still hold malice for her?"

"No."

"Then why?"

"My dearest Kaliope…" He lifted an acetic, reaching to cradle her face.

But she slipped away before his touch could find her. Tears shimmered in the cold water as she whipped her fin and darted from the chamber, fleeing into the vast, frigid blue toward the upper currents.

Khione remained motionless, the cavern around him heavy with unspoken fears. His heart ached, but his resolve did not waver. He told himself his silence was an act of protection—for Kaliope, for the kingdom. Yet in the depths of the ancient waters, a current was already shifting. Naida's destiny would not be contained.

King Bao glided back toward his kingdom, the great currents parting around him in hushed reverence. Tucked within the folds of his sleeve, Kutoka's tiny stone form pressed cool and certain against the fabric. The sea lay strangely still—calm as a held breath—until the Temple of Xorri came into view.

From within drifted the sharp, untempered voices of youth. Brimsey and Naida were locked in a quarrel that ricocheted through the coral columns like the snap of storm-whipped sails. Brimsey's outrage boiled over; he could not accept that the hybrid child had unraveled his magic without a trace of his involvement. Naida's fury burned just as hot. He had stolen her memories without asking, and she would not forgive the violation.

At the center of their clash hovered Yvina, her delicate acetics flicking in helpless agitation. She tried to calm them, but their tempers leapt like sparks on dry driftwood. In that moment, she saw Naida not as a creature of legend but as a child.

Their voices tangled in the water for hours. Even as King Bao entered, their argument showed no sign of breaking. He waited, listening to the relentless back-and-forth until patience thinned to a single, taut strand.

"Quiet!"

His roar cracked through the chamber like a seismic wave. The Makaras froze mid-motion; schools of fish scattered into the shadowed arches. Yvina flinched and slipped behind a column. Outside the temple, the Lorelies bowed their heads in wary silence.

Brimsey and Naida turned toward the sound. Their bravado melted. They could not make out his eyes, not even the faintest outline of his face; he seemed to have materialized from the ocean itself. The vastness of his presence pressed against them until words abandoned their tongues.

King Bao drifted closer, the water thrumming with quiet power. From the sleeve of his robe he drew forth Kutoka and, with a care at odds with the force of his entrance, placed the tiny black-and-gold statue in Naida's trembling acetics.

"Your majestic creature," Bao intoned, his voice deep as the ocean floor. "You are one with it."

"Attanga? She is a hybrid!" Brimsey cried, his voice carrying the uneven timbre of a boy whose tone had not yet settled into manhood.

"I owe you no explanation," King Bao replied, the deep resonance of his words cutting through the chamber like the slow toll of a bell. He regarded the young boy's audacity with an icy disapproval.

"I–I understand, King Bao… please forgive me." Brimsey bowed, but the confusion in his eyes betrayed him. The thought gnawed at him: a hybrid, granted the privileges of the purebred? It defied every lesson he had been taught.

Naida's gaze widened, curiosity flickering across her features. "What is it?" she asked, her voice soft but edged with wonder.

"You will not return to these depths until you have mastered your mageía," King Bao said, his tone final, leaving no room for protest. "Kutoka will guide you."

Before Naida could draw breath, the world shifted. She blinked—and the warm ciders of the deep were gone.

The surface of the Makara Kingdom unfolded around her, a realm unlike the frozen North. There were no drifting sheets of ice, no cloudy, powder blue or grey skies. Instead, a warm breeze whispered through trees heavy with petals of every hue. Leaves shimmered in the moonlight: crimson and violet, burnished gold and deep sapphire. It was as though an unseen hand had spilled a painter's palette across the land.

Grass flowed in soft waves, each blade tipped with dew that caught the moonlight like tiny crystals. A wide river curved through the valley, its glassy surface gleaming with pinpoints of reflected starlight. Above, a mountain loomed, its peak faint beneath a sky brushed in lavender and midnight blue.

A slender bridge arched over the water, so delicate it seemed spun from silver mist. Petals drifted from the trees, spiraling down in slow, hypnotic circles to settle on the river's skin. They floated there like scattered jewels, each carrying the faint scent of something sweet and unearthly.

Naida clutched the small stone figure to her chest. The breeze stroked her skin—soothing, almost merciful—yet Riko remained silent within her mind, still nursing his quiet resentment. She turned the carved figure over in her acetics, tracing the intricate grooves, searching for meaning she could not yet name.

Her voice was barely a breath. "What is a Kutoka?"

The name reverberated off her tongue. In the next instant, the statue dropped with a hollow plop into the dark water. Startled, Naida plunged after it. Warmth rushed over her skin as she searched the dim below, heart hammering. For one breathless moment she feared it had vanished.

Then the water itself began to quake.

A low rumble rolled through the riverbed, shaking the silt into clouds. Before her eyes, the stone figure swelled, fissures of blue light spidering across its surface. The shape broke apart and reformed until a living creature loomed just beneath the surface, vast enough to shadow the trees.

At first glance, it resembled a bear—massive shoulders, broad head, a stance that belonged to the wild—but the illusion ended there. Its body was sheathed in a lattice of black, fishlike scales that caught the moonlight in slick, metallic glimmers. Webbed paws spread like dark fans, each claw thick and curved like forged iron, ready to rake soil or churn water with equal force.

Its eyes—two fathomless pools of midnight—held a watchful intelligence, calm and unnervingly sure. The broad muzzle flared as it tasted the air, lips set in an expression that offered neither menace nor mercy, only the quiet confidence of something ancient.

Upon that scaled brow rested a circlet of pure gold. The crown's polished rim glowed as though it had drawn light from the heavens themselves. At its center, a sapphire burned with the color of the deepest sea, flanked by smaller gems that winked like captured stars.

The contrast was breathtaking: a creature born of abyssal waters and primeval strength, yet crowned like a monarch—a living paradox of raw power and sovereign grace. It erupted from the water with a force that sent waves crashing along the shore. Droplets arced through the air like liquid crystal. The beast shook its massive head, sending torrents of water flying, a tremor running through the earth with each motion. Its roar followed—a thunderous, cavernous sound that seemed to shake the very marrow of her bones.

Naida floated at the edge of the current, frozen between awe and caution. Should she move closer, or let the creature command its own dominion? The beast, unconcerned with her hesitation, paddled toward the surface with measured, unhurried strokes. Each movement carried the weight of absolute authority, as though the shoreline, the river, and the moon above all belonged to it.

Then it spoke.

"Naida."

The single word rumbled from its jaws like stone grinding against stone, low and resonant. It rolled through the air and sank into her chest, vibrating through her very bones. Each syllable seemed to bend the world around her, leaving no doubt that this creature was no ordinary being.

Watson felt ill-prepared, a feeling he despised.

The Queen's sudden request for a private meeting with the president carried the sharp scent of impulse, as if driven by emotion rather than reason. The usual scaffolding of diplomacy was conspicuously absent.

There had been no advance planning—no careful choreography between Buckingham Palace and the U.S. State Department to decide the agenda, the talking points, or the ceremonial flourishes. The White House Social Secretary and the Chief of Protocol, normally the architects of such occasions, had received no word. Rehearsals were standard for royal visits: the precise moment of the monarch's entrance, the formality of the announcement, the exchange of gifts, the seating arranged down to the inch. Every detail, ordinarily plotted like the steps of a state ballet, had simply... not happened.

It felt, to Watson, as if Queen Emmary wanted the meeting to seem born of sheer necessity—something that materialized of its own urgency, untouched by the usual theater of diplomacy. But what game was she playing? What was she deliberately leaving unsaid?

He watched in silence as the Queen ascended the narrow steps of the private aircraft, her generals forming a silent guard behind her. Her fingers were lightly intertwined with those of young Mary, who matched her stride with quiet determination.

The girl was dressed like a doll stepped out of a portrait: a sky-blue tweed dress falling just below the knee, white stockings and flats that gleamed against the tarmac's dull grey. Her ginger hair, parted cleanly down the center, had been gathered into two neat ponytails, each bound with a white ribbon.

Mary was beginning to carry herself like a lady of the court. Where once she would have lingered at the edges, she now issued small, confident instructions, learning how to speak her mind without waiting for permission. The transformation was striking—a reflection of the Queen's own steel.

Watson sat upright in his No. 1 Dress uniform, every detail exacting. The dark jacket bore his rank insignia on each shoulder; a neat line of medals and decorations caught the cabin's muted light. Gold aiguillettes curved with precise symmetry across his chest. A scarlet-banded peak cap rested on his knees, its badge polished to a hard gleam. The Sam Browne belt crossed his torso in a diagonal of brown leather, the buckle square and unyielding, as if even the strap carried its own discipline.

Enu, seated opposite, wore an almost identical uniform, though her insignia told a different story: a single crown set above three stars marked her rank with quiet distinction. Her medals shone just as bright, her bearing every bit as composed.

She watched Watson with the practiced stillness of a soldier trained to read more than words. It wasn't the uniform that caught her attention, but the subtle pattern of avoidance. Each time Mary's gaze wandered toward him, Watson found some reason to look elsewhere—checking a buckle, adjusting his cap, staring at the window's black reflection. No accidental brush of a sleeve, no glance allowed to linger.

The behavior struck Enu as odd, though she couldn't name the reason. Beneath the steady thrum of the aircraft's engines, her curiosity sharpened.

However, Watson exhaled at last and leaned back, letting the headrest cradle him. He closed his eyes as though hoping the darkness behind them might grant what the world would not—seven unbroken hours of sleep, and perhaps, the brief mercy of forgetting whatever kept him from the child's eyes.

Back in London, Noah had transformed his flat into the rough outline of a campaign headquarters. The dining table, stripped of any pretense of domesticity, bore a whiteboard streaked with hurried scrawl, papers stacked in precarious towers, and pens scattered like fallen soldiers. Pushpins bristled from corkboards where half-formed strategies clung in uneven clusters.

Their first gathering at the countryside cottage had ended with only a vague sense of purpose, yet Noah had recognized an opportunity. The Equal Species might actually serve him, even if he had to feign sympathy for their cause. He needed allies—he could admit that much—but nothing had prepared him for the raw urgency in their voices. They longed to become the spark that would ignite change between humans and Modiri. He found their idealism naïve, even laughable, but he couldn't ignore their reach. They could bring him before the public—and, perhaps one day, before the King himself.

A brisk knock interrupted his thoughts. Alice and Linus stepped inside, balancing iced coffees and plates of beans on toast.

"Greetings," Noah said, holding the door as they entered.

Alice's gaze swept the room. Linus paused mid-step. It wasn't the slums they had imagined, but a sour odor lingered, subtle yet unmistakable.

"Sorry about the smell," Noah said quickly. He resumed his restless pacing, papers rustling beneath his shoes. "I've been busy and let the trash pile up. Took it out earlier, though. Windows are open. Should clear soon."

The living room—little more than a narrow space doubling as a dining area—held a modest couch pushed against the wall. Alice settled in without ceremony, Linus easing down beside her, their coffees sweating rings onto the wooden table.

"No worries," Alice said, taking a bite of toast as she brushed crumbs from her lap. "I've spoken with the others. They're on their way."

The scent of roasted beans mingled with the city air drifting through the open windows, a fleeting hint of comfort against the charged anticipation gathering in the room.

"Great, thanks," Noah said, leaning against the edge of the table as the last crumbs of toast disappeared from Alice's plate.

Between bites, Linus studied him with a quiet intensity. Finally, curiosity won out. "Why the new name? I didn't get to ask before."

Noah exhaled, eyes flicking to the whiteboard as though the question had been scrawled there all along. "It's… complicated. My father isn't the best man. I needed distance. This country means a lot to me, and I can't stand watching it like this—fractured, angry, lost. People have every right to be furious. I guess"—he gave a small, self-conscious shrug—"I feel some duty to them. Maybe because of him. As wacky as that sounds."

Alice wiped her fingers on a napkin and tilted her head. "Have you spoken to him lately?"

"No." The answer came sharp and final, the kind that closed a door.

A knock broke the brief silence. The door swung open to reveal Willow, Preston, and Piper. The moment Piper crossed the threshold she wrinkled her nose. "Oh, for goodness' sake. What is that smell? What do you even do in here?"

Flustered, Noah strode to the windows and shoved them wider, letting the cool morning air sweep in. "I've just been busy, that's all. Sorry about the smell."

Willow barely glanced up from her bag as she pulled out a laptop. Preston dropped onto the sofa without a word.

"Good morning," Willow said brightly, as if Piper hadn't spoken.

Relieved by her steadiness, Noah returned her greeting. "Good morning."

Willow settled the laptop on her knees. "Right, let's get started. I took the late shift today so we have time to cover everything."

Noah clapped his hands, his earlier embarrassment already fading beneath a surge of excitement. "Perfect. Oh—by the way, I had campaign pins made. If you'd all like to start wearing them…"

He passed the pins around like Halloween candy, a grin tugging at his mouth. No one shared his enthusiasm. Alice and Piper exchanged a glance.

Piper bit her lip to stifle a laugh.

"Who does he think we are—fans?" she whispered.

"Oh, be nice," Alice teased, nudging her friend with her elbow.

Willow's eyes swept over the group, her gaze urging them to settle into silence. She cleared her throat, her voice firm yet measured.

"At the moment, I know you're eager to launch your campaign, Noah, but we're not there yet. Campaigns are complex—planning, strategy, public perception. And, ultimately, it's the people who decide if you're fit for the role."

She paused, letting her words sink in. "Right now, we know a few critical things, the most important being the King's health. If we can shed light on that, reveal some evidence, and simultaneously peel back the monarchy's secrecy and their insidious machinations, we can begin to rally the people. You need to become a leader, a voice for their grievances. Once they see you as someone on their side, they'll invest in your rise—all the way to Prime Minister. As of now…" Her gaze softened on Noah. "…you're just a nobody."

The words hung in the air. The campaign pins, once gleaming in eager hands, were now quietly set aside. Noah's response was measured, almost resolute.

"I get it. I'm not angered by the truth—only motivated by it. How do we change that? What's first? Where do I go? What do I do?"

Willow leaned forward, outlining each step with precision. "First, we draft your stance: the King is dead. That's our anchor. Next, we dismantle the monarchy's illusions—the lies they've spun to convince the people otherwise. Then comes evidence, and finally, the solution. We repeat this process, city after city, until the message sticks."

Alice, Linus, Preston, and Piper nodded in unison, the determination mirrored in their eyes. "Yep. Sounds good to me."

"Brilliant," Linus added, a small smile tugging at his lips.

Noah exhaled, letting a hint of humor slip through his nerves. "A grungy politician, eh?"

"Yes," Willow replied quickly, her tone serious. There was no room for pretense here. Despite the sting of her honesty, there was something in her clarity that made her trustworthy.

"Okay," Noah said finally, a spark of resolve lighting his features. "Sounds good. When do we begin?"

"Why not today?" Alice interjected with infectious enthusiasm.

And just like that, the room sprang to life. Flash cards were drafted, notes pinned to the whiteboard, speech cadence practiced, and wardrobe choices debated. They were amateurs, no doubt, but their energy filled the flat with purpose. In that moment, they didn't just plan a campaign—they began shaping a politician.

Meanwhile, the air in America was unlike anything the party had encountered in the United Kingdom. Despite centuries of time and progress, their country still carried a dampness that clung to the skin, a cool, heavy moisture born of its own maritime temperament. It was a contrast to America's warmer, drier climate.

Their arrival bypassed the usual pomp. There were no military bases bristling with soldiers, no international airport rituals, no 21-gun salute. The Vice President, First Lady, Secretary of State—none were present. Instead,

Queen Emmary, Mary, Watson, Enu, and a contingent of royal guards deboarded the aircraft with quiet efficiency. They moved swiftly, boarding two concealed, heavy-duty hovermobiles whose route had been meticulously cleared just twenty-four hours prior.

The Queen's orders were unequivocal: no detour to Blair House, no casual greeting. Her destination was the Yellow Oval Room. The matters she wished to discuss with the President could not wait.

Enu felt the grumble of her stomach, a sharp reminder of her human limitations. Watson caught her eye, offering a small, knowing glance. Was she ready for this life of constant discipline, of navigating spaces so far removed from the rhythm she knew? No. But could she endure it? Absolutely.

Lady Mary, on the other hand, had slept most of the flight. The landscape rushing past the hovermobile's windows enthralled her, every skyscraper, tree, and glint of sunlight igniting her curiosity. Her excitement bubbled uncontrollably, but she quickly realized there was no one around to share it with. Queen Emmary remained inscrutable, a fortress of composure. Watson observed the young girl closely, disappointment fleeting across his face as he saw her enthusiasm curbed by protocol and decorum. He longed to intervene, to be the one to let her breathe freely, but he held himself back. Drawing a deep breath, he pushed the images of Kovos and Emaline from his mind, forcing his focus on the present, on the precise choreography demanded by the Queen's will.

The hovermobiles glided forward, silently and purposefully, carrying the weight of centuries, duty, and expectation as the unfamiliar American terrain unfurled around them. Every detail reminded them that they were far from home, and every tick of the clock was bringing them closer to the careful negotiation between power, discipline, and the unknown.

Lisa K. Stephenson

BOOK 3
The Embers of the Ice (Available Now)
&

'The Naida Saga' Book Soundtrack

Buy. Download. Stream.

8 Original Songs | 3 Ballet Movements | 1
Choreographed Video

YouTube: 'The Snows of Khione Ballet Academy'

BOOK 3: THE NAIDA SAGA

THE EMBERS

OF THE

ICE

LISA K. STEPHENSON